Lim

Limehouse Lady

Irene Roberts

PIATKUS

Copyright © 1996 by Irene Roberts

First published in Great Britain in 1996 by
Judy Piatkus (Publishers) Ltd of
5 Windmill Street, London W1T 2JA

**The moral right of the author
has been asserted**

*A catalogue record for this book is available
from the British Library*

ISBN 0–7499–3400–X

Set in 11/12 pt Times by
Create Publishing Services Ltd

Printed and bound in Great Britain by
Mackays of Chatham Ltd, Chatham, Kent

Part I

Chapter One

Thirteen year old Moira O'Malley sat mouse-still on the lino, a newly polished stair rod forgotten. Her hands were clasped around her knees, her delicate face half hidden by her cloud of cinnamon-coloured hair. Her golden brown eyes, like dew-wet pansies, now held pain.

She had been up since the crack of dawn, busying about her chores. She had been halfway down the stairs, when she heard Flo and Maisy Noice at it. Mrs Noice was the daily and Flo was speaking in that hard way she had when specially fed-up. It was going to be one of those days.

At times like this she wished she could run away, but knew that she never would. There were too many authorities out there, with evil, beady eyes. All waiting and watching and hoping to whisk her away from Jordan Lodge. This was an ugly detached lodging place behind a brick wall at the end of Jordan Street in Limehouse. It had ten large rooms and the usual offices. Flo Williamson, the owner, Mrs Maisy Noice who came in to do the rough, and Moira the skivvy saw to them all. There was also a large back garden, and a laurel-shrouded front. And, too, there was the large basement where Freddy and Moira slept. All in all the Lodge was a palace compared with the rest of the houses in Jordan Street. However, its only beauty was the garden that Freddy loved.

Freddy, a lot older than Moira, was a slow, fair-haired gentle giant of a man. He was the gardener cum handyman, cum chucker-out. He, like Moira looked on the Lodge as his refuge. Unlike Moira, he never thought of the place as a prison. Moira had lived and slaved in the building, having been abandoned there by her father when she was two years old. It was now 1920.

Clearly Flo was suffering a hangover. She must have been drinking port, which always turned her really foul. If she could escape for long enough, Moira would sneak off in search of Freddy. But here, on the stairs, her retreat was cut off. And if she made a sound now, she might be discovered and there would be hell to pay. Freddy was the only one on God's earth who could make Flo act gentle. Especially when his eyes filled with tears. Freddy had often shed tears on Moira's behalf.

Moira looked frail. Above all she knew when to keep quiet. But deep down she had a fighting spirit that had helped her survive no matter what the odds. In spite of everything she loved the tough, tarty woman who had taken her in, even though Flo had rages and was apt to lash out when the mood took her. Flo had tried to protect her from the world and gave her a rough kind of affection ... most times.

But when suffering a hangover it was always the same. The loud moaning and groaning that rose up into raging and ranting on about the past. It was then she would hit out, physically, and it was usually Moira that got in the way.

Moira's heart was going at it hammer and tongs. She was being talked about again. Flo's voice could be heard all over Jordan Lodge.

'I sometimes sodding-well wonder what I'm doing here,' Flo's voice wafted upstairs. 'Bloody good, innit?'

'Life's what you make it,' came Maisie's gruffly feminine voice. 'You've got a good home, that's more than most can say.'

Flora Alicia Ruth Williamson was determined to have her say. She had taken Moira in when the child's 'Lousy no-good dad' had cut and run. Every so often Moira was reminded of the fact. Of that and the reality that she must work for her keep – which meant skivvying from dawn to dusk.

Penalties for slacking were wallopings. Once it had been a great deal worse, the cellar. Deep, dank, and worst of all, dark. To the frightened child Moira had been, it had held all the devils in hell. The cellar never happened now, thanks to Freddy's tears on her behalf.

Flo's voice raised higher.

4

'That little cow upped and lipped me again yesterday. After all what I've done for her too. Stood in front of me and said as how...'

'She didn't want to work in no wash house from eight to nine?' the daily remarked. 'I know! Freddy told me about the right old how d'yer-do there was. Gawd, you ain't half got a nerve. Young Moir does more'n her fair share.'

'It'd help pay for her keep.'

'What keep? When you booze all your cash away, she starves. I know it all, believe me. Freddy might be a bit slow, but even he knows how many beans make five. And thank Gawd young Moir's learned to back-answer. She'd be a dead duck else.'

This was true enough. These days Moira, the naturally quiet, dreamy youngster, had learned the hard way that she must stick up for herself. Must pretend that she had a skin as thick as a rhino's, and act as though sarcasm and slights just bounced off her hide.

Through the years she had learned to ape Flo. This even though her greatest joy was to sit quietly with Freddy and read anything and everything that came to hand. To drink in all that Stavros Sella the Greek taught her. And to remember all the things she must be and do to become the little lady of Lime-house. The lady that Stavros told her she was, must be, to rise above her present situation.

At the present she was a mere skivvy, beholden to Flo who had been drunk last night. It was always the same afterwards. Then the shouting and hollering began, the slapping, and the podgy finger poking against her own chest. Moira loved and hated Flo according to the treatment she received at the woman's hands.

Flo wasn't half bad when sober, and when in a jolly mood she was a wonder on earth. Her two chins wobbled when she laughed, and her ample bosoms heaved up and down like balloons floating on waves. Flo was Moira's saviour, protecting her from the wicked School Board, and keeping her out of the way of Officials. These faceless ones had power. Really terrible power at that. 'They' could put one in a Home, a Workhouse, or make one go to School where they gave you the cane. Where other great big bullying kids laughed and poked fun and made your life sheer torture for endless hours.

Moira was terrified of the outside world, and of Jordan Street, which was a hyphen between Burgess and Locksley streets. It boasted the Hare and Hounds at the Burgess end, and at the other, Jordan Lodge. The large old building all but hid itself behind tall, secretive brick walls. It was Flo Williamson's domain, left to her by her harlot of a mother. Unlike her home, Flo wasn't retiring at all. Everyone in Jordan Street knew her.

Smack in the middle of Jordan Street stood Dave Dilley's Late Fry, which spread its mouth-watering aroma throughout the area. A torture for the tired and hungry who had not even a ha'penny to spend on a few chips. On the opposite side stood Anne Cherry's second-hand. Apart from these, small wretched smoke-grey domiciles leaned against each other like so many down-trodden gnomes. The slummy, overcrowded two-up and two-downers held grim-faced people with a grudge against the world. Poverty led to helplessness or aggression. There was lots of aggression going on in Jordan Street, and Moira would scurry along it on errands, with her heart in her mouth.

In contrast all was peace and bliss in the Lodge basement. There, on the floor opposite Freddy's bed, Moira had her own horsehair mattress. Moira treasured her sanctuary in Freddy's domain. Loved the sense of companionship there. And Freddy, who understood, would smile and ruffle her hair and call her Iddy in his slow, kind way.

Freddy was grown up. Supposedly another stray Flo had taken in all the world knew that Freddy was Flo's illegitimate son and Maisy Noice's nephew. Freddy was rather backward. His world entailed Flo, the garden, and the American comics which a sailor gave to Mrs Noice's dock-worker husband. He in turn brought them home for Freddy. Mrs Noice would huff and puff when she brought them in for Freddy and Flo would ooh and ah and be very pleased. Flo loved Freddy but seemed to hate Maisy Noice at times. Not that the woman cared.

There came a crashing sound from the kitchen and Flo was swearing. Now she's dropped the serving tray, Moira thought, or was it Maisy that caused it? Oh crumbs, this is going to get worse! She wished that she dared creep upstairs and hide in Stavros's room. But fear held her frozen to the spot.

Stavros Sella was the most important lodger in Flo's establishment. The old Greek, a retired tutor, had been teaching Moira reading and writing from the moment he realized that learning to her was like water to a sponge. Hearing him talk made Flo wrinkle her nose, look to the ceiling and think he was nuts. Moira held him in awe.

The other permanent guest in Jordan Lodge was a complete contrast to Stavros. Mr Binks was a joker, a rogue and a thief. Like Mr Sella he paid his dues regularly and that was all that Flo cared about. Mr Binks and Stavros got on surprisingly well. They enjoyed a certain rivalry too; Mr Binks deliberately scorned Stavros's beloved ex-pupil Yani in order to over-praise a couple of youths of his own acquaintance. It was all good humoured, and the two old blokes wrangled for hours. Smiling as she went about her chores, Moira would listen to them back-chatting.

'Gawd!' Mr Binks would sigh, 'For a brainy bloke, you don't know how many beans, do yer? That milk-sop what's been born with a silver spoon in his gob don't stand a chance against life. I mean real life! Chumley now, he's a eel! Knows all the tricks. And his mate Conor can throw a punch to break a donkey's jaw.'

'One cannot beat a good education, my friend,' Stavros habitually replied, only to hear Mr Binks scoff.

'Cor bloody hell mate, you don't know the half!'

For the rest, a trickle of lodgers came and went, faceless strangers from places all over the world. This was a dockland area and foreigners abounded. All they meant to Moira was just that much more hard work...

'Gawd, my head!' Flo was yelling. 'As if I ain't suffering enough, you clumsy cow.'

'If it's aching that bad, you shouldn't shout,' Maisy Noice observed. 'And suffer you do not.'

'It's all right for you. You've got a bloke. I ain't. I have to graft to survive. What's more, I reckon that pissing notice up the office has gone missing. Moir could have done an 'and's turn up the wash-house for a couple of hours. It wouldn't kill her. If I don't get more blokes, if it's left to them what I can grab meself at the Hare and Hounds, we'll all be in the workhouse. When I think of what might 'ave been!'

7

The office? Moira wondered, her lips beginning to tremble because first or last, she knew what was about to come. The office? Then she remembered. Those needing a roof knew of Jordan Lodge because of the notice Flo had pinned up outside an office in the docks. She had been allowed this priviledge for a favour given. Flo was very generous with her favours at times. So her notice stayed put.

'Another thing,' Flo was beginning her usual tirade. 'The more I think about Seamus, I—'

Moira put her hands over her ears. How endlessly moments like this went on. She wished she could fly away, up in the sky, get away for ever from this place that was like the Styx that Stavros was always on about. She wanted to cry because it hurt her, the knowledge that she had been dumped like an unwanted parcel. Flo was nice about it sometimes, but today she was feeling rotten. Moira knew only too well just how the conversation would go. Flo was always ramming the painful truth home. About her life, her losses, and living in this God-awful place.

In her mind's eye Moira thought about the area in which she lived, where men came and went, arriving and leaving like the waves of the river that raced to the sea. All around in the wretched streets, life went on the same for the teeming poor. Beyond, there was the noisy mass that made up the great, sprawling docks.

Dockland, a world apart it was, of grimy wharves and warehouses. Where cranes like huge bony monsters toiled endlessly, heaving and groaning as they hoisted boxes of cargo onto the quayside. Dockers and stevedores shouted and sweated and swore, muscles heaving, working as only they knew how. Giant steam presses thumped and crashed, adding their powerful voices to the day. And all around there was the noise and smell of mud and machinery, water and wood.

Looming over all, great ships tapped their heels in choppy water like impatient matrons. And then those same ships moved away, slow and dignified, taking their crews with them. Just as all those years ago, one had swallowed up Moira's father and left her with Flo.

Trembling, defeated, Moira uncovered her ears because her hands were unable to block out Flo's strident voice. Then she heard the fierce rattling sound of the poker in the grate. She held her breath, then flinched because now she heard Flo banging her fist on the table in rage. There was to be no stopping her now. The only blessing was that on these occasions old Maisy took the time to answer Flo back. Usually she'd sniff and look as immovable as an ox, and just go on about her business in her stolid, down to earth way. But she defended Freddy and Moira as a matter of course.

Moira felt herself squeezing up inside. The hateful truth seeming to echo up the lino-covered stairs. The brown lino was held firmly in place by brass stair rods – shone like gold they did, and heaven help Moira if they did not.

'The whole bloody world passes through my door, Maise,' Flo was saying harshly. 'You'd have thought that out of all them rotten bleeders I'd 'ave known better than to 'ave been taken in by that sodding Seamus O'Malley.'

'I still think as how he weren't so bad.' Maisy replied and sniffed. 'I think as how—'

'Not only that,' Flo cut in, 'I get saddled with his motherless kid! I ask you? I must have been mad!'

'You could 'ave said no,' Maisy Noice pointed out, 'and told him to take her back to her mother's lot in Ireland.'

'He said he'd marry me when he came back, you know he did. He promised me that—'

'Promises are made to be broken. Anyway, I don't know why you're carrying on. All that happened donkeys years ago.'

'And even the war's been over since eighteen,' Flo exploded, 'so he couldn't give that as an excuse. I've had Moir on me back for over ten years, and all that time I've waited and hoped. No, he won't never come back now, even though I've—'

'Refused to accept that he went down with the *Aesop*? That was the name of his ship wasn't it? And it went down with all hands only a few months after Seamus joined the crew.'

'I weren't notified.'

'You weren't no relation, Flo. The times I've told you that! To the guvenors what count, you was only the woman what he lodged with.'

'Moira was a relation. His kid!'

'Well, we'll never know what he intended to do about you and her now, will we? Nor what really happened. Clearly Moira weren't registered nowhere, else you would 'ave heard by now. So it's a case of just carrying on the same as always.'

'It's all right for you to talk!' Flo was getting more rattled and beginning to shout again. 'But where the bloody hell does that leave me, eh?'

'Where you've been since the *Aesop* went down off the Azores. And if you ask me, you're a bit soft in the 'ead to have been hoping against hope all this time. D'yer know what I think? You've made Seamus O'Malley your excuse. You've been saying as how you've been waiting for him, and hanging on to his kid like a limpet for all these years, just because it goes down so well.'

'Put a sock in it, Maise! I ain't hung on to Moir to make her an excuse for anything and . . .'

'You knew damned well what the authorities would have done if they'd found out. If they'd learned about a poor orphaned child with no blood relations to hand! They'd have stepped in. They'd have shoved her in an orphanage. Anyway, they would have snatched her away from you.'

'Seamus put her in my care. He—'

'He just asked you to look after her and you said yes. But you don't have no proof of that, Flo. Nothing was written down and signed. It'ud only be your word, and they don't take no notice of what the likes of us say. In their eyes you ain't got no claim on Moira at all.'

'I gave Seamus my solomn oath and that's why I've been stuck here in this place, on me own, for all these years.'

'Oh, for Gawds sake! That's your story, and you'll stick to it no matter what. If you ask me, it's the yarn you spill because you ain't never got your hooks into some other poor bloke to take Seamus's place. Fate's been against you in that respect, Flo.' Maisy Noice's tone was flat but forceful. 'But it ain't never been your fault. It took someone with real guts to hang on to Freddy and—'

'Piss off!'

'Suit yourself.'

There came the clattering noises of Maisy Noice collecting bucket and scrubbing brush, and the heavy sound of her boots making their measured tread across the kitchen floor. At any minute Flo might decide to come up the stairs.

10

It was time to make herself scarce. Moira stood up and quietly slipped the stair rod into place. If she wasn't discovered perhaps she could go in and sit with Stavros for a while. If he wasn't too busy with his writing, he would allow her to stay and read. Then when Flo came storming upstairs to find her, he could tell her that he had asked Moira to do an extra chore or two. He had made excuses like that for Moira many times.

Stavros did not answer her tentative tap on his door. She turned away and went along to Mr Binks. She knocked and went in, knowing very well that he had not come home the previous night, but experience had taught her that it was always best to be on the safe side. Mr Binks's room was neat and clean, dusted, polished and the bed made up, simply because Moira had made it so. The fat little man had probably stayed with his lifelong friend Harriet, who had a place down Market Street. Thieves kitchen, Flo called it in her usual forthright way. Then she would add mysteriously, 'And there's some very funny stories going round about that woman, believe me. Gawd, Moir, you don't know the half of what goes on!'

Safe for a little while, intending to keep out of the way until Flo calmed down, Moira sat on Mr Bink's chair and began dreaming of the photograph Stavros had on his table. It was of a handsome boy who had eyes as dark hair as his hair. He had even white teeth and his smile was quite wonderful. Of course he did not look like that now, Stavros had told her, for he was a few years older than Moira, and was a student in a very, very posh school. The picture showed how he had looked when Stavros had been his private tutor.

It was Moira's delight to fantasize over Yani, for that was his name. Soon he would be coming back to join a business college much nearer home. Then, Stavros said, she, Moira, would meet the young Greek gentleman. His father was a rich man. So, in Moira's mind, Yani was a Greek prince who would, one day, come to carry her away to a fairyland of riches and abundance, where there were vineyards and olive trees...

'Moira? Where are you, girl?' Flo's voice, calmer now, wafted up the stairs. 'Get a move on. We ain't got all bloody day you know.'

Moira sighed and walked out of Mr Bink's room, then went slowly down the stairs. The house closed round her, warm and

11

welcoming now, for Flo's tone showed that she had got over her bad mood.

'Here you are!' Flo said without rancour when Moira entered the kitchen. 'Skiving again, were we?'

'I was giving Mr Binks' room a once over.'

'I don't know why you fuss over him and the Greek. Keep you at it, they do. There's other people in this house, and work what needs doing. I want you to go down Popsy's for me and get round her to let me 'ave some stuff on the book. Get me a loaf, a pennorth of jam and some of them eggs. You know, them what are ten a penny, all cracked. Here's the cup for the jam, I'll owe her the tuppence. It'll be all right, so don't look at me like that. And I don't want no dawdling.'

As Moira hurried down Jordan Street, eyes down because it was perilous to look any of the doorstep harridans straight in the eye, she didn't know whether to laugh or cry. The usual panic assailed her, for Flo's warnings about "Officials" out to get her had taken root a long time ago. She never felt safe outside Jordan Lodge and going on errands made her hands go sticky and her mouth dry. On the other hand, a penny cup of jam from Popsy's General Store meant luxury. So did the eggs. It meant she would eat as well as the lodgers tonight, and so would Flo. It would mean smiles and beams all round the kitchen table. Not that Freddy did anything but beam – unless Flo ordered him to do otherwise.

She bit her lip as another reality hit home. Jam and eggs on the book wouldn't be forthcoming. The woman in the shop had said so, at great length, only the day before. That spelled disaster. Flo would be off and away to the Hare and Hounds, scrounging drinks from the blokes and come back plastered. Then let everyone watch out! Of course, if she picked up a bloke ready and willing to pay for her charms, well and good – for Flo. It never turned out to be too handy for the man in question though. That's when poor Freddy came into his own.

Moira found herself praying that Flo stayed on gin. Most of the women found comfort that way. Dockland ladies had nothing much to lose.

The vast docklands themselves had a vibrancy not found elsewhere. It was the point of arrival, where people of many races came to settle and begin a new life. Once, rich merchants and other men of substance built houses on a grand scale in Limehouse. A long time ago, a wheezy old merchant fallen on hard times, had owned Jordan Lodge, until Flora Williamson's pro of a mother had got her hooks into him of course. Then many years later, Seamus O'Malley's footsteps had led him to Flo's door. But then, Moira thought, aggrieved, the whole world eventually made its way to Flo's. Yes, the whole shitty universe no matter what the colour or creed.

Chapter Two

The Hare and Hounds was crowded. It was hot and stuffy inside and smelled of cheap cigarettes, pipe tobacco and beer. Lots of Irish dockers were there, yarning about the 'Auld Country', or else carrying on about the guerilla warfare in their homeland, where the Reparations crisis was acute. Things were getting loud, a glass or two shattered, a thin little man was squaring up to bloke three times his size. An old man cackled and called them a stupid pair of sods. Another yelled out, "'Ere Arty, do up your flies!'

There was ribald laughter at that, and vulgar remarks, and the tension died down – for a while. The pianist began to play Danny Boy. Voices rang out in song, some blubbed in their beer, others drank deeply and shut their eyes, others began to cuss out loud. "Mother Macree" followed and "Phil the Fluter's Ball" and everyone was having a good time until Bert Yeats yelled:

'Put a sock in it, why don't yer? We ain't all bleeding Spud Murpheys in here.'

Some began to scowl and swear, and muttered among themselves. Everyone, Cockneys or Spuds, hated Yeats's guts. But he was built like a tank, had the strength of ten men, and could all but crush a man in half. No one back-answered him, though the singing carried on.

As the evening progressed, "Tipperary" and "If you Were the Only Girl In the World" was defiantly roared out while hobnailed boots were pounding the floor in rhythm with the words. Irish voices rose higher, glasses were raised, there was laughter and jibing and devils dancing in eyes. There was going to be a shemozzel, it was brewing all right.

Marcus Shaw, the landlord of the Hare and Hounds was watching the bestial Yeats family, who came from 313 Jordan Street, and were the worst trouble makers of the lot. He was also keeping a weather eye open for Flo Williamson.

The woman was, as usual, making a spectacle of herself. Thank God, she was in a soppy but happy mood. She'd been plied with drink by a bloke who'd enjoyed himself with her somewhere outside for fifteen minutes or so. Then he must have buggered off. Flo had returned alone, hat over one eye, hair a mess, and her front chest buttons undone.

'One for the road, luv,' she said to the barmaid, 'an' then I'll be off back 'ome.'

She downed her drink in one go and coquettishly eyed up a chap or two. Her luck was out, since quite clearly the men had other things in mind. They were squaring up, ready, blood racing through their veins. It was going to be great, a real whiz of a punch-up. A right old barney would be breaking out any minute now. It needed only one word out of place for the shenanagins to begin, and every full-blooded bloke there was just raring to go. Flo recognised the signs and knew it was time to leave them to it.

In a haze of good humour, Flo began the walk down Jordan Street. She feared no one. Not even the awful bruisers in number 313. Even they knew how it would be if Flo set Freddy on them. Flo had begun the rumours herself many years ago – that Freddy could go crazy, do murders in fact. No one dared to put him to the test and believed the story that when he was all fired up, Freddy had the strength of ten men. So Flo was safe down Jordan Street, as was Moira, and anyone else that Flo took under her wing. One word from Flo and Freddy would go at it hammer and tongs.

Nearly home, Flo thought merrily as the outer brick wall that shut Jordan Lodge off from Jordan Street came to view. The only way inside was through the tall green door. She frowned, non plussed. On the ground, in a dead faint directly in front of the door, there was a young foreign woman. Hovering over her there was a Chinese child, a girl who looked to be about four years old.

15

'Oi!' Flo was pulling herself together fast. 'Oi! What are you doing down there? Get up you stupid drunken fart-arse bitch!'

There came no movement from the young woman. Flo nudged her with her foot and nearly fell over, her arms flailing as she reached out to the wall to steady herself. Her feathered hat slipped down to half cover one bleary eye.

The young woman came to, and tried to rise. Flo saw, in the hazy street light, that the stranger was also Chinese, and by the look of it, in a very bad way. It was nothing to do with booze.

Flo made up her mind. The whole bleeding world was spinning round. She needed a shoulder to lean on and the Chink would do as well as anyone else. She peered owlishly past the crazily tilted brim of her hat.

'Can you walk?'

'Hai,' came the quiet reply.

'Good.' Flo slurred. 'Well you can come along and help me.'

The young woman stood up and waited patiently until Flo, still weaving, found her shoulder.

'Gawd,' Flo said, 'you ain't nothing but skin and bone.' Then she swore loud and long and let go again, and fumbled about in her over-large handbag until she found the key. At last, and after a struggle, she turned the key in the door. It swung open. The drink was wearing off, but still needing help, Flo hiccupped then, with drunken impatience, 'Come on! Don't stand there gawping.'

The path to the front of the house gleamed like a black river, and was flanked on either side with tall dark laurel bushes. Flo, her helper, and the small child went up the four front steps and into the house. The Chinese woman made to turn and leave, but Flo smiled and shook her head.

'You helped me, there ain't that many as would bother. Come right in and have a cuppa with me.' The young woman hesitated, unsure. Flo smiled in a stupid but kindly way.

'I won't bite you, or your nipper. Come into the kitchen. We can have a little chat, eh?'

The Chinese lady's face still held fear. Flo, used to having her own way, gurgled.

''Sallright! I'm not so far gone as you might think. You helped me, and Flo Willi – Flo always gives as good as she gets.'

She nudged the woman in the ribs, looked meaningful and laughed, 'Know what I mean? Good or bad, I always return favours. Come on, Chink, let's have yer. Sit down!'

She led the two Chinese into the kitchen and saw to it that they were sitting at the table. The kettle was lazily steaming on the range and Flo, sobering up with every moment that passed, made tea. Something made her take down cups from the dresser rather than use the everyday mugs.

'Now,' she said, 'I take it you're starving? I've got some bread and marge. You won't turn your nose up at English food?' She reached out for the tin of condensed milk to add to the tea, but the Chinese woman stopped her. 'No milk?' Flo giggled as she handed over two cups full of hot tea. 'Bloody funny lot you are. What's going on, eh? Where do you come from? We don't like Chinks much round here. Chinks is opposite to us in every way. You smoke opium, don't you? Don't you, eh? And you go in for white slavery, and all kinds of weird things. What's your name?'

The young woman, who had begun drinking the tea as if it was liquid gold, said something, very quietly, her eyes downcast.

'My Gawd!' Flo's eyes crinkling up, her brows raised. 'Really? Is that your name, honest? It don't sound foreign at all.'

'Is name of own lowly self,' the young woman whispered and looked over her shoulder in a frightened way.

'Well I never! Come on, drink up while its hot. Would the kid like a crust? Gawd help us, what a funny name to have! Now tell me all you can about yourself, and about how you come to be sprawled out like twopennorth of Gawd-'elp-us outside my door.'

Flo drank strong tea and reached for the teapot again. She was pulling round fast, her mind growing clear. The two Chinks intrigued her. She had never met their like before.

The Chinese, she knew, hung together, crowding out places that they turned into little China's. Most Chinese immigrants stayed in secret communities of their own kind; round the dockland area they had made Limehouse Causeway their own. They dressed odd, the men in long silk robes and women in trousers. They hung funny notices outside their doors, all red

17

and gold, and their little tumbledown shops sold strange things. They prayed to mysterious gods and had the nerve to call the English foreign devils. That didn't stop them crowding the shores even so. They were cunning, yellow-faced and slitty-eyed and up to all the tricks and treachery in the world. At least, that was what Flo had heard.

Flo could judge character. She knew that all that rubbishy talk could not include the delicate-looking pair hovering fearfully in her kitchen now. The Chinese woman did not have a pigtail, but instead wore her hair upswept and pinned in a knot on the top of her head. She wore trousers and a padded jacket in dark navy-blue and had a refined air. Her daughter was a small replica of herself.

'Tell me about yourself,' Flo said and refilled the cups. 'I ain't come across your sort in the whole of me life. Now I want to know all about you. All right?'

The young woman began to speak in faulty English, but Flo was able to get the gist. And all the while the kid was watching with a straight, pinched expression on her face. Her wide almond-shaped eyes giving nothing away.

After a while, and when the speaking had stopped, Flo raised her brows and spoke slowly and very carefully.

'I'm soused as a 'erring, I reckon. Pickled and daft with it, since I really believe as how you're telling me the truth. So ... you can stay here. It'll be rough, and you'll have to pay me, but you can hide away here if that's what you want.'

The woman began bowing her head, and clasping her hands together and shaking them, and acting as though Flo had offered her manna from heaven. Flo let her get on with it and went to the door in the hall that led to the basement and shouted down for Fred...

Moira couldn't take it all in. Had Flo finally gone mad? A Chinese child and her mother were staying in the attic, and had been there all last night!

'They want to keep themselves to themselves, Moir,' Flo said, leaning her elbows on the kitchen table and staring hard into Moira's face. Moira, standing as always, and drinking a mug of tea, looked down at her toes. Her heart was sinking, because she knew by Flo's manner that there was more to

18

come. 'And since that's the case,' Flo went on, 'and since I ain't no charity, Liverpool's gotta pay. So, I've put a word in already, and the woman's got a full time job. So it looks like you're going to be the one as looks out for the kid.'

'But I—'

'In between all your other work of course. And you've gotta keep your lip buttoned while you're at it. Oh, and when you're not with her, the kid'll have to be locked in.'

'How – how did the lady get a job?' Moira asked feebly. 'There aren't any jobs and—'

'Let's just say as how I heard of a full time stint going in the wash house. That's right, the same as what was going to give you a couple of hours at nights. Their regular dropped dead, scrubbing the concrete floor she was. They do say as how it was the old dear's heart.'

'And yet you...'

Flo raised her brows and shrugged. 'All right, I'll admit it's a pig of a job. But you could have handled it, even though it's hard and rough.'

'I don't want— I never did want—'

'Don't know when you're well off, you don't.' Flo snapped impatiently. 'Turning down work? My Gawd, Moir! Don't you know there's hundreds of women what would chase after it if word went round? Anyway, we ain't lost out today after all. I got Freddy to go round Maisie's and scrounge half a loaf and now we've got a regular. The Chink's money will come in handy, eh?'

'How did you find out about the job, if...'

Flo grinned and her voice held a sly humour.

'Use your marbles, Moir. I've got the manager by the short and curlies. I've done him favours several times. So the Chink gets the job. And if it don't work out the way I want, the manager's wife is all set to learn a thing or two. Yes, about her bloody old man! And that, my girl, would be curtains for the randy old sod.'

'I'm glad that you can help her,' Moira said uncertainly, and scraped the toe of her shoe along the floor, 'but I don't see— I mean—'

'You don't have to see nothing, Moir. The thing is, you're going to have to make a spot for yourself up there with them.

19

Liverpool wants someone to keep an eye open for the bread-snapper while she's not here. She's scared for the kid. I think someone's after her. So, I'm going to get Freddy to take your mattress up there, and I'll get a couple more off Anne Cherry. Oh, and don't forget, the kid's got to be kept safe.'

'Safe?' Moira asked and felt herself going cold with despair. 'By being locked in? Don't you mean that she's a prisoner?'

'Don't talk rubbish. You'll do as I say or else!'

'Flo, I – I don't want to go and sleep in the attic! There's rats up there and—'

'Don't be such a silly little cow. You've gotta do as you're told. Anyway, you're too old to share a room with Freddy now. You and the Chinks will manage all right, I know you will.' Flo looked into Moira's downcast face and grinned. 'Here, Moir, ain't Liverpool a bloody funny name for a Chink?'

Desperately uncertain of the future, Moira stood and watched Freddy chugging upstairs with her mattress. Her few pathetic belongings had been bundled into a cardboard shoe box. And that was all there was to it.

Feeling like a pariah, Moira got on with her chores for the rest of the day. And all the time she worked and slogged she felt her bitterness against the Chinese woman and her child grow. Because of those rotten foreigners, she must leave Freddy's room. Must exchange his cosy muddle, and his lovely quiet companionship, for a cold bare attic. Worse, she had to stay with the kind of people that would frighten her half to death! It was all their fault!

Late that night, exhausted, Moira climbed the attic stairs, clutching a key in her hand. Then she saw the woman and child for the first time. They were sitting side by side on one of the horsehair mattresses, and were very quiet and still.

The Chinese mother looked proud, with her hair piled high on her head, and her face was smooth and oval, and rather nice. The little girl looked sweet too. Thoroughly disgruntled, Moira hated them with her eyes.

'It's all right for you,' she burst out. 'But from where I'm standing, it's just not good enough!'

'You not like us?' The young woman breathed sorrowfully. 'Is sad!'

'It's more than sad,' Moira replied heatedly, 'It's downright unfair! And I'll tell you this, Liverpool, or whatever your name is, if you think I'm going to wait on you hand and foot, just because you're paying your way, you can forget it.'

'Liverpool,' the young woman replied quietly, 'is not true name. I not understand.'

'That's your name, Flo said.'

'I am Liver Pearl.'

'Pardon me?' Moira felt ungracious and it showed.

'Liver Pearl.'

'I've heard of black pearls,' Moira said nastily, 'but never pearls the colour of liver before.'

'Not say name that way!'

It took several times and finally the penny dropped.

'Oh so that's it!' Moira said, 'River Pearl! You have trouble with yours Rs.' She shrugged, loathing and detesting the fact that she was up here in the cold unfriendly attic, shut off from everyone. Stuck in with strangers who were definitely odd. 'Well, don't worry,' she said dismissively, 'I don't suppose we'll have much chance for talking. I'm tired out, so I'll just get myself ready for bed. Goodnight.'

Fighting her tears, Moira settled herself on her mattress. She saw the woman putting the child down on a mattress of its own, then firmly closed her eyes. It felt awful up here, it was dank and musty and she had a very real fear of rats. And she wasn't all that certain about the two strangers either. But rats! It came to her that she would get herself going in the morning and have a thorough scrub through. Perhaps Freddy would help and if there were any vermin around, he would sort it all out.

She bit her lips together, suppressing a sob. Freddy was wonderful, kind, and he was her mate. She liked him more than anything. And what's more, he would side with her about these rotten, lousy Chinks.

Then in spite of everything, she felt a wave of guilt. She was being horrible, really and truly awful! It wasn't the little girl's fault. And it wasn't the mother's either. It was Flo! Stupid, drunk as a skunk Flo, who'd let herself be hoodwinked into

21

having yellow skinned people in her house. Foreigners who were scary with their slitty eyes and—

Moira tried to sleep, but she was grieving. She was now even more of an outcast! Just as much as were the two strangers. 'Still,' a small voice at the back of her conscience whispered, 'the little girl looks sweet enough in a strangely distant way. Perhaps she's scared stiff and hating all this business as much as I do.' Her sympathy abated. 'I don't care! They're nothing to do with me. I shall do what I have to, but after that, I'll jolly well ignore them...'

It was not so hard to ignore River Pearl during the weeks that followed. The young woman, having received Moira's message loud and clear, kept herself very much to herself. Yet, in spite of everything, Moira found herself being drawn to the little girl, who she referred to as Thingy, and in an awkward, diffident way, she began to try to make friends. It was hard going all round. River Pearl went out early and came back late. She was always courteous and ultra polite. Moira secretly wished that she had not acted in such an ungracious way in the beginning, but was relieved that River Pearl seemed to trust her, at least where her daughter was concerned.

In spite of being warned not to let anyone know about the youngster, Moira sneaked her down to Stavros one morning. He smiled and ruffled the child's hair and offered her some bread and jam. The little girl held out her hand. And although she did not smile, it was clear that she had taken to the old man. And suddenly she relaxed completely and took to Moira too. She began to look for her, to run to her, to get close! She made Moira feel needed, really and truly necessary. This wonderful feeling made Moira glow.

Moira's care and concern for "Thingy" grew. Although of necessity, River Pearl was away for so long, one thing was perfectly clear. She truly loved her daughter and when they were together, acted like her adoring slave. Even so, her job kept her away from Jordan Lodge from dawn to dusk. She would return to the attic exhausted and looking harassed. Moira began to feel sorry for her. She and the lady even got to the point of exchanging shy smiles.

Flo acted almost as though she had forgotten the Chinese couple's existence these days. She reverted to her usual mouthy, sometimes downright rotten self. Moira, as ever, the butt of her anger, her confidences, her sarcasm, her finger poking and sudden spitefully flying hands.

'So sorry!' River Pearl whispered in sympathy one night.

'I'll live,' Moira replied and tried to laugh away her tears.

Chapter Three

Above the hissing and drumming of the rain the sound of merriment could be heard. Raucous voices accompanied by the beating of feet, and the high cackle from drunken women in the Hare and Hounds. The wind gusted and its icy edge seemed to cut through Moira like a knife. She huddled in a doorway, shivering and tired. If only Flo would hurry up. She was cold and hungry and Flo had promised! But promises were made to be broken, all the war-returned soldiers knew that!

A new world, a land fit for heroes? Not in shitty old Lime-house, Moira thought pithily and shivered as she tried to shelter from the rain. Grown-ups daft enough to believe what the papers said, deserved all they got. At least that was what Stavros thought.

Would the night never end? Life was the very devil at times. The odour of crisply frying fish came again from Dilley's Late fry. Moira lifted her head to sniff in the smell and felt the gnawing of hunger pains. Damn Flo and her way of making you do what she wanted all the time. It just wasn't fair!

Still, Moira tried to comfort herself, she had little Thingy to love, and she, Moira, and River Pearl were coming closer to being friends. Even so, you could never tell with that secretive lady. It wouldn't be so bad if Flo would speak about her two strange lodgers, but she always clammed up whenever Moira tried to bring up the subject. However, knowing Flo, Moira would have bet a pound to a penny that the China lady had promised Flo a fortune to make sure she and Thingy were kept safe. And of course there were always her wages for Flo to grab.

River Pearl worked like a dog, all hours, washing and ironing, never speaking by all accounts. Always afraid and looking over her shoulder. Why? And what was the little girl's real name? Perhaps, Moira thought, she would never get to know.

Flo, having been pointed out her initial mistake, now called the mother Pearl – and usually acted as though she wasn't there. And the poor thing took it, never even trying to fight back, Moira seethed, unaccountably finding herself fully on River Pearl's side.

She found herself swearing to God that one day she, Moira O'Malley, would rise above all this misery and be the lady that Stavros promised her she would be. The Lady of Limehouse she thought sourly, that was a laugh for a start! Ladies never felt as she did now, shivering in the rain.

Every so often, as well as the noises coming from the pub, the night was spliced with the melancholy sirens emitting from ships in or around the Docks. They sounded bloody awful, them ships, Moira thought, and shivered. Like grey ghosts wailing. Like warnings of the kicks and cuffs to come if port had put Flo in a hateful mood.

Moira crouched back in the shadows and started praying, with all the might of her old-young being, that Flo had picked up with a bloke. Flo always put on her simpering best if she'd got a man in tow. A sailor with money to spend – and money to steal the moment his eyes was closed. Then Freddy Noice would be called in. Big simple Fred who did what Flo said without question. And so Fred would sling the poor devil over his shoulders and take him to some dark lonely alley and leave him there to sober up.

Moira shivered right down to her shoes as she waited. She thought she saw demons lurking in the shadows. Officials waiting to reach out and snatch her away. At least in Jordan Lodge there were familiar faces. And at least, with Flo watching out for her, she was safe. And thumping and yelling and being worked to death wasn't half so bad as being thrown onto the streets to fend for oneself. Besides, like it or lump it, she was getting to enjoy the way young Thingy clung to her when Flo let off steam. Hiding against Moira's thin frame while Flo got on with her yelling and screaming. All this while River Pearl was away of course.

Moira knew that Flo was mostly all mouth and trousers.

Since being turfed out of the homely basement and up to the attic, Moira had vowed many times, just what she'd do to Flo – when she was grown up. Indeed on the bad days, it was her only pleasure in life, thinking up terrible tortures for Flo. Yes, today was a bad day and Moira was cold and miserable and out on a limb.

It came at last, chucking out time, and the doors of the Hare and Hounds swung open to let the stream of people pour through. They came in groups or pairs, laughing, wise-cracking back and forth with cockney humour, singing, shouting, swearing, scuffling. Then the inevitable fight broke out. Used to it, caring only for the mouth-watering smell coming from Dilley's Late Fry, Moira sidled forwards. She'd had only the scrapings of the porridge saucepan and a crust of bread to eat all day, and the promise of a ha'porth of chips was like the thought of Paradise. Flo was having a good time. She was clinging onto the arm of an equally big, heavy, round-faced man who stared down at Moira in an owlish way.

'What d'you want?' Flo asked and playfully pushed Moira so hard she fell back against the pub wall.

'You promised me—'

'I don't promise skivvys nothing, Moir.' Flo said impatiently, 'Push off! You're talking to the lady of the house, remember?'

'You promised me a ha'penny for chips,' Moira said desperately. 'You said if I looked after Thingy an extra hour I could have—'

'Are you daring to back-answer me?' Flo reached out, and began poking the thin cold girl hard on the chest with every word she spoke. 'Don't – you – give – me – no – cheek. I give you a roof over your head and feed and clothe you and —'

'All the poor little cow wants,' the big man growled, 'is a few bleedin' chips. What's the matter with yer?'

'If you're so sorry for the kid, you give her the money,' Flo giggled and ogled up at him. 'If only to show the world how well your pocket's lined.'

The big man fumbled in his pocket and handed Moira a penny. A whole penny! She could gorge herself. As she ran off to the chip shop she heard Flo beginning to screech at the man. Calling him all the filthy names she could put her tongue to.

This because the man, watching Moira's hasty retreat had growled out that Flo must be a right miserable old bitch what wouldn't give a poor kid a few fried spuds.

Moira all but fell into the fish and chip shop. Dilley, a tall, plain bean-pole of a man, leaned over the counter. He looked down at the small person whose coat must have once belonged to a boy much bigger and richer than she. He took her penny from her cold, wet outstretched hand. She looked up at him, her heart in her street-wise golden-brown eyes, her long cinnamon hair clinging wetly against the sides of her thin pretty face.

'So!' he said, 'Flo's seen you all right, has she?'

'The man,' Moira gasped, still out of breath, 'he gave it to me.'

'A man, eh?' Dilley looked down his long nose. 'Bit young ain't you? Still, if Flo Williamson brought you up, I suppose you know it all. Well, I'll tell you what I'll do.' Dilley's thin lips stretched in a sly conspiratorial smile, 'I'll keep your penny, so's you can come back for some more tomorrow. It's closing time now and and I've got a few left over that no one else seems to want.'

'Oh, Mr Dilley,' Moira could hardly believe her luck. 'Thank you!'

'And there's some batter chitlings too. Now while you wait for me to wrap them up, go through and get yourself warm and dry.'

Moira scuttled through the brown hessian curtain that divided the fish-fry and Dilley's living-room. The sofa was set before a warmly glowing fire. She sat down, having undone the buttons on her overlong, overlarge outer coat, silently thanking God that she had reached the chippy in time. She noted the gleam of a hearth-set. Heavy it was, brass, with a shovel, coal tongs and a poker with a round shiny handle and a large fancy knob on the top. She sat on an old sofa that had horsehair spilling out of it, and looked round. It was cosy and warm, dark and homely with the gaslight burning low. There was a table and two rickety chairs and a dresser that had shelves spilling over with all kinds of odd bits and pieces of crockery, ornaments, old newspapers to wrap up the fish and chips, hooks holding jugs and cups, even a small saucepan, and, even more out of place, Dilley's shaving mug.

27

The mantelpiece over the iron grate was also full to over-flowing with anything and everything. A cheap Woolworth alarm clock that had a loud, bouncy tick, held pride of place. Also there were pictures of Dilley's long dead wife, Martha and her twin brother Stan Jones who'd had his lungs burned by enemy gas. Stan now spent his time wandering the streets with a begging bowl. This had cut Dilley to the quick, his brother-in-law refusing his offers of help. It was common knowledge that this was because he blamed Dilley for killing his sister. Mrs Dilley had died trying to give birth to Dave's child. Everyone said that Dilley was daft to mind about Stan, and that it served the gassed-up old fool right if he finished up dead in a gutter somewhere. If he wouldn't take a hand-out from good old Dill, he'd never make old bones.

Dilley came in with hot chips and batter chitlings wrapped up in newspaper and handed them to Moira.

'Here you are! Get this down you. Want a cuppa?'

She nodded, already stuffing her mouth full.

He smiled a thin smile and, shaking his head sorrowfully, he went over to the black stove in the corner. He lit the gas under a battered old tin kettle, then cut a doorstep of bread off the crusty loaf standing on a wooden board.

'Fill yourself up with this, girl,' he told her, handing her the bread. Then, having sat down on one of the chairs, asked, 'How comes you're still skivvying for Flo Williamson?'

'I've always been with her, Mr Dilley. She's not so bad.'

'Dave. That's me name.' He wagged his finger at her in a mock playful way. 'Friends ain't we? You say always? Always with Flo? You ain't hers are you?'

'She told me that my Dad, a mealy-mouthed out-of-work Paddy, stayed at her lodgings for a while. She liked him a lot– at first. He told her that my Mum died when I was a year old and that he'd tried to do right by me, an innocent child, ever since. Then he got a job, on a ship. He– he told Flo that if she looked after me, he'd marry her and give her half his wages when he came back. Trouble is—'

'He never turned up, did he?' Dilley looked sadder than ever. 'So little Miss Moira O'Malley got to be her chief cook and bottle-washer! You're on your feet all day long, ain't you, at everyone's beck and call? Now this! You're never expected to get tired, or hungry, and you have to drag heavy coal scuttles up and down the stairs. I can guess how it is.' He got up because the kettle had boiled, and made tea in a chipped enamel pot. He then poured out two mugfulls, added sugar and condensed milk, stirred vigorously, and handed one to Moira. 'What time do you have to get up in the morning.'

'Half past five.'

'Then what do you do?'

'Light the fire in the range, then I help do the breakfasts, then wake people up and do the rooms, things like that. After that there's the steps, and housework. Of course, old Mother Noice comes in to help with the rough, so I don't do it all. Besides, nowadays I spend a bit of time looking after the kid.'

'What kid's that?'

'She belongs to a China woman.'

'What's it's name?'

'I call her Thingy, but she don't, I mean doesn't have a name.' She beamed at Dilley, grease shining round her lips, her eyes bright. 'Sometimes, when Flo's around, I wouldn't mind if I didn't have a name myself. It's Moir, do this. Moir do that. Moir get out of the bloody way.'

'What about school?'

Moira shook her head, mouth full, happy, her eyes twinkling now.

'I don't go.'

'All children have to go to school.'

'I don't. I've never been registered, so I don't have to go. Anyway, when I'm fourteen I'll be safe and sound and out of the reach of school board men.'

'You should have gone. They teach you to read and write, and how to knit and sew. And all kinds of clever things.'

'And they're welcome. Stavros teaches me all I want to know. I never wanted to go to no school.' She lifted her chin in a determined way, remembering all that Flo said. 'They make you sit on a bench with your hands behind your back. If you don't learn nothing they hit you with a cane. You have to sit still and not talk and— And I'd hate school!'

Dilley was watching her closely. There was colour in her cheeks now, and her long hair was beginning to dry and glimmer with hints of gold. Her eyes were the same goldy-brown as the wallflowers he'd once grown in his back yard. He hadn't bothered with growing flowers after his wife had died. Hadn't bothered with anything very much, except the frying, and keeping body and soul together. Now, faced with this tough little street-wise kid he was beginning to think, to feel!

'What would you say,' he asked her, 'if I told you I was thinking of seeing Flo and asking her if you could be my little companion and helper round here?'

'And I could have chips?'

'If you lived here with me, you could have fish with your chips.'

'Every day?' She couldn't believe what she was hearing. To eat hot food every day? To belong to Dilley instead of Flo? 'Oh, Mr Dilley,' she stammered, 'I'd think I was in heaven.'

'I'll see her in the morning,' he promised. 'In the meantime, you sleep on the couch. I'll get you a blanket so you'll be nice and warm. I'll talk to Flo tomorrow. All right?'

She nodded and ate the last crumb of the bread and the last tiny bit of crispy batter, the chips having long gone. She drank the tea, leaving only the grouts, and sighed with bliss. Dilley was watching her and smiling his funny thin smile. She beamed up at him, seeing him as God. To belong to Dilley. To eat good food. To sleep warm instead of on the damp mattress in the attic at the top of the freezing house. She was in Paradise. She had to be.

'I'll just poke the fire up and make it nice and hot for you,' he told her, 'then you can get ready for bed.'

He made a great to-do of poking the fire and fussing round after that, going up the stairs or somewhere, then coming back with a blanket, and finally saying, 'You can settle down now.'

He went out of the room and left her to it.

Having divested herself of her coat, and dress and liberty bodice, retaining only knickers and vest, Moira curled herself round in the blanket Mr Dilley brought down to her. It was multi-coloured and composed of many knitted squares. It was soft and warm and wonderful. Moira closed her eyes and dreamed of her father, whose name was Seamus, coming home from the sea. He had made a fortune and was going to take her to a lovely place to live. Her father had a face like Mr Dilley. Her father was cuddling and kissing her. Her father was—

He was pulling down her knickers! His mouth was at her unformed breasts. He was licking her. His hands were— His hands were feeling round her penny-parts! He was trying to— He was going to—

Her mind was racing. She had to keep still, not let him know she was awake. He was making little growling sounds deep in his throat. He was only thinking about what he was doing, not minding about her. She had to catch him unawares. She had to get away.

Her eyes fell on the poker. It was almost in her grasp. With a movement swift as lightning, and with all the force she could muster, Moira grabbed the poker and smashed it down on Dilley's head. Then she wriggled free, grabbed up her clothes and ran out to the fish fry area. She opened the front door and was outside, running in the rain, chest heaving, heart pounding, distressed and terrified.

She stopped at last, sobbing with relief because he was not following her. She put on her clothes, realised that she had forgotten her shoes, and felt sick, knowing that Flo would half kill her for that alone. Panting and near exhaustion, she reached the green door set in the brick wall, opened it and, quietly now, ran along the path. It was shrouded with tall laurel bushes, but unmindful of their ghostly appearance and the sharp stones under her feet, she crept back to the house and let herself in by the side door.

The journey up to the attic, trying not to make a noise, seemed to last a life-time. Then she was on her mattress, set on the opposite wall to where the Chinese woman and her daughter slept. Or was River Pearl sleeping? Did she perhaps, just for one instant, open her eyes to look at her, see the state she was in, and show concern?

'Is all right?' River Pearl whispered. 'You want speak?'

'I'm fine.' Moira mumbled in reply, feeling dirty, ashamed, and too shocked to want to confide. Shivering with cold, unable to sleep, afraid she would dream of what had happened, Moira drew her knees up to her chin in an effort to get warm. And all the while she was thinking of Dilley's tongue crawling over her like a wet and slimy living thing. And with all the might of her thirteen-year-old soul she made an oath. She would pay

Dilley back. If it took her the rest of her life, she'd get even. And she would make all men pay for being the animals they were . . .

It was still dark when Moira crept downstairs to the kitchen. Big it was, with a large wooden table and chairs set round it. A stone sink, a huge dresser holding crockery, and a large two-ovened cooking range that shone with the black-leading Moira did every day. She lit the gas lamp, liking the little plopping sound it made as it flared to life. She raked the grey ash out of the grate, screwed up paper, placed firewood on top and then small pieces of shiny black coal. Putting the match to paper, she blew gently, carefully, watching the whole thing hesitate, beam pale yellow and blue, then flare and take hold.

Now Moira replaced the heavy iron pot that contained mutton stew from the day before. Measured to within an eighth of an inch, even a spoonful would be missed under Flo's all-seeing eye.

Flo never wasted a thing. There'd be fresh carrot, onion, turnip and suet dumplings to go in once the gravy was boiled, anything filling, to keep the payers satisfied. Those that had no money went without. Moira had no money. The lodgers stew was sacrosanct. Still, even on bad days, she received what Flo thought she could afford. Flo never ate if her staff could not. She was a fair old thing in that way. When the lodgers had had their share of the stew, Moira could have what was left; in the meantime she had to make do with scraps.

Moira filled a large saucepan with water and tipped in the porridge oats that Flo had measured out and left in readiness the night before. Flo came from Scottish stock and was a great believer in oats. Here paying guests never had bacon and eggs unless they paid, and paid good. Good payers seldom chose to stay in Jordan Lodge. No matter, Miss Flora Williamson was a great believer in porridge oats. The oats saucepan took its place on top of the range.

The kettle went on, directly on top of the hob, once Moira had filled up with coal. She began praying for it to grow hot quickly. Her bare feet were blue with the cold on the stone floor. She thought of Dilley and shuddered and felt sick. She thought of Flo's rage when she realized that Moira's shoes were gone. Good stout shoes that Flo had bought from Anne

Cherry's Second Hand; Flo had made sure that Seamus's kid was fully clothed, and had been particularly proud of the liberty bodice.

'Don't you forget, Moir,' she had warned, 'to tell them that if you ever get found out. Tell them as how I've always treated you nice and kept you well fed and clothed. D'you hear me? You tell them that! They'll see for themselves of course. There ain't many kids round here what have nice warm coats. Shawls or bits of blankets for their shoulders if they're lucky, that's what they have. Not nice warm coats. So, if they catch up with you—'

'What will happen to me if – if they ever find me out?' Moira had asked fearfully.

'An 'Ome, that's what. A sodding 'Ome. They'll put you in an orphan's place where you'll be beaten and starved. Even worse, they'll put you in school! 'Orrible place that is. They make you remember things, and when you can't remember, you get the cane. Black and blue they make you. All up and down your legs. I did you a favour, keeping you on here, and don't you forget it. And if ever your Dad comes home, you tell him that too!'

'I don't think he'll ever come back,' Moira had burst out once. 'I reckon you did me a favour, 'specially keeping me away from school. They – they won't make me go will they?'

'Who knows what them upper-crusts do? Just you keep your mouth shut, that's all.'

'I will, I will!'

'That's all right then. Now get on with your work and remember that you're doing all this to pay me back for keeping you. Yes, safe from the 'Ome even though that mealy-mouthed swine of a Seamus O'Malley upped and left.'

'Swine of a Dad!' Moira said out loud, her voice harsh with tears. 'All men are rotters, specially the Dave Dilley kind.' Then she bit her lip because she heard Flo coming down the stairs.

The round-faced man had blacked Flo's eye, and given her a bit of a time of it, at least by the looks of things, but strangely Flo seemed to be in a good mood. She was looking smug as she took the kitchen cupboard key out of her pocket. She opened up and took out the larger half of a cottage loaf. She cut off a doorstep sized slice and handed it to Moira.

'Here, take this. Better than we had yesterday, eh? Things was a bit sticky till old man Stavros came home last night and give me his cash. Now on top of that Will is very well off. Emptied his pockets for me he did, and there was no need to call on Fred.'

'Is he the man that gave me a penny?'

'Yes. A real man is Will. Knows what's what, he does. A penny, eh? That was fair, very fair. A ha'penny would have done just as well. We've gotta make a fuss of Will, Moir. And we've gotta make him want ter stay. All man, he is, and don't take no nonsense, but he's my cup of tea, girl, make no mistake.'

Flo cut herself a slice of bread and sat at the table. Moira munched while standing. It was more than she dared do, step out of line.

The kitchen door opened quietly. River Pearl seemed to float in, silent, on her thin cotton shoes. She put her hands in her jacket sleeves, and bowed her head to Flo and gave a swift half smile to Moira before going to the dresser and taking from it a small bowl. This she took to the side shelf, where a tureen full of cold cooked rice stood. The small bowl was filled with rice, then from out of her sleeves she pulled chopsticks. She sat at the opposite end of the table to Flo, lifted the basin almost to her lips and rapidly ate the sticky rice which she formed into balls. Moira walked to the range; the water in the kettle was barely luke warm, no good for tea-making, but better than nothing. She filled a cup with water and took it to River Pearl. It was accepted graciously and with twinkling eyes. It was good that Moira and River Pearl now got on.

'She's a strange one,' Flo remarked when River Pearl had gone back up stairs, taking a dish of rice up to her daughter. 'Still she knows what's what and don't cause no trouble. When she's left the house, you go up and see the kid's asleep, then you go and do for Stavros. You really like the old boy, don't you?'

'He's been learning, I mean teaching me how to speak properly for years,' Moira openly admitted for the very first time, 'And to read and write. He says that he is teaching himself all the time, and that it helps him just by helping me.'

'What else does he do while you're up there all cosy-like in his room?' Flo's eyes were narrowed with suspicion now. 'Don't you take no nonsense, d'yer hear?'

'He's a Greek gentleman who used to be the tutor in a rich merchant's house. Mr Stavros taught the son and even the grandson of the Bertos family. But when Yani was sent to a posh English school, Stavros was pensioned off. It's only a small pension, he says, but it comes regular and he still gets to see the grandson, Yani, who he loves like his own.'

'Proper little know-all, ain't yer?' Flo teased. 'Well, thank Gawd for Stavros! I was on me uppers yesterday, but he paid me last night. Come on, spit it out. What else does he tell you?'

'About the island where he was born. He lets me sit by his fire and he tells me and Thingy stories and—'

'He knows about her?' Flo's cheeks were flushing red. She jumped up from her chair and grabbed hold of Moira and shook her hard, 'I told you, don't breathe a word! Didn't I tell you? Who else knows about the kid?'

'Only – only Dilley.'

'Dilley? Since when did you get talking to him?'

'Last night. Ow!'

Flo glared down, at Moira's foot, now red and grazed where Flo had unwittingly stepped on it. Then the older woman's face went the colour of beetroot as she shook the girl's thin frame even harder, till Moira's teeth rattled and she couldn't breathe, and the whole world was spinning round and round. And all the while Flo was shouting and raving fit to burst, about no one knowing about the kid. That terrible Chinamen all slit-eyed and evil would come and chop them all to bits if they found out that Pearl was here. Then with a dagger-look and murderous intent Flo snarled:

'And what the bloody hell are you doing down here without your perishing shoes?'

She let go, and Moira fell back, breathless and dizzy. Then, as the woman leaned forward menacingly again, she panted,

'I got my feet wet and Dilley saw and said I could sit by his fire while my shoes dried out a bit.'

'And what else?'

'Nothing. Nothing, I swear!'

'Then how comes you ain't got your shoes on now?'

'It was getting late.' Moira gasped desperately, 'You half

killed me that time I was late back with your chips, remember? Told me never to be late again. I – I fell asleep, yes asleep in front of Dilley's fire. And when he woke me up and told me the time I run out of there as fast as I could. I was nearly home when I got to notice I'd left my shoes.'

Flo folded her arms and smiled a mirthless smile. In a half-scared but triumphant way Moira saw that Flo believed her. At least her brassy hair wasn't standing on end – when Flo was furious, Moira always swore she saw the fair frizzy hair rearing up, almost alive, and sparking and spitting out Flo's rage.

'So,' Flo smirked, 'I scared the shit out of you that time, did I? It's good you remember my words. Don't you never forget what I tell you, d'yer hear? And I'm warning you, don't you ever breathe on about Pearl staying up top. They're after them two, them Chinks, and they'll slit our gizzards from end to end if they find Pearl and her sprat here. Now, get down to Dilley's. Tell him you want your shoes and there'll be hell to pay if you don't get 'em. All right?'

Moira stood there, mind racing. She was sure that she had killed Dilley stone dead. If she went back, they'd know she'd done it. They'd take her away and hang her for murder. It must be terrible to be strung up by rope and be hung by the neck until you were dead. Even worse than getting a back-hander from Flo, or a shaking, or even a good thrashing. Anything was preferable to the slimy feel of Dave Dilley's tongue.

'Won't do no good, me going to Dilley's' she said defiantly, 'he won't be back from the fish market yet. Can't I go later on?'

'All right, all right!' Flo shrugged her fat shoulders, 'It's you with freezing feet, not me. You what's without shoes. You get them back, that's all. And don't ever let this happen again.'

'Never ever again, Flo. I don't know what got into me.'

'Don't think you're getting round me. Old for your age, you are. Been here before, ain't you? Well just you remember this. I bought you good shoes and they've gotta stay on your feet, wet or not. You've grown into them now, and they're worth their weight in gold. Now I think I heard the door go, that means Pearl's left for work. Go up and see to her kid. Give her some more of the rice and some of them vegetables from the stew. It ain't the poor little sod's fault, none of it, and Pearl would give her life for that child.'

'What's her name?' Moira asked daringly, as she put rice in the bowl and went to the stew pan and began fishing round for carrot and peas. 'I never know what to call her. And why is she and her Mum hiding here? River Pearl and me are talking now, but ... I don't like questioning her too much. If she thinks I'm being nosy, she'll go back into her shell again and—'

'You are prying, and curiosity killed the cat, Moir. As for the rest, I dunno.' Flo shrugged casually, 'I think Pearl overheard something she shouldn't have. It ain't wise to see or hear things you never ought. Well, Pearl knew it'd be curtains if she didn't do a bunk. Don't know how she found this place. All I know is, she finished up on my doorstep with enough money to pay me for three weeks. I didn't know that when I got her the job up the wash-house! But me and her have an arrangement. Now, Nosy Parker, you know as much as me.'

'But – she never calls the girl a name. Never! It's as if she's scared to say something that might ... Oh, I don't know, but ...'

'Who the bloody hell cares about either of them? Don't you get mixed up in nothing, d'yer hear? They're lodging here and nothing to do with us. That's what you'll tell anyone what comes. Especially anyone with a yellow face. As for the kid, all I know is Pearl told me once that her daughter is as precious as Jade. And that's why she pays me extra, to make sure I look after her. But she's never said nothing about a name. Anyway, what's it to you?'

'I'll call her Jade,' Moira made up her mind. 'I don't want to call her Thingy, or kid no more. She seems to have taken to me.'

'Gawd! That shows she's daft as well as foreign,' Flo said with heavy humour, 'how out of luck can you get? Now don't push it, buzz off, else you'll feel the back of my hand.'

Moira hastily left the kitchen and all but ran up three flights of stairs.

She reached the attic door and turned the key in the lock. Moira opened the door and went in. The Chinese child was lying on the mattress, a small, dark butter-ball, she was so wrapped up in her padded clothes. She saw Moira, sat up, and held out her arms.

37

'What a lot of cupboard love,' Moira teased and smiled, 'it's only because you know I've got your breakfast. Here you are, and with a spoon. I could never get on with them chopsticks of yours. Why don't you talk, eh? You're a big girl and should be chattering nineteen to the dozen. There's kids on the street who live rough, and who know how many beans make five, a sight younger than you. Come on! Cat got your tongue?'

The child remained silent, having bowed her head slightly as a thank you when Moira handed her the food. She began eating quickly, quite at home with the spoon, since Moira always made a point of insisting on it.

'When you've finished, we'll go and see Stavros, shall we? We've got to listen to him, and learn things, like he said. Then they'll never make us go to school.'

The little girl stopped eating long enough to give Moira a wide eyed stare. Moira winked at her and grinned.

'Why don't you say something?' she teased. 'Why won't you speak to me so's I can understand? You talk to your mum all right, I've heard you, but I don't know nothing about Chinese. Say my name. I'm Moira and you're Jade.'

Jade held her half-filled spoon in mid-air and stared, and for the first time ever, gave a ghost of a smile. Then dark almond-shaped eyes sparkled and rounded rose-bud lips curved upwards again as Jade's face spilled over with delight. She burbled something in a foreign tongue, but it didn't matter. Moira's affection-starved heart melted.

After all this time! Moira thought. Me and Jade really are one!

For the first time in her life Moira felt she had someone who loved her for herself, without Flo's violent contradictions and conditions which had made her young life such a misery of insecurity. At that moment Moira made an oath. She would look out for, care for, even lie and steal for the China child.

Then in a high, light, lovely way, Jade tried to say Moira. It didn't matter that it wasn't quite right, it was good enough.

'That's right!' Moira told her, delighted. 'You're a clever one. Almost as clever as me! We'll get on like a house on fire, won't we? And I'll always look out for you while your mum's not here. There's nothing to be scared of, Jade. That I promise

38

you. Good! You've ate it all up. Just wait till I make sure Flo's not around and then we'll go and see to Stavros.'

Jade held up her arms, but Moira laughed.

'You've got to use your own two legs. You might be a little tot for your age, but I'm not your Mum, waiting on you hand and foot, and carrying you around. Come on!'

They went down the ill-lit stairs together, knocked and went into the room that Mr Stavros Sella called home.

Chapter Four

Stavros was a small man with thick, bushy white eyebrows and kind eyes. He was already up and sitting at the long, narrow oak table that ran almost the length of his room. The table was highly polished and clearly treasured. Indeed, the table, purchased by Stavros himself, was his life. He used it as a desk, an eating place, a school for Moira, a debating point, a home for all kinds of writing materials, a base for a huge dictionary, resting place for various Greek artifacts. In pride of place was a large framed and signed photo of the stern-faced man who had employed him as tutor for his son. There was another picture of the three Bertos men together. Father, son, and grandson Yani. All dark-eyed and very handsome indeed.

Now he looked over at the two young people and smiled.

'*Kalemera* my little ones.'

'And good morning to you, Mr Sella,' Moira replied politely and gave him a wide, all-embracing smile.

'You are growing up now and you are my friend,' he told her, wagging his finger in a reproving way, 'you must call me Stavros. A tutor must, above all, be a friend. Must be close.'

'Flo said school's terrible and she hates teachers and will to her dying day.' Moira replied carefully. 'I know I'd hate school.'

'Miss Williamson is a product of a system that believes obedience and knowledge will be achieved by fear. Little one, fear merely makes a creature vicious and on the attack. Fear is not good.'

This was above Moira's head, so she dismissed it, saying, 'It's funny the way you go all polite and call Flo Miss Williamson –

40

and get her to call you Mr Sella.' She smiled a little wickedly, adding, 'Mind you, she don't call you no Mister behind your back! You keep her in her place all right. But you call me my full name and you tell me to call you Stavros. Why?'

'Because she is not my friend and will never be a lady. On the other hand, you are both.'

'And Jade!' Moira lifted her chin firmly. 'She's with me.'

'Ah! You have discovered the little girl's name?' He beckoned the children towards the fire. 'Get yourselves warm. Moira, may I ask, where are your shoes?'

Moira chose to ignore the question and replied, 'I don't know her proper name, but I like Jade because her Mum says she's as precious as jade. So that's what I call her.'

'A very good idea. Names should mean something. My favourite is Amanda. Once, a very long time ago, I knew someone of that name. Alas, it was not to be. In Latin Amanda means "Lovable".'

'Ha!' she said fiercely, 'I'm not lovable, Stavros. I'm an unwanted thing that was left behind like a parcel. I was dumped and if it wasn't for Flo I'd be out on the street with the rest of the urchins. I'd hate that, I really would. There are wicked people out there. Men!'

'I'm a man.'

'No you're not. You're Stavros what learns me things and—'

'Not too well, I'm afraid.'

'What?'

'We shall have to begin at the beginning again. You are forgetting a great deal. You will go far in the world, I have every faith that you will. But you must learn to speak properly. Has Miss Williamson given you breakfast?'

'I had a doorstep, yes, but I'm still hungry. Thank Gawd you paid her last night. She got a loaf and—'

'God.'

Moira stopped in mid flow.

'Do what?'

'Not Gawd, Moira. God!'

'Oh that! God then. So she must have bought it last night. Went round to the back door of Popsy's Corner shop I suppose. Popsy often obliges when everywhere else is shut.'

'Would you like a piece more bread?'

'No ta, I—'

'No thank you!'

She smiled across at him, her face rosy in the firelight.

'Oh my Gawd, Stavros, you don't half go on! Are you going to have porridge? It's real nice and hot. I'll run down and get it for you now if you like.'

'Very well. Ask Miss Williamson for my largest bowl. Fill it because I am extra hungry, eh?'

'And you want milk and sugar don't you?' Moira asked and looked greedy.

'Today I am rich and Miss Williamson has been paid, so yes, my dear. Milk and sugar if that is what you want. Later, if you will, perhaps you will go to Popsy's for me?'

'I'd go to the ends of the earth for you,' she told him earnestly, 'and so would Jade.' She smiled down at the child who was standing close against her side, 'Wouldn't you, Jade?'

'Hai,' Jade whispered.

'Yes,' Moira said firmly. 'You've gotta say yes!'

Jade's lips remained obstinately closed. Even so, the little girl sat down obediently and waited.

Moira ran down the stairs. She opened the back door to scoop up the large, cleanly scrubbed slop pail and set it down while she took Stavros's own large soup bowl off the dresser shelf. She filled the china bowl, which was decorated with vine leaves and purple grapes, and filled it with porridge that was keeping warm on the range. She added sugar and the much prized cow's milk that was ice cold from the step.

'You little bitch,' Flo snapped, coming in just at the wrong moment, 'you didn't shake the bottle. You've given old Stavros all the cream from the top.'

'Well, he paid you last night, didn't he?' Moira replied and glared back, 'You was able to get a loaf up Popsy's and I thought—'

'You do too much thinking, you do. Cheeky sod. If you don't watch your lip my girl, I'll—' Flo stopped mid-sentence to snarl at Mrs Noice who had just come in. 'What kept you, Noice? I pay you half a crown to come and work first thing, not halfway through the bloody day.'

Mrs Noice, large, tough, with beefy arms and legs that matched her red face, impatiently pushed a strand of greasy black hair under the man's cloth cap she wore. She sniffed and looked down her nose. There was nothing subservient about Mrs Noice, because she was Freddy Noice's aunt, and the whole world knew that Flo doted on Fred.

Mrs Noice wore serviceable black boots over thick woollen stockings and long, well-worn, no-nonsense navy-blue clothes. She took off her outer coat, donned a voluminous coloured pinafore. Her feet made stolid clumping sounds as she went to the old yellow stone sink. She opened the cupboard door underneath and reached for the scrubbing brush, the bag of soda, yellow soap and pail.

'Water 'ot yet?' she asked and looked to see if the kettle on the range was steaming. 'You ain't getting me to do nothing without some heat. It's monkey's outside, make no mistake.'

'You should 've been here an hour ago,' Flo was going turkey-cock red, 'and I'll have you know—'

'Someone up the road's frying bacon.' As usual, Mrs Noice was taking the war into enemy camp. 'Fair made me drool it did. Can't you send Moira up Popsy's for some bacon? I know Stavros paid you last night, so you could give Freddy something better than porridge for a change.'

She smiled in a sour, bitter way, 'Still that don't cut no ice with you, does it, Flo? You've spent the lot up the Hare and Hounds, just like you always do. No wonder you don't get no good paying customers. No real gent would stay in a place what's filled with drunken caterwauling every night. Another thi—'

'Shut up, you mouthy bitch.' Flo shouted, 'For two pins I'd—'

Moira snatched up the slop pail and the porridge bowl in the other hand, and beat a hasty retreat. She pretended not to hear Flo yelling, 'Shut the bloody door!'

Moira's hands were full and she did not intend stopping for nothing or no one. She continued her race up the large flight of stairs and setting down the pail, opened the door and burst in.

Stavros's room was a haven of warmth and comfort now the coal had fully burned through. Moira paused for a moment, just to look round. At the book case filled with Greek books. The little wall shrine to Saint Spiridon, and on the mantelpiece an icon of the Mother and Child. Stavros's bed that served as settee by day, was as yet unmade, but Moira would soon see to that.

She knew that the tall cupboard was bare apart from Stavros's one and only black suit and his well polished shoes; he had old slippers that he used most of the time. Stavros also had two well laundered shirts and two sets of underclothes. The old oak sideboard that for most of yesterday had been empty, would for a few days at least hold food, extras that Stavros enjoyed, and quite apart from the plain, no-onsense fare supplied by Flo.

Most of Stavros's spare money went on writing things, he was always writing about the people he met on the streets. It would be a book one day. But mostly he haunted the second-hand book stalls in the market. When he had a little left over, he indulged in chunks of crusty bread dipped in olive oil, and there would be onions and tomatoes, and feta cheese, bought from a special shop he knew.

As Moira entered, he was holding the top half of the cottage loaf Flo had bought, and taking it to the table. He had already poured olive oil into a saucer. He smiled over at Moira and waved to the bed.

'Sit down and share the porridge between you. Hurry up before it gets really cold.'

'Thanks ever so much,' Moira said and twinkled at him. 'I couldn't half have done with this yesterday.' She climbed onto the bed and Jade clambered up after her. Jade refused the porridge, but Moira wolfed it down. 'I hoped as how Mr Binks will pay today,' she said between mouthfuls. 'Your rent will have been sunk by now. Thank Gaw – God, she was on gin.' She looked across the room, entreaty on her thin, rather lovely face, 'When I've seen to Mr Binks and done whatever it is Flo wants, can me and Jade stay down here with you for a while?'

'It will be no problem,' he told her, 'and we will begin to speak properly, and learn to read and write a few more words. Perhaps, in the meantime, Miss Williamson and I will have a short conversation.' He cut off a piece of bread and dipped it into the oil and before taking a mouthful, added, 'I mean to find out if the woman has taken it upon herself to sell your shoes.'

'No! She's done nothing of the sort!' Moira's swift look of horror merely confirmed Stavros's fears. Then as the memory of the horrible Dave Dilley rose to grin like a spectre in her mind, she burst out, 'I hate this old Jordan Street, and this house and – and men! I don't know why you stop here when you've got a pension, and you could go home to Greece. If I had a pension I'd be off like a shot!'

'What is it?' he asked, and his piercing eyes were very direct. 'And why are you so fiercely against men? You quite liked us yesterday.'

'I still like you,' she panted, 'and Mr Binks and Freddy. And that new bloke of Flo's is all right, he gave me a penny for chips last night and— I don't like chips Stavros.' Tears were scalding against her lids as he gasped out again, 'I think as how I hate chips now!'

'Why? Tell me. You are like my kori, Moira.'

'No I ain't, I mean not,' she said fiercely, 'I'm not like anyone's daughter. And now I'll get on with my work.'

She jumped off the bed, swung Jade down and plonked her on the floor by the fire. Moira's chores were always the same. She completed them without thinking, quickly and dexterously. She turned down the bed clothes, leaving them to air while she got on with other things. She emptied the contents of the chamber into a slop pail. Emptied the water from the wash basin into the chamber, rinsed and poured out. She tipped water from the jug into the basin, wiped it round, emptied, then dried. She made the bed, having beaten the bolster and replaced the pillow, tucking the blankets in, two bright red ones that had once seen service in a hospital, together with top and bottom sheets. Then she threw over the white tasselled bed-spread, that was put in the copper to boil once every four weeks.

It was Flo's proud boast that Jordan House was scrupulously clean. Bugs had short shrift in Flo's place and it was one of Moira's tasks to search them out and kill, kill, kill. Fleas were powdered out of existence the second they hopped into view, and the kitchen cockroaches were always having to regroup, being under unceasing attack. Even so, Stavros took his own precautions. This room was his world. One which he cared for very much. Unlike Mr Binks who didn't give a damn.

Leaving Jade and Stavros to mind their business while she got on with hers, Moira grabbed up Stavros's rag rug and the slop pail and went out.

Half way along the passage a splinter of wood ran into her foot. It hurt a lot. She said 'Shit' and pulled the splinter out. Further along she dropped the rug down outside Mr Binks' door and walked in without waiting. Normally she loved seeing him, he was a laugh. But today was a bad day, her foot hurt, and she didn't much care whether Mr Binks was in a good mood or not.

He was sitting at his small square table, as supplied by Flo, eating his porridge that had been taken up by Mrs Noice. Only Mr Sella and Mr Binks were served breakfast in their rooms. But they were regulars and paid well, Flo had to look after them! If she didn't the Hare and Hounds would lose out.

Mr Binks looked up and winked when Moira entered. She gave him a half smile and began her chores, exactly as she had for Stavros, whisking about, methodically, unthinking, conscious only that the splinter had gone in deep and that her feet were cold. She could all but feel Mr Binks watching her. He was waiting for her to speak, but she wouldn't. She couldn't. She just didn't damned well care. She knew all about old Binksy, oh yes!

If the truth was known, she could spill the beans about a whole bunch of them in Jordan Lodge. She had been put on this earth old, so Flo said. Well today was an old grey day. Mr Dilley was probably still where she had left him, all dead and horrible on the floor. They all said that Mr Dilley was a good man. Well he wasn't. They said he was well respected, which was a laugh. They might have been nearer the truth if they'd looked up to and thought good things about the man watching her now.

Alfy Binks, known by the police, yet popular even so, was fat and jolly. He had salt and pepper hair, and piggy little eyes that always seemed to be twinkling and teasing and darting about. Mr Binks wore a large gold pocket watch that he swore had been his father's though everyone knew that it had probably been pinched from some poor unsuspecting nob. He wore bright coloured waitcoats and baggy trousers and a too large jacket; all had previously seen life in Anne Cherry's Second Hand.

Mr Binks haunted the markets, picking pockets and taking what he could with consumate expertise. He did it all with a merry quip and a jolly grin on his face – most folk agreed that he was a very likeable man. He and Stavros got on well and spent many a pleasant hour together, talking about this and that, especially the rival merits of their young friends. Stavros was always boasting about Yani Bertos, while Mr Binks laughed and crowed about the tricks young Chumley Potts and Conor MacCluskey got up to, both youths being Mr Bink's ragamuffin friends. Moira was intrigued by the sound of all three. She understood that they were all several years older than she.

'Cat got your tongue, Moir?' Mr Binks asked and winked again. 'Where the bloody hell's your shoes? It cold 'nough to freeze the balls off a brass monkey, and there you are, flitting about like a tit in a trance. Why ain't you got nothing on your feet?'

'I forgot them,' she said crossly. 'Mr Binks, why don't you mind your own? I'm sick of everyone carrying on about my shoes.'

'Oh Lord!' he groaned in an exaggerated way, 'got out the bed the wrong way, ain't we? Never mind, Moir, I'm all on your side.'

'It's a good job somebody is,' she snapped, then collected the slop pail and his rug and went outside to collect the one from Stavros's room. She lugged the lot down the next flight of stairs, along the passage and into the kitchen. She intended to go through to the yard and empty the pail down the lav, and then she would beat the rugs free of dust. Instead she stopped in her tracks and froze.

Flo and the large, round-faced Will were sitting at the table – listening to Dave Dilley!

Dave Dilley looked taller and thinner and sadder than ever, and he had a whopping great bump on the side of his head.

Flo was squinting and her cheeks were red. She stared at Moira hard, then looked contemptuously up and down and all over Moira's thin frame. Then she thumped her fat fist on the table, which made the shoes near her hand bounce. She almost hissed as she said menacingly, 'Come here you little trollop. And let me, Mr Fenning, and Dave know just what you've got to say for yourself.'

It wouldn't do any good to say a thing. Moira could tell that.

47

They were all against her and she couldn't win. With all the longing in her young soul, Moira wished the three of them dead. Dead and done for and burning in hell.

Saying nothing, her face set, she began to move towards the back door. Once safe outside, in the yard, she could beat the living daylights out of the rugs. She wouldn't cry and she wouldn't be scared. Old Dave Dilley had said things to get them on his side. He had told lies all right. Well she could tell a lie or two for herself if it all boiled down to it. Deep inside she knew that today was going to be a "Lie to the bitter end day".

She heard the chair scrape back and flinched as Flo jumped up and caught her by the shoulders and spun her round. She glared defiantly up at the woman. Flo began to shake her hard, which made the slops over-spill. Then Flo finished by giving her a stinging blow across the face. Moira's eyes became twin brilliants with unshed tears, but she continued to glare, her cheek burning with Flo's finger marks. Raging at the injustice of it all, she plonked the bucket down and dropped the rugs, then clenched her fists tight against her sides.

'Are you stone deaf?' Flo yelled and slapped her again. 'Answer when I'm talking to you. D'you hear me? You cunning little cow! How could you do it? Especially when I look after you so well.'

'You don't look after me,' Moira rapped out, and took a furious step forwards. 'You just let me stay here and work! Everyone knows that. Even Dave Dilley.'

'What?' Flo's eyes were glittering red. 'How dare you mention a gentleman's name.'

'Gentleman?' Moira was shaking with fury as the words spilled out. 'He ain't no gentleman. He's a rotten foul pig, and he reckoned my life here was so horrible he offered me a place in his house.'

'Don't lie to me!' Flo began her finger poking again. 'Do – you – hear – me – slut? Do – not – lie – to – me!'

'I ain't. On Jade and Freddy's life, I ain't!' Moira's voice rose higher as she back-answered. 'He said that if I stopped with him I could have chips and fish every day. He said he wanted me to be his little helpmate and companion. I told him it would be heaven if he meant it. He said to sleep on his couch by the fire and he'd see you about it today. I undressed and went to sleep and I woke up when the dirty old devil started fingering me.'

'What?' Flo swung round to face Dave Dilley who was looking more mournful than ever. 'You didn't, did you?'

'Miss Williamson,' he all but wrung his hands, 'you must understand! She told me that she had already earned money from a man. She stood there, large as life, and held out the money she had taken from a man.'

'She ain't never had no time for that sort of thing,' Flo was now looking at Dave in a mean and thoughtful way.

'I thought,' Dave Dilley was frowning, looking puzzled and even more sorrowful, 'I mean, I believed that –' He lifted his head and stared hard at Flo, then continued in a firmer, far more convincing manner, 'It's like I've just told you. She egged me on. She ogled me and wriggled her hips and made me think things. She went out of her way to make me think she'd let me – if I gave her chips today as well. That she'd stay with me if I promised her fish and chips all the time.'

'My Gawd!' Flo was gob smacked and it showed.

Dave Dilley warmed to his theme.

'I am a lonely man, very lonely, so I said yes. I meant to wait till I'd talked to you, but I kept thinking of her, the way she was flaunting herself, and so I went down and—'

'Tried it on?' The stone faced Will rasped. 'She's just a kid, you dirty bastard. Just a poor little cow what's—'

'What's been here before,' Flo cut in, rounding on him. 'Knows a trick or two does our Moir. Mind your business, Will. This ain't got nothing to do with you.'

'Bloody hell, Flo,' the warning cut no ice with Will, 'ain't you forgetting something? She's had to learn the hard way by the looks of things, and she's still only a kid!'

'A man gave her money. She told me.' Dave reiterated and managed to look even more miserable. 'That's how she came to be in my shop, with her smiling and simpering, and giving me them knowing looks.'

'She had a penny,' Will snarled across the table at him, 'a whole bleeding penny what I gave her.' He looked at Flo. 'Kick the dirty bastard out. He ain't worth the air he bloody well breathes.'

'Hold your horses, Will,' Flo flared at him, and suddenly

49

there was calculation in her eyes. 'I believe him. Moir's no better than she should be, and I don't think Dave's lied any more than she has herself. Else why did the little cow tell me that she just fell asleep while her shoes were drying out in front of Dave's fire? That when he woke her up and told her the time, she run like hell back home and quite forgot her shoes?'

'Are you going to kick him out, or shall I?' Will was standing up now, not as tall as Dave, but three times the man Dilley was in build and intent. But Flo was no sylph and with three quick steps she was between the men, red-faced and furious and snarling at Will, her black eye gleaming purple in the light.

'*I'll* chuck out them as ain't welcome, in me own good time, Will Fenning,' she shouted. 'D'yer hear me? It's up to me who goes and who stays.'

'The dirty bastard's a—'

'Sod off!' Flo had made her choice. 'D'yer hear me? Who goes and who stays is up to me. Mind your own business, you ain't nothing to do with us here. You've just told me that you're only staying for two days, then you're off to your ship and only might come back. Might!' She tossed her head, incensed. 'No nice promises, eh?'

'A seaman can't—'

'Ha!' Flo's tone became bitter. 'Don't bother yourself. I've had promises before, and seen what they've come to in the end. But no one's ever been so cold and cruel and callous to a woman as you. You're only sticking up for Moir because you're dying to have a punch up to show how you can use your fists. I know as how you can with women! Now you want this bloke and it don't make no odds that he's a skinny thing what 'ud drop at a touch. That's the way you like it, ain't it?'

'Mind how you talk to me!' Will's tone became menacing. He jutted out his chin and looked evil.

Flo's dander was up, and she was far from impressed. She took a step forward, fists clenched and raised in readiness.

'Know all about your sort, I do,' she said in a dangerous voice. 'So get out!'

'Glad to, you ugly old tart.' Will snarled, 'I was soused as a herring to take you on.' He was sneering and looked ugly as he viciously jeered, 'Yes, I must have been bloody hard up!'

'You weren't never hard, nor up!' Flo replied sarcastically.

She put her hands on her hips and threw back her head and laughed in a coarse and vulgar way. 'I've seen better dicks on two-year olds. Crooked, weedy little thing you've got. You're a joke you are, make no mistake.'

Will Fenning went puce, his eyes bulged. Flo had hit him below the belt, Moira thought wildly, laughing at his manhood like that! She wasn't a bit surprised when the round faced man turned tail and walked out of the kitchen in a silent, stiff-backed way. Flo, for all she had said that Will was all man and perfect for her, had impatiently dismissed him. All of her attention was now on Dave Dilley.

'So,' she drawled, and contrived to look vampish, 'you're lonely, are you, Dave? Fish and chips you said? What, every day!'

'Yes,' Dave replied, brightening a little. 'That's what I said.'

Moira's heart was thumping. She tried to run out of the kitchen, but her legs wouldn't move she was so afraid.

'Stay where you are!' Flo snapped and threw the shoes over. 'Put them on. Cost me, they did. Go on, put them on!'

Moira gave Flo a wide-eyed look of pleading, and bent down to do as she was told. Flo was once again concentrating on Dave.

'Let's sit down,' she told him in a falsely bright and friendly way, 'make yourself comfy.' Then she ordered over her shoulder, while still smiling at Dave, 'Oi! Moir, you hurry up and make me and Dave a cuppa. Hot and sweet with plenty of condensed.' She gave Dave a playful nudge with her elbow, 'That's how I like it, hot and sweet. And you?'

Dave Dilley was brightening with every second that passed. He nodded slowly and sat down at the table, curling his long legs under it, leaning thin bony elbows on the surface before him. He looked across at Moira and she glared at him, not realizing that her eyes were like large crystals, and that fear had made her beautiful. She turned her attention to the teapot, emptying the grouts into the slop bucket, which made a wave of stench rise.

'For Gawd's sake get that outside,' Flo ordered and herself moved towards the range, taking the teapot from Moira's shaking hand. 'Then come back and listen to what's being said. D'yer hear?'

Moira wordlessly did as she was told. She emptied the bucket down the lav, took as much time as she dared to rinse it out and clean it under the outside tap. It was freezing cold, but she lingered, terrified of what might happen next. Then Flo bawled out.

'You, Moira, get your arse in here!'

She walked back into the kitchen, shivering, and sidled towards the range, standing with her back to it, her hands behind her and stretching out towards the fiery glow. Flo had made tea and poured out. She had calmed down and wore a thoughtful expression on her face. Seeing how cold Moira was, she jerked her head towards the teapot on the range.

'Pour yourself out a cuppa, the condensed is on the dresser. Hurry up about it. Me and Dave want to talk.'

'I have the upstairs to do and–' Moira mumbled as she poured out a mugful of tea and went to the dresser to add two teaspoonfuls of condensed milk, 'I mean if you want me to get on with the other rooms—'

'You stay where you are. Drink your tea, listen, and shut up!' Flo turned back to Dave. 'Now 'ere's where we get down to brass tacks. You said as how you're lonely for a bit of love, eh?'

'I'd treat her well and—'

'No,' Flo's silky tone was almost sick-making Moira thought, and felt relief. When Flo used that tone, she meant what she said, and nothing would change her mind.

Dave was beyond replying because Flo was formidable and it would take a stronger man than he to argue. He'd just witnessed someone as big and beefy as Will going off with a flea in his ear. Dave was in trouble and he knew it, Moira could tell by the hunted look she was seeing in his face. She felt a thrill of glee flushing her cheeks. Flo was a one, make no mistake, she would soon whittle Dave Dilley down to size. And knowing Flo so well, Moira knew that what Flo had in mind would not involve her own small self.

'I think you know why I came here, Miss Williamson,' Dave said as piously as he could. 'To bring back her shoes and to ask you if she could come and live with me from now on.'

'I couldn't stand the thought,' Flo replied sweetly, 'she belongs here, in this house. Like me own daughter she is, and like me own daughter she stays.'

Dave made as though to get up from the table, but Flo shook her head and smiled in a merry, vampish way.

'Listen to what I'm going to say, Dave. All this is Fate. Yes, good fortune for us both. You're lonely and I'm lonely. I also get hungry and so does Moir here – and so do my two regulars. So here's what I think should happen. You move in with me!' She giggled, which made her double chin wobble. 'I don't know why you and me haven't got together long before this. What do you say?'

'I think not,' Dave said sadly, but he had a wary expression in his eyes. 'I have my business to run.'

'Well most men have to leave their beds to go to work. You can do the same.' Flo leaned across the table in an ingratiating way. 'You're a fine figure of a man, Dave, and I pride myself on how I look when I'm all done up. So? Don't you think we'd make a fine couple?'

'I don't know what to say,' Dave's tone was getting shaky, 'I've never thought of taking up with another woman since my dear wife—'

'Until my girl came in your shop, Dave. She ain't fourteen yet and it's against the law, ain't it?'

'I didn't, I never—' Dave was now very aware of the threat underlying Flo's smile, 'I swear, I never even...'

Flo turned a beaming gaze in Moira's direction.

'Look at her!' She turned to face Dave again, 'Ain't she sweet and innocent-looking? You want to see her all togged up in her pretty best clothes.'

What best clothes? Moira thought and sniffed disparagingly.

'Sweet and innocent ain't in it!' Flo went on, warming to her theme. 'When she goes up before the beak and tells them what you did, what you said, Dave—' Flo's tone became conspiratorial now – 'And you've already learned what a fibber she can be!'

'There's been a mistake here, and it would be best if—'

'No,' Flo cut him short, 'I think it's best if you string along with me.'

'I'm sorry, Flo.' Dave Dilley was openly desperate, 'I'm not the marrying kind no more. I know the honour you've done me, but I can't live away from my own place. It has memories, you see, and—'

53

'All right, Dave.' Flo's tone remained bright. 'I understand!
Tell you what, I can come and live in with you.'

'I don't think—'

'And neither do I,' Flo was all business-like now. She spoke
over her shoulder to Moira. 'Go down the basement and get
Fred. I need a witness to the agreement what me and Dave are
going to make. Hurry up!'

Moira turned tail and fled, grinning.

Freddy was sitting in a raggedy red armchair. An oil stove
blasting away sent out a suffocating heat and heavy fumes, but
Freddy was blissfully cosy. He was looking at a comic and did
not hear Moira come in. His basement home was decently
furnished, dark, and a bit of a muddle all round. Even so, it was
a palace compared to the freezing attic. Moira clattered over to
him and he looked up and smiled. His eyes were very large and
blue, yet when angered they could all but glow red. It was a
good job that he had not been in the kitchen when Will had
been insulting Flo, the sparks would have flown then and no
mistake.

'Freddy,' Moira said and put her arm lovingly round the
massive neck, 'Flo wants you upstairs in the kitchen. All right?'

A man of few words, Freddy beamed, put his comic down in
a slow, careful way, then swung Moira in his arms as he stood
up. Laughing and carefree now, she beat him with her small
fists, which made Freddy's smile grow broader than before.
With effortless ease, he carried her up the short flight of stairs
and into the kitchen.

'Here you both are,' Flo's tone was jocular as she turned
back to Dave. 'Ain't it nice to see how dear Moir is to Freddy's
heart? Kill for her, he would. Do out and out murders if anyone
so much as looked at her wrong.'

'I can see that, yes.' Dave replied and looked longingly
towards the door.

''Nuff about that,' Flo said breezily. 'Now, here's what we're
going to do. We are going to give you, Dave Dilley, an ever
open door to Jordan Lodge. Understand? Because you're so
lonely, you can come here any time you want and get your
comforts. Yes, I mean bed and all, from me! D'yer get it? From
me! I promise you, I know a trick or two that'll keep you well
and truly happy. In return, I'll have you deliver me as many

chips a day as I need. I mean every day! And on and Fridays you can bung in five bits of rock eel as well.'

'Five?' Dave was getting hot under the collar. 'Five?'

''Course. For Freddy, Stavros, Binksy, me and Moir.'

'But—'

'And since everything's so friendly like, we won't have to tell the police what happened last night. Agreed?'

Suddenly Flo's good humour had gone. She sat on the opposite side of the table, still-faced, sharp-eyed, cold and mean. 'Do I make myself clear?'

Dave Dilley got up; he was looking sorrowful, afraid, but suddenly there was a small calculation gleaming in his eyes. He seemed all but hypnotised by Flo's ample, heaving bosom.

'You are quite a woman, Flo Williamson,' he said and gave his thin smile, 'I wonder why we haven't met before? I've heard about the Lodge of course and the goings on, but never quite dared – I will be happy to send you round six penn'orth of chips every day, and on Fridays, fish as well. And that means?'

'You can come and sleep with me nights, unless I'm otherwise engaged, of course.'

'I was thinking of Sunday night most particular.'

'If that's what you want, Sunday nights regular, that's how it will be.'

Dave Dilley stood up.

'Then I'll go now. Must get on. Must get on!'

'Too right!' Flo agreed. 'Freddy, show Mr Dilley to the door.'

'I will,' Freddy said in his soft, slow way. 'Mr Dilley?'

When they had both left the kitchen, Flo put her hands against her sides and laughed.

'Ooh, Moir,' she spluttered, 'I'll have you go and do some vamping and ogling at old Marcus Shaw next.'

'Marcus Shaw?'

'He runs the Hare and Hounds. We'd have it made if we could con him out of a load of free gin! Gawd, it's a funny old world. *You* wiggling your hips and making sheeps eyes? Oh my Gawd!' Convulsed again, she bent over, ready to split her sides.

Moira turned tail and left her to it.

Chapter Five

'Moir,' Flo said expansively one morning, having had a very good night with Dave, 'his wife had it made! The flat upstairs ain't used much, but it's full of lovely stuff all covered with dust and going to waste. There's a marble clock what I'd give me eye teeth for, and that's just the start! I've got me hooks in that man and I ain't ever going to let him go. In fact I can't think of the future without him.'

'You love him?' Moira asked, incredulous, her heart dropping like a stone.

Flo put her hands on her ample hips and laughed.

'If you mean liking me belly full of fish and chips, if you mean getting regular presents of bottles of gin, then yes, 'course I do. Make no mistake, you've got to look out for the main chance in this world, and Dave Dilley's mine.'

There was to be no getting rid of Dave Dilley then.

'Would you marry him?' she asked quietly one morning, daring to voice the question because Flo was in a good mood.

'No, I wouldn't.' Flo replied. 'I'm too long in the tooth to care now. I minded rotten once, but I stuck it out. Faced all the bleeders that was so full of scorn, and I snapped my fingers in their faces. Now no man's going to get the chance of grabbing a snitch of what I own.'

'Haven't you ever met someone you really liked, Flo?'

'The only man I would have taken a risk for, and was set to marry, was your Dad. Had the silver tongue of all the Spud Murphys, Seamus did. Got a little bit of the Irish in you too, now I come to think of it. Fair took me in he did, with his promises. I ask you, me what knows what's what! So, I took you in while he went off on his ship. I ain't too sorry though.'

'You're not?' Moira felt humbly grateful for those few kind words. She usually got more kicks than ha'pence from Flo.

'You ain't so bad. You're a help round the house and you're the only one in the world I can let me hair down to. You can't have a real talk with Freddy because sometimes what I say just don't sink in. No, you're the nearest to a mate I'll ever have.'

'I – I didn't know you liked my father – that much. I thought he was a no-good and—'

'Looking back, Moir, I can see now that he loved your Ma, and then you in that order.'

'He couldn't have loved me all that much!'

'He did, and he managed to do what he thought best. Like leaving you all safe and sound instead of tramping the streets alongside of him.'

'I thought you said he went off on a ship.'

'He did, but not before you was safe. Couldn't take you with him, could he? Not to sea!'

'But he never came back!'

'And we'll never know why. There was talk of course, but I didn't believe it then and I don't now. About as how he drowned.' Flo's good humour was vanishing fast. 'All I know is that the war didn't happen till six years after he disappeared, so he couldn't have that excuse. Of course, he really could be dead and done for, but we'll never know for sure. So don't you go making no hero out of him!'

'I don't think about him,' Moira said with quiet honesty. 'There was a time when I dreamed dreams, but not now. You are the one what – I mean who, took me in. And Freddy, Stavros, and Mr Binks have always been my family too. Now I've got Jade as a little sister, and,' here Moira's voice dropped and almost held a note of awe, 'River Pearl actually treats me like a friend now – and we even have a giggle sometimes ... When she's not dead tired of course. But sometimes Jade says some really funny things. Jade tries to remember what Stavros tells her, but she's only a little girl. I'm getting very fond of Jade and River Pearl.'

'Shut up, Moir!' Flo looked over her shoulder in a quick, nervous way. 'Don't you start getting tangled up with no

Chinks, d'you hear? Don't get took in. Ain't you sodding-well learned nothing yet? They're a quiet, secretive lot with their slitty eyes and pigtails. Stavros says as how they think all topsy-turvey. Opposite to us in every way. They treat their women like dirt and have them dressed in trousers while the men wear long silk robes!'

'Stavros knows everything,' Moira had to admit. 'And he says that learning's never ended.'

Flo sniffed.

'Well he oughter learn his own people a trick or two. The Greeks ain't much better where their own women are concerned. Their poor cows slave in the fields while the men drink that bloody awful ouzo. Yes, they all have a sodding lovely time, drowning their sorrows, while the poor down-trodden bitches get on with all the hard labour.'

'Stavros would never be like that!' Moira told her doggedly. 'You can't believe all the things the sailors tell you.'

'Got no reason to lie, have they? You don't know the half, Moir. But I'll tell yer this, at least Greeks are open and arrogant with it. Slit-eyes are different. They're quiet and sly and you can't tell what they think. But everyone knows what they get up to, oh yes! Drinks and opium dens, and white slaving is the business of them cunning, quiet Chinks. An' they make promises what you can't believe in.'

'River Pearl and Jade—'

'Belong to them! So how can yer believe in rich husbands what will turn up out of the blue and give you a fortune for saving wife and nipper, eh? Truth is, them two are on the run, oh yes! So you've gotta keep your mouth shut, understand? If you get on the wrong side of that lot what's after Pearl, it'll be nothing short of slit your bleeding throat time. Yes, curtains for you, and me, and all of us.'

'If you don't believe that you'll get a fortune one day, for looking out for River Pearl and Jade,' Moira argued, 'why have you let them stay?'

''Cause I'm a gambler what believes in the big pay-off one day. That Pearl's probably lying in her teeth, but there's a faint chance. Yers! Just a faint chance.'

'China people can't all be bad, Flo. After all, we learn lots of strange stories about folk in different lands from the men that come and lodge here and— Well, we don't know if they're telling God's truth, do we?'

'Oh my Gawd, why won't you listen to me?' Flo was rapidly losing her temper. She always did if Moira dared to question her. 'Get out of my sight, thick-head. With all your sucking up to Stavros, you ain't really learned a thing, have you? What's more—' Flo stopped to bawl over her shoulder to Mrs Noice, 'And I don't pay you no half a crown for dawdling about behind me back, ear-wigging me words neither!'

Moira smiled to herself. Flo was trying to cover up the fact that she had her weak moments. Flo on gin was sometimes quite good-hearted. Obviously the moment she had said River Pearl might stay, she had reverted to type. Yes, made sure that she came out of the deal far better off. Living in hopes of the big win, and in the meantime accepting payment for favours given. That was Flo's way.

'What you up to, Moir?' Flo bawled out. 'You dawdling again? Get on with it else you'll get me toe up your arse.'

Moira decided she had best make herself scarce. She began her chores, the bathroom first. She swept the floor, rubbed the brass taps to make them shine, wiped over the yellowing tiles. She washed the lavatory basin, using Monkey brand soap to remove the marks. She pulled the chain so that the clean water flushed, scrubbed with a brush and pulled the chain again. Some of Flo's guests were not very particular, she thought wryly, but she was used to worse. It was when they returned from the Hare and Hounds that things got really messy.

There were those that wondered how the mouthy, vulgar Flo came to be the owner of such a place, but Moira knew. Flo had let the whole story drip out over the years. Usually when she was drunk and maudlin, and spilling the beans.

'You don't know the half of it, Moir,' Flo had slurred, full of self-pity once. 'I was a cross my mum had to bear. Dragged up, I was and had more kicks than ha'pence. Mum's "girls" if you could call them tarted up bitches that, were a hard lot, and tough as old boots. Their sweet, simpering ways were put on for the men. And there were millions of men sneaking through our bloody green door, I can tell you. And I hated them all. Swore I'd get me own back one day.'

'You've done that all right,' Moira had replied soothingly,

59

knowing full well that in Flo's own words, she had, 'Used the bleeding fools from the day I was old enough to open my legs, Moir.'

'And – and didn't your mother mind?' Moira had asked.

'I don't know and I don't care. All she wanted to be sure of was taking her cut off her "girls". I used to watch them at it, I did. Butter wouldn't melt in their mouths, if you know what I mean. But as soon as the customers were out of the way, it'd be the booze and the foul talk, and their favourite pastime, getting back at my Mum by pinching and teasing and being downright cruel to me.'

'And your mother just let them?'

'My mum was the wickedest moo of all, because she just didn't care. Shoved me out all the time she did. Even to school. I'll never forgive her for that. The teachers hated me, because of what she was, though they couldn't prove it, of course. And me class mates all gave me hell, poking fun at me. I got me own back though.' Flo sniggered balefully, 'Told each of 'em in turn that I'd seen their Dad, or their big brothers in our house. Made up a whole pack of lies about how disgusting their men were. That shut 'em up, I can tell you.'

'You must have wanted to kill them!' Moira had burst out, wanting to defend that lonely long-ago girl. 'Thank you for not sending me to school where they have such rotters all round you, and teachers what – I mean, who hate you for things not your fault.'

'It was hell on earth, Moir, make no mistake. But I think I hated Mum's "girls" most of all. Them painted-up harlots left my Mum the minute she took sick. And stupid, bloody me stayed on and looked after her. Riddled with disease she was. Horrible! But even though she always shoved me off out of the way, I had to do me best. Weren't her fault that it was bad for business to have a kid snivelling about the place. Died raving mad, she did . . .'

'And you had no friends, not a single one?'

'Yes. His name was Frank, and him and me took to each other – just in that way, if you know what I mean.' Flo nudged her and winked. 'Big he was, you know, big! Him and me were young and soppy and though I weren't in love I hoped—' Flo shrugged and looked sad. 'Died he did. Of fever when he was

60

seventeen, and I was your age and up the duff. I survived, took it on the chin and cocked a snoot at them all. My Mum had left me enough cash to see me through so I was able to blow raspberries at the bloody common-as-muck Noices what had the cheek to look down on me!' She had sniggered then, 'Now you know why I make his sister-in-law Maisy work like ten bleeding tigers for her half a crown. Gets right up her old man's nose, that does. But he daren't argue with ol' Mais. Gawd 'elp us, she seems ter need the half crown...'

As Moira went from room to room, emptying slops and doing a hundred and one other things, she found herself wondering if being Flo's skivvy was all that life had to offer her. It would be wonderful, she thought wistfully, to go and be a housemaid in a posh house like the one where Yani lived. There, according to the old Greek, they gave you special clothes to wear and a little lace cap. She would work just as hard, probably even harder than here, but the people would be nice, lady-like, and you could hold up your head and feel proud. Not creep about like a thief in the night in case old Dave Dilley sneaked up. Every time she saw him she felt sick. Yes, she would give anything to get away.

But deep down Moira knew she was stuck. Jordan Lodge was her home and held people she was fond of – and there was young Jade who she loved, and River Pearl. She was wholly on their side, no matter what Flo said...

Moira walked slowly and unwillingly towards Dave's on an errand for Flo. She knew that they all hated Flo and herself simply because these days the folk in Jordan Lodge lived well. Everyone knew what Dave Dilley was up to, and he was seen, slinking down the street, heading for the Lodge, too regular to disguise. Besides, one could smell his fries from a mile away. Torture for the hungry it was, nothing but bloody torture! Nearly everyone in Jordan Street hated Dave Dilley's guts. He was a have, and they were the have-nots. It wasn't only his gassed-up old brother-in-law who wanted to sort him out. Dave Dilley was a well-got, a bloke who was always full of grub, who put on a sad face because that was the only expression he dared use. A happy face would have exposed him as a cock-sure bleeder intent on showing off!

61

Moira, feeling dread, loathing Flo for sending her to the Fry, hung about until she saw a customer go into Dave's. Then she followed, making certain that she wouldn't be there alone. But the woman, though garrulous, was soon served and gone. Dave looked at Moira and leered. She glared at him and warned:

'Come it once more, and I'll fetch Freddy. I mean it!'

He changed tactics.

'Coming to something when they come in for chips and go straight home and add them to the last of the mutton pie!' he said mournfully. 'Made my head ache again she has. Like it always does since the day you clobbered me with me own brass poker.' He leaned forward and nodded like a clockwork doll as he added meaningfully, 'One day, a poker what ain't brass will be used on you and—'

'Oh for Heaven's sake!' she acted impatient and superior at one and the same time. 'And in my book, that woman's family are very lucky. She's spoiling them!'

'Not from where I'm standing. Told me that, straight to my face she did. We all have to make a living. I ask you, is it fair?'

'It's called making ends meet,' Moira replied tartly, 'And a penn'orth of chips between four ain't actually spoiling anyone. Come on, Dave, I ain't got all day!'

'It's all right for some,' he was playing for time. Was he waiting to make sure that no one was around before coming out from behind the counter. Her mouth went dry with horror at the thought. 'That sort,' he went on waspishly, 'make me lose all me profits.'

'You can get a brown paper bag full to the brim of potatoes for a penny from the greengrocer's,' Moira snapped. 'And you get *your* spuds lots cheaper even than that since you buy in bulk.'

'You look good enough to eat,' he told her and his mouth twisted in a thin-lipped leer as he tried to get personal again. 'Did Flo get that floral dress for you from Cherry's?'

'That's my business!'

'Come round the back with me and I'll give you—'

'No, Dave,' she replied perkily, valiantly hiding her loathing and fear. 'It'ud amount to nothing against what I'd give you! Only harder than last time, eh? Now stop mouthing on. I'm here because Flo is asking can she have a pennorth extra tomorrow, half fish, half chips.'

'Why?' Dave was on the offensive at once and looking mean. 'She ain't feeding up no man at my expense is she? I'll kill her!'

'I'd like to see you try! No, it's just that Stavros is going to have a guest tomorrow and Flo is after making everything really nice for the old man. He's our best payer and Flo wants to let him see that she values the fact. She's making apple dumplings and custard for afters. Afters, just think! Everything's going to be real posh. And before you start moaning, here's the penny. And Flo said that it had better be good helpings seeing she knows the profits you make – oh, and don't forget the gherkin.'

'Who's the guest?' Dave snarled, his long skinny fingers shooting out to snatch a gherkin out of the jar and re-wrap the goods. He passed the newspaper-clad food over the counter and snatched the penny. 'If any conniving mongrel's sniffing round, I'll—'

'A young man named Yani.' Moira's face was glowing with excitement now, her discomfort gone. Dave Dilley was far from cocky now! 'He's home from college, a real posh place, and he's insisted on paying a visit. Stavros is all of a flutter, I can tell you. Stavros used to teach Yani's Dad a long time ago, and he taught Yani too. Yani's a toff and shouldn't be anywhere near our street, but according to Stavros, he's a very willful young man.'

'Well don't let him make sheep's eyes at you, that's all,' Dave warned her nastily, 'because one day you're going to get poked good and proper, my girl. Know what I mean? Poked in and out, hard and fast – and I want to be the first.'

Moira tossed her head and laughed at him in a bright mocking way. She was feeling braver by the minute because a coalman, covered in coal dust, chose that moment to come in.

'Well I never!' she said cheekily, 'Getting above yourself again, Dave? Let's hope that Flo never finds out.'

She whirled round and left him standing there. Once outside she breathed in the hot dusty air that was filled with impure, unmentionable smells. Some coming from the soap factory, others from the tanners, yet others from where kids had piddled up against the wall. All of which were vying with that of frying fish. Moira felt she was suffocating, but it was nothing to do with unsavoury odours. In spite of her outwardly casual air, Dave always affected her that way.

It was stupid, and in broad daylight too! She tried to get calm. But he had meant it, when he had been carrying on about her getting poked, she thought desperately. He really had! Well she would die before she ever let him lay his hands on her. And she would see him dead too! One day she would brain him, even if they hanged her for it, and she'd use something a darned sight heavier than a brass poker!

She ought to tell Flo what was going on, Moira thought wildly, about the things Dave said, the nasty things he whispered to her every minute he got the chance. Yes, Flo ought to know! But if Flo's bubble of good fortune burst, the whole lodge would suffer. Life would be hell on earth, it always was with Flo on the rampage. No, best let sleeping dogs lie. She, Moira O'Malley would manage on her own as best she could.

If only she had a knight in shining armour, she thought wistfully. A knight she could turn to. Anyone! A thought struck. Of course! She brightened visibly; she could always ask Mr Binks to help. Mr Binks had hundreds of good mates, market people, and he also had two young favourite scallywags he called his chaps.

Chumley Potts and Conor MacCluskey, who were according to Mr Binks 'Real daring young scamps, and a damned sight better than la-di-da Yani. One fine day Moira, me gel, you'll meet them both because they've promised to visit the same time as Stavros's young mucker. Can't 'ave old Stavvo getting one over on me, eh? So it'll be all mates together, an' you can come too.'

Now it was all going to happen. It was something to look forward to, Moira thought. But most of all she would at long last be coming face to face with Stavros's fine young friend. The one Flo was apt to dismiss as that young greasy Greek, this behind Stavros's back of course. But that was Flo all over, curling her lip and looking down her nose.

Stavros stood for reading and writing and learning things. Flo, who could only barely read and write owing to her fear and loathing of school, felt threatened by those who were more educated. She did not like the idea of Moira being taught by the old man, but had seen sense a long time ago. This when Stavros had quietly asked to know the whereabouts of the local school. That had stopped Flo in her tracks and no mistake. She pretended ignorance of the tutorials Moira received, but would have liked to have stopped them. As it was, Stavros had his way in most things, and paid handsomely for the privilege. At his insistence Moira was to be off duty for Yani Bertos's visit. But that was not until tomorrow.

Tonight was another matter. Moira and River Pearl enjoyed the brief times they had together. Moira remembered the first time the ice between them had really thawed. It had happened late one night when River Pearl had magically provided a box full of new candles. A whole box. Luxury, since before they had to make an inch piece last for at least three nights, Flo being the skinflint she was. Now, wonderfully, the attic became bathed in light. Moira and River Pearl had smiled at each other and clapped their hands, then laughed aloud.

'I bet you never got that little lot from Flo,' Moira had said.

'Own humble self bought them in shop,' River Pearl replied. She spoke shyly and nervously at first, then openly and warmly. Now it seemed that she and Moira had always been close.

River Pearl could speak English in a funny, foreign way, and Moira thought her enchanting. She learned from the start that River Pearl had been taught English by a Christian missionary in China. Also Moira had been given to understand that in her own country, River Pearl had been very high born.

Tonight River Pearl had promised that she would tell Moira the story of her life, and of Jade's, and of the adventures they'd both had. In return for this, Moira had to make a solemn oath to always look out and care for young Jade. To even, if necessary, give up her own life in the attempt.

'No problem!' Moira whispered the vow out loud. 'I'd do that without River Pearl asking. I can't wait for her to get back tonight.'

She remembered how nice and private the attic now was, and cosy, now the weather had turned warm. It was as greatly appreciated as Freddy's basement had once been.

Dismissing Dave Dilley from her mind, Moira pushed her way through a crowd of children playing hopscotch, and made her way home.

Chapter Six

On entering through the green door Moira saw Freddy lumbering towards her. He was smiling, his blue eyes filled with pleasure.

'Wait in the garden, Iddy,' he said slowly, 'I am going for ice cream.'

'I can't,' she replied sadly, 'Flo said that I've to—'

'In the garden. Flo said so. You wait.'

Flo hadn't said a word about her joining Freddy in the garden, Moira knew this very well. But then disobeying Flo wasn't new to Moira – and with luck, she'd get a lick of Freddy's ice cream. She watched the big man amble up to the door and through it into Jordan Street. Then she slipped round the side of the house and into the back garden. She loved it out in the sunshine, seeing the colour of the flowers. Not that she often got the chance!

Moira inhaled the perfume of stocks and relaxed. It was like a secret world here. As apart from Jordan Street and its surrounding mean area as shit from cream. Moira was not usually allowed five minutes at peace in Freddy's domain. There was always too much to do – at least Flo saw it that way.

Moira sat on a piece of coconut matting, looking rather like a flower herself in the dress that Flo had bought her from Cherry's. For once it was a decent fit, a pale primrose yellow with a pattern of deep pink roses and forget-me-nots. She had a sneaking suspicion that Stavros had something to do with it; Flo was sufficiently under the old Greek's thumb to make sure he was given what he needed, and a key to his door. Only those actually invited ever entered Stavros's domain.

For just a moment the sun went in and in spite of herself, Moira found herself thinking of Freddy and how he would do anything for her, anything! Even choke the living daylights out of the evil Dave Dilley. She only had to ... 'No!' her heart cried. 'I musn't!' Not put Freddy in that kind of position. Never Freddy who had always been so wonderful and kind. She remembered how it had been when she had first arrived in Jordan Lodge as a tiny wide-eyed tot.

'You are our Iddy-Biddy-Baby,' he said in his slow, lumbering way. 'You belong to us now. Freddy will always look after his Iddy-biddy.'

According to Flo, she had never heard him string so many words together before. He had progressed from that day, and had adored Moira from the moment she had held out her arms to him, waiting to be picked up. He had been a youth then, and slow, simple in outlook, but never, ever, daft.

Moira frowned. Freddy must never know the truth, that Dave Dilley scared her half to death. That he skulked and prowled and sidled up and reminded her of something from the unnatural world. Freddy must never know that given half the chance, Dave Dilley would play Flo false and grab her, Moira, and use his tongue and ...

'No!' her mind shuddered away from the awful thought, 'Please God, no!'

She had to admit to herself that Freddy did not like Dave Dilley at all. She could tell by the look he gave the man. That he kept himself in check was a blessing. For the moment at least he saw Dave as necessary to Flo, and the means of getting regular fish and chips. For Freddy, who lived for the moment, that was enough.

The memory of the ghoul-like fish fryer made Moira shiver again in spite of the warmth of the sun. But the memory of the man, his sibilant remarks, made her feel trapped.

There must be another way of living, she thought desperately, where there were no flying fists and sneaky, disgusting old men, and a hateful rotten cruel world.

She was filled with worries and woes and unsolved grievances. She was alive with passions and conflicting emotions. She wanted to run away from Jordan Lodge for ever. She hated the drunken seamen; the nights Flo got spiteful and filthy tongued on port; the daily grind and misery; the times when Freddy sneaked through the green door with a boozed up man slung over his back. Above all, the thought of the evil, skinny, ghosty Dave. Dear God, must her thinking always involve him?

It was costing the fish-fryer a great deal, tangling with Flo, Moira thought. For the time being, the mistress of Jordan Lodge had the man exactly where she wanted him. And because of this, she, Moira need never actually go hungry again. Dave had to cough up food, not money. Thank goodness for that.

Life in Jordan Street was horrible and vulgar and crude. There was no escape. And Moira found herself wanting and needing to escape again. Yes, even though she was sure of a good ha'porth of chips that night. To think that she had been happy earlier on; that the sun had been shining, and flocks of sparrows had looked like a host of small feather dish-mops as they fussed and fretted in the privet hedge. But everything changed so quickly. Now the world seemed grey and frightening and she was on edge.

She was just about to get up and return to the house, defeated, when the sun blazed out again. Then everything was changed, her mood, her sense of impending doom, her horror, for now the golden light gleaming down like a slow, brilliant river had bathed the garden in gold. Relaxing, she was aware that life went on, and lifted her face to feel the summer's glow. She heard Freddy's footsteps scrunching over the gravel pathway that led along the side of the house. Then her smile blazed out as joyfully as the sun. Freddy was back and holding not one ice cream but two. He handed her his gift, then lowered himself down carefully to sit beside her.

'Freddy! Thank you!' she licked the rapidly melting ice cream rapturously. 'Who gave you the money to buy this?'

'Flo.'

'I don't believe that!'

'Stavros gave money to Flo.' Freddy said slowly. 'I was there to move the big table.'

'Never!'

'Away from the wall.'

'Mr Sella would never allow anyone to touch his table.'

68

Moira felt a flare of horror. 'He isn't going to leave us, is he? He wouldn't do that. He couldn't, could he? I'd hate it if—'

'I had to pull table back,' Freddy explained, 'for Flo to clean the wall.'

'Oh of course!' she felt an upsurge of relief. 'He's to have a visitor and he gave Flo extra money to make sure there were no bugs around. That nice old Stavros is very particular, Freddy, and he loves Yani as much as I love you.'

Freddy's large blue eyes were soft and sparkly at that. He smiled an ice-creamy smile.

'You have very nice eyes,' Moira said. 'Now tell me what happened.'

'The Greek told Flo, "Some for Fred." He was very stern.'

'So Flo gave you a copper or two and you thought of me? Oh Freddy!'

She kissed him, beaming. 'This is such a lovely, lovely day . . .'

'Oi, Moir!' Flo bawled from the scullery door, 'Is that you out there?'

'I'm with Freddy.'

'You move your blooming arse in here! We ain't got all day!'

'Coming.'

'Now!'

Moira stayed where she was until she had bolted down the last of the ice cream. Then she beamed at Freddy, jumped up and ran back into the house. It wasn't until she was feeling the back of Flo's hand for dawdling, that Moira felt smothered with guilt. She had ate that ice cream like a pig! She hadn't given Jade a single thought!

She stopped turning the mangle, filled with consternation. Flo's enormous pink drawers dangled unheeded; they were caught between the rollers, dripping water from one end and squashed flat at the other. She came back to the moment and ducked as Flo made to bash her again. Then, scarlet-faced, she lipped back.

'Hit me again and I'll fetch Freddy!'

'You little cow!' Flo let loose a string of foul epithets, but kept her hands to herself. This only because she couldn't bear seeing Freddy pucker his lips and his eyes fill with tears. When

Iddy was in trouble with Flo, Freddy was always immensely sad...

Anyone would have thought the King was coming, Moira thought late that evening. She had been on the go all day, dusting and polishing like a maniac, not forgetting metal-polishing the hundreds of stair rods of course. They were the pride of Flo's life, gleaming like precious metal as they held the brown lino in place.

'One day,' Flo had told Moira earlier on, 'I'll have carpet covering them stairs. I wish I had some stair carpet now! I'm not too happy about that bleeding Greek inviting all his posh friends.'

'It's only a young man he used to teach,' Moira told her. 'His name's Yani and he isn't all that much older than me. Since when have you cared about kids?' She had ducked away from Flo's waving fist yet again and childishly poked out her tongue behind the woman's back.

In spite of what Moira had said, Flo had even gone so far as raiding Freddy's garden. Proud blue lupins and a sunflower or two were placed on a table in the hall. They would be the first thing Yani would see.

'What a shitty old show-off!' Moira whispered to herself indignantly. 'Flowers indeed. I bet her pinching them lupins made Freddy really sad! Still, Flo's got to make good I suppose.'

Moira was ready to drop by the time she was allowed to creep away. Even so she was feeling a tinge of excitement. Going up to the attic was never a hardship these days. In a moment of weakness, having been given a fresh bottle of gin from Dave, Flo had said expansively, 'Know something, Moir? We wouldn't be living so high if it hadn't been for that silly sod trying to mess with you.' She had put her hands on her ample hips at the thought, and tossed back her frizzy hair as she laughed, 'Gawd that thick-head! A kid like you, and he tried it on, eh? Poor old Dave don't know much about women, that shows up a mile. Still, we've got him now, and I'll make sure we keep him, but in the first place it was all down to you.'

'Don't remind me!' Moira had gasped. 'He still scares me, Flo.'

'Hark at you!' Flo jeered, 'He don't have no eyes for you now I'm around. Still, it's through you I got him, so what about me doing something for you, for a change? What would you like?'

'The attic made more nice,' Moira had replied without hesitation.

'Bloody hell!' Flo pulled a face. 'That was quick.'

Moira jutted out her chin.

'You asked!'

'So I did – and don't glare like that or you'll get me toe up your arse. Oh, all right, I'll see what I can do.'

True to her word, Flo paid a visit to the local Aladdin's cave. Anne Cherry's Second Hand was as dingy and tumble-down as its neighbouring hovels. Filthy and full to the brim with anything and everything, it was the place to rummage through, to pick and nick, and turn over to the heart's content. And Anne Cherry, henna-haired, quick-eyed, bossy, ruled her domain like a long-nosed predator. She had a punch that could knock one for six – as would-be thieves soon learned to their cost. Even Flo minded her Ps and Qs where Anne Cherry was concerned. As did the ragmen, the dustmen, and the manager of the local refuse tip, three sources of the Cherry Second Hand supply.

Flo spent the lordly sum of two shillings and sixpence at Cherry's. Money that should have gone to the pawnbrokers to get back her mother's diamond ring. But the ring, Flo's standby, had remained where it was, safe in the shop with the three brass balls trademark hanging outside. The ring had bought many bottles of gin in its time, and kept the wolf from the door. But just this once, Flo left the ring where it was. This she had never allowed Moira to forget.

Moira, River Pearl and Jade's horse-hair mattresses were now covered with red blankets. They were marked up as belonging to the fever hospital, but who cared? There was a rickety wash-stand with a black marble top on which stood a white china hand basin and matching jug. There was a large rag rug on the floor, now clean and warm, though it had been moth-eaten and filthy before Moira had half killed herself working on it. There were also three wooden orange boxes. Up-ended and with a shelf in the middle, they made handsome cabinets. Freddy had covered them with paint left over from the green he'd used on the gate. Candles from River Pearl's box were stuck in the tops of wine bottles and surrounded the room. Moira had two real and true friends. A Chinese lady and child who were happy to see her when she came in.

'Hello you two,' she greeted them both and beamed when her chores were finished at long last.

After River Pearl had put her hands inside her sleeves, bowed, and courteously asked had Moira spent a happy day, they sat together. All on River Pearl's mattress, in a circle of candle-light and shadows. Jade between them, serene and content and safe.

'Tell me about your country,' Moira began. 'It all seems so strange and so far away. And explain how you come to be here of all places.' She never tired of listening to the stories River Pearl told in her high, thin voice, for once the ice had broken their talk was endless. '"Out of the mud cometh Beauty,"' River Pearl began pensively, 'That is what we say. For with the eye of faith we foresee the pink and white of lotus-flowers. They rear their heads out of miry ponds when Winter is gone.'

'Don't talk about Winter,' Moira told her, 'You know how freezing it gets up here. Now what's all this about foreseeing things?'

'I meant that I, faithful and obedient number three wife of Lord Li Tzu, await the coming of Beauty, for there has been much mud. Oh, how my heart breaks to be once again in the beloved Flowery Kingdom!'

'Number three wife? Number three?' Moira was frowning. A look from River Pearl's sickle-shaped eyes made her hastily change tack. 'Where is the Flowery Kingdom by the way?'

'That is what we call China,' River Pearl told her. 'It is the centre of the world. And it is the only place where I can be truly happy. In all the heaven and earth nothing can be more lovely than my homeland in Spring.'

'Yes,' Moira agreed, 'we have bluebells and daffodils and things like that. In the country of course, which I haven't seen, but the pictures are nice and – well, you know!'

'Spring in northern China is wonderful with its rivers and willows. On the dreary brown plains, there come little faint, dotted lines of golden green. The willows are showing leaf – not the dull grey-green hue of this land, but golden in their budding, with oval leaves scattered like beads down the long, thin

72

branches. And then the willows spread out their leaves and bow in homage to the earth in their full glory, but that last Spring was very bad time.'

'What happened then?'

'In my country, there are many grievances and these are hard times. Some men believe in being loyal to the Dragon Throne. Others believe that ordinary people should hold the power. My lord husband is the Honourable Li Tzu who believes in royal throne. It is my duty to care for Li Sweet Precious Jade, his only child by Li Golden Plum, number one lady of his house.'

'Are you telling me that you're not Jade's Mum?' Moira asked, amazed.

'I am honourable nurse and guardian of my lord husband's only child. She is our greatest treasure. I am privileged above all others to have her in my care.'

'But – but why are you here – in this dump?' Moira was taken back at the turn of events. 'You told me once that Jade's dad is very rich and that— I just don't understand!'

'Is not easy for young foreign girl. I tell you that the life long rival of both my lord husband and honourable father, is one Kung Chin. In spite of this, Kung Chin's number one son, Kung Yat-sen was greatest friend of Li Pang, my lord husband's younger brother.'

'If you expect me to understand that lot of funny names, you're barking up the wrong tree,' Moira said feelingly. 'What with all your Kungs and Pangs and Chins, you're making my head spin.'

'Is important to know that Kung Yat-sen and Li Pang were students in Peking. There was also another in the group. A working student named Chou En-lai and Yat-sen were members of the same society to do with Marxists, which I do not understand. What is clear, they on opposite side to Li Pang, a Nationalist like my lord husband. Even so, all three young men remained friends. That was until the men in charge stepped in.'

'It seems that guv'ners are the same the world over,' Moira said wisely, 'bloody minded is what Mrs Noice says.'

'The three friends were ordered to part. Then one day there came an uprising, all very terrible. Men went crazy with anger and many died. One of them being Yat-sen, who before he

73

succumbed, cried out for the presence of Li Pang, who he loved like a brother. He took a long time to die and he begged to see Li Pang with tears in his eyes. Chou En-lai, who was very brave, tried to reach Li Pang, but was turned back. When he told the dying youth this, Li Pang cursed the war, and everyone who took part in it. Many men heard his awful words.'

'He was right to curse war. You can see what's left of the poor devils who went through our Great War. Grey-faced, dried up, washed out – beggars on the streets.' Moira warmed to her theme. 'Horrible it is, horrible!'

'Hai. All very sad. Kung Chin lost face when his number one son cried, and called out for Li Pang. Great dishonour fell upon the House of Kung.'

'Why? Was it a crime to wish to see a mate just once more?' Moira was indignant. 'What a rotten shame!'

'When the uprising ended, Chou En-lai and others were taken to court, then imprisoned. The story of the death of Yat-sen and his manner of going, came out. Kung Chin blamed it all on Li Pang and swore revenge. Nothing less than the death of all members of the House of Li would do. Yet my lord Li Tzu was here in England, on business, during that time.'

'Your lot don't half get het-up about things, don't they?' Moira said, 'Losing face and all that sounds daft to me.'

'Gentleman in this country shoot themselves with pistols rather than lose honour,' Pearl replied quietly, 'all same thing!'

'I suppose so,' Moira hastily agreed. 'When did the row between the two sides really start?'

'Long time ago. But the uprising itself was on the 4th day of Pearl in the year of 1919.'

'So near? I suppose all this has caused your husband a lot of bother?'

'He still might not know whole story. He went on a ship to far away America. He travel the world on matters of business. He might not have learned that the Kungs fell upon the noble House of Li and killed many people. They cut off serving men's heads and put women in cages after torturing them. I had time to gather all the silver nuggets I could, and my jewellery, and I ran outside and hid with Sweet Precious Jade in the gardener's underground nursery.'

'You keep your babies underground?' Moira was outraged. 'That's awful!'

'Nursery for dwarf plum-trees.' River Pearl laughed and clapped her hands at this, while Jade, who had remained silent throughout, smiled. 'The little trees live there until is time to take them up to the light. I could hear the screams and cries of the dying. And the ladies wailing to be killed, for they were in terrible pain. When the gardener told me that the Kungs had gone I ran outside. There were many dead, cut to pieces, and great pools of blood. A disgusting scene for small child's eyes.'

'And I thought Jordan Street was hell on earth,' Moira said quietly. 'Fancy Jade seeing all that! Looks like your Flowery Kingdom isn't so pretty after all.'

'One of first to die was Golden Plum.' River Pearl went on. 'Before she went to Other World, she beg me to care for Sweet Precious Jade. By this time, the House of Li was burning to the ground. I had the silver nuggets and jewellery, and with the help of the old gardener, I took Sweet Precious Jade and escaped.'

'I bet you were scared stiff!

'Tried to tell myself that the Lord Buddha was watching over us. I tried to remember all wise words of Confucius, but I was very afraid. Was long and very terrible journey, but at last we reached a ship which brought us to this pitiless land. I found place where many China people stay, but soon learned that the Kungs had followed, and that they have sworn to kill us in revenge. I still do not know how to find my lord husband, and I did not know then. So I ran away and came to this place, and the Honourable Number One Lady has let me stay ever since. She is good, kind person.'

'You're joking!' Moira said sourly. 'So, the message is that we run like the devil if we see any Chinamen hanging around.'

'Hai!'

'And Jade's Dad?'

'I will look for my lord husband until the day I die,' River Pearl said quietly. 'He will take care of us. He will know what to do. Now you make a promise?'

'If I can.'

'If anything happen to me, you look for the Lord Li Tzu? I

give you a letter for him. You go find a funeral shop in place named Limehouse Causeway?'

'Nothing's going to happen to you,' Moira told her stoutly, 'we're like a castle in here. We have the wall and there's only the one gate and—'

'You make solemn oath to do this thing?' River Pearl asked urgently. 'Go to funeral shop?'

'I don't hold with no coffins and such-like,' Moira objected, 'and I don't—'

'Coffins? No coffins! Beautiful things cut out in paper, to burn so that smoke joins spirit rising high to join noble ancestors. Outside shop there are strings of red lanterns and many Chinese signs.'

'Yes, but—'

'Venerable gentleman in shop knows our story. He has promised to try to find where my husband is. Find old gentleman and tell him that you must take Sweet Precious Jade safely to her father. If she is not made safe my soul will wander throughout all of the ten thousand hells in torment and wailing. Moila, give word of honour. Make oath!'

'It won't be worth a brass farthing, River Pearl. I don't worry about honour and losing face and all that stuff. It takes me all of my time just getting through the days. So – don't you go expecting too much of me.'

'You are a good person, and you give Sweet Precious Jade much love!' River Pearl insisted, entreaty in her eyes.

'Oh, all right!' Moira capitulated. 'But cheer up! It's a pound to a penny, nothing's going to happen to you. Now let's forget all this misery-guts stuff. Tell me some more about your Flowery Kingdom that's set plum in the middle of the world.'

'Go to your bed and close eyes, and I will tell you about the greatest god of all.'

As she closed her eyes to hear all about the greatest god in the world, Moira thought of River Pearl's story. It was a bit too much to take in, to believe. It came to her that her friend had made the time pass by very skilfully. That the China lady had been spinning a yarn, that was all. She smiled a little, obediently keeping her eyes tight shut. River Pearl was very good at telling stories. She made life worth living with her colourful tales.

'His name is Lord Buddha,' Pearl's high, lilty voice held awe.

'And He had a thousand arms. And in each of His thousand hands there is an eye. And because He has so many eyes, He can see everything, the whole world, and even into our souls. I would like, just for once, to ask Him to lend me one of His arms. Then I should elongate that arm over the wall of this Lodge, being very careful not to drop the eye, and I would send my vision and hand far away, travelling, travelling and elongating exactly as He once stretched out to take hold of the sun.'

'Why do you want to do all that?' Moira murmured.

'So that my Buddha arm could pass over many lands, across the iron mountains of Russia, and the silver-birch forests of Siberia, over the desert of Gobi with its glittering rainbow pebbles, to the plains about Peking, and the first faint gold of the willows on their river-banks. And there I would see my ancestral home, and my beloved mother, and in his own private rooms, my honourable father.' Pearl's voice became sad. 'A bride belongs to her lord husband from the moment she dons the red wedding robe. I have not seen my parents from the time I was married to the Lord Li Tzu. I would wish to see my parents once more before I die.'

'You're never going to die,' Moira murmured. 'I won't never let you, River Pearl. Sing me a song about the moongate in the sky. You have a really pretty voice.'

And so River Pearl sang about the moongate in the sky, and the star daises, and the goddess of the moon until both Jade and Moira fell asleep.

The next morning, in the early hours, Moira got up and went about her usual chores. Then she ran upstairs to see River Pearl and give her a cup of hot, weak, milkless tea. Moira now regularly stole a pinch of tea from the caddy every day for this purpose alone. She had discovered that her friend liked it, and so sneaked up this one tiny luxury every morning.

Before she made ready to leave, River Pearl handed Moira a short bamboo tube,

'If anything happens to me,' she said urgently, 'and old gentleman in the funeral shop has learned the whereabouts of my lord Li Tzu, take him this. There is a letter inside for his eyes alone. You give word?'

''Course I do,' Moira replied easily, slipping the bamboo

tube under her mattress, 'and stop worrying. You're safe over here. You won't find no mad Chinks waving swords down here in Jordan Street. All right?'

'Hai,' River Pearl whispered and left for the wash house and her day of hard labour.

But now Moira realized that work wasn't the only reason why River Pearl left so early and stayed out so late. She must be traipsing around trying to find her husband. He must be a real pig, Moira though sourly, not to let his number three wife know where he was. This even though River Pearl had made it clear that all Chinese men were lords, and that women were on the earth merely to serve their masters. Chinese girls were brought up to believe their duty was to exist only for their lord's pleasure. Even the peasants in the fields had to obey their men, poor things.

Moira thought of the tough old girls in Jordan Street and their unattractive, generally skinny little runts of men, and smiled her private pixie smile. She tried to imagine Maisy Noice, in her black boots and man's cap, bowing to her lord, a casual Dock labourer, and chuckled out loud. Now, remembering the expression she had seen in River Pearl's eyes as she handed over the bamboo tube, she realized that the situation was not funny for her.

Once Pearl had gone down stairs, leaving Jade still sleeping, Moira slipped the string from her neck on which swung the heavy old key, and secured the attic. Then she returned to the kitchen and her heart sank. Flo was sitting at the table, looking the worse for wear.

'Gawd!' she moaned irritably, 'you're late, ain't you? What have you been doing up there? I've got a head on me like an elephant's arse. Get me a Beecham's, girl, and pour me a cuppa.'

'Did you have a good night?' Moira asked as she busily did as she was told, and surreptitiously poured herself a cup too. 'Can I have a slice of bread?'

'Keep me poor you do.' Flo took the tea, winced, then handed Moira the key to the kitchen cupboard. 'All right, one slice. Then you can make extra porridge. Can't have you fainting with hunger on the day old Stavros' guest comes calling, can we?' Her tone was sarcastic, 'Though why the silly old sod insists on you waiting on him hand and foot today is beyond me. Since when have you been his slave?'

Moira did not mention that she longed for Stavros' call. Sometimes even prayed for him to ring his bell. The Greek gave her food for her mind, and food for her tummy, and he treated her like a lady. His moods never changed, at least towards her. Being with him was never like living on top of a volcano ready to erupt all the time – which was the feeling one had while dealing with Flo.

Moira went to the cupboard, cut herself a slice and spread it with marge. The bread and the hot, sweet tea felt good. The sky was lightening and there was already a rosy glow in the East. It was going to be another nice day.

Brisk, efficient, she sped about doing the chores, only listening with half an ear to what Flo had to say. Clearly Flo had spent half the night in the Hare and Hounds and was even now regretting the drink she had downed.

'It was that pork pie what caused it,' she moaned, 'I shouldn't have had it, but he insisted on treating me.'

'Who? Dave Dilley?'

'Gawd 'elp us, no! Squeezing them bloody taters and a bit of fish out of him is like squeezing his life's blood. No, there was this bloke what...'

Moira closed her ears to the rest of the sordid tale. But she heard enough to know that the man who had treated Flo to the pork pie had passed out before he had reached Jordan Lodge's green gate. Flo had rifled through his pockets, found nothing, and left him lying there. She had fallen down once or twice getting back inside the house, and had the grazed and bloodied knees to prove it. She had been sick, very sick, and was feeling at death's door now.

Knowing that she had better keep well out of Flo's sight, since Stavros was too busy to spend time with her, and Mr Binks had gone out, Moira got to it. She scrubbed the step, the outside lav, did the last minute dusting and polishing, having made the porridge, and seen to Jade. She did a million and one things to keep herself busy and out of harm's way. Then, just after three came the dreaded call.

'You up there, Moir?' Flo yelled. 'What the bloody hell are

you doing, eh? You cunning little cow. If you think you're getting out of things you're very much mistaken!'

Well at least her headache's gone, Moira thought wryly and made her way slowly down stairs.

Flo was still looking pasty-faced. She was standing just inside the kitchen door, waiting. She peered at Moira through screwed up eyes.

'Look Moir, none of your messing, eh?' she said in a cold, mean voice. 'That young Greek bloke will be coming soon and everything's got to go well. But we're in trouble.'

'We are?'

'A boy's just brought a message from Dave who's heard some sort of lies about what happened last night.' She smiled in a sourly triumphant way. 'Seems the silly old sod's narked because I got a skinful last night and palled up with a fella. Dave don't like it because I left a message that he wasn't to pay me no visit. Got up his nose, that has! My Gawd, you'd think we was married!'

'What am I supposed to do about it?'

'Dave will be here in about an hour's time. That's when the Greek kid's due. I don't want no scenes and I don't want to face Dave simply because I can feel me temper rising. It wouldn't take much for me to give the old bastard a back-hander – and we don't want to do that, do we?'

'I don't see why not,' Moira was brightening up at the thought, 'after all, who does he think he is, bossing you about?'

'He's the bloke what gives us fish and taters. I need to hold on to him until me ship comes home. So this is what's going to happen, Moir. You've gotta keep Dave down here in the kitchen, smarm round him, give him a bit of the old toffee, say and do anything to keep him quiet. I'll do the waiting that the Greek insists on. All right?'

'Stavros wants me special,' Moira protested, her skin crawling at the thought of the monstrous Dave Dilley. 'He asked me most particular to take the—'

'I ain't going to argue, d'you hear me? I want to hang on to Davey-boy, but I ain't up to coping with him right now. I can kiss the old Greek's arse if it comes to it and—'

'You'll upset Stavros,' Moira argued frantically, 'and you need his rent more than you need fish and—'

She tried to duck, but wasn't fast enough. Flo's hand reached out. Large and beefy, it hit her face so hard that tears sprang to Moira's eyes. Then Flo's finger began to poke her in the chest.

'You – will – do – as – you – are – told – All – right?'

'I hate Dave,' Moira panted, 'and I hate you! And one day—'

'One day you can rot in hell, girl, but today you'll do as you're told . . .'

Chapter Seven

Moira's heart was thumping hard and she clenched and unclenched her hands as she heard Dave Dilley's footsteps coming along the passage. She found herself wishing for the millionth time that Flo hadn't given the man the keys to the green gate and the front door. It was awful that he could come and go as he chose. Thank God he could never enter the attic, that it was locked at night, for safety's sake against murderous Chinks – who couldn't in a million years be worse than Dave.

He came in, long and thin and bony, mournful faced, and his eyes that glinted lecherously when he saw her there.

'Moira,' he said, 'this is a surprise. You were waiting for me?'

'Flo said to give you a cuppa and you're to – to put up with me. She – has a lot to do right now.'

'Oh?' Dave's thin lips made a straight line in his face. His eyes glittered. 'Who's giving her a poke?'

'Flo is waiting on Stavros's student friend. The young man's name is Yani and ...'

He was eyeing her scarlet face and noticed the rapidly forming bruise marks of Flo's fingers across one cheek. He stepped towards her and Moira moved backwards, finding to her dismay that she was pinned against the wall. He had forgotten Flo and was intent on her; his expression was strange, his cheekbones jutting out and his large Adam's apple was jerking about as though it were on a string. His hands were now clenched on her shoulders and she could feel his fingernails biting through her dress.

'Come and live with me,' he said softly. 'Don't you know that thoughts of you are driving me mad?' His voice grew more hoarse as he went on, 'Live with me and let me do things to you. Lovely, wet things what will make you come alive as you've never been before. Let me touch you and feel you, and you can touch and feel me. I'll give you everything you ask for. I'll—'

'Get away from me,' she panted, feeling her gorge rise. 'Do you hear? If you don't get away from me I'll scream blue murder. Freddy will kill you stone dead.' She could feel her rising hysteria and gasped, 'And I'd like that! You're evil! I'd like him to kill you and I'd—'

'Laugh?' He gave a thin smile, though colour burned high on his cheekbones and his eyes were staring in a terrible way. 'Freddy's out, but you know that, don't you? As always you're just putting on an act, egging me on. You're playing hard to get, knowing as how it turns me on. Yes, all your struggling's more exciting than even your usual knowing looks. Come 'ere, girl, let's have you.'

She kicked and struggled, but his hands were like a vice. His bony body was pressing against her and forcing her back. His knee was lifting, pushing, trying to get between her legs. His awful voice dropped to a whisper.

'Come off it, girl, enough is enough. I see you smile and simper when that half-wit's around. Strong though, ain't he? Do you let him finger you? Does he poke you good and hard? I can do better. I know how to do things what will make you . . .'

His face was lowering, his tongue first running round his lips then coming out, like a live thing, towards her.

She flinched away, frantically twisting her head from side to side and all the time he was wearing her down. He began whispering in her ear, filthy things, awful things that made her cringe. She wanted to vomit, to scream, to die, to go utterly mad, but it all had to be so quiet. Flo had threatened her with the gutter if she made a fuss. She had to do as she was told and butter up Dave Dilley! But the gutter was surely better than this?

She opened her mouth to scream and he bent his head down, and his tongue, like a fat snake, was reaching between her lips. She bit him, shutting her jaws as hard as she could, snapping them together with all her might. He grunted and let her go — then she was running like a mad thing, out of the house, along the path and through the tall, green gate.

Jordan Street swirled round her. A jungle of mouthy women. A grimy, grey place jam-packed with screaming kids, and boys apeing their elders with their leering and swearing and suggestive remarks. Jordan Street was the jaw crushing outside world of unnamed terror and jeopardy and now she, Moira O'Malley, was part and parcel of it all. 'No!' Moira's heartbroken wail seemed to be echoing in her soul, 'No, no, no!' She needed Flo and the security of being behind that old green painted door, and above all, she wanted Dave Dilley dead, dead dead.

A sallow-faced man with a woodbine clamped in the corner of his mouth, lurched into her. For a split second his world-weary eyes looked into hers and showed a spark of sympathy, of decency and concern. She gasped and sobbed and ran into Burgess street, and on. She reached the busy main road. It was hot, dusty and alive with people and smells. She caught whiffs of horse-dung, perfumed hair oil, the fish being trundled along by the barrow-men, the scent of flowers from a handcart parked in the kerb.

Ignoring the street-singer's outstretched hand, she ran on. Past an organ-grinder and his monkey, horse-carts, trams and, every so often, cars. Shops spilled their goods onto the pavement, open invitations to ragged urchins. Many haunted the market area.

A filthy young rascal cannoned against Moira. She knew that in that instant, nimble fingers would have searched her empty pocket, knew, but was too soul-weary and scared to care. Most times she would have cuffed him round the ear, repeated a few of Flo's favourite words, brave in the knowledge that there but for the grace of God . . .

Her sides were aching. She was finding it hard to breathe. She pressed on. Unmindful of where she was going, beyond caring, Moira thought only of putting herself as far away from that evil, slimy tongue as possible. But the noisy thoroughfare pulsating with life around her was the kind of place where the Dave Dilleys of the world lived – and the fish-fryer belonged in hell!

She reached a more gracious area. Ahead, a tall, wide wrought iron gate came to view. It stood a little back from the road, half open, a kind of invitation into the coolness beyond.

The gate was like a lace-patterned black screen dividing the present from the past.

Chest heaving, mouth dry, Moira stopped running at last. She crept by the gate and into the grounds beyond. Everything seemed cool after the burning street outside. Here the air was filled with the smell of flowers. The grass was green, the trees tall, graceful and richly endowed. There was a sense of eternity here, of smoothness, of God's endorsement of the correct conclusion of things. And the old grey church, with its up-sweeping spire, held a silent promise of even better to come.

Moira forgot Flo's sarcastic remarks as, hand on hips she would declare, 'I don't hold with no do-gooders, smarmy lot!' Or, when the bells rang out, 'That sodding church!' else, even more fiercely, 'All that praying and caterwauling is a lot of bloody codswallop!'

Flo had got it all wrong, Moira thought tearfully, and rubbed her knuckles against her eyes, conscious of the smell of roses and the sweet undertones of newly cut grass. She remembered the fleeting sense of peace she had felt in Freddy's garden the other day. Now she walked carefully along the gravelled pathway separating velvet smooth lawns. This is holy ground, she thought, and felt small stones scrunching under the well-worn soles of her shoes.

Moira began looking at marble angels, then at the austerely grandiose mausoleums. These were separate, enclosed by iron railings. Snobbery, even in death, she thought and sniffed contemptuously, reacting exactly like Flo. Here and there among the white headstones, were ancient lichen-covered slabs, markers for those long gone. But to Moira, the most moving of all were the small, barely distinguishable green mounds. Some, covered mere babies by the looks of things. All sleeping peacefully and for ever, safe away from the harsh gun-metal drabness of the every-day world.

Emotionally drained, Moira found herself a secret resting place. Now, half hidden under the sun-gilded curtain of a weeping willow tree, she sat down on the grass. At her side was a small, mossy green mound on which sweet peas had been placed. There was a brass plaque which read, "To beloved Robby, aged three." By the date the boy had died five years before. Five years! Yet there was still someone who

85

remembered, who grieved, who made offerings of sweetly scented flowers. Robby had been rich, endowed beyond compare because quite clearly, he had been deeply and everlastingly loved.

Fresh tears came then. For a father who had done his best, but who had vanished for ever. And a mother who slept far away in the emerald isle. And for herself, unable to visit and pour out her heart over their graves, or offer little bouquets to the parents she had never known. More tears flowed. Even for poor old Flo, her protector and tormentor, who was forever living in her fool's paradise. And then, too, new scalding tears of guilt and remorse.

Moira found herself remembering Jade.

Perhaps the Chinese child was looking for, and truly missing her own cowardly self. She had given River Pearl her word of honour, but had instead cut and run. The small girl must still be alone and locked in the attic. River Pearl wouldn't be back for a long while yet. When she found out what had happened, the gentle lady with her lovely, sickle-shaped eyes would retreat into her world of silence again, and never, ever forgive the one who had so let her down. But then, Moira thought miserably, River Pearl didn't know about Dave Dilley, the horror and downright awfulness of the man.

How long she sat there, torn with doubt and fear was hard to tell. But gradually the timelessness of the churchyard took over. Her sense of outrage and revulsion abated and was replaced with a quiet determination not to give in. She had to plan, to think about what was best to do. As her courage grew, her chin lifted and her cheeks flushed. Was she, Moira O'Malley made of jelly? No! Was she going to take the fish-fryer's nonsense lying down? No, no, no!

She stood up, whispered goodbye to Robby, and slowly began the walk back, finally turning into Burgess Street, rather than walk through the rougher area further on.

It was dark when she finally reached the pub on the corner. Now, worn out and weary, her courage left her. The Hare and Hounds was full it seemed, and rousing choruses of "It's a Long Way to Tipperary" and "Pack up your Troubles in your old Kit Bag" could be heard reverberating through the walls. The door opened, sending out a shaft of light, a rush of heat and smoke-swirling air. A man wearing a greasy cap and choker for all it was summer time, stumbled out. He was holding onto a women who seemed as far gone as he. They were singing at the tops of their voices.

'My old man, said follow the van and don't dilly-dally on the way.' The loud, unlovely voices cut through the air. 'Orf went the van with me 'ome packed in it. I followed on with me old cock linnet. I dillied and dallied, dallied and dillied, I lost me way and . . .'

'Shut up that bloody row!' a woman yelled from a top window. 'Ain't you got no sodding 'ome to go to?'

'Arse'oles!' came the drunken reply.

There came the sound of someone tipping the contents of a bucket out of the window.

'You bleeder,' the man roared.

'Shit!' screamed his companion.

'That's right!' the unseen person from the top window agreed and laughed out in a loud and vulgar way.

I can't walk the length of Jordan Street, Moira thought. It's a hell's cauldron down there, and I can't make myself go by Dave Dilley's. He might see me. He might—

She retreated into Burgess Street, with its mean houses and hosts of fly-specked windows that glinted down on her like evil eyes. Then finally she was back into the High Road once more.

Tired and dispirited she walked along towards the market area, flinching as a couple of old men, stinking of beer and Navy Twist tobacco, offered to buy her "wares". She ignored them and walked by with her nose in the air. They were cackling over their own devilment, convulsed at their own daring, and would have dropped dead if she had faced them and pertly said yes. She knew it, and they did too. Her lips curled with contempt. Men!

Stretching before her were tawdry shops and dark doorways, alleyways and furtive-looking night people. She hurried on, past abandoned booths, the acetylene lamps now extinguished, but the acrid smell of carbide still clung in the air. There were other odours, mostly unpleasant, of stale, wet fish, urine, and rotting vegetables. Market stalls now closed down looked like black skeletons. Empty chip wrappers rustled along the kerb while homeless cats, eyes glittering, ceaselessly prowled.

Moira left the market area and reached the shops that were

big and glass fronted and on far grander scale. The Picture House was spewing out its audience; nice people, she thought wistfully, who smiled and talked together. Ordinary folk whose two-up and two downers were scrupulously clean, who had pretty curtains at the windows, who laughed richly at witty cockney jokes – who were probably as poor as the people in Jordan Street, but had self-pride and dignity just the same. One couldn't judge the whole world by the scruffy lot round Jordan Street.

Just then a gang of drunken youths pushed through the drifts of picture-goers. They were out for mischief and it showed by their loud laughter, filthy tongues and unsteady gait. They came face to face with Moira, a girl on her own. They jostled against her, their eyes suddenly cruel. She felt hot breath against her face and the stink of stale beer. She was being backed against a wall. Decent folk hurried on with averted eyes. It was the nightmare of Dave Dilley's attack all over again.

'Let's 'ave you, girly,' a brutish-looking young boy stepped too near, intent on showing off in front of his mates.

'Giss a look!' another teased amidst a chorus of rough laughter. Someone's hand lifted her skirt.

Moira screamed, high and wild. She was fighting back, furious and afraid, but losing the battle, her spirited defence merely egging them on. Their prankish air was fading, being replaced by lust. They were getting rough, inflamed, and she was helpless against them. They were crushing her. There seemed to be millions of hands touching, pinching, probing. She felt sick with horror and self-disgust. And with every fibre of her being she was wishing herself dead. Dead and done for, and lying at peace under a weeping willow tree.

The world spun round in a dizzy, crazy manner. There seemed to be an extra dimension to the shouting and shoving, but now it all seemed far away. Then the nauseating hands trying to pull down her knickers, let go. There was a crunching sound and a muffled 'Ow!' and, 'Bastards!' and 'Pissing hell!'

Then strong arms held her high and very close.

'Iddy,' Freddy said quietly, 'don't cry!'

Laughing and crying, Moira clung to him. She heard old Stavros carrying on in his fiery Greek way, and Alfy Binks being more "Gor-blimey" than she had ever heard him before. There were others there too. Three young men all looking just two or three years older than herself. But they didn't matter. Nothing mattered except that she was safe.

Breathing a deep sigh of relief, Moira relaxed against Freddy's broad shoulder, for the moment content to let the world go by. She was vaguely aware of them all turning into Locksley Street and walking down until they reached the corner that swerved round into Jordan Street. The green gate was swung open and Freddy scrunched purposefully along the gravelled pathway, past the hunched up old laurel bushes, and finally into the Lodge. Moira found herself set down with infinite care onto a kitchen chair. Then Freddy was making tea with water already boiling on the range. There was the faint smell of boiled cabbage, undisguised by the tang of the carbolic Mrs Noice always used. The fire in the range blazed orange through the bars. The crockery and huge blue and white china tureens on the dresser glinted under the light. Everything was cheerful and warm and homely.

Moira's rescuers were all taking seats round the large, well scrubbed kitchen table. They were grinning and boasting, being very pleased with themselves. There was no sign of Flo.

'I never knew,' Moira quavered, 'how lovely this – this kitchen was till now. Thank you for—'

'Thank Freddy,' Mr Binks teased. 'Gawd 'elp us! Scattered them saucy little sods like chaff he did. Like chaff!'

'And Yani was good, very good too!' Stavros said firmly. 'It was he who saw what was going on when he passed the open door of the kitchen, and ran up to tell me. More to the point, I am amazed at his knowledge of fisticuffs.'

'Chumley and Con weighed in and socked 'em for six as well,' Mr Binks said stoutly, not to be out-done, then added delightedly, 'an' didn't our Fred turn up trumps? Like a steamroller mowing 'em all down he was. A ruddy great engine what no one could stop!'

Glowing, feeling warm and wanted, Moira, her eyes swollen and face tear-stained, looked round at them all. She saw that Yani Bertos was slim and olive-skinned, with eyes as large and luminous as polished black grapes. His hair was black and he looked a gentleman. He was very noble-looking, even more

89

handsome than she had imagined, and very Greek. A bit
tousled now perhaps, since his jacket was torn, and he had a
tell-tale smudge of blood on his nose. A toff! And he had
fought for her! Moira could hardly believe it and felt honoured.
He was smiling at her, and she felt her heart skipping in a
strange and crazy way.

''Ere, I give one of 'em a loverly black shiner,' Chumley
Potts, Mr Binks' favourite of favourites, boasted. Everyone
guffawed.

Chumley was foxy-faced and had small boot-button eyes
glinting brightly under thick dark brows. His mouth was thin,
his chin firm, and he had a knowing street-wise air. He was a
right'un and no mistake, but there was something very likeable
about him even so. Now, chuffed, he was grinning a yellow-
toothed grin at his mate, 'Did yer see, Con?'

Moira looked from Chumley to Con. Although sitting, she
could tell that he was the tallest of the three. He had roguishly
twinkling dark iris-blue eyes surrounded by thick black lashes.
His unruly wavy hair fell onto a broad forehead. His face was
lean and hungry-looking and his sensitive mouth was uptilted
at the corners. He had a devilish Irish lilt to his voice as he
answered Chumley.

'T'will be blacker than a bog come morning,' he agreed. 'By
Jaysus, we showed them!'

'Oh my Gawd,' Chumley groaned, 'there's nothing like a
good barney to bring a light to your eye. Right Spud Murphy
you are.'

Con cuffed him one in a lazy, affectionate way. Grinning,
Chumley ducked, took a mock punch back at him, then called
over his shoulder to Freddy, ''Ere, cock, need any help? I'm a
dab hand at making cha.'

Freddy was concentrating very carefully on what he was
doing, but paused long enough to smile and shake his head.

'This is an occasion,' Stavros said, beaming, 'excuse me
please.' He left them only to return shortly with the remains of a
fruit cake and a plate of chocolate biscuits.

Dismissing thoughts of Flo's whereabouts for the time
being, Moira relaxed and knew deep down that she never, ever
wanted to leave Jordan Lodge again. No, not for Dave Dilley
nor anyone!

Over tea, cake and biscuits, the talk became general and Moira was content to sit close to Freddy and listen and watch. Yani seemed to be taken with Mr Binks' two favourites and they, strangely, didn't seem to dislike him. They were from different worlds and poles apart, but a mutual interest and liking seemed to be born.

Everyone was having a high old time until Stavros took out his pocket watch.

'My friends,' he said, 'I must remind you that very soon now the Hare and Hounds will be closing its doors and Miss Williamson...'

'Gawd 'elp us!' Chumley said, 'I've heard all about her! Come on, Con, let's be off!'

Con turned to Yani.

'Do you live round here?'

'A ten minute walk, that's all. I could take a taxi, but,' he smiled widely, 'I have rather enjoyed all this, so I think I'll use my own two feet.'

'We'll tag along if you like.' Conor MacCluskey offered.

'A damned good idea,' Chumley agreed perkily, 'they might be hanging about – and although you're good with your fists, you'd be on your own. 'Sides, mate, we ain't got nothing better to do.'

Yani turned to Moira and held out his hand. She took it, trembling and momentarily shy.

'I hope that we meet again soon,' he told her and looked as though he meant it.

'Surely and I'm sorry for your troubles,' Con added easily. Moira blushed scarlet, acutely conscious of his strikingly dark blue eyes. She half nodded, confused, liking them all, but wanting rather desperately to escape before Flo came staggering in.

'Tata, ducks.' Chumley put in, then added breezily to the other two, 'An' if we don' want that scary woman's toe up our arse, we better get a move on.'

'I'm with you,' Con replied. He blew a kiss to Moira and followed the other two who were already bee-lining for the front door.

The three young men left without a backward glance. They were talking about football as though nothing had gone before.

'I'd make myself scarce if I were you,' Mr Binks observed, 'an' let the old girl sleep it off. She was looking all 'orrible and hateful when she left and if she's been on the port...'

'Ah!' Stavros agreed. 'Perhaps we should all make our way upstairs. Miss Williamson knows what happened here and is suffering from hurt pride.' He coughed behind his hand in a politely apologetic way, 'And my child, she is not a happy lady.'

Giving her two old friends a frightened stare, and Freddy a quick hug, Moira ran out of the kitchen.

Amazingly, River Pearl had not yet returned, so it must still be quite early. Pausing only long enough to see that Jade was safe and sleeping soundly, Moira gratefully slipped under her blanket. For a moment a vision of Yani, so handsome, lithe and noble like a god, floated before her eyes. She felt little squiggles of delight curling her toes. He had said that he hoped to see her again. Perhaps, oh please dear God, perhaps he actually meant it! Her eyelids fluttered, then she slept...

Chapter Eight

'Here, what did you think of that Moira?' Chumley asked Con as they walked back to Harriet Jones' place.

'What sort of question is that?' Con replied easily. 'She's young, but getting ready, so I'm thinking she'll be all right . . . so far as girls go.'

'And that's all?'

'Aye. The way she was trying to defend herself was grand. Reminded me of my young sister, Peg. Like a tigress she was. There was not a man within a million miles who'd dare to so much as look at Peg MacCluskey. Then along came Myles Fitzpatrick and that was an end to it.'

'They've got a kid now, ain't they?' Chumley asked. 'Is that why you send all your money back 'ome?'

'I wouldn't dare. Myles is a proud man and built like a barge. No, the little I have I send to my mother.'

'I ain't never had no mother.'

'I don't believe that,' Conor laughed. 'A poor wee woman must have had something to do with you in the beginning.'

'Fat lot of good she done me, then.'

'You've not needed a mother to help you survive. You're a fighter so you are, like me.' Con smiled. 'And we didn't do so badly with our fists tonight.'

Chumley's mind was not on the fight.

'It was her hair,' he observed, 'that Yani couldn't take his eyes off her. Took a shine to her, he did.'

'And that's where it'll end,' Con replied carelessly. 'Didn't you see that grand house of his?'

''Course I did,' Chumley was aggrieved, 'and I still don't

know why you refused point blank to go in and have a chin wag with him like he asked.'

'Ah! It couldn't be anything to do with your taking ways? You'd have left with more in your pockets than you had when you went in.'

'Are you saying I'm a tea leaf?'

'And wouldn't that be the truth of it?' Con playfully punched Chumley's arm. 'And it's a good job I know you so well, us being such firm friends. The Greek's all right, but the Yanis of this world don't belong with our sort. They're as helpless as lambs when it comes to being taken in. And yes boyo, I think he knows it as much as we do. He'll forget the girl as easily as he'll forget us. We've had a decent time of it tonight, now it's over and done with. Come on, let's get back to Harriet's.'

'What's the rush?'

'The pitch outside City Park will be taken if I'm not up with the lark.'

'Did you get them coloured chalks you wanted?'

'Harriet saw to it.'

'Bleeding hell!' Chumley's jaw dropped open. 'Did you kiss the Blarney Stone or something?'

'Not at all. She came along and saw my work. Looked down at the pavement so she did, and said, "Did you draw all them pretty pictures of mountains and sheep and things, Con?" "Twas none other" says I. "Then I'll put a penny in your cap." She meant it, I could tell, so bold as brass I told her, "I would prefer some more chalks, Harriet, if you've the mind." "Chalk it is, Con," she replied, and that's how it was.'

'Good on yer, mate.' Chumley threw back his head and laughed. 'Never alter will you? I remember how it was when you first came here. Determined to make a go of it, for all you'd been let down. Did yer ever hear from them friends of your ma's? Them people what were supposed ter look out for you, but did a moonlight instead?'

'No, but I'm sure they had their reasons.'

'Rotten sods could have hung on. They didn't oughter have left you, a stranger to this land, on the street all on your own.'

'Wasn't such a bad thing. You came along and that was the end of my troubles.'

'Didn't do much,' Chumley demurred.

'Only took you to Harriet and practically went down on me bloody knees.' Chumley grinned in his wicked way, 'And that was all you needed mate. Don't give in do you? You was always being told there was no work, but back you come like quick-silver, not letting nothing get you down. Then you saw that old man—'

'Holy Mother!' Conor's voice held disgust. 'He was getting pennies in his hat for drawing horses that looked like pigs with snouts and all. I knew then what I had to do. I'll find myself a place, I thought, and show them a horse that's long legged and adventurous and full of fire. And I'll draw pictures of my homeland, and see to it that I get pennies in my cap. I'll be better than that old man to be sure.'

'And you are – and you're getting known, and you're making money. What's more,' Chumley added stoutly, 'one day, my old cock sparrow, you'll be as rich as the Greek. Oi, don't you honestly reckon he'll be at the pub tomorrow like he said?'

'Of course not, boyo,' Con laughed. 'And who cares? We'll be there and that's all that matters.'

Hands in pockets, shoulders hunched, they began whistling merrily as they made their way home...

It seemed as though a million sparrows conspired to wake Yani. He blinked, for the morning sun shone directly in his eyes. He yawned, stretched and sat up.

Cissy, the skinny maid of all work, knocked and came in with his breakfast tray. Neat and homely in her black dress and white apron, she set the tray before him.

'Good morning, Cissy,' Yani said easily. 'It looks as though we're in for another nice day.'

'Yes, sir, looks like it,' Cissy replied dutifully.

'And did you have a nice evening with your young man, Cissy?'

'Yes, sir,' her cheeks reddened and her lips twitched a little. All the servants in the Bertos household liked master Yani, for all he was spoiled rotten. He was a real decent sort, like Mr Christos, his dad. It was sad that Mr Christos spent so much time away from home. It wouldn't be so lonely for the young master if his mother would come and live in London, but she preferred to live on the Greek Island called Kerkyra because the English weather made her ill. Not that Master Yani ought to be tied to his mother's apron strings, but it wasn't fair, all them years and hours he had to do learning at them toffee-nosed schools. Her boy-friend Vic had a much better time of it. Being a worker from the time you were fourteen helped a lot. Vic was an experienced eighteen-year-old man.

'You're blushing, Cissy,' Yani told her, his dark eyes laughing into her's. 'What did you and your Victor get up to I wonder? You must have stayed up until the early hours.'

Cissy opened her brown eyes very wide.

'Are you joking, sir? I've been up since five, working. I mustn't stand here, sir. You know how it is!' She went cold at the thought of crisp, business-like, no-nonsense, Mrs Lines who even scared the local bobby half to death. The house-keeper who ruled over all. 'And please sir, eat your toast. If you don't, Mrs Lines will swear it was cold and I'll get ticked off. I always get ticked off!'

'Then I'll eat and drink the lot if it kills me, Cissy,' he promised. Then, casually, he asked, 'I say, how well do you get on with Wally?'

'The handyman's all right,' Cissy replied all hoity-toity, 'just as long as he remembers his place.'

'Now you're mimicking Mrs Lines! Come on Cissy, would you say that Wally's jacket might fit me?'

'Pardon, sir?'

'It might be a bit large,' he said thoughtfully, 'but it will do. Cissy, the moment you can, tell Wally that I need his jacket. That's today if you please.'

'Yes, sir,' Cissy replied and looked curious.

Yani smiled his wide, warm smile.

'I am going to wear it, Cissy, that and my oldest trousers. I rather want to look like a bit of a scruff tonight. I'm going slumming with a couple of very interesting chaps.'

'Oh sir,' Cissy was horrified, 'that wouldn't do. Besides it'd be impossible for you to look...'

'Nothing's impossible, Cissy. So bring me Wally's jacket when you come to collect the breakfast tray.'

Cissy left the room thinking of Master Yani slumming it, and of poor old Wally who looked like he was going to lose the only jacket he had. They're really nice in this house, Cissy thought, and I'm lucky to have such a good situation, but it's true what they say. The toffs just don't know how us other half live!

She went down the wide, graciously curved stairs, to the large, well-appointed kitchen, and out of the back door. She had to find Wally, who would be tinkering in the shed in the back yard. For poor old Wally, this was not going to be a happy day . . .

Flo bore down on Moira like a ship in full sail. Her frizzy hair was all but standing on end, and her face was was beetroot-red with fury. Moira stood there, heart thumping, her eyes defiant.

'So, you bloody little bitch, egged him on, didn't you?' The lethal finger shot out and began poking Moira's chest. 'You – cunning – little – cow! He – was – telling – the – truth – all – along – wasn't – he?'

'I'm sorry, Flo,' Moira's mouth went dry as she tried to placate the woman. 'But I did tell you! I – I begged and begged you to let me go and wait on Stavros and—'

She flinched and gasped as Flo's hand whipped out to smack her hard across the face. It's not fair, she thought wildly, it's just not fair! Suddenly furious and on the defence, Moira drew herself up and jutted out her chin.

'Like it or lump it,' she panted, 'your darling Dave Dilley's nothing more than a filthy dirty rotten old man!'

'You saucy moo,' Flo screamed. 'I'll wring your scraggy neck for this. I'll kill you stone dead! I'll—'

Fat, furious hands were beating wildly at Moira now and she staggered back, tring to shield her face. But the pasting went on, and in spite of being afraid of being thrown out of Jordan Lodge, Moira could take no more. She ceased retreating, straightened up and took a fierce step forwards. Now she was glaring up into Flo's face and hating her with her eyes.

'Don't hit me again, d'you hear?' she cried. 'Don't you dare hit me again! I'll have the law on you, I will, and I'll tell Freddy all about you.'

'Leave my Freddy out of this!'

Flo raised a clenched fist this time, but Moira stood fast, her eyes twin brilliants in their fury, her cheeks on fire, her hands clenched. Flo's mouth dropped open because Moira on the war-path was a novel sight.

'Freddy's the one who brought me back!' Moira panted, her voice harsh with unshed tears. 'Yes, Freddy and Stavros and Binksy! And also there was Mr Yani Bertos who you made so much of yesterday. Not forgetting Binksy's two friends as well.' The words were tumbling out now, and as she tossed her head, her hair swirled out like cinnamon bathed in light. 'And what's more, they were all fighting a crowd of rotters that were trying to rape me. Yes, rape! Just like shitty Dave was trying to. And how you can stand such stinking men I just don't know!'

'You lying little—' The fat fist was raised, about to strike, when a voice rasped behind them.

'For Gawd's sake, Are you two cats spitting at each other again? Bloody well cut it out!'

Moira and Flo swung round as one, to look at Will Fenning. He stood in the kitchen doorway, his braces hanging down and over his trousers. His blue and white striped shirt was rumpled, his hair was on end and he was unshaven. But he was leering and confident and as he stepped inside the kitchen, Flo dropped her fist and looked unnerved.

'You!' Moira whispered, amazed, 'I – I never thought I'd see you here again.'

'Had to prove meself, didn't I?' he smirked. 'Had to show the missus here a thing or two. Said things about me manhood last time, didn't she? In front of you and that bastard from down the road. He won't trouble you no more, girly, believe me. And I don't think as how he'll trouble anyone else for a while.'

'You ain't—' Flo began in quick alarm, 'You ain't put him off me for good have you, Will? It's all right for you, going off to sea, but I've gotta stay here and—'

Will's face went dark, he scowled, then made a grimace of a smile. With cold deliberation he looked Flo over, and then round at the kitchen, then back at Flo again.

'What if I didn't go?'

'What if the Thames runs dry?' Flo's hands were on her hips now and her tone held sarcasm, but even so, a hint of hope.

'How about me taking the chippy's place?' Will said in a smarmy, superior way.

'Sod your luck,' Flo said all cold and hard now, hope replaced by the need to survive. 'Leopards don't change their spots. All right, you've proved yourself! And I'll tell the world you've got a big dick, if that's what you want. But you've also got a right wallop in your fist and I'll have none of that!'

'Gar'n, you enjoy it,' he told her, daring her with his eyes. 'Every bit of it, Flo. You like a barney, and you've got a fair old wallop yourself. I was black and blue the morning after I left here. A bit of hammer and tongs makes you all hot and fired up. Go on, admit it. You're quite a woman, luv.'

'Shut up. You can't get round me, you mouthy devil.'

'Come on, tell the truth for a change! That chippy's got about much guts as haddocks water, and he must have left you at screaming point every time you and him had it off. *I* know how to satisfy a woman. At least you know you've been good and had while I'm around.'

'Piss off!'

'Now look here, Flo—'

Moira, aware that they had both forgotten her existence, gratefully slipped away.

She ran upstairs, unlocked the attic door and swept Jade up into her arms, then hot-footed it down to Stavros. He was expecting them and was beaming. And oh joy of joy, he held a large bag of Strutts creamy toffee in his hand . . .

Chapter Nine

It was Friday, the evening Moira dreaded. The year was now growing old, and River Pearl was no nearer to finding her lord husband. But she still kept faith and continued her ceaseless searching, but she was scared, Moira could tell.

A cold wind was blowing hard down Jordan Street. Heart thumping, hands sticky and mouth dry, Moira hurried to Dave Dilley's Late Fry and went in. Relieved, she found many people patiently waiting for the fish to be cooked. With luck there would be other customers to follow her and she need not be in the shop on her own.

Moira was still afraid of Dave Dilley, deathly afraid. She could never forget that first night's visit, after Will had bashed the fish-fryer black and blue, and neither could Dave!

Moira had never told a soul about the nastiest part of the conversation that night, but Will's words blazed like letters of fire in her mind.

Will Fenning, still holding her fast, had waited until the shop had been empty, then he had moved round to behind the counter.

'While we're here, shit-pants,' he'd rasped, 'we'll have fish tonight as well. And every Friday you'll bung in one gherkin, get it? A gherkin what's as long and green as your face. And when I eat it with me rock eel and taters, I'll be thinking of you. As how that gherkin is you! And I'll bite it bloody hard and hope you'll know that's exactly what I'll do to your miserable little dick. Yes, that thing what you call your manhood. Clean bit off it'll be – if you ever so much as look at Flo or this poor little cow again. Get it?'

Dave's face had in fact changed to a pea-green colour, Moira remembered, and he went bug-eyed and stared as though hypnotised into Will's flinty orbs. But Will was enjoying himself too much to let it go at that. He grabbed Dave by his shirt front and pressed home his point.

'And every time Moira comes here to get our order she'll ask you most particular-like, not to forget the gherkin! And that should remind you, that I'm in the background just hoping and praying that you step out of line.' He had turned away from Dave then, and grinned down at Moira, 'Now girl, what's the favour you want off this bastard? He's gotta pay for what he tried to do to you. Come on, speak up!'

'No – nothing,' she had stammered. 'Honestly!'

'Come on girl. How about a pound or two out of his takings tray? There ain't nothing wrong with having a bob or two to yourself.'

'I'd die before I took money off him!' she had flared up at him. 'Enough is enough, Will Fenning. I want nothing off this man. Nothing!'

Will's hand was gripping her like a vice. Harder, so hard that his fingers were biting into her flesh. She had winced.

'You've gotta!' he snarled. 'I'll not leave here till you get your dues.'

Then Moira remembered something she had always thought most unfair.

'I – I'd like an extra helping of chips, and fish on Fridays, please,' she had whispered, shame-faced.

'Gawd's truth!' Will grinned. 'What a greedy guts.'

'Not – not for me,' she choked, wanting to scream and run and get out of the shop at any cost, 'for – for River Pearl.'

'Bloody hell, don't she get nothing? A regular at Flo's and she don't get nothing?' Will turned to glare at Dave. 'Make that a good helping, mate, or you're for it. All right?'

'Please,' she had been unable to control her spurt of angry tears, 'can we go now, Will?'

And the big, rough, round-faced man who'd spent half a lifetime as a stoker on ships, glared at Dave threateningly once more. Then he marched her out of the shop. On the way back to Jordan Lodge, cold-bloodedly snarling, he barged any luckless person in his path out of the way. When they neared the lodge he relaxed sufficiently to warn her.

'Don't you ever forget, girl. It's you what's got to get the taters, and the fish. And you what's got to say, "don't forget the gherkin." If you don't say it, I'll find out and then there'll be trouble. D'yer hear what I say?'

'I hate him!' Moira had thought wildly, but nodded weakly just the same.

As the weeks had gone by, then the months, she had noticed something different about Dave Dilley. Oh, he looked the same sad-faced ghoul as always, but there was a red glint of hate at the back of his eyes every time he took a gherkin out of the huge glass jar of pickles standing on the counter. Dave Dilley would never rest until he had paid his enemy back, she knew that. And deep down, she knew too, that the man's sick desire for her own young self was growing as much as his detestation of the man who had usurped him. Above all, Moira knew that the day would come when she would have to pit her wits against the fish-fryer...

Moira's heart sank. The chip shop was empty apart from the proprietor. She had to walk in and face the tall, string-bean of a man. She saw his expression change as he turned from his vats of boiling fat and saw her. Now there was a sly, evil look in his eyes. Hiding her fear, she tossed her head, lifted her chin and stood boldly in front of the counter waiting to be served. But he pretended not to see her and said 'Evenin' Mrs Bloomfield,' to a lady who entered just then, and who was closely followed by other customers. He deliberately saw to everyone else first. Then she was alone and praying that Will might think she had been away too long and come looking for her. She felt sick because Dave's gaze was roving all over her as he undressed her with his eyes.

'Well, well,' he said, his voice dripping with oil, 'here you are again, my dear. Preening and vamping as always, and with them wanton, knowing looks. The day will come when I give you what you're asking for. You know that, don't you?'

'All I'm asking for,' she told him quietly, 'is for the usual order – and the gherkin of course. We musn't forget that must we?'

The man made haste to serve her after that, glowering as he placed the hated gherkin in with the rest. He did not look her in the eye as he handed over the hot, savoury smelling meals. Moira heard herself saying, 'Thank you!' in a polite, distant way. Then she walked out of the shop with the large parcel of newspaper-wrapped food held close against her chest. The Jordan Lodge order would just about take all Dave Dilley's profits away she thought and suddenly, quite absurdly, even though it was wicked, she wanted to laugh.

Moira walked on, feeling the ice in the heart of the wind. It made her gasp and hold the fish and chips up against her freezing nose.

It would be Christmas quite soon, she thought, not that the festivities meant much more than extra hard work. But sometimes Mrs Noice gave her and Freddy a tangerine orange each. Mr Binks always gave a small bar of milk chocolate. Usually Stavros would give a pencil and notepad. The previous year Flo had gone so far as to give Moira a box of three handkerchiefs. White they were, with lace round the edges and tiny mauve violets embroidered in one corner. They were just too beautiful to be true. Pristine in their little box, they were Moira's greatest treasure, kept neat in her orange-box cabinet, there for all the world to see. Certainly not hidden under the mattress like the bamboo tube held in trust for River Pearl.

A huge lumbering figure walked towards her and her lips curved upwards.

'Freddy,' she said as he reached her, 'were you too hungry to wait any longer?'

'You were a long time,' he replied, 'I wanted to – make sure.'

'With you looking out for me,' she told him blithely, 'I'm as safe as houses. Come on, Freddy, let's hurry. It's freezing out here.'

Friday night was feast night. Moira having finished the last of her chores, took River Pearl's and her own fish and chips from the range oven where they had been keeping warm, and finally went up to the attic. It was out of the way, all lovely and homely. A place where all three felt safe. New candles were glowing, and Jade and River Pearl, who Moira considered to be like her own little family, were waiting. They looked up as she entered and were smiling and loving her with their eyes.

They settled themselves on their mattresses with their blankets wrapped around them. The fish and chips plus doorstep of bread each, were shared with Jade. It was their weekly luxury, one to be thoroughly savoured and enjoyed. And looking at River Pearl's thin face, so lovely in the flickering candle light made Moira's heart full.

'Have you had a good day?' she asked.

'Same as usual. Is good to be home.' River Pearl replied in her high, thin voice.

'Still no news?'

River Pearl's expression became sad.

'Think that honourable lord husband has fallen off the side of the world,' she said mournfully. 'Is all very worrying. Not know which way to turn.'

'It'll all turn out right in the end,' Moira comforted her. 'And the world is round, Stavros said so. It has no sides for your lord and master to fall off!'

River Pearl's lilting laugh rang round the shadowy attic like the chimes from small bells.

'Confucius, he say, knowledge is key to virtue.'

'Who or what is Confucius when he's at home?'

'Is sage.'

Moira's pixie smile uptilted her lips and sent golden laughter lights twinkling in her eyes.

'Sage? You mean the stuff Flo uses with onion to put in our Christmas turkey? Sage, River Pearl?'

'You know that I mean very wise man.' River Pearl protested, going along with the joke.

'Say very again.' Moira commanded. 'I like the way you say it. Velly rhymes with belly and for tonight at least, we have very full tummies. All pushed out and fat, look!'

She made her stomach stick out as far as possible and this had the desired effect. Jade, usually very wide-eyed and self-contained, chuckled out loud.

'You never serious!' River Pearl protested, laughing and clapping her hands.

'Say serious again.' Moira jibed, 'You can't say your R's at all, can you?'

For a while after that there was much teasing and laughter and using lots of words with Rs until Jade, full-up and exhausted, closed her eyes and slept. Then Moira, watching how tenderly River Pearl wrapped the child up in her blanket, said quietly:

'My mother died when I was born and I never knew her. But if I had, I know she would have been just like you, River Pearl.'

'And if gods had blessed own humble self,' River Pearl replied, 'I would have chosen a number one daughter like you. Sleep now. Getting late.'

Where Moira enjoyed defying Flo as much as she dared, she always obeyed River Pearl instantly. She went to her own mattress and wrapped herself up warm. She had come to adore the young Chinese woman by now, and also to admire her quite tremendously for her unstinting loyalty to a man who had upped and left all his lovely family in the name of business! Who, so far as River Pearl knew, still did not realize that his wives, relations and servants had been killed all that time ago. And if he did know, didn't care! River Pearl had said life was cheap in China, but didn't he care that his big, posh house had been burned down? That only River Pearl, Jade, and an old gardener who kept little trees under the ground, had survived? Some honourable lord!

Moira felt that she would just love to meet Mr Li Tzu. She would tell him exactly what she thought. Men! They were all stinkers, they really and truly were! She said as much to River Pearl, who replied,

'Honourable Mr Sella is man, and also Mr Binks, Freddy, and the young masters, Yani, Chumley and Conor. All of them are your friends. Not all men are same.'

'Oh, let's forget it,' Moira answered and gave in gracefully, only to wheedle a moment later, 'Tell me a story – please?'

She closed her eyes and listened quietly to the gentle voice telling a tale about the saint Bodhidharma. And even though she didn't believe a word of it, Moira loved the story and the way River Pearl told it.

'And the saint would sit cross-legged in the stillness for long, long time,' River Pearl said. 'He wished to let his soul fly away to higher place. He wanted to be at one with universe and to learn from the gods. But in afternoons, was very hard. Bodhidharma kept falling asleep ... Are you asleep yet?'

'No. Please go on.'

105

'Should sleep! The saint grew anxious about being unable to stay awake, so he cut off his eyelids one afternoon, and he threw them away.'

'That was a terrible thing to do!' Moira, horrified at the thought, sat up. 'And it must have hurt him, and—'

'Whatever Bodhidharma did always meant good for the world,' River Pearl said smoothly. 'Put head back on pillow.' She waited until Moira did as she was told and lay facing her, then went on. 'One of the honourable one's eyelids fell onto the ground. Next morning there had grown a lovely little shrub with eyelid-shaped leaves. And something made the saint pick the leaves and pour boiling water on them. Then he drank it. And from then on he could keep awake for ever because he had invented tea.'

'So when we have a cuppa,' Moira refused to be impressed, 'we're drinking eyelids? Ugh!'

'Not joke! Tea a great miracle,' River Pearl said reprovingly. 'And tea also meant needing cups. So the men of Flowery Kingdom invented the beautiful porcelain from which they made cups. And the peoples of the Western world copied us and –' here River Pearl giggled behind her hands, '– and you still call your cups and saucers china-ware! Is that not a strange and laughable word?'

'I hadn't thought about it,' Moira replied honestly, 'but I will from now on. What's more, I—'

'Go to sleep now,' River Pearl told her. 'Is time!'

River Pearl left her mattress long enough to go to each candle and snuff it out. Moira heard her friend's dainty footsteps going over the cold floor, and the rustling as she returned to her place and settled down.

And Moira went to sleep dreaming of men cutting off eyelids that turned into tongues. Tongues that grew and grew until they turned into Dave Dilley. A terrible ogre of a Dave Dilley that was bearing down upon her with murder in his soul. Moira woke up, her heart pounding and her forehead was beaded with sweat . . .

It was still very early and already River Pearl had gone. And looking at the empty mattress made Moira's panic grow. She didn't quite know how she'd carry on living without the loving companionship she and River Pearl shared. It came to her to be really terrified then, because she was remembering the tale River Pearl had told of the vengeful Kung Chin.

That night River Pearl returned safe and sound and Moira began to relax.

Her life now settled in a not too unpleasant routine. She worked hard from the crack of dawn to late at night. But it was all spaced out with visits with Stavros, and chit-chat between her and Mr Binks. On some occasions there were the meetings with Chumley and the handsome, rascally Con who had taken to blowing her a kiss whenever he left. And over and above all, there were the odd occasions when Yani turned up. She was very aware of the growing admiration she saw glowing at the back of Yani's eyes.

Moira began weaving impossible dreams. Cinderella stories about herself and the handsome Greek. They could never come true, she knew it. He was a toff and above her, she knew that too. But the dreaming helped the days go by, as did Stavros' lessons, and the love she had from Jade. And most comforting of all, the close companionship she shared with the charming River Pearl.

By the middle of December Jordan Lodge was bursting at the seams. Sailors ashore, but with no homes to go to. A huge rabble of seamen, all set on having a whale of a time. And if that meant teasing Moira, and making eyes at Flo, and getting as drunk as skunks every night in the Hare and Hounds, so be it. Will had a good time of it too, enjoying punch-ups like there was no tomorrow. And all the time there was Flo, ooing and ahing and preening like a parakeet. This because she had convinced herself that all the manly battles were over her.

Christmas was good and warm and charitable; Moira was overwhelmed by the unusual number of gifts she received. A warm woolly cardigan from Flo, writing things from Stavros and chocolate from Mr Binks. Chumley shoved a Woolworth's brooch in her hand in a shame-faced way, leaving her stuttering with surprise. Yani, home again from his posh college, presented her with a box of marzipan shapes. Then Con found her working in the kitchen and gave her a bottle of perfume.

'For you, mavoureen,' he told her, 'since you're like a flower yourself. Growing up, so you are, and beautiful to be sure.'

107

'Oh, thank you!' Moira had whispered shyly. 'And – and what is the name you called me?'

'Me darlin' of course.' he teased.

'I – I have never been someone's darling before,' she replied. 'It's – nice!'

'Better get used to it, then, for to be sure you're a peach. Why, wasn't Yani saying that very thing only the other day?'

'Oh, stop your blarney,' she replied and ran upstairs to stand the bottle of Devon Violet perfume on her orange-box cabinet. Loving the look of it, and the smell, and wishing deep down that Yani had thought to give her something more grown-up than sweets.

And above all she wished that she had been able to give lovely presents to those she loved, instead of the Christmas cards she had so painstakingly made. But presents cost money and she did not have even a halfpenny to her name. Still, one day, Moira consoled herself, if all that Stavros told her came true, she would get a fine paying job in a really nice place, and then she would be able to be independent and take a step up in the world.

But the hard slog during the bad weather took its toll. Flo was on the rampage wanting everything just right. The Lodge was full, some nights men sleeping four to a room.

Moira fell to sleep each night too exhausted to hear River Pearl's colourful tales. But she never forgot to take one last peep at the most precious gift of all. It was a small picture of almond blossom that had been embroidered on silk, River Pearl's present to her, given shyly and in a depreciating way. Moira had wanted to cry at the exquisite delicacy of the picture and she knew that she would treasure it all the days of her life.

The New Year's celebrations exploded in a final blast of eating and boozing, with Moira at the beck and call of everyone. This was her life, Moira thought, skivvying and clearing up after drunken sailors. This was her future, the emptying of slops, the scrubbing, the lighting of the range in the wee small hours, the doing of a million things. But it was not so bad, the long haul of the daily grind, because she herself made it busy and bright. She smiled a lot, and felt warm and wanted by her friends.

These days, as Maisy had pointed out, she seldom had to

worry about Flo's poking finger, or endure her wild, port-induced tempers. And for the moment at least, Moira had come to terms with the dreaded visits to the fish and chip shop. She was even able to push her deepest dread to the back of her mind. Of Kung Chin's men catching up with River Pearl ...

After the New Year's celebrations everyone settled down again. Life became drab perhaps, but determined not to let things get her down, Moira bustled about doing her chores, longing for her moments with Stavros, and her late evenings with River Pearl and Jade.

And there were significant changes occuring to Moira herself. Ever since Con had given her the bottle of scent and smiled so roguishly into her eyes, she had felt different. Had thought differently, become more self-assured. She held her head high and had a strange dignity about her when Flo started to rave. One day Flo stopped in the middle of a particular breath-wasting mouthing to say,

'Bloody hell, Moir, you're getting all grown up!'

'Yes,' Moira had beamed and said in her best Stavros-trained way, 'I rather think I am.'

'Get away with yer, cheeky little mare,' Flo said and cuffed Moira round the ear. Moira chuckled as she ducked out of harm's way, and got on with emptying the slops.

Time passed by and River Pearl still ceaselessly searched, even though Moira told her over and over again to just give up. That no one would come after her after all this time, especially since the honourable lord husband seemed to have vanished off the face of the earth.

'Those rotters you told me about could have killed him too,' she pointed out once. 'For goodness sake, take time out to have a life of your own. You're killing yourself!'

'Is not true,' River Pearl replied. 'And not to persist in honourable duty towards Lord and Master is to lose face. Own humble self will never lose face!'

'What am I going to do with you?' Moira sighed, then hugged her friend. 'Oh all right then. Have it your own way.'

The depression became more acute, but inside Jordan Lodge every day things continued more or less the same. The work, the guests, folk from other worlds it seemed, came and went.

Moira would class them as either good or bad according to the messes they left behind for her to clean up.

Stavros avidly read the newspapers that lodgers left behind and discussed the contents with Moira and Jade. They enjoyed many animated discussions, even including the owl-like young Jade whose solemn remarks often made them laugh. Stavros also chose library books for Moira, using his own membership card. All kinds of books, on art, fashion, history, geography, saying in his wise way, 'My kiri, if you fight shy of the world, then I must insist on bringing it to you.' And loving him, trusting him, needing him more than he would ever know, Moira found it in her heart to thank God for sending her this wise old man.

He listened to her, tried to assuage her fears for River Pearl. After all, the death of Kung Chin's son had occurred a very long time ago. He even convinced her that her own future would hold truly wonderful things. That nothing was impossible, providing one refused to accept it as such.

Moira went along with him gladly, his handmaiden in every way allowed. But she knew that in spite of all his learned words, Jade too felt fear, even though her bland expression hid her real emotions from view. After all, unless things had altered dramatically, Sweet Precious Jade was the lord Li Tzu's one and only child. As such, her death would perhaps be recompense enough for Kung Chin. But the dark threats of revenge were always there, dancing like macabre demons in the back of Jade's mind, just as was the ever present spectre of the fish fryer lurked behind Moira's eyes. She, Jade and River Pearl had an understanding, felt rather than spoken. One that held them intuitively close, a bond that deepened as time went by.

Moira recognised and understood how deeply River Pearl's fears had affected Jade, though she would never show it. Jade would die rather than lose face. Now seven years old, the youngster was still very aware of the fact that her whole family had been murdered. Moira had heard her whispering in her sleep. In Chinese mostly, but River Pearl's translation had not been necessary, the child's intonation had been enough.

Now at sixteen Moira was old enough to live her own life, apart from all her friends, and outside the walls of the Lodge. She was even old enough to marry – Yes, she could marry Yani if he asked. But marriage was not all it was cracked up to be, she thought, seeing the tiredness in River Pearl's eyes, knowing how she searched. Always and always she crept about, going who knew where, in the endless search for her lord.

No! All things considered, Moira now preferred to stay safe with River Pearl and Jade. Spending their nights in quiet companionship, together in the attic that had become their own very special space.

Besides, though not a word had been spoken, Moira knew that Flo had no intention of letting her go.

Part II

Chapter Ten

It was summer already, and hot. Now heading towards her seventeenth year, Moira was lithe, lovely and had large expressive eyes. Her hair, long and free, flowed like a waterfall of bronze gold. Jade was seven, or could she be six, eight? They did not seem to have proper birthdays in that exotic far away land. But Jade was Jade, exquisitely pretty, like a little Chinese doll. She was without question the apple of Moira's eye.

Now holding a bunch of sunflowers and daisies Moira walked along the main road and felt peace. She had escaped all the prying eyes and was now off and away to her secret place. The place she had discovered quite by chance all that time ago. St Stephen's, old and beautiful, above all serene, was now her refuge and joy. Here she could daydream about Yani. About being carried away to a magical place where olive and cyprus trees grew, and sea and sky were bright and clear and incredibly blue.

She never tired of listening to Stavros's tales and descriptions of his homeland. Of how the golden glory of mimosa grew in the open air, huge bushes or trees of it and never in little spriglets as bought from the florist to intermingle with spring flowers. And every so often she would sneak in questions about Yani, how he had been as a little boy. About his home, his parents, likes and dislikes.

Yani was even more of a man now, and head and shoulders above her. He wanted her, she knew it. Stavros would never allow it, she knew that too. Stavros had warned Yani, Chumley and Con in turn that she, Moira, was a young lady and was to be treated as such.

Moira's cheeks crimsoned with annoyance, remembering the now very tall Con's grin and his exaggerated bow as he teased:

'She's a princess to be sure, Stavros, and it's a good man you are to remind us of the fact.'

Stavros had nodded, lips twitching, as ever liking Con very much. Chumley had laughed and shrugged, but Yani's dark eyes had looked into her's and Moira had wanted to faint with excitement at the expression she saw lurking there. But he had gone back to his own life as always and she was left with her dreams. Her lovely gentle pie in the sky flights of fancy that no one could steal.

Moira went to her place under the willow tree and took the empty glass jar from Robby's grave to fill it at the tap a little further away. She returned, and placed her offering of flowers where sweet peas had once been. Alas, no one but Moira had visited Robby for well over a year.

It was warm and wonderful, just sitting there on the grass, half hidden under the down-curving branches. It was good to be alone for a little while, happy in the knowledge that Stavros was caring for Jade and that Flo was off out with Will somewhere. Flo who was now a warmer person all round, who wasn't above showing a rough kind affection for Moira now that she was settled with Will. 'Dear old Moir,' she was apt to say to him. 'Like me own kid, she is. I tell you, Will, they don't come much better than her, and I ain't never going to let her go.'

'Then Gawd help the poor little cow.' Will had replied and tipped Moira a sly sort of wink that said, 'Your goose is good and cooked, ducks. Make no mistake about that!'

Moira closed her eyes, just thinking of Yani and cradling her secret dreams to her heart. Then she slept.

It was late when she awoke, shivering. The sun was going down and the grass under the tree was now damp. But the hairs at the nape of her neck were prickling as she felt an upsurge of fear. Someone was watching her. Someone, she felt, who had been watching her for quite some time.

Moira jumped up and left her hiding place, looking round at the shrubs and roses, at the dark railing-enclosed mausoleums, the stone angels and white crosses. Everything was still under the scarlet weight of the sunset. The air was heavy with per-

fume, of summer jasmine, flocks and carnations, all mingling
with the sweetness of new-mown grass. It was lovely, but eerie
too, as the shadows etched inky outlines, and made smudgy
phantoms round graves.

Moira saw no one, but her panic did not subside. Someone
was hiding and still watching. She could sense the awful stare of
those unseen eyes.

Memories of Flo's dire warning about 'Them evil, slit eyed
Chinks what want to do for our Pearl and Jade,' came to her
mind. Could the wicked Kung Chin have found her – and
through her River Pearl and Sweet Precious Jade who was so
dear to the not-so-honourable lord Li Tzu?

'Please dear God, help me.' Moira breathed as she picked up
her heels and ran pell-mell out of St Stephen's. She did not stop
until she was in the crowded area of the High Road...

'Now I know!' Dave Dilley muttered to his dead wife as he
stepped from behind a giant yew. 'After all this time I've found
out, Martha. Yet she and me must have been coming here lots
of times and I never realised. So this is where she meets all them
men. She was all abandoned and waiting for someone what
didn't turn up. Her and her enticing wanton ways! I should
have – I could have—'

His thoughts flickered back to the sight Moira had been,
sleeping peacefully on the grass under the willow tree. So
beautiful that his mouth had gone dry and his heart had beat so
loud he thought it would, no must, wake the dead.

She's all grown up now, he thought, forgetting about Martha. And worse than any scarlet woman. One day, he promised
himself, I'll give her the poking she's asking for, once I've
punished her of course. But that won't be nothing to what I've
got in mind for Fenning.

Strange lightning shapes began dancing in his mind and he
tried to blink them away. But they, and the weird noises
lurching and heaving behind his ears, grew more pronounced.
He began to sweat. He looked over his shoulder, half expecting
to see ghosts of the dead. Ghosts nearly as real as the goblins
always gibbering and giggling and picking at his brain. And
one of them was Martha, all grey she was now, and floaty like
the veil she'd had on her best Sunday hat. And Martha was

117

always whispering to him that her brother Stan was like her other half. That having married her, Dave must always swear to look after her twin when he came home from the war. And that it cut two ways. Stan would always look out for him!

Stan had been a hero once, before he breathed in all that gas. It was the gas that made Stan lay the blame for Martha's death at his own sorrowing door. But all that was years ago. Stan must have softened up by now. Stan must be found. Stan must be told that Martha wanted him to do for her dear husband's enemy – Will Fenning. Stan had been a soldier and he could kill a man stone dead. Yes, he must find Stan! Stan would know exactly what to do.

Dave Dilley stood there, in the ever-darkening shadow of the yew. In the wide, crowded loneliness his was the only living figure. His expression was mournful as he inhaled, then moved on to where Martha lay under a veined marble slab. He looked down, the diminishing sunset making his eyes glint red as he said low and clear, 'Make him do what I ask, Martha. Just you make him do what I ask!'

There was no reply, only the sound of a night breeze rustling a million leaves together. They sounded like evil djinns sniggering, like wanton devils cavorting, like ghouls all giggling and jeering at him.

He left Martha and walked quickly towards the gate, yet in his manner there was nothing purposeful, only an angry aimlessness. His tall hunched figure a punctuation mark in the brooding, holy grounds of everlasting sleep.

He left St Stephen's, a string-bean figure, disappearing in the absorbent darkness and reappearing for a moment, palely theatrical beneath the downcast radiance of the lights of the High Street. He flapped his arms awkwardly, his lips moved, but made no sound. For a moment, with his thin neck pushed forward, he was a travesty of one of the buzzards to be found in London Zoo.

The devils were dancing in his head again and he heard himself cackle, low and evil. A passer-by looked over his shoulder and hurried on. Someone else walking past with a girl on his arm, muttered, 'Come on, stop gawping. The poor sod's crackers, not drunk!'

Shocked, Dave Dilley pulled himself together. He stopped

118

under a street lamp and fumbled in his pocket for a packet of wilted cigarettes, and in the spilled light his face was thin, bitter and soured with hate. He was glad he'd taken on Don Compton and his Mrs to manage the shop and the cooking. They'd once had a place of their own. They were pathetically grateful, for they now lived in the room behind the business and they were worth their weight in gold. Because they had set him free. Free to think, work out and plan his revenge.

And the next step was to find Stan Jones, the one-time hero who was now nothing more than a gassed-up old fool. But he'll do, Dave Dilley thought. He'll do nicely. And once Will Fenning's out of the way I'll have the girl where I want her – and then let her watch out!

He began sniggering as the shapes and lights in his head began flickering on and off again. He spat into the littered gutter, then went on, his footsteps striking sharp discords against the increasing emptiness around him. He carried on, arms waving, lips loose, head pushed forward on his long thin neck.

Time had no meaning for him. The world was a vast nothingness, for everyone was asleep. There was only an endless maze of empty streets. Yet the night was breathing. There was something living in the black silence, it was as intangible as a dream. Like a great pulse rising and falling to the rhythm of the seconds and the minutes and the hours. And through it all the floating vision of the pouting, sensual face of the girl with cinnamon-coloured hair.

Unmindful of his whereabouts, Dave Dilley walked on. He felt as though the buildings around him were crouched in a fearful trance, waiting hypnotically for dawn. Then the sun rays would leap down from the sky. Rays that would rend and hammer and destroy all the sweet escape one had in night time fantasies. Like the visions he had of holding the girl in his arms. Of breaking into her, and bending her to his will – and after that, the delicious punishment he would mete out. Oh how he would enjoy paying her back for torturing him with her knowing looks and wayward, wanton ways.

He continued more slowly, for his limbs were weary now, but he had no desire to return to the dank upstairs flat in Jordan

Street and the lonely echo of its rooms. Yet somehow he had reached the silent, blanked-out-looking Hare and Hounds.

A movement ahead caught his attention. He stopped and slunk out of sight in the shadowed porch. Watching the slip of a woman who had been hiding out in Jordan Lodge for years. Who he had often seen scurrying about her silent, secretive business well before the streets were aired. He had noticed her a long time since When coming home from the market one day.

It had often occurred to him even then to wonder what she did at that hour. The wash house never opened before eight. A secret lover? His lips turned down. Nothing exciting about a China woman. Sniffing around her wouldn't make a man come alive like he would with a girl with dull, red-gold glints in her hair. Moira, whose little breasts stuck out delicious and inviting. Who had great pansy-brown eyes and a body that could drive a man mad.

Then Dave Dilley smiled. This China woman was important to Moira. She must be, because of the way she had spoken about the lodger in the attic all those years ago. The woman had a child who no one had ever seen, but who Moira was fond of.

Perhaps— Perhaps he, Dave Dilley, could get to Moira O'Malley via the little Chink that was scurrying past him now.

Dave Dilley waited until it was safe and then he began to follow River Pearl . . .

Chapter Eleven

It was Saturday and sunny and crowds were out walking and taking their children to the park. And part of the day's enjoyment was to stop and look at the wonderful pictures the young artist had made on the pavement outside the great park.

Tall and slim he was, with smiling eyes of darkest blue. His black hair was unruly in an attractive way, and because of his handsome looks he ought to have been on the films.

'Only cruel fate brought me down to the drawing with chalks,' he was wont to say to admiring young matrons. 'And wasn't I given the tutoring of a real artist when I was back home? But then it is hard times for us all. So I'm thinking that the pictures might brighten the day.'

At this point someone always threw a copper down. 'Thank you, me darlin', 'tis a beauty you are,' Con would say in such an all-embracing manner that it could surely melt stone. 'May the Holy Mother smile on you and yours.'

It always worked. Halfpennys or pennys, sometimes even threepenny joeys would clink their way into the cap he'd placed alongside the magnificent country scenes he portrayed. Scenes with horses. Always, somewhere, there would be horses.

Chumley never tired of watching Con at work. Con had an expressive face that could show anger or displeasure at the drop of a hat. He was strong and wiry with wide shoulders and thin hips. If trouble came looking he could put up a dandy of a fight. Would-be pitch-stealers were well aware of that fact! And yet there was something fine-looking about Con. Something thoroughbred, there was no other word for it. Con reminded Chumley of the long-legged colts he drew so often. Clean-limbed, sleek and magnificent. Always ready to run wild and free. Colts that, Con said, he had watched at play back in Ireland, on the estate where his father had worked in the stables with the colts, mares, foals, and even a champion or two.

Con never tired of telling about Marcher, the great black stallion that had been the king of the Ingram Estate's stables. Marcher who had been like wax in his father Thomas's, hands. And because Thomas MacCluskey had so impressed Mr Ingram, he had allowed the MacCluskey children to share his own family's private tutor. And it had been that fusty dried-up old man who had fostered Con's love of painting, had made him presents of books on the great artists, and above all had taught him everything he knew.

It had ended when Thomas suddenly took fever and died. His exalted position had been quickly filled. Mrs MacCluskey, Peg and Con had to leave their home. Mrs MacCluskey now lived in a small cottage outside the estate and took in washing. Peg married her Myles and lived elsewhere. Since there had been no work to be found, Con had come to London, and in spite of the odds, was doing very well. His quick wit and ready charm, and above all his talent, helping him to become a popular character known and recognised by all.

'Gawd help us,' Chumley said, late that summer evening, 'you've kissed the blarney stone all right. You don't half put it on when there's folk hanging round. What wouldn't I give to have your silver tongue? I've been hanging about watching you charming all the old girls. Bli'me, cock, it's a wonder your tongue don't drop off.'

'It's the truth I've been telling them, nothing but the truth.'

'That you had lessons?'

'Aye.'

'Then why tell Yani that you didn't take none of this picture drawing business serious? Why get all tight-lipped and shrug off his offer to help? Bloody hell, Con, he wanted to set you up in a place where you could do proper paintings! Ones you could frame and sell. What did yer shut him up for?'

'Because I'm proud.' Con replied easily. 'Because I'll take no hand-outs from a friend we see on and off, and only when it suits him. He's playing a game in that jacket of his. And the moment he takes it off, he's Yani Bertos who is way out of our class. Besides, wouldn't you be knowing that I'm me, and that I'm after doing things my way.'

'And you think that—'

'Taking a mean advantage of a mate, even a fair-weather friend like Yani is the devil's own doing. I'll not lean on him, no more than I'll lean on you, nor anyone come to that. The world is big and round and full of opportunity. I'll make my own chances, take my own risks, and by them I'll stand or fall.'

'I remember you not being too proud to let Harriet buy you chalks once.'

'And paid back she was, the very next day.'

'Got an answer for everything, you have,' Chumley snorted, then gave his foxy grin. 'I'm going over Yani's place tonight. Coming?'

'What, just to watch you making a play for Cissy again? That game's as old as Patrick, and I want no part of it. You'll get her into trouble, boyo and you're in no position to buy a wedding ring.'

'No, but I could pinch one instead,' Chumley quipped. 'Cissy will do for me. I'm glad she told that Victor to buzz off.'

'You like her like that?'

'She's a John Blunt like me, down to earth, and a game'un. Yes, I like her like that. Though its a pound to a penny she thinks less than nothing of me.' He looked searchingly into Con's lean, good-looking face. 'Ain't you got anyone special in mind? You don't take none of them women what come after you serious, do you, Con?'

'I've enjoyed a moment or two, nothing more. Fun while it lasted, but that's all. And neither should it. A man must be well into his thirties before thinking of settling down.'

'Yani hankers after Moir.'

'There'll be no joy for him there.' Con said carelessly, 'Stavros is like an old hawk where that wee girl's concerned, and I'm glad. Yani will have to do as his father wishes in the end – and marry the one chosen for him way back on that Greek island of his.'

'He says not! Says he'll defy his old man.'

'Jaysus, you two *have* been letting down your hair! But I'm telling you, he'll not have Moira O'Malley.' He grinned at his mate. 'What the devil's all this talk about?'

'They can get married as early as fourteen in Greece,' Chumley insisted, 'and Moira's a sight older than that. So if he uses his loaf, old Yani might click with her after all.'

'No. He won't.'

'How comes you're so cock sure?'

'She'll not play games with any man. She hates the breed, she told me so. Her father upped and left her, and Dave Dilley set the seal on her feelings. And she's none too keen on Will Fenning either, which I fully understand. No, it'll take a champion to bowl over Moira O'Malley.'

Chumley looked at Con hard, then,

'Could it be that you're sweet on her yourself?'

'She's a darling girl and I love her like a sister,' Con replied firmly, closing the subject. 'Now stop acting the fool. Get your mind on things more important than the Cissys of this world.'

'Such as?'

'Making our fortune for a start.'

'Get away with you,' Chumley said.

They stood there, grinning at each other like the couple of great mates they were. It was Chumley that had the last word.

'Gawd help us, you can charm the birds of the trees! Tell you what, see us both in clover. Why don't you go and marry a very rich woman?'

'Have you even seen a wild horse in a stable?' Con teased back. 'He kicks and screams and fights like the devil to get free. There's no woman that could hold me. Jaysus! The mere thought of it makes my blood run cold.'

'You'll get your comeuppance one of these days, me ol' cock sparrer,' Chumley warned. 'And when that happens I'll remind you of the rubbish what's just spilled out of your mouth. Are sure you won't be coming to Yani's with me?'

'Quite certain, but I'm thinking a half pint of the best might go down a treat.'

'You're on!' Chumley replied and scooped up Con's case of chalks. 'Let's get cracking then.'

They began companionably making their way to the good old Hare and Hounds.

Moira paced the attic floor. It was stifling hot and there were no windows to open. Jade had gone to sleep at last, believing

Moira implicitly when she'd said that River Pearl was on the way home. But River Pearl had not arrived. And because the small, delicate Chinese lady always made a point of being on time, Moira knew that there was something desperately wrong. Even the pubs were shut by now.

She made up her mind at last and left the attic, carefully locking the door behind her. She hurried downstairs, to the small room beyond the kitchen, which Flo and Will called their own. This and their bedroom upstairs, were sacrosanct. She knocked on the door and waited for Flo to bawl out impatiently, 'What is it now?'

'It's me, Flo. I want to ask you something.'

'Can't it bloody well wait?'

'Not really. I mean—' She stopped short, for the door was swung open in a furious way and there was Flo, hair all pinned back and make up all smudged and messy. 'It's about River Pearl.'

'What's up with her?'

'Nothing, but – but she hasn't come home.'

'Well?' Flo's tone was mean and she lowered her head in a belligerent way. 'What's that got to do with me?'

'I think there's something wrong, Flo.'

'She'll turn up, like she always does. I don't know what gets into you sometimes, Moir. All this fussing about that Chink and her kid don't help matters. You ought to leave well alone if you ask me.'

'River Pearl wouldn't—'

'Stop using that stupid name! The woman's handle's Pearl and she's up to her neck in hot water with her own kind. I've give her a roof over her head and that's more than most would do. As for the rest, it's up to her.'

'Flo!' Moira was glaring back now. 'You won't give an inch, will you? After all this time, after her regular rent, after her not causing you even one little spot of bother, you still don't care whether she lives or dies! She's like my big sister. She's sweet and kind and loving and – Flo, you make me sick!'

That was like holding up a red flag to a bull. Flo stepped forwards and began poking Moira furiously in the chest.

'Let – me – tell – you – bitch – I'll—'

125

Moira would have none of it. Furious, she slapped Flo's hand out of the way.

'Don't! I'll have no more of that, not ever! Now, listen to me!'

'You little mare,' Flo screeched, 'I'll have your guts for garters if you ever back answer me a—'

'Be quiet, Flo.' Moira cut in urgently. 'Listen to me! River Pearl's in trouble somewhere and I don't know what to do. I've come to you for help!'

Flo looked into Moira's tear-filled eyes and saw her very real distress. She called impatiently over her shoulder. 'Will?'

'What now?' he bawled out.

'The Chink's gorn and Moir here's worried sick.'

Will came to the door then. As usual when he was at home, his braces were hanging down and his shirt buttons were undone. He needed a shave and his hair was on end. A hand rolled cigarette was hanging from the corner of his mouth. His breath stank of beer.

'What is it, Moir? It ain't something worth getting your knickers in a twist for, is it?'

'Yes,' she choked, 'I know there's something wrong!'

'Well did Pearl ever tell you anything?'

'Only that her family is in the middle of some kind of feud. That her husband's enemies were on the rampage, and that above all she was scared for Jade.'

'Nothing else?' he asked with heavy humour.

Moira snapped back, 'Isn't that enough?'

But Will's words had made her think. The bamboo tube, that had remained safely hidden under her mattress all this time. The tube that Moira had come to believe would never have to be used. Now she was remembering the oath of secrecy River Pearl had made her swear to.

More composed, Moira stepped towards Flo and said quietly.

'Flo, I – I want to go out. I need to look around to see if I can find her. There's a favour, though.'

'What a sodding surprise!' Flo groaned.

'I might be a bit of a while. I mean, I'll plod on if it takes all night. I might not be back in time to do my work, or to look after Jade, but I've got to go. I must try!'

Flo opened her mouth to argue, but Will cut her short.

126

''Course you must, girl. You do your best, like we all do where mates are concerned. Flo and Maisy will manage just fine.'

'Thank you!' Moira breathed, and turned away.

As she raced back up the stairs she heard Flo letting fly, and Will roaring back. They'd be going at it hammer and tongs for hours.

Moira knocked on Stavros's door. He was a long time coming and when he opened the door she could tell that he had been asleep.

'I'm sorry,' she said rapidly, 'so very sorry, but I need your help. River Pearl hasn't come home and I'm about to go looking for her. Stavros, dearest, this is important. I'm just going up to see that Jade's comfortable and still sleeping, then I'll come back and give you the attic key. Don't let anyone near nor by Jade, except any of us! Promise?'

'You cannot go searching the streets on your own, my child.' Stavros was now wide awake and very concerned. 'You really must—'

'Only to the wash house and round that area,' she fibbed hastily. 'I've got to do something, haven't I?'

'Then let me call Mr Binks, or Freddy. Both would want to help.'

'I can't wait. Tell them if you like, but honestly, Stavros, I can't wait!.'

'Foolish child,' he began, but Moira had whisked away, back upstairs, staying just long enough to glance lovingly at Jade, snatch the bamboo tube from under the mattress, and run down to Stavros with the key. Then she was haring along the path, by the bushes that looked like hunched-up old animals, and finally through the green gate.

Fear for River Pearl having far outweighed her own fear of being alone on the streets at night, made her hurry on. She reached the wash house which was empty and still, just as she knew it would be. She went on, her footsteps rapid in the night.

As she left the area of Jordan Street behind her, Moira felt the beginning of unease. All the horror stories Flo had told her of opium dens, white slavery and secret societies rose to the fore. But she had given River Pearl her promise – that she would do exactly as she was about to do now.

127

'Never wait!' River Pearl had said. 'The moment things seem to be wrong, go to Mr Chung Weng at 16 Limehouse Causeway where he lives at the back of his shop. Give him the bamboo tube. He will read the message inside and will know, better than either of us, what to do.'

Moira hurried on, ignoring the people swirling around her. It was late, but a few revellers sang bawdy songs, and the odd, furtive looking customers sneaked down dark alleyways. Prostitutes stood on corners, painted and hard-eyed, waiting for whoever came along. Gas lights spewed down pallid light, illuminating sordid scenes: a drunken youth peeing up against a bakery wall; a woman tramp sleeping on waste ground, her worldly possessions tied up with string and piled in an old pram; a couple having sex standing up in a shop doorway. A mangy dog snarled, but slunk back as Moira impatiently shooed it away as she passed.

Down Dock Road Moira went, and finally she came to Limehouse Causeway. Her heart sank.

She saw a line of about twenty-eight dingy and decrepit buildings, some with Chinese signs hanging outside. She could see no light for shutters were firmly closed, but she could smell smells that were different somehow, spices and a whiff of some kind of smoke. Was that incense? It smelled just a little like the faint aroma that drifted from St Stephen's sometimes.

A faint thrill of fear and excitement went through Moira then. She had reached the Chinese quarter at last. These people were Jade's and River Pearl's. Flo's awful tales deserved to be thrown into the bin, for at number 16, so River Pearl had said, could be found Chung Weng, an old and very venerable gentleman.

Even so – did she dare go along and find number 16? To knock on the door, a total stranger, and spill out all her worries and woes? It was so late! It would be an intrusion, but— Might there be a chance that River Pearl would be there? Could the old man help?

Drawing in a deep breath, Moira walked along the untidy street until she reached number 16. She hesitated outside the ramshackle door and bit her lip. She had the uncanny feeling that many a hidden person had been watching her from the moment she had entered the Causeway. Even from behind shuttered windows and closed doors. Yes, all of them! The Chinese people who had made this into a tiny China Town. And they were not friendly at all. She was an intruder and didn't belong. Panic now rose to the fore. Moira's mind was racing.

River Pearl had said to keep everything secret. But an English girl being here, so late and alone, was hardly keeping things quiet! If the truth were known, she, Moira O'Malley, was sticking out like a sore thumb. There was still time to turn back...

Moira lifted her clenched fist to knock on the door of number 16, but the blow never reached home. The door opened silently and remained so. Without thinking, Moira stepped into the ensuing gloom. Then, to her relief, she saw someone coming toward her, holding a lantern high. She caught a glimpse of an old woman, stick-thin and brittle, with a wrinkled face and tired eyes. The woman gestured for Moira to follow her.

In the filmy, murky lantern light, Moira saw many shapes hanging from posts and on the walls. The floor was crowded with objects. There was a bench running along one wall, and on it small statues of gods. Paper shapes hung from the ceiling, frozen cut-outs hanging there, still but with a kind of waiting still-life of their own. The smell of burning joss sticks hung over all.

The old woman held the lantern high and pointed to a step going down; beyond it there was another door. The woman stepped aside. Moira nodded a thank you, pushed the door which swung open silently, and went into a well-lit room.

Moira stood there, blinking, then gradually her eyes became used to the light. She was in a room that held little furniture. The floor was covered with straw mats, and on the far side wall, a long thin god in a flowing robe stood in his shrine. A single lily floating in a blue bowl had been set before the god. For a moment Moira thought she was alone, then a movement to her right made her turn her head.

An old man was sitting at a square black japanned table. On the table there was a tall vase that held what looked like a dead twig, all twisty and gnarled. There was also a blue and white basin that held dried fruits. The Chinaman looked distantly regal, and was clearly of the old school. He had slanting eyes,

129

high, prominent cheekbones and concave cheeks. His hairline had been newly plucked, cut cleanly across the crown of his head, his hair falling back in a thick, loosely plaited queu. His high-necked dark tunic was richly embroidered in scarlet and gold. He fitted River Pearl's description perfectly and Moira knew that she was looking at Chung Weng. A man who had once been rich, but had fallen on hard times, and for some reason had had to flee his beloved Flowery Kingdom. A quiet, unreadable person indeed. One who, she felt, did not belong in a Limehouse funeral shop.

Chung Weng rose from his seat and bowed slightly and very politely. His hands were hidden in his long sleeves. He seemed to be shaking his own hands in a kind of greeting. He began addressing her in English, speaking in a civil, long winded way. And remembering River Pearl's word of caution, Moira stood there, humbly; not wanting to stare at him, she found herself looking at the blue and white dish. Fighting impatience, she let him get on with it.

'Honourable missy would do me much honour and accept lichee?' he asked finally.

He probably thought she was hungry and was clearly trying to do the right thing by an English girl. Yet Moira sensed that he neither liked nor trusted her too much. She looked up at him and smiled. Not fancying eating something she knew nothing of, she shook her head, then tried to look deferential. Inside, she was thinking, China men and me will never get on. Honourable missy indeed!

She wanted to shiver under his sudden rapier-like look. She felt fear and uncertainty then, but contrived to look calm. His mouth makes sounds that don't match up to the look at the back of his horrible eyes, Moira thought. He hates me, and probably loathes and detests all of us English people. Well I'm not too happy with his sort neither! Nor them horrible looking things in that dish. He wants to poison me, I know.

'You're very kind,' she heard herself replying, 'but no thank you.'

'Then perhaps honourable young lady would tell own humble self that all is well with her, and all of those sharing her gracious home?'

Moira nodded and smiled and replied to all his long-winded

130

courtesies, but inside she wanted to yell and run, say and do anything to get away. In this house it was like being in a strange land and she felt that she was the foreigner. Indeed, one who was under close scrutiny, who was being weighed up and found wanting!

At last he got round to asking, in a very grave and refined manner, just what was it that she had come to see him about?

Casting caution to the four winds, Moira opened the floodgates and told Mr Chung all about her friendship and love for River Pearl. About her fear for her, and how she was hours late and that she, Moira, was scared silly in case something terrible had happened. That, in the event of anything untoward happening, she had promised River Pearl to come here, to Mr Chung, and hand over this very special bamboo tube.

Chung Weng accepted the tube, graciously excused himself, unsealed the tube and drew from it a roll of silk. He unwound it, and Moira glimpsed Chinese writing and a symbol of some kind. Chung Weng examined the silk for a very long time. His expression was inscrutable and suddenly, her nerves stretched as taut as wires, Moira wanted to scream at him, and yell that wasn't it about time that the old chap hurried himself up? That River Pearl might be in deadly trouble somewhere, and all he was doing was standing there like some Chinese wop-wop doing nothing at all.

And then Chung Weng was speaking quietly, carefully, explaining that he had never really believed River Pearl's story. That he thought she must be in league with Kung Chin or his kind.

'How could you?' Moira grieved. 'River Pearl would as soon lie as cut off her own head! She's the sweetest, most lovely lady in the world and— Oh, for heavens sake! I take it that you believe her now?'

'She has sent me the proof, Honourable Missy. Is pity she not let me see this before.' Chung Weng looked at her in an oblique sort of way, 'But had reasons no doubt. All big puzzlement.'

'The puzzle is, where is River Pearl now, Mr Chung?' Moira's tone was aggrieved. 'And how is it that her husband has taken so long to come and find her? He could have made some effort -- and the thing is, she just about adores him!'

131

'The lord Li Tzu believes River Pearl perished along with the rest of his family. That was what the old gardener said.'

'You mean the man who looked after little trees?'

'Hai. He was questioned closely, but gave nothing away. He told the officials that everyone had been killed. That no one was saved.'

'But, don't you see?' Moira was trying to keep her patience, 'he refused to speak in order to keep River Pearl safe! He must have been scared that— Oh dear! Kung Chin's people are here, as you know, wanting revenge! River Pearl is always so afraid. Now she's gone and I – I can't help being scared for her. Isn't it about time her husband was told? Shouldn't he down tools at once, and come and make sure she's somewhere secure?'

'Leave matters in my unworthy hands,' Chung Weng told her. 'Will see what I can do. Is time for young missy to go. Not come again. Not safe. Number one son will follow when you leave. Keep a look-out for your sake.'

'I'm not worried about myself, don't you understand?' Moira beseeched him, once again near to nervous tears. 'Mr Chung, there's something very, very wrong about all this. I know that Kung Chin has sworn a terrible revenge.'

Chung Weng looked unperturbed and said: 'Before setting out on revenge, is wise to dig two graves.'

'Really?' she flared and wanted to hit him.

And then somehow Moira found herself outside in the street again, seemingly alone. Her heart was pounding, and she wasn't quite sure whether she trusted the old man or not, in spite of the fact that he had come to believe her in the end. She was very certain of one thing, she was glad that she had kept Jade well out of the conversation. If River Pearl's honourable lord put in an appearance, well and good. But in the meantime, Jade was going to be kept safe and sound by staying exactly where she was.

Her feet seemed to be made of lead as she walked away. A long time seemed to have passed since she had left Jordan Street. Had she managed to do any good? Had venturing into what amounted to a tiny sliver of China, actually helped? Probably not. China! What a strange sort of upside-down land. Yet, mysterious and wonderful too. And one day, yes one day she, Moira O'Malley would see River Pearl in a dress just like the one she had always yearned for and had often described in their bedtime talks in the attic. A dress that River Pearl's lord husband considered to be so great an heirloom that it went with him everywhere. And only someone very highly prized indeed was allowed to see it, let alone try it on. Moira remembered the look of yearning on River Pearl's face as she spoke of the treasure that had once been worn by the princess, wife of one of Li Tzu's honourable ancestors.

'It's sleeves are wide, immense.' River Pearl had whispered in awe. 'Is cut so full that it could wrap around me at least three times. The vermilion silk, is thick and durable and such quality is rarely seen today, and the embroidery! A treasure of colour, cherry, jade, amber, gold all in the four flowers of the season and two huge butterflies. One on the bosom, the other between shoulders. Most important, butterflies.'

'What's so grand about them?' Moira had asked, intrigued.

'They show that robe is used for wedding. Chinese people love to pun, and the two little monosyllables Wu and Fu for Butterfly and Happiness can easily be mistaken when breathed softly. So the two butterflies stand for Married Bliss.'

'Ha! We don't see much of that round here!' Moira had said pithily and this had made River Pearl put her hand over her mouth and laugh.

'English ladies not show feelings,' she told Moira. 'But all wives show blessings of marriage no matter what their land. That is why on the knees of wedding dress there are embroidered most glorious peonies bursting into spring fullness. Speak of enlargement and maturity. The flowering of hope into fulfilment. You understand?'

'Some hopes!' Moira had retorted. 'All the old girls round here think is "Oh my gawd, I'm up the duff!"'

They had had a fit of the giggles after that. What a dear friend River Pearl was!

The streets ahead of her were inky, indigo, and cucumber green. Suddenly Moira felt the depths of despair. Night shadows were in her eyes, fear was a heavy weight in her heart. And high above, the stars burned like cold crystals with no feelings at all.

133

Chapter Twelve

Moira knew, yes knew that she was being followed. It made her feel ill, but Mr Chung had given his word that his son would see her all right. The idea was creepy just the same. But over-riding all else was her fear for River Pearl.

She had come to look to River Pearl as instinctively as she had turned to Stavros. For she had recognised and, above all, experienced, their kindness and understanding. She never needed to be watchful for an unexpected blow from either of them. Nor an insult. Neither had she been taken for granted and looked on as a skivvy placed on this earth purely to do exactly as she was told.

Both her friends listened to her, allowing her to have ideas of her own. And she had listened to them. Oh how greedily she had learned and listened!

River Pearl, Moira found, was as wise in her way as Stavros. Her honourable father had been a great scholar, which put him among the highest ranks in the Flowery Kingdom. He had strong convictions, which was why he had allowed his daughter to go to the mission school, even though "foreign devils" were immensely hated in his land. He had encouraged his beloved number one daughter to be in his presence, and quite often he would speak to her as he never would to his wife or concubines.

'Was so sad!' River Pearl told Moira once. 'Honourable father taught me many things. Spoke to humble self as though she was important. But even then I knew that above all, I must obey him. Woman are born to serve our fathers and husbands since they are our lords and masters.'

'Have you heard Flo "obeying" Will?' Moira had chuckled. 'It was with a rolling pin last time!'

They had sat on River Pearl's mattress and laughed and laughed, while Jade, between them, had sat wide-eyed, her expression grave.

'Tell me more!' Moira had pleaded. 'You're so funny at times!'

'Was learning about tea on most terrible day. I remember so well. Was when he finished telling me about Occidentals and their attitude towards tea.'

'Occidentals?' Moira had asked, and River Pearl had smiled her sparkling smile and bowed low in a mocking, playful way.

'You, Moira, all Western peoples! In China, tea drinking has gone on from the time—'

'Your old saint cut off his eye-lids, I know that!'

'In your country not until the 1600s. Honourable father, he told me that in year 1615 an Englishman named Wickham wrote to Macao, in Flowery Kingdom. He was asking for a "pot of best chaw." Chaw is the Chinese word for tea.'

'Get away!'

'You be surprised when you learn that even by Georgian era, tea was worth its weight in gold. Only the very rich could drink it. I remember my honourable father telling me how wicked, greedy English men used to make tea double its weight by mixing it with ash leaves boiled in strange chemicals, dried hawthorn, or even sheeps dung. Made many peoples ill! I will never forget the day I learned these things. Was a little later on my father made lowly daughter feel ill, and sad, and very afraid. He told me I was to be sent to my husband.'

'I thought you loved your old man – sorry! I mean, honourable lord.'

'Oh Moira,' River Pearl's tone became tragic, 'I do! But did not know I would love him at the time. Had never met him, nor had he set eyes on own humble self. And, the thing that made me have feelings that I dared not show – because China girl must never lose face – was that once a daughter goes to husband's house, she is no longer part of her father's family. I – I have never been to see my parents since I was married to the honourable Li Tzu.'

'I would have shouted and screamed blue murder, if I'd had a

135

mum and dad I loved,' Moira had said stoutly. 'I would have kicked and struggled and refused to go.' Then, with rising anger, 'Men are not our lords and masters! And believe it or not, River Pearl, it's not a crime to – to what you call lose face!'

River Pearl's lips had curved upwards, touched at Moira's explosion on her behalf.

'Not get cross! The gods smiled upon me. My husband is a kind and most wonderful man...'

Moira came back to the present. Wonderful? she thought. Ha, I can take that with a pinch of salt! It's through her precious honourable lord that she's in this pickle now.

She went on, straining her ears to hear the follower that she was certain was there. If only she didn't feel so alone. She pictured Yani, but he was far away in Greece on holiday. If only she was far away, and in a much different place. Not surrounded by glowering old buildings, dark alleyways and shop doorways that looked like empty pits of hell.

It felt awful really, the upsurge of panic in her now. She wanted to pick up her heels and run. Race like the wind as did the colts that Con was always on about. She wished Con was here with her. His eyes would sparkle and he'd tease her and say, 'Run for it, mavoureen. Kick over the traces and run!'

She almost did, then decided against it, in fact did not dare. She had the uncanny feeling that her follower was just longing to give chase.

During the long, seemingly interminable walk, she ached to see other people. The night streets were so empty, so shadowy, so threatening somehow. And whenever a solitary person walked by she felt her heart swelling with thankfulness. Relieved that a night worker or two on unsociable shifts were going swiftly to who knew where. Not forgetting the odd whore at a loose end. She saw one here and there, haunting dark corners, for ever on the prowl. Their powdered white faces and dark red lips made them look like haggard clowns.

These individuals looked at her spitefully as she passed. Moira hurried on, nose in the air, her feet clicking over the pavement making sharp, punchy fire-cracker sounds. Sounds she felt sure that were as audible as the huge pounding of her frightened heart.

She had been walking for ever it seemed, and was nearing the

136

wash house where River Pearl worked, when she saw a familiar figure walking slowly towards her. All of Moira's heartbreak and fear spilled over as she cried out – and ran to Freddy, throwing herself into the safety of his enormous arms.

He began telling her off in his slow way, for worrying him sick, for keeping him searching the streets for hours, for not waiting for him – that if it hadn't been for Stavros he might never have known about this, his Iddy's latest escapade. That she was never, ever to do such a thing again.

'It wasn't any use, Freddy,' she whispered mournfully. 'I haven't found her, I don't know where she is, but I know that, just as sure as God made little apples, she's in dire trouble somewhere . . .'

Three days and three nights and now Moira was beside herself. Too worked-up to realize just how uneasy Flo was. Flo's remarks about cunning, vicious slit-eyed Chinks grew more vehement. She swore she looked over her shoulder every time she went out.

'I tell you,' Flo went on, 'just going down Jordan Street's trouble enough at times, but now! I feel crawly all over. You never know what's lurking in them sin-bins down our street. There's those who'd skin a turd for a ha'penny, or their own mothers. So giving house room to a Chink 'ud be no trouble at all. I hate going down our street!'

'Then let me go out for you,' Moira replied impatiently, 'or Freddy if it comes to that. And not all Chinese people are the yellow devils you seem to think. Really, Flo! I'll shop for you any time you like. I don't know why you're keeping me here at home all of a sudden. Just like a prisoner in fact. You used to jeer at me when I was so scared of them all, when I hated leaving this place. You forced me! I'll never forget the first time you insisted that I went out late, and in the dark, to the Ham and Pie Shop. What's so different now?'

'Are you stupid? Because it might have got round that you're Pearl's friend, that's why. You can't tell about nothing these days.'

'How could they? Besides—'

'Don't keep on! You're to stay put and make it your business

137

to see to the girl. If you don't take her over I don't know who else will.'

'No one's to take Jade, do you hear, Flo? No one but me!'

Moira fled to the attic after that, just to make sure the little girl was safe.

Jade clung to Moira even more on River Pearl's disappearance. Not speaking much, showing neither unease nor fear. But then, Moira thought thankfully, she seldom did. A quiet, contained serious-faced child, who usually kept her thoughts to herself, Jade was little taller these days, but not much. And she could, when wanting to, speak well and lucidly, because of all the learning she had done at Stavros's knee. Apart from asking once or twice where River Pearl was, she did not seem too concerned. Jade's greatest worry was if Moira herself stayed out of sight for more than a minute or two. She had said as much to Flo. Touched because of the trust she saw in the solemn, sickle shaped eyes, Flo just shrugged.

Early next morning, as was the practice now, Moira left Jade with Stavros. She went about her chores, then Flo came down to the kitchen. Moira hastened to make tea, chatting about her young charge as she did so.

'Tough little moo, ain't she?' Flo sniffed, while she and Moira were drinking at the table. 'And you're telling me they ain't all the same?'

'She doesn't understand!' Moira replied in quick defence of her darling, and settled herself more comfortably in the chair. Ever since Will had come to the lodge she, Moira, had been allowed to join Flo at the table. And was indeed treated just like one of Flo's own.

'Thank Gawd she don't understand,' Flo's tone was dogmatic. 'I reckon Pearl's gorn and had her throat slit by now. And if them Chinks find us out, they'll do for the lot of us too.'

'Don't say such terrible things,' Moira said in quick alarm. 'Don't even think them, Flo!'

'She'd have been back by now if not.' Flo leered. 'Unless she's found her precious lord and he don't want the kid. You never know with Chinks.'

'Don't be silly,' Moira flared and tossed her head so that her hair swirled out. 'You of all people should know better. We've had sailors from the seven seas stay here at one time or another,

138

and some of them real pigs too! So how is that you have such a down on people who, generally speaking, are probably as kind and gracious as River Pearl?'

Flo narrowed her eyes and her frizzy hair began standing on end. With studied care, she pushed the cup back, leaned on her plump elbows and glared across the table.

'You want to hear yourself spouting off lately,' she said nastily. 'The way you talk, you sound quite la-di da. Like you're getting too big for your boots in fact.' She jumped up, spritely in spite of her size, and knowing she was for it, Moira stood up too. Then Flo began her finger poking.

'Well – let – me – tell – you –'

Furious and near to tears because of Flo's taunt about River Pearl's throat being slit, Moira fiercely pushed Flo's hand away. She took one short step nearer to the woman who never failed to rub her up the wrong way. Who wounded her every time she went on and on about how it was she, a poor homeless creature, came to be living in Jordan Lodge. And as for that good-for-nothing Seamus O'Malley!

'I don't want you telling me any more, Flo!' Moira said, her anger the more pronounced because her voice was now so cold and quiet. 'In fact I think it's time I told *you* a thing or two. I love River Pearl! Just watching the way she loves and cares for Jade makes me want to melt. I often find myself wishing that she had been my mother.'

'I've done my—'

'I'm not interested in listening to what you may or may not think and believe, Flo. I am having my say for once. Do you know how cruel you are? Don't you understand that hearing about my father's desertion all those years ago not only hurts you, but also flays me alive? To this day I hate the melancholy sound of ships sirens. Do you know why? They're like grey ghosts wailing. Like warnings. Like sad, agonised last good-byes. And I find myself wondering whether they are the last thing on earth my father heard. At least I try to understand, and believe I meant something to him. I hope I'm more kind-hearted than you are. That I—'

Shocked and outraged, Flo was at high tide now. Red faced and rushing out the words, shouting remorselessly.

'You're nothing more than a kid what got dumped by her no-good dad, and if it hadn't been for me—'

'I know,' Moira cut in gravely, 'and in that way I'm in the same class as River Pearl. Her father got rid of her too, and—'

Surprised at Moira's stance, Flo deflated suddenly, and sank down onto the chair Moira had vacated. Then she breathed in hard, took her second breath, and glared up at Moira who had so completely taken the wind out of her sails.

'Just as it looks as if I've been got rid of, girl,' Flo said harshly. 'D'you hear me? That bloody Chink ain't the only sorrowing figure in the world.' Her face was now even more beetroot-coloured, her eyes glittering with furious tears. 'Will told me, just like that! He's going in the morning. Sodding off and leaving me.'

'No. He can't be!' Moira was taken back and immediately concerned for Flo.

'Yes, Will, what's my life! Got a ship he has, signed on again and never a word to me. Says he'll be back, but he won't. He's going to be just like your father! So who the hell do you think you are? Jawing the hind leg off a donkey, and going on about ships' sirens?'

'Oh Flo!' Forgetting her own troubles, knowing how deeply Flo had come to care for her Will, Moira put her arm comfortingly round the older woman. 'What brought this about? Did you have a fight?'

'Me and Will always fight,' Flo all but whimpered now, thoroughly unnerved. 'It's not that. It's his pride. He run out of money ages ago, but I – I made him hang on. But, you know men! "I'm orf," he says, "and I'll be back when I've got something in me pocket to show I'm a good'un. I ain't never going ter be no kept man."' At this point Flo clutched a hand against her ample bosom. 'Oh my Gawd, Moir, what am I going to do?'

Before Moira could reply someone else put in a word.

'Not take on Dave Dilley again I hope,' Maisy Noice said firmly as she clumped into the kitchen. 'He's a poisonous swine. And did you know that he only serves in the shop the nights Moir has to go in? The Compton's work and live there these days.'

'Sod the fish fryer!' Flo yelled. 'And sod you! Since when did you go sneaking round ear-holing on mine and Moir's talks?'

'Don't need to sneak,' Maisy sniffed, 'since you've got a voice like a fog-horn. Where do I start?'

'Anywhere, everywhere. Use all the elbow grease you've got. You've gotta do Moir's work as well as your own. From now on she's got to keep her eye on that kid.'

'Right you are,' Maisy said, her tone implacable. 'An' if it helps, I'll tell you that he'll be back, your Will.' She sniffed loudly. 'Bad pennies always turn up and Fenning's a know-nothing brute, but let's face it, he seems real stuck on you.'

Flo looked eager.

'You really think that, Mais?'

'Yes – and I also think the man's ruddy mad. Oh, and so are you, if you think you'll be getting hand-outs from Dave Dilley from now on. He's only been coughing up because he's shit-scared of Will.'

Eyes victorious, smiling her long-toothed smile because for once in her life she'd had the last word, Maisy Noice gathered the scrubbing things from the cupboard under the sink and went about her business.

'Bloody hell,' Flo breathed, 'I hadn't thought of that.'

'Me neither,' Moira replied quickly, 'and don't think of asking me to go there from now on. If we need fish and chips that badly, send Freddy.' Then she simply had to add, 'Though to be honest, Flo, I never did agree with all that business. It was nothing short of blackmail.'

'Don't be so daft!' Flo snapped. 'You ain't never going to get on in this world.'

Well before dawn the next morning, Will Fenning, navy-blue kit-bag slung over his shoulders, peaked cap pulled well down, strode along Jordan Street. He looked neither left nor right. A huge round-faced man, beefy and proud. He did not look back . . .

'CHINESE WOMAN FOUND DEAD IN DOCK ALLEY.' the headline screamed. The article went on—

'Unidentified female of aproximately twenty-eight

141

years was found, bound hand and foot and strangled to death, in Shaft Alley, a place where down and outs are known to gather. Before her demise the young woman had been severely mis-used. As yet the police have no leads to the person or persons who perpetrated this heinous crime. Would anyone who believed they knew the victim please come forward. Help is needed for enquiries.'

Moira's hand shook as she took the newspaper back from Stavros, who was looking very grave.

'Dear God in Heaven,' she choked, 'they have found River Pearl!'

She sped from the room and down the stairs to the kitchen.

'Flo,' she sobbed hysterically as she ran to her, 'I – I found this newspaper in one of the rooms. The one that the ships' mate took for the night. Look. Look what it says!'

'I don't know what it says,' Flo retorted. 'You bloody well know I can only barely understand a couple of words. And calm down!'

'I'll try,' Moira gasped, trying to compose herself, but unable to stop her tears. 'I'll read it out for you.'

Her hands were shaking so that reading the paper was impossible. She sank down on a chair and began rocking herself backwards and forwards, the paper now crumpled up on the kitchen table. Her whole body was racked with sobs.

'Stop that!' Flo snapped. 'Pull yourself together, girl.'

Gasping and choking, but shocked back to reality, Moira sat there, taking in great, trembling breaths.

'Now, read the paper,' Flo commanded, and pushed it into Moira's shaking hand.

Almost blinded by tears and with a great lump in her throat, Moira stumbled through those terrible words again. Then she let the paper drop, turned wildly and clung to Flo, again bursting into heart-broken sobs.

'Flo,' she gasped eventually, 'they need someone to go forward. I've got to go. I must! And—'

'Oh no you don't,' Flo replied, cold and clear. 'You stay exactly where you are.'

'I won't listen to you,' Moira sobbed passionately, 'I'm going to go to the station and tell them—'

'Where you come from?' Flo snapped. 'Where River Pearl came from, and where the Chinese kid still is?'

'Oh, no, no, no!' A terrifying picture was now flashing in Moira's mind, of poor, torn River Pearl, all crumpled and alone. 'Flo,' she whispered hoarsely at last, 'they must have beaten her most horribly. The Chinese make life time oaths about revenge.'

'I told you never to get mixed up with the likes of her. I warned you...'

'I don't care!' Moira lifted her pain-wracked face, agony in her eyes. 'Who else on God's earth do I have to really care about? I'm not made of stone. I loved looking after Jade while River Pearl was out slaving away in that wash house, and for ever searching the streets. Oh God, I can't bear thinking of how she must have felt. She was tied hand and foot! She wasn't able to move or defend herself. Sweet Jesus...'

'Stop talking like that Moir. Sweet Jesus indeed! That ain't posh like what old Stavros teaches. Shut up and let me think!'

'All I know,' Moira gave in to wild sobbing again, 'is that they've found River Pearl, and I'll hate her honourable lord till the day I die.'

'Get a hold of yourself. It might not be Pearl. Go back upstairs and look after the girl. And don't show your nose down here till I say, d'you hear me? I've told yer, I've gotta think!'

'What about?' Moira panted. Now her tears were angry and she brushed her hand across her eyes, before continuing reck-lessly, 'Just where your money's going to come from? Blood money that you took off River Pearl? Money that she sweated and slaved for? For a lousy, rotten attic and a dish full of rice?' She jumped up, her slight figure like a coiled spring, 'And here's the biggest laugh, Flo. She actually believed you to be honour-able and kind!'

'You don't know the half of it, Moir.' Flo's tone was full of bile. 'She told me all about it. Told me exactly how things were. Why d'you suppose I've sounded off so often about her kind? What makes you believe you're the only bloody shining light round here? You're just a kid, yet you stand there mouthing on,

143

as though you're a sort of saint and I'm the lice in the wood pile.'

'You never put yourself out to—'

'My Gawd, I'd clip your ear for you if it wasn't a waste of time. Oh, and I never took every penny of her wages. She kept some separate, to keep safe in case things went wrong. For Jade's keep, she said. And if you want the proof, you'll just have to look through her things.'

'I'd die before I'd look through her private belongings!'

'Suit yourself,' Flo said, then added impatiently, 'now buzz off. Your death's-door expression's getting on my nerves.'

Moira ran upstairs, all the way up to the empty attic, thanking God that Stavros was looking after Jade. Dear Stavros who was such a friend, who was so wise and kind. It was all a terrible dream, she though wildly, there must be some mistake. Flo was right, of course she was, there were lots of Chinese women living in and around the docks. It couldn't possibly be her own beloved River Pearl.

But it was, deep down she knew it, and the raw-edged nerves of her grief throbbed naked and bleeding. She slowly slid down on River Pearl's mattress, feeling more lost and alone than she ever had before. Grief, so deep that she felt physically sick, gripped and clawed at her stomach. She wanted to die herself. And over and above all, she was picturing River Pearl, so alone and afraid, suffering terrible indignities and pain. Gentle River Pearl who had risked all, and finally given her life for Sweet Precious Jade, her lord husband's child.

Moira found herself praying then, that things had turned out exactly as her friend had believed. That her soul had wafted away and risen to join the ancestors she had so greatly revered. That the lord Buddha had leant her one of His many arms and lifted up the small butterfly-like spirit of River Pearl and carried her away. Over the endless plains and mountains, above the beating seas, and finally to the almond blossom and cherry trees of the Flowery Kingdom she loved.

Moira stayed alone in the attic for a very long time. It was late evening and dusk when Flo came up the stairs, walked in and spoke in a crisp no-nonsense way.

'Pull yourself together, girl. You've been skulking in here all day. But enough is enough, and I'll give us a treat. I want you to go down Dave's.'

'I'll not go,' Moira replied, feeling wooden and drained. 'Not now, not ever.'

'You'll do as you're told,' Flo said, rearing up. 'Otherwise I'll—'

Suddenly Moira was filled with a terrible anger. She jumped up and stepped towards Flo, near enough to see her face plainly in the gloom.

'Yes, Flo, just what will you do?' she asked icily, 'Throw me out? Poke me in the chest again, smack my face? Give me the locked in the cellar treatment you handed out to me when I was a kid? Well go on! Bash me stupid if you like, but I'll not give in. I'll not forgive Dilley, nor my father, above all, Li Tzu. Dear God, how I hate men! Everyone!'

'Shut up that caterwauling and get down stairs. I want you—'

'No!' Moira said, even more fiercely, and looked so tight-faced, that Flo gave her a shove. It was hard enough to send Moira sprawling backwards. Then Flo swung round and left Moira to it.

A little later, a grim expression on her face, Flo shut the green gate behind her. Jordan Street seemed quieter than usual, a grey, alien place. But Flo's mind was on other things.

'Little bitch!' she muttered to herself. 'Fancy her refusing like that – after all I've done for her too!'

Flo pushed down the sense of betrayal that kept creeping insidiously into her mind. Gawd, she thought, you'd think that Pearl's shit don't stink the way Moir goes on. Liked that Chink better than she liked anyone, did Moir. She'd just said she hated everyone else. Which includes me no doubt. The thought cut to the quick and Flo sighed in an exasperated way. What with all the strange goings on, and talk of murder, and Moir sparking up like she was ready to explode, the world had gone mad. And not having Will around made things a million times worse. Above all a survivor, Flo took in a deep breath, thinking, but I've got Freddy. At least he won't never let me down.

The fish shop was crowded. Dave Dilley wasn't there. Flo stood back, narrow-eyed, watching the two newcomers at work. The Compton's were a pair right enough, and slow.

She'd be there all night by the looks of things. The woman enormous, with at least two double chins and the man was a weedy little shrimp. They reminded her of something. Knowing that she had to kill time, Flo let her thoughts wander away.

For an unknown reason, her mind went back to when Freddy was a boy. He'd been ill, and she'd been scared she might lose him. When he recovered she'd given him a treat and taken him for a day's outing. He'd loved the steam train and had gazed entranced at the passing scenery, eyes wide at the sight of cows and sheep. And he'd chuffed out loud, along with the sound the wheels made as they pounded over the rails.

'Chu-chu-chu—char. Chu-chu-chu—char. Chu-chu-chu—char'

How he'd gone on, dancing and alive like she had never seen him before. And real taken by the rhythm too. Flo had smiled down at his earnest face, thinking she'd have to build him up since he'd lost weight. Then, right out of the blue, she was aware that in all that crowded carriage, she was the only woman without a man in tow. It hurt that did. Stupid perhaps, but it really did hurt!

At long last the train had pulled in at the station. It had reached the Londoners Mecca, Southend-on-Sea. Southend, or else Kent's hop-fields, being to East Enders what the South of France was to the toffs.

Well, Flo thought, remembering, it had been all right perhaps, but not all that much! She cast her mind back and saw again the pebble beach over which the cockle men scrunched, with their wide trays slung round their necks. Just about everyone rushed to buy a saucer filled with cockles in vinegar. She had herself. Small saucer it was, too, for a penny Flo had thought sourly, far from impressed. It was her opinion the seafood was gritty and tasteless. She had said as much to Freddy who had plumped for ice cream.

The whelk stalls were a bore too. And also the mud stretching as far as the eye could see when the tide went out. Mud teeming with baby crabs which the children scooped up, popping them into jolly little buckets like they were so many gems.

Yes, Flo thought and sniffed, the pier had been too long, her deck chair too flimsy, the blokes too daft, with their rolled up trousers and knotted handkerchiefs covering their heads. And the day seemed too long.

Freddy, intent with his seaside bucket and spade, was in a world of his own and she had sat there, in the deckchair, without a man at her side. Without anyone, apart from Freddy, who she could really call her own. This realization had soured everything. Even the smells had been too much. Sausage, mash and onions, fish and chips, then the subtlety of cakes baking, and the pepperminty aroma of the pink stick of rock she held in her hand. Sweet and savoury odours all mixed up with the smell of people. Yes, she had thought, her lips curving down, all those people who'd been swimming and were now drying out, cooking and smoking themselves like so many kippers in the sun.

She had taken Freddy onto the Pier, the longest in the world, they said. But Freddy had not liked the feeling of being over and above the water. He had stiffened with terror, and had not been persuaded by the side shows, the fortune tellers, the clowns and the puppet show, and the laughing sailor had horrified him. They left the Pier and decided to walk along the main street and look at the shops with their over-spill of buckets and spades, celluloid windmills, balloons, and water-wings and blow-up rubber toys for children to take floating in the sea.

Feeling washed-out and weary, with Freddy dragging his heels and lagging behind, Flo had pressed on. Hot and sweaty it all was, she remembered, as she and Freddy had walked along. There was a small crowd of people looking in a shop window, they heard ripples of merriment, sudden spurts of giggles, and open chortling from men. Curious, Flo had pushed in. And then there they were. Picture postcards, string upon strings of them, greatly amusing the crowds. Vulgar, funny and good for hearty belly laughs.

Her spirits lifted, Flo had looked at them. The drawings were mostly of big fat wives and little shrimpy men – who were always looking at half naked, well-bosomed lovelies walking by. You didn't have to read the captions, because mostly the pictures told all. Not that she'd had to bother, Flo thought, because the crowds milling round were reading out loud, and guffawing fit to bust. One that was very popular was of two old

147

ladies in a museum of some kind. They were each looking at different things. One, at an octopus with long waving black legs, the other, eyes popping, at the statue of a Greek god who was particularly well endowed.

'Look at his tentacles!' one old dear was saying, while her companion, open-mouthed was nodding in a hypnotised way.

''Ere, Gert,' a bloke roared, and poked his missus in the ribs, 'she's thinking as how her old aunt said testicles!'

Yes, Flo thought, them postcards had brightened her day. So much so that she and Freddy had gone along to Peter Zanchi's, and had one of their good shilling dinners instead of the fish and chips she was going to buy.

Flo came back to the present, wondering what had set her thoughts on that particular moment in her life. Then she realized the truth of it. The Comptons looked uncannilly like those funny couples depicted on the Southend picture postcards. Fat and thin they were, and right now, red-faced and working like dogs. Flo folded her arms, stood back and waited until the shop was empty. Then she said, all friendly-like to the woman:

'I'll take the order for Jordan Lodge now, ducks.'

'Oh, no yer don't!' the weedy man snapped. 'Mr Dilley says as how we weren't to serve no orders to Jordan Lodge. Not now Mr Fenning's gorn back to sea. What's—'

'Is that so?' Flo cut in, butter-smooth. 'Well, if that's the case, I'll just take what I need.'

Ignoring the pair of them mouthing at her, she walked behind the counter and began scooping up liberal helpings of chips. Blubbery Mrs Compton tried to barge her out of the way, but Flo's hair was beginning to stand on end, and her eyes were mean. Mrs Compton hesitated, then stepped back.

'I'll call the police,' Mr Compton, the smaller, but now the braver of the two sparked up.

'Go on then,' Flo jeered. 'I'd like you to, because then I'd spill the cops yarns about your boss that'll make their toes turn up. And let me tell you something else, my old cock sparrow, Dilley wouldn't thank you at all if that was to happen! In fact you'd be out of here with his toe right up your arse.'

'But—'

'And you tell him that Flo called. And that I said as how

148

what went for Will goes for Freddy and me.' She leered then, in a menacing way. 'Just say the word gherkin to him, ducks. He'll know what I mean!'

While she had been speaking, Flo had been wrapping her ill-gotten gains in newspaper and flounced out of the shop. Big and nimble, she was fast enough to catch a glimpse of the watcher skulking in Anne Cherry's doorway.

A Chink. Yes, a Chink! Flo's blood ran cold. There was no doubt about it. All dolled up he was, and unable to hide away from the light coming from the street lamp. White socks, he had, white! And black slippers, and a jacket with what was called a mandarin collar. Even worse, he had a pigtail hanging down.

'Oh my Gawd!' Flo gasped, and felt herself beginning to shake.

The Chinaman melted away so fast that she could have been dreaming, but she knew that she was not. It could only mean trouble for young Moir, apart from the kid. No slit-eye was going to get within a mile of Moir, but even so . . .

'That's caused it,' she muttered as she hurried back home. 'That's bloody well caused it and no mistake!'

Chapter Thirteen

Con walked down the street unmindful of his surroundings, a tall, fine-looking man who had a sense of purpose in his stride. Eventually he reached the address he had visited just once before – to hand his pictures in. A woman servant had taken them, nodded, and shut the door in his face. It had not been a good sign.

The house lay back from the street and was one in a row of Victorian buildings. He loped up the three steps and rang the door bell that was set in the mouth of a gruesome gargoyle.

The door creaked and groaned a little and then a woman stood before him. She was small, rather plump, her figure encased in a long multi-coloured gown. She was neither young, nor old, just in between, and although not good looking, her eyes were friendly. Her skimpy, peppery hair was held back by a wide, flowing band of material as bright as her dress. She had large gold hoops dangling from her ears. She wore many bangles and beads. Her Eastern-style slippers were exotically embroidered.

She smiled at him.

'Would you be Mr Connor MacCluskey?'

'I – er – yes, I'm afraid I am.'

For the life of him Con could not have controlled the apologetic note in his voice. He wondered just what was going on in her mind.

Vivien Bentine watched him. The tall, well-proportioned young man towering over her remained silent. Unlike so many others, she thought, this one was refusing to plead his cause, had not resorted to the gift of the gab. Yet she knew that this moment was, to him, more important than life itself. There was a stillness, a rigidness about him that hinted at self-control and yes, of loneliness.

Big as he was, Vivien saw him as the boy he once must have been. Long and lean and out on the limb, fighting for survival, a sensitive, artistic person who, according to Yani Bertos, had had to fend for himself as well as for his sister until her marriage, and above all, his beloved mother, who still remained his greatest concern. Even so, he had knuckled down to it and never complained. And now, mad as it seemed, he was using his enormous talent to earn a living as a pavement artist.

She had gone along to his pitch, surreptitiously of course, right at the beginning, to look at the young man's work. Had stopped, stared and felt excited. The horses he drew were alive and free, their muscles rippling, manes flying as they raced over fields. Just as the clouds he depicted scudding across the skies above had a marvellous airy feel about them. This young artist made everything he drew seem very invigorating, compelling and alive. He needed some direction of course, someone who knew how to refine his technique, but yes! Yani Bertos had not been wrong. This young man was a find.

Con pulled himself together. Mentally throwing his hat over the mill, chin lifted, he grinned his devil-may-care grin. At that moment he and Vivien became friends.

She led him to a large room in the front of the house. The floor was covered with an ancient Persian carpet and there was bric-a-brac everywhere, all arty stuff Some pieces seeming to Con at least, rather outlandish, the creator's intentions utterly obscure.

There were books everywhere, and magazines about art. There were unframed canvases standing with their backs against the wall, easels holding paintings, and hanging above, all but cheek by jowl, watercolours. These, finer than the oils, were behind glass, and were mostly studies of still life. However, the flowers were lovely and inspiring in their delicacy. They bore the signature Rowena Wray.

Smack in the centre of the room and its surrounding mishmash, there stood a massive desk. This was piled high with mail, printed bills about exhibitions, and writing materials.

151

Vivien Bentine began rifling through some letters. He stood there, nonplussed.

One swift glance and Con could not see any of the six pictures he had slaved over for the past year, worked and concentrated on, all but sweating blood over for hours. This, long after his day's stint on the pavement outside the park.

Landscapes they were, wide and commanding, and of course always containing the fine animals he had known so well. Creatures he had come to learn about and love, and even now, saw through his father's twinkling Irish eyes. It had been his choice to paint the scenes and the animals his father had been so close to. His father, Thomas, the large man with the big hands, the gentle touch, who would breathe into a wild young thing's nostrils and make it his own.

So, it had been the joy and the ache, the toil and the triumph to work in oils. And before the actual paintings, the rough drawings. Of thoroughbreds, hunters, plough horses, stallions, shires. The great drays pulling the beer barrels through London town. The prancing little mares between the shafts of oilmen's carts, indeed carts of any kind. He made sketches of colts, fillies, yearlings. So many, he loved them all. The oil paintings he achieved were part of him, the brushes he used carrying his heart and soul. Yet he felt he could have done better with every one. Then had come the day of reckoning.

Con had chosen six he thought best and brought them along to this address. It had been scribbled on a scruffy piece of paper, yet handed over by Yani before he left for Greece as if it held gold.

'Here's to your fame and fortune, my friend,' Yani had said.

Now the two weeks Yani had said were necessary were up, and here he was, like a kid before the Head, Con thought with disgust. What the hell had he been doing, listening to Chumley and finally giving in? Not forgetting the way Yani had been droning on about chances too good to miss. He should have stuck to his guns and never put himself under someone else's thumb. Now he was here, feeling a fool. The six pictures that would supposedly hoist him onto a higher rung of the ladder, had been hidden out of the way.

A step up in the world, Yani had insisted. Some hope! Why

the hell he'd gone along with the Greek's smooth talking he'd never know.

The silence, apart from the rustling of paper was hard to bear. Con cast his mind back all those months ago.

'You are my very good friend,' Yani had told him, 'and I know you well enough to accept that you must do this on your own. But in the name of St Spyridon, paint some real canvases! Do the kind of things that the old man in Ireland taught you.' He had smiled his white-toothed smile, 'And they had nothing to do with chalks, eh?'

'He was a dabbler himself.' Con explained. 'Portraiture was his joy. He showed me how to use the medium of oils. I used to paint pictures of the horses – and my father working with them. They were good days. Happy!'

'Then get yourself some oil paints,' Yani had ordered. 'Beg, borrow or steal if necessary, but do it! Paint the animals with all the feeling you've got in your voice now. Don't hesitate. Set yourself up with all that is necessary and—'

'I haven't that kind of money. Canvas, oils, brushes, varnish – it's beyond me, boyo.'

'If you won't let me help you, you've got to make yourself get the stuff. You could be earning yourself a fortune later on. You must look ahead, Conor. You are worth better things. Don't be like Chumley and take each day as it comes—'

'Chumley's fine,' Con had said stoutly, 'and he has his feet set firmly on the ground.'

'Chumley is as great a friend to me as he is to you,' Yani had replied dogmatically. 'But he is different. He is his own man – and you are your own man. What's good for him is not good for you. You can and must get on in the world – if only for your mother's sake. You've got to do this. Let me help with the money and—'

'Devil take you!' he'd snapped, incensed, 'I'll rot in hell before I jump onto another man's back to get me across stream.'

'Sorry!' Yani had hunched his shoulders and shrugged in an exasperated way, 'I meant that I would like to help, that's all! But that's neither here nor there. It's important that you work in oils. When you've got six that you're happy with, I will give you the address of the woman I've found.'

153

'Never!' Con's pride had again reared it's head. 'I'll not—'

'This will be no favour, Con.' Yani's tone had become impatient. 'The woman is an agent. She will look at your work and assess it! If it's good, she'll tell you. If it's bad—' Yani had shrugged again. 'Then you will know.' He had reached out and embraced Con in his very Greek, very expressive manner. 'Bear with me, Con. It's just to get you started. There'll be no problem. No problem at all ...!'

Now here he was, Con thought, just as Yani had directed, and terrible it was, to be sure. Worse, it rankled. It rankled like hell. The woman's silence was driving him mad.

In spite of telling himself for months not to get too wound up about all this, he had felt like a coiled spring. And now? Now he felt flat, disappointed, let down. It was no go! It had to be because the woman in front of him had seen fit to shove his pictures out of sight.

Con silently cursed to himself again for listening to Yani's pie-in-the-sky ideas. Devil take him. If he'd been here right now, instead of on that Greek island of his, he'd give him the tongue-lashing he deserved.

'Ah! Here it is!' Vivien found the paper she had been looking for. 'Sorry about that. Please take a seat.' She sat down herself and smiled across her desk. 'Now we have some rather good news ...'

Con walked towards home, his movements fluid, his iris-blue eyes shining. His lips pursed as he whistled high and clear as a lark.

He reached the stalls area of the High Road and turned into Market Street where the over-spill of traders carried on in their usual cheery, back-chatting way. A group of Pearly Kings and Queens, looking marvellous with their clothes smothered in designs made from pearl buttons, were gathering together, as always, ready to work for charity of some kind. A greengrocer was raucously bawling out to the women that passed.

'Happles, a pound, pears. Happles a— 'Ere you are luv! A penny ter yer – an' yer won' get no better hany ol' where! Happles a pou-end, pears ...'

Con reached Harriet's place, a tall, gaunt building with extensive living quarters behind a glass fronted shop. From there on it stretched upwards for another two floors. Right at the top, a short flight of steps led to the attic, which Harriet had now allowed Con to rent. Chumley retained the small, rent-free, poky back room, and was glad to at last have it to himself.

Home, Con thought with great satisfaction. Sure and it was good to be home at last. And the telling of the tale would be as joyous as making Patrick throw back his head and laugh.

Harriet Jones was standing behind a counter holding jewellery of all descriptions. All around were art objects, statues, busts, gilt frames holding pictures of historical times, ornaments, anything and everything that was old, second-hand but nice. The stuff she received that was worth only a copper or two, she passed on to Anne Cherry of Jordan Street.

Harriet was olive-skinned. Her oval-shaped face was strong-featured and good-looking. Her mouth was wide and generous, her eyes large, velvety-dark and slanting. Her black hair was cut short and worn with a fringe and she looked rather Egyptian in her mid-blue dress, set off by a wide, gold neck band that matched her gold, crescent-shaped earrings that bore blue stones. She was one of those women it was impossible to put an age to. One had the impression that at ninety she'd look about the same.

Harriet was used to having her own way, and she was also a fine lady – and Gawd help anyone who thought otherwise!

'Well?' she asked Con, in an all but belligerent way, 'What happened?'

'They're hanging on a wall in some galley,' Con told her, eyes sparkling. 'A little out of the way place, so it is, and probably the paintings will be mouldering away there for years. But it's good to know that Vivien Bentine reckons I'm a natural. She tells me that I'll be getting better all the time.'

'A woman!' Harriet's lips curled with contempt. 'So that's it!'

'A suspicious person you are to be sure,' Con laughed. 'She'll be old enough to be my mother, and not the flirty kind at all. She's all for Art, Harriet, and what she doesn't know on the subject would barely cover a postage stamp.'

Harriet raised her brows casually and thought things out. Smiling, breathing in the familiar leather and polish smell of the shop, Con watched her.

Harriet was great at surviving, and ready to use all the

cunning tricks necessary. She did not suffer fools gladly. And quite clearly, she was now thinking Con a fool. She distrusted men, and treated them like dirt. She had taken Chumley under her wing to please Mr Binks. Then in turn, Chumley had wangled a place for Con. Harriet, putting up with them as callow youths, was kind in a cool way. But, over the years had often told them, 'One day you'll be fully-grown blokes. When that happens you'll not be worth the air you breathe.'

They were men now, and knew the way of the world. However Harriet still saw them as callow youths. So, they considered, that was all right. They both got away with murder, well all but! And Chumley treated her as he would a mate.

'Have a heart,' Chumley's response to her nagging was always the same. 'You're all mouth and trousers, Hal. Like it or lump it, you've got a soft spot for us. An' know something else? We're daffy over you too.'

Harriet would glare such a glare that Con, before he became used to her, had wanted to curl up. But Chumley would just roar out laughing, toss Harriet something nice that he'd pinched off some unsuspecting person, and go whistling on his way.

It had taken Con quite a while to come to terms with the fact that Harriet's building was an Aladdin's cave filled with anything and everything that she could sell. Piled up it was, in every room, some things having been there for years, inherited from her father, who had been in the business and was wily as they came. He was a receiver of stolen goods; everyone knew or guessed. But it was something, up till now, the police had been unable to prove.

'Cat got your tongue?' Con asked, surprised at her lack of excitement on his behalf. 'I thought you'd have more to say. It's a great stride forward I've taken in life.'

'Ha!' she sniffed. 'So that's what you think. What else did this so-called expert say to make you look so pleased with yourself? Buttered you up, did she? She's let someone put your pictures on their wall and you call that good? Where's the spondulicks? The money you deserve? God, men are such fools!'

'They'll take a percentage of any sales made,' Con explained, 'but what matters is that they think my work worth hanging!'

156

'I could have told you that – and did. What else did that woman say, apart from the fact that your pictures are good enough to steal?'

'Not steal, handle! She told me that I must work to perfect my style. That I must specialise, and that I'm a natural. That I have a good eye!'

'It strikes me I knew that all along.' Harriet remained unimpressed. 'In fact from the moment Chumley brought you here.' She smiled in a grim way. 'Like a skinny, bedraggled young rat, you were, and wet behind the ears. Not believing that the folk that promised you a roof could be so heartless. That they had done a moonlight, and so let your old mum down.'

'But you came to my rescue, darlin'. I'll never forget that!'

'Stout-hearted you were then, ready to work if it killed you, roaming about the streets like a restless wild wolf when there was nothing to hand. Then you saw that old boy drawing on the ground and it clicked for you. And from that day you've done well.' She sniffed disdainfully. 'I went along with you right from the start – and I'm no expert! So that woman don't know no more than I did all them years ago. Well, don't stand there grinning, what are you going to do from now on?'

'The same as before.' Con told her easily, 'Work in chalks for my Ma, my rent, and my keep. And after that, I'll be using the oils to please me and me darlin' dad. God rest his soul.'

'You'll have your work cut out.'

'I'll be enjoying the challenge!' He was clowning now. 'After all, Harriet, isn't that what life is all about? And don't you find that your own days hold many challenges? Risks of many kinds?'

'And you are a devil,' she replied, hoity-toity now, and far from amused. 'Don't think of getting above yourself Conor MacCluskey. If you do, I'll soon sort you out!'

'That sounds promising.' He bent down and kissed her, teasing her with his eyes.

Out of all those she had dealings with, Con was the only one who would dare. Not even Chumley or Mr Binks would risk actually touching her. She hit him then, a fair old wallop. Still laughing, he left her and ran up three flights of stairs to the attic that was now his workshop and home.

He had a three-foot-wide bed, a cupboard, chest of drawers, a table and kitchen chair. There was a saggy armchair that had stuffing spilling out at the sides, and a few other odds and ends, but above all the place screamed it housed an artist, for a large, second-hand easel held pride of place. Painting gear was spread all over the table.

A gas ring jutted out from the skirting board, just a few inches above the floor. Con knelt down and lit the gas ring which took one medium-sized kettle, and prepared to make tea. His mind was racing. He felt pleased but not certain whether to write and tell his mother. She would smile, be proud, say all the right things, but secretly wonder why he was putting his mind on fanciful things when he should be going all out to get a proper job. Just as his father had all those years ago.

Deciding not to do anything for the moment, he cut off a thick wedge of crusty bread, a chunk of strong cheddar and sliced an onion in half. A meal fit for a king. He grinned to himself, thinking that for all his mother's ideas, chalking on pavements didn't do half bad. Didn't do half bad at all . . .

Moira sat on her mattress, her arm round Jade. The little girl clung on to her, her eyes on Moira's sad face.

I must pull myself together, Moira was thinking dully, for Jade's sake! I've got to stop picturing River Pearl being treated so badly and – and being dumped in that alley like a discarded broken toy. She must have been fighting and struggling and— Moira's mind darted away from the terrible pictures her thoughts made. But she couldn't get away from her grief for River Pearl. The sweet, delicate lady whose high, lilting laugh was as cheeky as the small brass bells they put on babies' reins. She could not rid herself of a deep aching sense of loss. Of course the dead lady was River Pearl. The only thing strong enough to keep her away from Jade was death. Yes, River Pearl was gone for ever and Moira could not suppress a sob, thinking how empty and unloving her own life would now be.

In spite of trying very desperately to quell her imagination, the knowledge of how River Pearl must have suffered came to crucify her thoughts. How terrified she must have been, and all alone too! That must have been the most awful part, to be away from Jordan Lodge with its safe walls, its air of sanctuary. For

River Pearl there had been only the filthy, rubbish-filled alley-way, and derelict people who were befuddled with meths. Awful, scarecrow-like men and women walking round her poor, lacerated body. God forbid, perhaps actually falling over her! Not understanding, not caring, neither seeing nor sensing the unbearably wicked, the impossibly sad!

Why did they have to kill her? Moira grieved. I know she would have refused to tell them where Jade was, that she defied them no matter what, but why, why, why did they have to kill her? If I ever catch up with those Chinamen, either Li Tzu or Kung Chin, I'll – I'll— She was floundering then. What could she do? Tell the police? Explain about River Pearl and her story? About her lord husband's home being torched, his family killed, everything? And in so doing, wouldn't she be giving the old man in the funeral shop away? Oh, she was not at all certain that she liked him, but he had sent his number one son to follow her, keep her safe, and— Safe from what? From whom? A thrill of horror ran through Moira, remembering that long, lonely journey through the all but empty night time streets.

'You are too quiet and too miserable, Moira,' Jade said uncertainly. 'I am not sure what to say.'

'I'm sorry, Jade. It's just that I miss River Pearl a lot. Don't you?'

'She will come back soon,' Jade said with quiet faith. 'She would never leave me here.'

The attic door swung open with a bang, making them both start. Flo stood there, closely followed by Freddy.

'Pack your things, Moir,' she said firmly, 'and the kid's. Wrap everything you can in your clothes. They'll be taken to your new place as soon as poss. We're getting you away from here.'

Moira froze, her mouth went dry. It wasn't a dream, she could tell by the look on Flo's face. The nightmare of all these years was coming true. Flo was throwing her out on the streets.

'What – what's happened?' she asked fearfully. 'Is it something too terrible to—? What have I done wrong?' Then desperately, 'Flo, I – I can't leave here! Why are you looking at me like that? What's wrong?'

'The place is crawling alive with Chinks, that's what! Some-

159

how they've found out where Pearl came from— She probably told them herself because she was forced. So, out you go!'

'We want to stay!' Moira felt terror for Jade, and fear for herself. Her tone was pleading now. 'Flo, you wouldn't dump us just because—'

'Shut up, you stupid cow!' Flo told her fiercely. 'I'd no more dump you than I would Freddy. But I've got to get you out of here to keep you out of harm's way. I ain't having no bloody slit-eyes choke you to death'

'But where are we to go?' Moira clung to Jade tightly. 'What are we to do?'

'Don't worry, it's all sorted. Me and the Greek and ol' Binksy's worked it all out, everything! Now pack your things – and look for them savings of Pearl's. The kid's going to need her keep, and you'll have to work for yours.'

'I can't, I won't—'

Flo strode forward to poke Moira who had jumped up from the mattress in dismay.

'Do – as – you're – told!'

Furious, frightened, Moira pushed Flo's hand away and would have hit her back, until she saw the expression in Flo's eyes. Flo *did* care! Flo was really and truly concerned for her safety.

'Oh Flo,' she gasped, 'Flo, I—'

'We ain't got no time to argue. Now get on with it!'

Heart pounding, feeling utter despair, Moira began gathering everything she could, putting it into her prized winter coat. It was old now, threadbare, but useful for many winters to come.

She found a small, dull-red japanned box under River Pearl's mattress. So, that was Jade's keep! She looked over at Flo, the woman who had not been so bad to River Pearl after all. Moira gave Flo one brief, scared smile.

'Take that with you,' Flo snapped. 'I don't want nothing to do with stuff belonging to poor old Pearl. What's that you've got?'

'A little picture painted on silk, Flo. River Pearl gave it to me and – and it's special. It rolls up into nothing, see?'

'Then stick it in Jade's box.' Flo looked curious. 'What's she got inside it by the way?'

Moira lifted the lid with shaking hands. There was an emerald brooch inside, and underneath this some one pound notes. She counted them.

'Five pounds,' she said quietly, 'Jade has five whole pounds! Oh, and this.' She held up the brooch. Flo shrugged.

'That's all right if you like that sort of thing. It might be worth something. Harriet'll soon know. I hope as how I'm doing the right thing in all this. Gawd knows what side them Chinks is on, but I ain't going to take no chances.' She smiled wryly. 'Know something? Pearl said I'd be given a fortune when her old man turns up. Some hopes! Still, I've gotta try and do right, so bloody well come on!'

It was all a mad rush after that and Moira was in a daze of shock. Jade just watched and listened, empty-faced.

'Wrap the kid in the blanket,' Flo ordered Freddy. 'She ain't so big for all she's growing up fast. Make it look like you're carrying a roll of carpet if you can. It's all but dark and no one's going to stare too hard, so with luck no one will see the difference. You know where to go?'

'Second hand?' he asked slowly, and looked sad.

'S'right. Anne Cherry's expecting you.' Flo turned to explain to Moira. 'Stavvy's over there now, paving the way. The old Greek ain't so bad at that! Binksy's gone to tell Harriet Jones what's expected of her – and believe me, that woman won't do no informing. Got too much to hide herself. For Gawd's sake, Moir, let go of the girl! With Freddy looking out for her she couldn't be in better hands!'

Moira let go of Jade who now had two tears slipping slowly down her face. After one, searching look into Moira's eyes, she obediently allowed Freddy to roll her up in the red blanket.

'Anne will tell you what to do next,' Flo told him. 'She's got a yard door that leads into Barrier Street over the back. No one in Jordan Street'll get their beady eyes on our Moir or the Ch—'

'Jade!' Moira cried fiercely through her tears. 'Her name is Jade, Flo. Jade!'

'Keep your hair on, Moir,' Flo said impatiently, but she continued to look at Fred. 'Anne'll tell you the next step once you've got Moir here over to her place in the same way.'

Freddy lifted Jade with consummate ease and strode out

161

with her well hidden inside the rolled up blanket. Flo turned to Moira, speaking with crisp authority.

'Got it straight? You've got to get to Anne's, so you'll be in Freddy's care. In the meantime, let's go to the kitchen and have a cuppa.'

'Jade will be frightened.' Moira whispered. 'Can't I go with her?'

'Freddy might be big and tough, and he could easily take the pair of you.' Flo smiled mirthlessly, 'But wouldn't they wonder about a bloke what's walking about carrying a carpet under each arm?'

Moira crept like a mouse, down the stairs behind Flo. She went into the kitchen she knew so well, and sat at the table. It was Flo who poured out the tea and handed a cup to Moira.

'Here you are, drink up. Hot and strong it is, with plenty of sugar. Make the most of it, Moir, because only Gawd knows when you'll be back.'

'Oh!' Moira said quietly, the blood turning to ice in her veins. 'You – you really are washing your hands of us, Flo!'

'Don't be daft. It's like I said. You're best out of the way for a while ... Since I don't want to see you, or that Ch— Jade, floating face down in the Thames.'

Moira shook her head and forced herself to drink the only cup of tea ever poured out for her by Flo. Tough as teak old Flo, who'd given way only once before to Moira's knowledge. When Will Fenning had left.

There was silence in the kitchen after that, apart from the ticking of the tin clock on the dresser shelf. Ticking that seemed to get louder as the seconds and minutes crawled by. Then Freddy came back, blanket in hand. Moira stood up. Not daring to look back at the now red-faced woman, she walked to Freddy. Dear old Freddy, who was quiet and woeful-looking. He never said a word.

Freddy wound the blanket tightly round her, leaving sufficient head space for her to breathe. Moira felt herself swung up, and though wanting to cry out, she remained mute, and held herself still ...

Chapter Fourteen

Con was sketching a country scene that he remembered from
his boyhood days. It had all been green and fresh, and empty
for miles. The byrn always rushing, running cold, crystal clear
and clean. And there had been space, so much of it, not like this
people-packed city at all, at all. But he wouldn't be anywhere
else, not now! This was where it happened. And if he missed the
loving and fighting, the kicking and cursing, the drinking and
singing of the MacCluskeys, he had Chumley, who was such a
good mate. And he had Yani, who was a decent sort after all.
Not forgetting Harriet of course, who a while ago had thumped
him hard enough to make his ears ring.

He was whistling as he worked. Thinking of nothing but his
picture until, suddenly, the gas light went out.

He put a penny in the meter and gathered his things together,
carefully cleaning his brushes in turps. Then he went down to
Harriet's sitting room, beat a lively tattoo on the door and went
in. He stopped short, surprised.

Mr Binks was sitting by the empty fireplace, whisky in hand.
This was not unusual, for though Binksy refused point blank to
live here in Harriet's place, he looked on it as his second home.
But not Moira and Jade!

They sat there, at the table, quiet, still, both looking strained.
Harriet was there, pouring milk into cups, prior to adding
sugar and tea. The thing that struck Con most at that moment
was the utter grief he saw in Moira's large eyes.

'Just the chap I wanted,' Harriet said without preamble.
'We'll need your help. I want some furniture moved round, and
Binksy here's not big enough to do it on his own. There's a bit

163

to do, and it'll be easier when Chumley gets back from mooning over that girl he's so keen on. But first, sit yourself down, Con, and have a drink. What'll it be?'

'Tea it is and I thank you,' Con replied, then turning his gaze onto Moira's stricken face, asked, 'What happened?'

Moira was unable to reply.

'We have a couple of girls come to stay with us for a while,' Harriet told him firmly. 'And it's going to be our secret.' She smiled at Moira, 'Isn't that right?'

Moira nodded, and reached over to take Jade's small hand into her own comforting grasp.

'You're not to worry about Jade,' Harriet said firmly. 'She and me's going to get on fine.' She handed a cup of tea to Moira. 'Here, drink this up, you look like death. What can we get this sprat, eh? Lemonade?'

'Thank you,' Moira found her tongue at last and quietly accepted the cup that had a poppy and cornflower design. Delicate china it was, pretty, unlike the heavy old enamel mugs that Flo chose to use most of the time. Moira knew that she would give her soul to be back safe in Jordan Lodge. This strange house was of the outside world and she wanted no part of it. If only she could be washing and drying Flo's enamel mugs right here and now. If only—

A wave of horror washed over her then as a thought occurred. Had it been Dave Dilley standing there, outside the green gate as Freddy had carried her by? Why oh why was that man always there, hovering like a spectre in her mind? Flo hadn't helped either, with her tittle-tattling. Why, only the day previously she had been carrying on about Dave Dilley being seen near his brother-in-law's dreadful digs. A derelict place Stan had taken over without a by your leave, it was a filthy hole, an old shed affair situated under a railway arch. As if anyone cared what Stan or Dave did. She, Moira, most certainly did not! In fact she loathed and hated Dave Dilley far more than she feared the Chinese people. River Pearl was Chinese, and Jade. Now all River Pearl's troubles were at an end, and seemingly her own just begun. Dear God, what was the matter with her? Her mind was going round and round like a squirrel in a cage...

164

'I said,' Harriet's voice cut rough-edged through Moira's cloud of panic, 'what shall I give the girl?'

She felt Jade's fingers twitching urgently round her own. She smiled at her in a comforting way, then politely replied, 'Jade likes tea, please. Could it be weak and without milk? That's how River Pearl gives – gave it to her, you see.' In spite of herself, Moira's eyes filled with anxious tears. 'Are – are you sure it's all right? Us staying here I mean? We really are safe?'

'Safe as houses,' Harriet's tone held conviction. 'It's time I had some girls around me.' She darted a piercing look at Jade, then she added, 'It's not good, being outnumbered by men. Know what I mean?'

Startled, Moira looked into her strong, good-looking face. Harriet's expression did not change, not even though Mr Binks and Con both laughed. Then they began teasing, saying that no matter how she put it she, Harriet, would go through fire and water to defend them, even though they were dreaded, down-trodden males.

'I'd as soon fend for a barrel-load of monkeys,' she told them. 'Now, who'd like some bread and real nice beef dripping?'

It wasn't long before they were eating and drinking and talking over the topics of the day.

Moira sat very quietly, only half listening, conscious of the fact that Jade was now slumped in the chair and fast asleep. No one seemed to be too bothered about moving furniture at all. Dear God, she grieved, was the world going mad? Here it was, the middle of the night, and every so often a tight-faced woman would come to tell Harriet there was someone waiting to see her. Harriet came and went while everyone else continued with their laughing and talking about stupid, unimportant things.

She looked at the dark-red japanned box she had brought and set on the table. It seemed to loom larger as the minutes went by. River Pearl had scrimped and saved and worked herself to death to make sure of Jades's keep. Well she, Moira, would look out for the little girl now, and give her own life if need be.

'I won't let you down, River Pearl,' she whispered deep in her soul. 'I'll look after Sweet Precious for you. I give you my word!'

Moira continued to sit where she was, at Harriet's table, feeling that her world had come to an end. She was beginning to believe that she was forgotten when Con caught her eye and winked. She tried to smile back, but it was hard to stop her lips from trembling. After losing River Pearl, the horror and terror of Dave Dilley – the man's name still brought dread flooding to her heart – and now here she and Jade were, in a strange place, with an unknown woman who seemed to rule her roost as powerfully as Flo ruled hers. So she and Jade were, to all intent and purpose on their own – or were they?

Moira felt cold, trembly and her forehead became beaded with sweat as she remembered. She couldn't be sure, but, yes, she believed it really had been the fish-fryer she had caught a glimpse of. He had been hanging around outside, in Jordan Street, when Freddy had left with her slung over his shoulder. Oh, her head had been hanging down, and she had been bumping up and down with the rhythm of Freddy's movements, and she had been well out of sight, but she had caught a glimpse of the street, faintly. And in a hazy kind of way, she had seen Dave Dilley's long figure. Unmistakable. Hovering, long and skinny and grey, like an evil phantom, always there. Habitually sliding his evil tongue over his lips in a wet and greedy way.

She came back to the present, conscious of the second, concerned glance Con had directed her way. Then he spoke to Harriet.

'It shows that you're not used to having lady guests under your roof,' he said easily, 'since the wee girl's asleep in her chair and Moira is looking all in.'

'A proper place must be made for them,' Harriet said crisply. 'The room I have in mind is cluttered up to the roof. Clearing it will take some time.'

'To move all those heavy old antiques you have hidden?' he teased. 'And the warehouse of stuff you keep around? Wouldn't it be better for me to move out of my bed for this once? We can't expect the young ladies to sit up all night.'

'Now that's what I call a good idea,' Mr Binks said. 'Moir looks fair worn out.'

'Suit yourselves,' Harriet replied carelessly, 'but I was thinking of taking Jade in with me. Besides, it won't hurt Chumley to give a helping hand for a change and—'

'Chumley's feet are still under Cissy's table, if I know him at all,' Con insisted. 'He's making the most of it now that Yani's away. He'll not be back for a while yet.'

'Do what you like,' Harriet replied, adding tartly, 'but only for now. We mustn't have our famous artist short of a bed, must we?'

'Cor bli'me,' Mr Binks put in, 'I forgot! Harriet's told me your news, Con, me boy. Good on yer, mate!'

'Thank you,' Con replied, then looking once more into Moira's white, tired face. 'Now I really must take care of this young lady.'

Young lady, Moira thought, was that how Con saw her these days? She was conscious of Harriet's whip-lash look, but she felt too down to care. She allowed Con to take Jade in his arms, and having politely wished everyone goodnight, she followed him upstairs.

'Cheer up!' he told her. 'Once you get used to it here, you'll find yourself enjoying a far better life-style. Harriet will lean over backwards for Jade. She's always telling Chumley and me off for being born boys. She always wanted a daughter you see.' He was leaning over the bed by the wall and settling Jade down. 'Now I'll leave you to it. Things will look better in the morning. Which isn't all that far off.'

He winked at her, waved, and walked out of the room. Moira waited until he had shut the door behind him, then thankfully undressed. She turned out the gas, felt her way across the room, then slipped into the bed and cuddled Jade close...

How long she slept she never knew, but there was a wide patch of sunshine coming through the skylight. Moira lay there, puzzled, wondering for the moment where she was. Then realization came, closely followed by fear. There was a movement in the room, stealthy, the floor boards creaked. She froze. Then heard Con's lazily pleasant voice.

'Ah, you're awake. Here, take this.' He handed her a cup of tea. She watched as he put a second drink on the table. 'We won't wake Jade, it's good for her to sleep.'

Conscious that she was not dressed, Moira blushed and tried to pull the sheet up with her free hand.

'Don't worry,' he told her easily, 'We're both grown up, eh? And know how many beans make five. I remember what you said about your feelings for all men.' He frowned and shook his head in a teasing, mocking way. 'It's a shame, because you've grown into a little beauty.'

'Con,' she whispered, utterly confused, 'I—'

'But I swear by the Holy Mother,' he cut in, 'that you'll never be troubled by me.'

'Thank you,' she replied, shaken. 'Thank you, Con.'

'We're mates, eh? And I'll not let you come to harm.'

'You – you promise?' she asked anxiously, her heart in her eyes. 'That you'll look out for Jade and me?'

'The wee girl will have no problems,' he told her. 'No problems at all. Seems that Harriet's set to take her off your hands.'

'No!' Moira sat up so sharply that tea spilled into the saucer. 'Jade is in my care. She always has been and always will be.'

'Are you forgetting something?' he asked, as he leaned against the table and folded his arms, 'Harriet has taken you both in. This is Harriet's place. Moira, my darlin', never forget that under this roof, what Harriet says goes!'

Never! Moira thought. No one's going to take Jade away from me. Never in a million years.

In that moment she began to feel even more afraid...

Three weeks later, and with a decent room she shared with Jade, Moira was still ill at ease in Harriet's place. Her whole existence had been turned upside down. She felt hopelessly out of place and inadequate. She had no money and lots of time to spare. Determined at all times to do her best for Jade, she finally plucked up the courage to throw herself onto Harriet's mercy. Harriet listened, her near-black eyes glinting with amusement as Moira asked for some halfpenny exercise books and pencils.

'Lord!' Harriet replied, looking amused in the hard way she had, 'I thought you were at least asking for the Crown Jewels. Of course you can. I'll get Con to bring some in. Why are they so important anyway?'

Colouring with embarrassment, Moira explained.

'I want to teach Jade all that I've learned from Stavros. You see, he explained to me over and over, that reading and writing and learning turns a person into a lady. Well, he's tried all his might with me. But – but Jade really is a lady, born and bred. I must do my best by her.'

'She certainly has an air about her,' Harriet admitted. 'I'm more than smitten myself. And I find the idea of an old Greek trying to teach a skivvy to better herself utterly intriguing.'

'Thank you,' Moira told her, hot with humiliation. 'But you don't have to – to rub it in, I mean. I do know my place.'

'For crying out loud! Sensitive, are we? Well, I'll tell you something. On top of all that learning, you need to go one better. Having a nice way of talking, and all sorts of knowledge in your noddle don't mean much to the outside world. You've got to look the part.' She snapped her fingers, adding, 'Which can't be a bad idea since it won't do no harm to disguise yourself.'

'Harriet, I don't think ...'

'Strikes me you think too much. I rather fancy the idea of changing you from the drudge of Jordan Street into the lady of Limehouse.'

'Oh no!' Moira began, colouring furiously. 'There's no need to poke fun and ...'

'Nonsense, girl, I insist! You're going to be "made over."'

It was utterly ridiculous, Moira thought during the next few days. And all the plans Harriet seemed to be making for her and Jade's's future were quite unnecessary. But Harriet was enjoying herself in her laconic way, and once, when Moira demurred, she stared straight down her nose and said, 'Making a silk purse out of a sow's ear is not so easy as it sounds, girl. Still, you've turned out a damned sight better than I hoped. Proper little sweetheart you are. I can see all the blokes sniffing after you now.'

What a horrible thing to say, Moira thought. "Sniffing after" sounds like dogs. And to think they believed living with Flo was a come-down! She smiled wryly to herself.

After that, Moira found it hard to accept that it was her own reflection staring back at her from the mirror. She was now dressed in smart new clothes. Her hair had been cut and styled

so that it framed her face in an attractive way. And she had new
shoes, and a best dress that she could change into. Her own
second-hand rags had been firmly dumped in the dustbin by
Harriet herself.

But Moira was still ill at ease; she had no role in Harriet's
house. Without her chores and Flo's bullying, now even simple,
everyday life seemed unreal. And most cutting of all was the
way that Jade seemed to be drifting away from her. Sometimes
even to the point of giving Moira looks of loathing when made
to do as she was told.

Jade with Harriet was a very different kettle of fish. For
Harriet, who was for ever buying her lovely new things, she was
all sweetness and light. Running to do the older woman's
bidding. Listening avidly to her every word.

Now dressed to kill, Jade looked charming, and she knew it.
Her hair had been cut and instead of a top knot, she wore it in a
long bob with a fringe. Jade had taken to being spoiled like a
duck to water. She loved the presents Harriet showered on her
and it showed. Even so, spoiled though she now undoubtedly
was, Jade was a lovely little thing.

Feeling proud of her charge, with tears in her eyes and an
ache in her heart because she was now so openly rejected,
Moira wished that River Pearl could have been there. How
happy she would have been to see her beloved number one
daughter turning into such a beautiful child.

Harriet was always going on about how gorgeous and fasci-
nating Jade was. Just like a besotted Mum, Moira thought
resentfully, and the woman praised Moira too.

'There's no doubt about it, girl,' she said on more than one
occasion, 'Con and Chumley's eyeballs all but pop out when
they see you, and I can't blame them. Nowadays you are quite
the little Mary Pickford. For two pins I'd box their ears – just
for being blokes.'

It was intended to be very flattering of course, but it all left
Moira feeling uncomfortable, and worse, suspicious of Harriet's motives. The kindness of her gesture in dressing Moira
well, was undermined by her determination to interest Moira in
young men rather than in Jade. The older woman seemed
utterly determined to take Jade away from her. She fussed and
fretted over the child like a mother hen. I suppose it's because

she'll never have a daughter of her own, Moira thought bitterly, and wished that she had the means of putting a stop to it all.

She tried to tell Harriet how she felt, but to no avail.

In a short space of time the result of her actions showed. Jade had become a very spoilt young lady and impossibly self-willed, showing off at the drop of a hat since she had Harriet firmly on her side. The greatest bone of contention became the daily lessons Moira insisted upon.

It was a fight, but Moira was determined to have her own way in this respect. Stavros's lecturing had gone home, she knew how important learning was. So from the outset Moira had made up her mind that Jade would, at the very least, know as much about reading, writing and arithmetic as she did herself.

'I'm sorry Jade,' she would say every morning, 'but you're going to sit up here with me until you've gone through your lessons. Just a little bit of work every day. Yes, just a little, I promise! But it's important. One day ...'

'One day my rich and noble father will come for me.' Jade replied snootily on more than one occasion. 'And he will find me a powerful lord husband.'

'All the more reason to ...'

'Then it will be my duty to take him to realm of Heavenly Bliss. He will not worry whether I can do sums!'

'I know that River Pearl told you all of those things, Jade.' Moira replied, shocked for all she had heard River Pearl say much the same things many times. 'Even so, she was delighted that Mr Sella was teaching you.'

'She did not ...'

'Now stop being such an obstinate mule. You have to accept that if you're nothing more than a soppy ha'porth when you're all grown up, your noble father will be ashamed. You will make him lose face. If that happens he won't even try to find you a rich and powerful lord husband.'

'But ...'

'Jade,' Moira lost patience then. 'Do as you're told!'

Melon-seed eyes blinked twice, then Jade picked up the pencil and obeyed.

Relieved, Moira knew that she was going to have a fight on her hands where Jade was concerned. The child was growing

171

more self-possessed by the day. Indeed, Moira sighed, Jade was now very different to the small butter-ball wrapped in layers of quilted cotton she had first known. Quaintly, River Pearl explained that hot weather was a One Coat Day. Warm weather, Two Coat Days. Cold weather was always Three Coat Days. Moira was prepared to swear that the first time she had seen the small Jade, she had been all but smothered under, not three coats, but at least four. Now, thanks to Harriet, Jade wanted for nothing.

When lessons were over Jade would hurry away to find Harriet, without giving Moira so much as a backward glance. But Con and Chumley at least knew that she, Moira, was alive.

Blackmail or not, tailor's dummy she might be, but still, the way Con had looked at her, and Chumley's manner when he had whistled long and shrill, had been rather pleasant. If only Yani could see her now!

Moira found that she didn't mind these particular men. They were her friends, just as Stavros and Mr Binks were. She tried to take to Harriet too, but something held her back. And worst of all, in spite of all the clothes, the lovely food, and always and ever the flattery, she was miserable. She was losing Jade, and to make things worse, she had nothing to do to take her mind off the fact.

From childhood she had been used to getting up at the crack of dawn and working through the day. Now her life was a vacuum. Her services were not needed in Harriet's place.

Harriet had a woman, Lizzie, a sort of relative and something to do with Anne Cherry of second-hand fame. Lizzie was thin and tight-lipped, had beady black eyes, and she was downright unfriendly. Lizzie was trusted by Harriet, and had freedom throughout the whole house. It was she who jealously saw to all the chores.

Moira did not like the woman and kept well out of her way. She wished herself back with Flo. At least in Jordan Lodge she felt at home. Even nicer, she had been Jade's greatest love. Now things were different and she felt helpless, quite unable to stop what was going on.

'I need to work!' Moira told Harriet on one sunny afternoon when she and Harriet were alone in the shop. After meat pie and pease pudding, Jade was sleeping off lunch. 'I must earn some money for my keep. I really need to do some housework for you. Besides, I want to pay my way.'

'You don't have to bother about a roof or food, Moira.' Harriet's tone was crisp, official. 'Anne told me that Flo said Jade's money was for the pair of you. Well a fiver will only go so far, but that emerald! No, girl, you can rest easy as far as giving me anything's concerned. That stone's worth a cool fortune, believe me. I know!'

'You – you'll be able to sell it?'

'Of course! But for the moment, I'm loath to let it go.'

Desperate now, Moira said,

'I've got to do something! I hate having all this time on my hands.'

'Then why not go to the park? Look out for Con. I know Chumley likes to visit him and have a chat. I thought the three of you, yes three including the Greek, were chums? Close mates in fact.'

Close? Moira still dreamed of Yani, yearned for him, imagined how it would feel to have him for her sweetheart, but that was like living in fantasy-land. Even she did not believe that real life would turn out like that!

Her three friends had turned out to be older than she had first thought, and were fully grown men. All had busy lives. Yani was in Greece, as ordered by his father. The other two breezed in and out of Harriet's place when it suited them. Chumley was smitten with a girl servant in Yani's home. Con was always in his attic, painting, when not actually making chalk pictures on paving stones.

'Cat got your tongue, girl?' Harriet persisted. 'Or is there some other reason you're not answering me?'

'I – I thought that you understood, Harriet.' Moira told the older woman. 'That's why Flo sent me here. I'm supposed to stay hidden!'

'What, a pretty girl like you?' Harriet scoffed. 'You should show yourself off! Not hide in here like a scared rabbit. It's only being with Jade that might give you away. And once you've given her lessons, Jade's staying with me. We play ludo, dominoes, stuff like that, and I'm teaching her card games, which she loves. We play for matches.' Harriet's tone became indulgent. 'You want to see the masses she wins. Matchsticks worth thousands of pounds. She loves such games and is a regular little gambler.'

'I'm not sure that – that gambling should be encouraged, Harriet. And Stavros said that—'

'To hell with that old man! You quote him almost as if you think he's old Moses. I know what makes Jade happy. Don't you understand that? She'll be fine with me.'

Oh yes, Moira thought coldly, Harriet is good at playing games and at bribing Jade. And it works every time.

Her own sense of jealousy and bitter loss felt like a physical pain.

'Dave Dilley might spot me,' Moira objected tightly, 'and the people who – who did for River Pearl. Besides, I can't leave Jade, not ever. I promised!'

'My God!' Harriet exploded. 'Have you heard yourself, girl? Don't you know that you're acting plain daft? The Chinese you're so scared of will be looking for you at Flo's and even she would be hard pressed to recognise you now!'

'I know that thanks to you, I—'

'And as I've already said, it's Jade they would have noticed, not you. I don't understand why *you're* so terrified of going out.'

'I – I have always felt threatened out there on my own, Harriet,' Moira heard herself reply in a tight, panic-stricken voice. 'And anyway, I don't want to go out and leave Jade. She was put in my care.'

'Oh come now...'

'Yes, my care alone!'

'When a girl like you acts afraid of shadows, I can't see...'

'It's you who can't or won't see how things are.' Moira replied, fighting to hold on to her control. 'But I do most sincerely thank you for all the kindness you've shown Jade and me. And I've never actually had new clothes in my life before!' She lifted her chin defiantly, adding, 'But what's outside can't change what's inside. And yes, Harriet, you *are* right. You can't make a silk purse out of a sow's ear.'

'No?' Harriet's black eyes held faint humour. 'I've not done so badly with you, though, have I? Speaking up for yourself now, aren't you?' She leaned over the counter to stare at Moira hard. 'All right, you tell me what's going on in that mind of yours.'

'All right!' Moira threw her cap over the mill. 'Yes, I have always been scared,' she went on furiously. 'Terrified in case Flo turned me out. I felt safe in Flo's, and in just one other place. I loved visiting St Stephen's.'

'Bloody hell! Not a church?'

'A church yard where there's grass and trees and flowers.' Moira laughed in a dry, harsh way. 'And being me, I always found getting there and back quite terrifying.'

'Why?' Harriet cracked out. 'You've been out and about since that business with Dilley, haven't you? You're not making sense!'

'I'm sorry,' Moira replied defiantly. 'I'm scared of being on my own outside, that's all. I have this nameless dread of strangers pouncing on me. When I was little, Flo used to hand out so many dire warnings.'

'About what exactly?'

'Mostly of being found out by Authorities and sent to The Home. Of being sent to The School where there were wicked witch-like teachers. Things like that. I suppose that over the years I – I have come to look at the world outside Jordan Lodge as – as a sort of enemy.' She laughed apologetically. 'Strange how such ideas take hold. They wouldn't have me at school now even if I banged on the door and begged. I am too old.'

'We've all known fear,' Harriet told her firmly and seemed to make up her mind about something. 'Come out back and we'll have a cuppa.'

Harriet came from behind the counter and shut the shop door. She led Moira to the sitting room and pulled out a chair for her. Moira sat at the table just as Lizzie poked her head round the kitchen door.

'A pot of tea, Liz, and some of those wafer biscuits,' Harriet told her, 'and have some yourself.' Then she turned back to Moira. 'I mean it, girl. We are all afraid of something.'

Moira stared unbelievingly at the striking woman who didn't seem to have a nerve in her body.

'I can't imagine that about you.'

'No?' Harriet's tone was suddenly metallic, her eyes hard. 'Well think about this. You had Dave Dilley to contend with,

175

and you managed to fend him off. I had my own father, and I was too young and scared to get out of his way! He used to threaten me with terrible things if I ever told. My own mother died not knowing, thank God. So my father, who started out just by pinching me and other spiteful little tricks, finally had his way with me. It continued all the years that my mother lived.' Harriet smiled a baleful smile. 'After a respectable time, and when I was old enough to work things out of course, I got my own back.'

'Harriet!' Moira was seeing Harriet with new eyes. 'I don't know how you can bear the memory. I'd want to shrivel and die. I—'

The older woman shrugged.

'Oh, I keep that lot pushed at the back of my mind, and just cling onto the fact that I made the old sod suffer in the end. Not a lot against all he did to me, but enough to give me a real shot of pleasure when I look back.'

Moira was watching Harriet now, understanding why the woman before her so hated, so loathed and detested men. Her own father! The pig! The beast! It must have been like having Dave Dilley actually ... She shivered thinking of Dave Dilley grinding her down, and his evil tongue licking and ...

'Harriet,' Moira heard herself whispering. 'What did you— I mean, how did ...'

'I murdered the bugger,' Harriet replied calmly. 'I shoved him down these very stairs as hard as I could. He thumped against every one. I can hear the noise he made even now. Banging thump, thump, thump down all fourteen. He landed at the bottom, unable to move. Then I pushed a whisky bottle into his mouth, and held his nose, making him swallow. And all the time I was telling him what he always told me. That it might hurt, but it was for his own good in the long run. That he'd feel better later on. My God, did I ram it home!'

'And – and he—?'

'He kept trying to move his head away – he knew. Oh yes, he knew what was happening all right! Knew how I was enjoying forcing him to drink. He'd always hated whisky.'

'Are those really the things he said to you?' Moira whispered and felt sick. 'While he was – even when you were just a tiny girl?'

'Yes, but I showed him! I kept that whisky pouring down his throat, and all the time I was wishing it was poison.' Harriet warmed to her theme and went on with relish. 'Nearly choked on it, he did. He was groaning, and I could tell he was snuffing it. And he had to lay there and take it, and listen! Oh yes, I told him a home truth or two, and he was scared! His eyes nearly popped out their sockets, he was so afraid of what I was going to do next. He was as terrified as I was on my eighth birthday when he started it all. Not pinching and punching. Raping me I mean.'

'Oh, Harriet,' Moira was almost weeping with sympathy now. 'You weren't all that much older than Jade. Still almost a baby!'

'Never had no babyhood in this house. He ruled my poor silly mother with a rod of iron, so she—' Harriet changed the subject of her mother abruptly. 'No, no babyhood. No childhood neither.'

'Harriet! I—'

'Don't fret ... I got my own back. I was laughing like a mad woman when I told him as how I hoped he'd rot in hell. He started to puke up, so I shoved the bottle in his hand. Clasped his fingers round it tight I did. It fell out of his grasp almost at once, but it didn't matter any more. I just put my coat and hat on, and walked out of this house.'

'Where did you go?' Moira barely breathed the words, she was so awed and overcome with Harriet's tale. 'What did you do?'

Harriet's brows were raised and her lips twitched.

'You look green! Almost as sick as my dad was in fact. Where was I? Oh yes! I stayed with Anne Cherry in Jordan Street. We went to the Hare and Hounds and had a right old time – with plenty of witnesses to prove I was nowhere near this place that night. And when Lizzie turned up next morning, all innocent-like, she found him dead. I had done the old bugger in good and proper, I can tell you. I had a hard job not to let the whole world know just how delighted I felt.'

'Weren't you scared witless?' Moira whispered. 'If they had found out that you were a murderess they would have hanged you by the neck until you were dead!'

'But they didn't, did they?' Harriet's expression was wicked, her eye's distended and almost black. 'They reckoned he was drunk and fell. Accidental death they said. Of course Lizzie swore that I'd arranged to be out all that night. And what with Anne, and all that lot in the Hare and Hounds, it worked! Anyway, he was dead and done for, and I've never ceased to cheer the fact.'

Lizzie came in with tea and biscuits, but Moira shook her head, and Harriet pushed the tray away. Watching her, Moira realized that she had accepted that Harriet Jones was a strong-willed woman. Hard as nails in some respects. She was certainly a law unto herself. But never in a million years had she thought her capable of murder.

'Forget it, Moira,' Harriet said and reached across the table to squeeze Moira's hand. 'Now you know why I can understand your feelings about the Dave Dilley's of this world. Admit it, when he was having a go at you, you would have killed him if you could, wouldn't you.'

'Yes,' she whispered. 'I – I think I tried. But the brass poker wasn't heavy enough.'

'There you are then! You and me are sisters under the skin. I'll always hate men. They're filth!'

'Even – even Mr Binks?' Moira asked quietly. 'Oh, surely not him!'

'He's different. He fished me out of the river when we were kids at school. Saved me from drowning, that little old butter-ball did. I never let on that I'd deliberately jumped in. Never said that I wanted to feed the fishes rather than put up with my bloody dad. But Binksy was – well Binksy, that's all. I'd trust him with my life. Him and Anne Cherry, another mate from school.'

'Didn't they know?'

'Not then, but they do now. Shocked?'

'Yes,' Moira replied honestly. 'But I'll not even try to imagine what I'd have done in your shoes.'

'Now you know my story, just as you also know that Jade will be protected by me. I promise you, no one will get within a mile of her. So go out and start looking at the world! See the streets as Con sees them. Alive and beautiful he says they are. God what a pain he can be!'

178

'I will try to do as you say.' Moira replied uncertainly. 'I – will go to the market and try to find Mr Binks. He . . .'

'Not wise.' Harriet was back to normal and smiling her hard-eyed smile. 'You just might foul up his business for the day. No, go and see Con. Pass the time with him. Start trying to see the world through his eyes. He's all right, though I'd drop dead before I'd tell him so. He and Chumley are – are like the sons I'll never have. Oh, for God's sake buzz off and stop wasting my time!'

Without a further word, and sensing that she had no other option, Moira walked out of the house. She had not wanted to leave Jade, but Harriet had given an order and, as Con had said, 'What Harriet says, goes!'

Almost at once Market Street swirled round her. She was mingling with others, walking past the stalls, heading towards the High Road. She reached it and the greater market area. One of Chumley's haunts, so it was said. But she didn't look for him. She wouldn't go and see Con either, she thought sombrely. She would make her way to St Stephen's and try to think. To analyse Harriet's awful tale.

It made Moira feel sick, and it made her afraid of what she herself had nearly done to Dave Dilley that night. Perhaps she could have been forgiven if she had killed him? She had delivered that blow to the fish-fryer's head with all her might and main. She had been terrified, wild to escape, wanting only to run away. But—

Harriet had waited, had planned, had committed murder in cold blood!

Although it was warm, she shivered, and looked about her, feeling unsure. She really was like a rabbit, she thought, always needing to hide away in its burrow, always needing a bolt hole. Oh yes, Harriet certainly saw her like that. Saw her as a cowardly kind of recluse, a willing prisoner. At least prisoners felt safe! But then Harriet was cold and calculating, and could wait for years to work things out. That was the big difference.

Rough and ready, fat and frumpy, loud-mouthed old Flo was a creature of impulse. Lashing out one minute, laughing the next, then handing out rough justice right, left and centre as she saw fit. But, unpredictable as Flo's temper was, you knew where you were with her. You wouldn't have to worry all the time, about what dark plans she was plotting underneath. Like trying to win over Jade. To make her into her own little girl?

Harriet said she had taken Con and Chumley on, as sons! What would happen if she really wanted to take the reins of Jade's life in her hands, officially adopt her? Only the Lord knew who the woman would talk to to try and achieve that!

It will not do, Moira thought desperately. Flo believes that Jade and I are safe here – somehow I feel that we are not.

She wanted to run to Flo. To feel the security of the lodge with its enamel mugs, Freddy's walled garden, the great old-fashioned black kitchen range and Flo's habitual bellowing. But she must come to terms with this new world, she knew it. It could take years, Moira knew that too. But she would try. She would do her best.

She walked on, unmindful of the people, the shops, the messenger boys on bikes, and the happy little mongrels lolluping along with their tongues hanging out. She was thinking of the stories she had heard. Of people killing one another. Of how River Pearl had died, and Harriet's father. And it reached home to her that she could never cold-bloodedly murder another human being, not even Dave Dilley. No, not in a million years! It occurred to her to wonder just why Harriet had told her that terrible tale. Perhaps to make her so afraid that she would do as she was told! Never!

Moira sighed. Ahead, now fully in view, were the great gates of St Stephen's. She reached them and slipped through them, grateful to have reached sanctuary at last.

Chapter Fifteen

Moira sat under the willow and felt treacherous. Robby had no flowers! The realization shook her to the core. What was she? Man or mouse? Had she been so weak, so stupid as to let recent events knock her completely off course? Harriet was right! She had allowed her grief for River Pearl, her fear for Jade, and even more horrible, her jealousy of Harriet's hold over Jade, to all but overcome her!

She drew in a deep, shivering breath. She had to think. Had to plan. Had to be like Maisy Noice and get on with life. But how?

What could she do? She had no money and very little chance of getting work. But, wait a minute, was she so certain that was the case? If only Yani were here. He would help, she knew he would. Just as he had known how to help Con. Of course, helping Chumley was out of the question. He liked his life, enjoyed the challenge of the nefarious things he did. He would get caught one day and go to prison, but he was prepared even for that! She had heard him saying so to Con.

Her jealousy? Moira bit her lip and felt ashamed. She and Robby shared this space under the willow. It was like their secret home.

'I don't think you'd like me very much, Robby,' she said quietly. 'And I've never felt so nasty before. I've been jealous about all the things Harriet's done for Jade. Jealous instead of glad! But, you know, I really believed that Jade loved only River Pearl. Then – then when River Pearl died I thought Jade would turn to me. It gives me a sinking feeling to know that Jade can dismiss me so easily. She's all for Harriet now and it hurts. This is silly, because she's only a little girl and you can't put old heads on young shoulders. Still ... know something, Robby? I feel so alone! I wish—'

She fell silent, frowning. What did she wish? To be back inside Jordan Lodge for a start! It was strange to admit it, but she actually, deep down, loved old Flo. Next? To have heaps of money so that she could buy things for Jade and so win her back. And if that proved impossible, she would at least be earning her own keep, would at least have her pride.

That was part of it too, her need for self-respect. It rankled that Con treated her with such a distantly lazy and casual air. He rarely teased her these days. Chumley breezed in and out as the mood took him, his mind mostly on Cissy. He was having a rough time of it there! And Yani was far away on the island of Kerkyra, trying to fend off the marriage his parents had planned for him.

Marriage? What of it? To live with a man all of your life, be part of him? At one? And what of the physical side? It couldn't be too horrible judging by Flo. Poor old Flo, who in her own way was lonely too. If wishes were granted, Moira thought, she would wish Will back.

When he was around, Flo literally glowed. Glowing just as she herself did when in the presence of Yani.

'He's not too much taller than me, Robby,' she told her small, sleeping friend. 'He's slim, and has such dark eyes. Soft eyes, not hard like Harriet's. Outside he is so elegant, even though he still hangs onto that old jacket for his outings to the Hare and Hounds. It's quite a stupid idea on his part, because they do have some very smart customers go into that pub in spite of its lowly neighbourhood. But Yani likes to play a part! He dresses rough, and acts cool and aloof. But I know him! He has a fire inside him, even though it is always controlled. But if he ever let that control go I bet the whole world would see how explosive his Greek temper could be.'

Moira frowned, trying to work out how she knew all that about Yani, or rather, sensed it! Yani could be a bit of a devil, she thought; then hope sprang into her heart. Perhaps Yani might have the power to defy his parents and not marry the girl chosen for him. If they tried to insist, perhaps Yani would lose his temper and—

'I reckon the only one who could stand up to him then would be Con,' she told Robby. 'I reckon Con could be as fiery as that black stallion he's always on about. The one his father so loved.'

She lay back and half closed her eyes. It was cool and sweet under the concealing branches of the willow tree. Like being in her own secret world. Her mind drifted back to River Pearl, to the tales she had told about the Flowery Kingdom. She felt unshed tears pricking against her eyelids, remembering the tiny Chinese woman she had come to love and now missed so much. River Pearl, who would never poke her finger in one's chest, and cuss and swear and clip one round the ear. River Pearl who had come to care for a skivvy named Moira just because the maid of all work so cared for Jade. River Pearl who was not evilly possessive at all. Most of all, River Pearl who would never, ever push an old man down and rant and rave and carry on while he lay helpless and dying at the bottom of the stairs.

Moira felt herself going hot and cold at the thought of Harriet. Had she been right to leave Jade in the woman's care? Oh yes. Plainly Jade was all right there – for a while at least. But she, Moira, would watch things like a hawk – for Jade's sake and for River Pearl.

How she wished she were here now, beside her, under the waterfall the willow branches made. She remembered her friend telling her of Chinese willows with their golden leaves falling down the branches like tears.

'Draw me willow trees,' Moira had begged. 'I know I would love them too.'

And River Pearl had carefully drawn not one but many of her favourite trees, saying, 'The artists of my country fashion little trees of malachite and hang them with slivers of green jade and pink tourmaline. These beautiful little willows are for the adornment of a writing table. My lord husband was gracious enough to buy me one. I treasured it, and I am sad that I do not have it now . . .'

'But we have our tree, don't we Robby?' Moira asked softly. A real living and breathing one. 'And we have each other. Next time I come, I will bring you some flowers.'

It was evening and getting cool when Moira left her sanctu-

ary and began the journey back to Market Street. She forced
herself to walk slowly, to look around, to try and see things as
Harriet said Con did.

She saw the road sweeper, old and gnarled, doggedly doing
his job. The street hawker with his wares arranged on a tray
hanging in front of him. He was selling shoe-laces, pencils,
combs, toothpicks, ink pots, cotton, tape, elastic, ribbon. A
hundred and one things all piled together, but instantly found
when the need arose. Flower sellers stood in the kerb, their
wares alive and bright and holding all the colours dear to the
heart. A match seller, disabled, but cheery just the same. Moira
felt sorry for him. There were many ex-servicemen around still.
Retired or disabled, often without a pension, they were forced
to take to the streets. Selling matches as a way of life was only
marginally better than begging, but it had to do. One could
always tell old soldiers, Moira thought, by their highly polished
boots.

She reached the more populated market area with its over-
abundance of traders. All yelling and shouting, chipping and
jibing, as lively as they come. Here thronged the women and
kids, the unemployed, the beggars and thieves. The market was
a ragamuffin world of its own.

Moira forced herself to walk slowly. Forced herself to look
life fair and square in the eye.

By the time Moira turned off the High Road and into
Market Street her self-confidence had returned. This was one
thing she could thank Harriet for with all her heart; she would
not have faced the world again if it hadn't been for Harriet's
orders.

Harriet was in the shop with Jade at her side. They both
looked up and smiled, Jade's eyes contemplative. No one can
tell what she's thinking, Moira thought, but she has guessed
how I feel about things. Yes, I'm sure of it. And she knows how
to play us one against the other too. Little devil!

Her mind was made up. She would speak to Con and to
Chumley the moment she had the chance. She needed
something to do, and perhaps they could help her make plans.
It really was time to get up and go!

Upstairs in the room she and Jade shared, she sat alone. She
was waiting to hear Con. He left his pitch quite early, for he had

oil painting to look forward to at the end of the day. She was thinking rapidly now. Con would give her paper and pen. She could at least write to Flo. Oh, Flo couldn't read very well, and on principle, rarely tried. But Stavros would do the honours, so in that way at least she could keep in touch. Why hadn't she thought of that before? Why indeed! She had been too busy feeling sorry for herself.

'Well no more!' she said aloud. 'No more!'

She heard Con's footsteps and sat where she was, her heart beating fast with excitement. She was getting ready to be master of her own fate. But she knew that, initially at least, she needed a little help...

Con looked about the attic, squinting against the flare of gaslight. He was analysing the tired old walls. Overhead, the patchy dusk gleamed through the grimy oblong of glass. On clear nights, it showed the sky festooned with stars. But this evening it showed nothing. Con found himself wishing for a studio where he had light. Clear, wonderful, natural light, to work by. One day, he thought, if Vivien has any luck, I'll get myself a decent studio.

He looked down at his palette and began to mix pigments with practised assurance. The picture he had been working on for a long time, the one most special since it was purely for him, was beginning to take shape and form. This was his own work of art, the one that he picked up and put down in between works created for Vivien. For Con was endeavouring to capture something of the wonder and mystery, the happiness and contentment, the pure buoyancy and exultation of those long ago days. The time when his father, Thomas, was there to put a huge hand on his own bony shoulders, and grin down at him, and say in his rough, affectionate way, 'Sure and you're a fine young man, Conor, and it is proud of you I am.'

Con went into his mind again, going back to when he was a boy.

Engrossed in his work now, trying to recapture the country scene, he lightly dusted the distant hills with a violet tinge. Con worked on. The picture would be good, he knew, but would it be good enough? He wanted the canvas to glow with feeling,

185

with the sense of timelessness he was experiencing now. He was conscious of an inner excitement.

It was as though he knew that something extraordinary was about to happen. Something that would make this picture come alive, would epitomise all that he had seen as beautiful in the world. The lush emerald scene, with its purply hills and silver streams, its dandelions like little butter balls, and daisies, numerous as stars on the milky way, was beginning to materialize.

There was a strange dream-like quality about the room and the painting now. And it was in that moment when everything stood still, when the London street sounds came as if from many miles away, that he heard a faint knock on the door and Moira came in.

Her dress was blue, and the lamplight made a nimbus round her hair. She was the most beautiful creature Con had ever seen. He felt his throat go dry. His heart was pounding. He felt as brash as the schoolboy he'd been all those years ago. Yet he towered over her and could have killed her at a stroke.

She stopped beside him, and looked at his picture. Con continued to make movements with the brush, even though he was now finding it impossible to see. An inner voice warned him to stay where he was and be perfectly still. She was afraid of men, distrustful. He must say and do nothing to frighten her away.

'That's beautiful, Con,' Moira told him gravely, looking up into his face, vaguely conscious that she had to look up a long way. 'I never realized how wonderful at painting you are.'

'Thank you for the compliment,' he heard himself reply. ''Tis a pity that you won't come and visit me at work. Perhaps you'll force yourself to come and see my pavement pictures one day?'

'I – I would like that.' She smiled up at him. 'Con, I have actually been out today. For the first time I . . . I left Jade with Harriet.'

'Ah!' he smiled down at her. 'I hope you're not feeling a bit pushed in the background where the wee girl's concerned? Harriet is a bit over-powering, but her heart's in the right place.'

'She seems to be smothering Jade.'

'Making a fuss of her, that's all. Harriet will never marry. Will never give herself to a man, therefore she'll never have a child of her own. She is making the most of having Jade under her roof, that's all.'

'I wish I was back with Flo.'

'When the nights get darker and Flo thinks it safe, I will take you to visit her.'

'You will, Con?' She had perked up now, eyes sparkling, lips uptilted at the corners. 'You mean it?'

'I swear it.'

'Thank you. Oh, thank you, Con! I – I feel safer with Flo and Freddy, no matter who's lurking in Jordan Street. And I'm sure that Flo imagined seeing the Chinaman and—'

'Anne Cherry saw him by all accounts, and others besides.' he told her carefully. 'No, Moira, you must stay here for the time being, and so must Jade. Holy Mother, we don't want you going the same way as the China woman went, do we?'

'I'm bored, Con. I don't know what to do! I came to ask may I have a pencil and some paper? I can at least write to Flo and—'

'You can have writing stuff, as much as you want,' he told her. 'But never be bored, Moira! The world is a wide and wonderful place. And even the market can be a bucket full of life in the raw. Why don't you go out and about? Don't worry about Jade, she's as bright as they come, and knows which side her bread's best buttered. Think of yourself for a change.'

'I'm waiting for Yani to come back.'

'Oh?' His eyes went still, watchful. 'Really?'

'Yes. I'm hoping he can help me as he did you. I need a job, Con. Any job. I haven't a brass farthing and I don't want to rely on Harriet all the time. It isn't right!'

'I don't think Yani knows much about jobs for young ladies, even though he likes them a lot,' he told her. 'So you needn't be waiting for him. If you'll be happy with a penny or two, you can come and spend a little time with me each day.'

'I can't even draw a cold sausage, Con!' She was laughing at such a ridiculous thought. Alive and bright and as perky as a robin now. 'In fact I was thinking of . . .'

'You don't honestly think that I'm about to ask you draw on paving stones?' he asked her, brows raised in a comical way.

187

'Moira, me darlin', have a heart!' He smiled down at her. 'Are you getting ideas of cutting me out already? I meant for you to mind the pitch, which is by the park railings.'

'Con!' She was delighted. 'I think you're kind and nice and – and – Con!' On an impulse she threw her arms round him and kissed him. 'Thank you!'

She whirled round and left him then. He stood there grinning like a fool. The kiss was sisterly, an innocent kiss meaning less than nothing in the fullest sense. But it made a warm glow flood through him.

'Twill be like treading on egg shells from now on he thought, and he would have to take care, but he'd teach her to love him. Show her what loving meant! Which was a damned sight different to the wishy-washy daydreaming she did about Yani Bertos, who she all but saw as God. He found it in his heart then to wish that his mate Yani would go to hell.

He picked up a sketch pad and began to draw Moira as she had looked just before she kissed him. Wide-eyed, sweet, full of hope and joy. She would be sitting there, wearing blue, in the foreground of his picture. With the beginning of a smile, at ease among the buttercups and daisies. She would make the picture live and breathe. Become, in fact, the epitome of a summer's day when there were dreams to be shared, and there was a quiet faith in the future . . .

Chapter Sixteen

It was October already and bitterly cold. The market was as brash and bright as ever, and the stall-holders in Market Street had come to know Moira well. Her luck had changed from the time she had stood in for Con, and in turn, he had spread it round that she would be available if anyone needed help. Inwardly nervous and excited, always feeling the need to be inside and safe, she hid her feelings well. Outwardly cool and adroit she had made many friends. At the outset, her instinct had told her how to behave. She knew when to be at one with them. She put aside the careful lady-like facade she used to impress Stavros, became herself, and mucked in with the rest. She gave as good as she got, stood her ground and made a niche for herself.

In a very short time Moira's services were in demand. She was honest and reliable and worked with a good heart. Within weeks she was making money. Oh, it came in dribs and drabs; copper or two, a threepenny joey sometimes, even a sixpence occasionally. It all added up. Now she was able to go home to Jade bearing gifts, strings of glass beads, hair ribbons and crossword puzzles, things that Jade really liked. And now, with the aid of out and out bribery, Jade was finally fired with real enthusiasm for her lessons. Quick and intelligent, Jade learned fast. Quite soon she was reading, and reading properly. Moira introduced her to books, having found a marvelous stall that sold a selection of second-hand editions.

Now Moira found herself sighing with relief. With books to hand and a willing and enquiring mind, with the added bonus of a marvellous memory, Jade would, one day, be able to hold her own in the world. How River Pearl would have rejoiced had she known. And how awed and taken aback Flo would be when she heard. The small gifts she had bought Jade, Moira thought, had been worth their weight in gold.

Harriet always bought bigger and more expensive presents of course, but now it did not matter quite so much. For now Jade had come to realize that she was not the only pebble on the older girl's beach, she became more willing to please. It had come as a surprise that at long last Moira had found outside interests and was not wholly dependent on her own small, proper little madam self. Without a doubt Jade was impressed. She valued Moira's gifts and was especially fond of a twopenny string of blue glass beads. Fake crystals, they glittered and gleamed, and Jade loved them on sight.

'Thank you, Moira,' she said and threw her arms round Moira's neck.

'Cupboard love, you little minx,' Moira told her, laughingly, 'and don't think I don't know it, miss!'

Suddenly, working in the market, and standing with Con earning the odd bob or two, gained an immensely important place in her life. She triumphantly offered to give Harriet something towards her keep, only to have it slung back in her face.

'Since when have I been unable to feed a stray cat?' Harriet said nastily; then her expression softened as she looked at Jade. 'Or a kitten, come to that? Keep your money, girl, and thank your lucky stars that I was at hand. You'd have been in the gutter else.'

Hurt and humiliated, Moira had walked upstairs to the room allocated to her and Jade. One day, she thought, one day!

It turned bitterly cold with winds that cut through them like a knife, but so far it remained dry. It would have been more comfortable to stay at home all day, but Moira, having spent the alloted time with Jade and her lessons, would make ready to go out. She spent most of her time helping various store holders these days. Con was still able to draw his pavement pictures, and so earn hard cash, but these days rain could and often did spoil things. By now he had quite a following, but people visiting the park area became fewer and the pennies and ha'pennies became scarce. On top of that the winds blew across the open spaces, so Con would send Moira off to the market where it was a little more sheltered.

Somehow or the other, no matter where she was, Chumley would find her and spend the time of the day. And Moira's eyes would dance at the sight of him, almost as brightly as they did at the sight of Con. Chumley was his own man, determined that he would always be so.

Moira could not come to terms with his thieving. No more than she had where Mr Binks was concerned. Chumley was like a brother, and she was afraid for him. She learned how bitter his earliest years had been, how fortune had shaped his way of life. But he had never lost his sense of humour, a rascally one at that. Ambling along he would come. Shoulders hunched, the peak of his cap at a rakish angle, whistling. Always whistling a merry tune.

'Wotcher Moir,' he said one freezing afternoon when he found her minding the hosiery stall. 'How's yer luck?'

'Fair to middling, matey,' she replied in the same light vein.

'More'n what mine is!' he said and moodily kicked the littered kerb.

'Oh?'

'Cissy's turned me down again. Gawd, you'd think she'd have a change of heart by now!'

'Well, treat her to a pair of these stockings. Only a shilling three farthings a pair. Look how fine they are.'

'She won't take nothing from me.' Chumley sighed.

Moira, who had heard a great deal about Cissy via her love-lorn Chumley, raised her brows and sighed with him.

'It's what you do, Chumley!' she told him gravely, 'Cissy's a fine and decent young lady by all accounts. You've told me so often enough. You can't blame her for being as she is about you – not since she knows how light fingered you are. You'll just have to mend your ways.'

'What makes her so different to all the other women in me life?' Chumley groaned, then stopped to wink across the way, at the woman on the haberdashery stall.

'Oi, you Chumley?' the fishmonger's wife shouted, 'Are you playing me false?'

'I wouldn't bloody well dare!' Chumley roared back, and everyone laughed.

191

'I mean it, Chumley,' Moira said when things had quietened down a bit. 'You'll come a cropper one day. Why don't you try the straight and narrow for a change?'

Chumley whistled and winked.

'You can be a right little marm-stink. You could even make a toff happy,' he added slyly. 'Yes, a toff like what Yani's turning out to be.'

'Don't take it on yourself to be so rude,' she flared, taken off guard.

'And as for Yani Bertos—'

'Crikey, you ain't trying to make out you don't like him, Moir?'

'Oh yes,' Moira agreed openly, and felt her cheeks flush pink.

Seeing the stars in her eyes, Chumley ruffled her hair and began chipping her in his lively don't-give-a-damn way.

'Poor sod's being made to learn the business, Moir. His old man's a right hard nut where that's concerned. And his ma's set on the wedding of the year over there on that island of his. But Yani'll get back to you soon as he can.' He had all of her attention now and his chest puffed out as he added, 'Oh yes, Yani will be visiting you – and I promise yer, I'll see to it he does. Of course, I can always take you over to see him.'

'I would never do that,' she told him fiercely, 'I would never lower myself to go calling on a man ...'

The year grew old and Yani never came near nor by. But Moira heard from both Con and Chumley that he still occasionally managed to join them at the Hare and Hounds on his brief visits from Kerkyra. He also went to see Stavros and Mr Binks at the Lodge.

Stavros wrote short notes regularly. He told Moira that things carried on much the same. That Flo was well, that they all missed her, Moira, very much. That she must stay where she was, for the time being at least. Moira's heart sank, remembering the watchful expression she so often saw in Harriet's black eyes. It was clear that Harriet was now regretting speaking about the death of her father.

The rain constantly washed Con's pictures away, so he left his pitch and resumed his painting indoors. Rather that stay in and take second place to Harriet, Moira forced herself to go out in the icy blast and ask for work. Trade seemed to have slack-ened, but she found that there would always be a penny or two to be earned. And everyone was working towards, and praying for, a pre-Christmas rush.

As the weather became more foul, brickies and others in the building trade took to hawking hot chestnuts and Irish dock labourers to selling fruit alongside their wives and children. Now the market suffered an over abundance of new traders, many touting substandard goods. There was increased yelling and obstruction from dawn to dusk as vendors were forced by falling margins to work longer hours.

'It's getting too bitter outside for you,' Con told her, 'and tempers will be flaring. I think it's best you stayed home in the warm from now on.'

'I once wanted to stay hidden behind the walls of Jordan Lodge for ever, Con,' Moira told him carefully. 'And given half the chance I'd be back there now, safe and sound.' She laughed shakily, 'I thought I would always be safe there. Since Flo sent us away I've taken over Jade's education as best I can – and believe me, there's times when she hates me for it. Apart from that my hands are idle. So I want to stay out here.'

'Well I like seeing you,' he told her. 'You brighten up the place.' He shrugged expressively. 'And there's times when a man needs a ray of light in his life.'

She looked at him sorrowfully.

'They haven't sold your pictures at all, Con?'

'There's been interest, so I've been told, but that, mavoureen, is as far as it goes.'

'It will all happen for you, Con,' she told him with certainty. 'I know it will!'

'And for you,' he told her and she saw an expression in his eyes that she had never noticed before. 'Oh, while I think of it, take these. If you're going to be pig-headed, you'll need them.'

He picked up a brown paper parcel and threw it towards her in a nonchalant way. She opened it with trembling hands, then looked up at Con, her face glowing. Woolly hat, scarf and gloves, coloured peacock blue. It was the most wonderful present she had received in her life.

'Con,' she breathed, 'it isn't Christmas! I don't know what to

193

say, how to thank you. I have *never* had a present like this before. Oh Con!'

'Now hop it,' he told her, grinning like a Cheshire cat. 'I don't want to waste any more of my time.'

'Thank you, Con. I—' She looked towards his easel and voiced the question that had been on her mind for some weeks. 'Why do you cover your picture these days?'

'Dust,' he told her sternly. 'Now Moira, off you go.'

Once she had put Jade through her paces, from eight until nine in the morning, Moira returned to the market. One hour, she thought ruefully, Jade allows me one hour of her time. A right proper little madam! But she's coming on. She's coming on fast.

Cosy in her new, warm scarf and gloves, Moira did not at first realise that tensions between established traders and the new street people were at crisis point. A huge beer drink-sodden man tried to barge Moira out of her space.

'Push off!' he told her. 'This is a man's world.'

She stared up at him, eyes wide.

'Excuse me,' she said politely, 'where's the man?'

'Why you little cow! I'll—'

'You'll hit me?' Moira jutted out her chin in her best Flo Williamson way, glared, and snapped, 'Try it!'

He raised his hand and rather than retreat, she stepped towards him, ready and willing to stick up for herself.

'Better be on your way, boyo,' Con said from behind him. 'Else you'll be as headless Pie Matthew's eels. Do I make myself clear?'

The man swung round to face him, and such was the look in Con's eyes, so coldly furious his expression, that he had to back off.

'And now you'll be going home,' Con said firmly.

Moira tilted her head to one side, laughing and lipping him. 'And you'll be going about your own business, Con! I could have handled him.'

'By Jaysus!' He raised his brows high. 'You really believe that?'

'I was brought up by Flo, don't forget. I like to be quiet and I usually am, but I can put my fighting irons on when I need to.'

'A little cock bantam, so you are,' he laughed. 'May Patrick smile on you for ever, mavourneen.'

The market situation worsened Now each district's coster-monger's 'king' and other 'pearlies' with him, saw off the more violent intruders. Sometimes it became really rough. On those occasions, Con always seemed to be around. A regular hero, Moira thought, feeling deep down that he was there watching her. Why couldn't he be more open with it? After all, he was like a big brother. What was he at? Daft thing!

She began wrinkling her nose at him because like it or lump it, she missed standing with him by the park railings. Missed watching him at work. A tall, perfectly proportioned man who could seduce young matrons with his eyes. Who, she thought, incensed, never took her seriously at all. Yet Con was full-blooded where his mates were concerned. If folk looked like being outnumbered the cry would go up.

'Send for the big Irishman. He's the boy for us!'

And Con would oblige, always siding with the regular stall holders. He would and did stand toe to toe with outsiders trying to push in, and it was they who backed down. And Moira would look up into his handsome face, straight into his very intense dark blue eyes and feel so proud!

'He's a rum 'un, your Con,' Bill the greengrocer was apt to roar. 'Soon sorts 'em out he does.'

'He's not my Con,' she replied on the defensive. 'I think he belongs to just about everyone here, even though his pitch is well outside the market. He is a fine artist and one day he'll be famous I'm sure.'

'He ain't like no artist what I know of, Moir,' came the reply. 'Likes a bit of a ding-dong, does our Con. On the other hand, his mucker's no market man. Nar! When the rukuss starts up and people's busy watching it all going on, it's pickings time for our ol' Chumley. Oh yers! He gets down to his nicking with never a thought for nothing else.'

'He's a decent—'

'Nar! He's a bloke what looks out for 'isself! And don't you never forget that, Moir!'

This was not strictly true, Moira thought. Chumley loved the market and mingled in with them all in his own rumbustious way. He was sometimes even quite careless where his thieving was concerned. Mr Binks was far more discreet. But Chumley openly admitted to enjoying "dicing with death" as he put it. Above all he enjoyed the market with its shouting and shoving. The end of season rowing, the fist fights, the rough and ready aggressiveness of it all. It was just that being a pick-pocket and out-witting the cops was life's elixir to him.

'How did you come to be at Harriet's?' Moira asked him one afternoon when they were standing together by the wet fish stall.

'Don't ask, ducks. You don't want to know!' he laughed, his face crinkling up, 'Do you want to weep tears of blood?'

'No. But I want to know all about you. About you and Yani and Con. Come on, tell me the truth!'

'Well you asked for it. I don't know nothing about my ma and pa, 'cept they bloody well didn't want me!' he shrugged. 'I was just dumped on a workhouse steps. They was hard in that place, but fair. The trouble started when I was fostered out. Gawd was I fostered! Plagued the life out of all them old cows I did. Binksy found me near unconscious one rainy night. I'd been beat black and blue by a foster mother what weighed about ten ton – and she used a rolling pin! Bitch!'

'No wonder you're so fond of Mr Binks!'

'And Harriet! Binksy took me to her, he did. She give me house and home for his sake. Soft on him, she is. But not in that way, if you know what I mean. If it ever boiled down to it, I'd kill for them both.'

Looking into his dark eyes and likeable foxy face, Moira found herself believing him implicitly.

'And would you kill for Con and Yani?'

'Of course. But old Con can look after himself. Yani?' Chumley shook his head. 'He ain't really one of us, Moir. He wants ter be, sometimes, but he ain't.'

'Oh he is, he is!'

'Suit yourself, Moir. You might look at things different to me, and good luck to you. I know one thing though, Yani's sweet on you!'

She stood there, glowing...

Chapter Seventeen

It was Thursday afternoon and early closing day. The market had shut down. By law, the sellers of perishable goods, like flowers and soft fruits, could stay. But without the others the market was a dead place and most traders preferred to go home – or pitch outside hospitals or anywhere else where they could earn a crust.

Moira, having bought a spray of bronze and gold chrysanthemums, made her way along the main road. She wore the thick woolly scarf round her neck and almost up to her nose. Matching gloves kept her hands like toast. It was a lovely warm set, luxury tossed to her in such a casual way, by Con. She blessed him every time she put hat, gloves and scarf on. But right now Con was far from her mind.

She was off to see Robby again. In a strange way she had come to believe that Robby was the only soul truly belonging to her. The only soul to whom *she* truly belonged! Everyone else had their own lives, their own thoughts and feelings. She was accepted by them, liked, but was hardly essential to their way of life. Jade was adept at ignoring her when it suited, and was consistently turning to Harriet and talking about the Christmas presents she would like to have. Moira knew that a fortune would be spent there! Flo had shoved her out without a second thought when trouble came. River Pearl had loved her, darling River Pearl whose spirit had flown away to foreign climes.

'Now I'm being just plain damn stupid!' she told herself fiercely. 'I should know better than come here feeling sorry for myself. And there is hope! I've just got to keep faith, that's all.

And if Chumley can be believed, Yani is sweet on me, no matter what.'

The very thought made her heart sing.

She entered the gates of St Stephen's and made her way to the now leafless willow tree. Taking off her gloves, she discarded the previous week's flowers, went to the tap to put fresh water in the jar, and arranged the chrysanthemums. They made a brave patch of colour there, lightening the gloom.

'Well, Robby,' she said quietly, 'it has been quite a time of it, hasn't it? I would still go back to Flo given a chance. I've written to her again, but I never get a real reply, because she can't write very well. Still, she does her best and sends messages with Con. When he's not too busy, Stavros drops me a line. He says that Flo isn't the same, even though she still makes a bee-line for the Hare and Hounds every chance she gets. I know what it is. She's lonely without Will. Lonely like me.'

Moira stared down pensively. Wishing that she had met Robby when he had been alive and well. She pictured him as slight and handsome with lots of golden curls. Like a Pears Soap little boy perhaps. But Robby was, she knew, wise beyond his years, and able to understand.

Although it was still quite early, it was growing dark. Moira turned to go home. She pulled her scarf higher so that it shielded her face, and replaced her gloves. Then she froze.

For one moment she thought she heard a ghostly laugh. But she relaxed as a fresh upsurge of biting wind crackled the branches and whistled through the evergreens. It had been her imagination playing tricks, she thought. Not surprising, because in this eerie half light even the pallid stone angels had acquired an awful sort of still life of their own. And the mausoleums had a menacing air. She hurried out of St Stephen's church yard without a backward glance...

Dave Dilley crouched by Martha's grave and sniggered and sniffed at the lichened headstone.

'You were right, old girl,' he was babbling and whispering. 'You told me I'd find her again if I refused to give up. You put the message in my head that I'd catch up with her here, didn't you? You understand that she's the only one I want in that way. She's the only one as affects me like you used to do. As for the other...' He looked furtively over his shoulder, then back at the grave. 'But that don't matter at all. I'll poke Moira O'Malley good and true, I will. Just like I've always dreamed! But I'll wait, by God.' He tittered behind his bony hand. 'Got plenty to amuse me otherwise, eh, eh? And outwitting that sodding Chinaman all adds to the fun. As for her with her smiling and simpering and knowing ways, she'll get hers, believe me. But I'll watch and wait because I've got all the time in the world.'

He stood up and cocked his head to one side. He was leering and listening to someone speaking, although no one was there. He nodded and cackled and agreed to what the unseen someone said.

'It must be the right time, eh? I must make me some fool-proof plans. Yes. yes! But I'll get her in the end. I've got to have her, Martha. Unlike the bone-bag ... eh, what's that? 'course, you're a bone-bag too, must be by now, but Flo's girl, Martha, she's even more of a beauty than she was before. Nothing will take away the itch that she's left between my legs. Her with her smiling and simpering, and her mocking wanton ways.'

Moira had gone from view and determined not to lose her, he began to hurry like a thin grey ghost in the rapidly descending night. He was still talking and arguing with Martha as he walked by graves. Finally agreeing that, yes, he would stay with Stan even though the poor gassed up old fool wasn't necessary to his plans. Stan had been meant to do for Will Fenning, but the sea had got the bastard instead. Now he must concentrate on the girl walking away so swiftly. He must find out where she was staying.

As he left St Stephen's at last, he wanted to laugh and jig and jeer at the slight figure that waited patiently at the gates for him, even though Dilley had cunningly given the Chinaman the slip several times. The Chink was a foreigner and stood no chance against a bloke born and bred in the district. He, Dave Dilley, knew all the alleys, the broken fences, the quick get-aways, and just where you could nip over back garden boundaries and reach other streets in no time at all. It had become the joke of the century, to give his follower a hard time of it.

The Chink, a silent, secretive figure had been shadowing him ever since he'd gone after River Pearl to Limehouse Causeway all those months ago. The fish fryer had soon cottoned on, oh yes! Hadn't been fooled for a minute. The small, slim Chinese youth hadn't caught old Dave Dilley, on the hop, oh no! Nor had any of the others of his kind that took up the challenge when the young one left off. Strange little runts they were too. More than one of his kind had been seen in Jordan Street by all accounts.

'They all followed me, Martha!' he cackled. 'Now ain't that strange? Didn't like me going into their territory up the Causeway, I reckon. How bloody tough!'

His eyes began to glisten. He caught sight of a gang of young thugs coming towards them. A group of rough-gut blokes out for mischief who'd ignore crazy old Dave Dilley, but who'd love baiting the Chink.

It didn't happen quite as he had expected. The ruffians had reached him and started off with their wise-cracks. They began to jostle against him, mouthing all the time.

'Wot's the matter with yer, got a screw loose? Shame! They didn't oughter let you out. Yer oughter be in with the monkeys up the zoo.'

'Let me pass you hooligans,' Dave Dilley spluttered. 'Martha, make them let go!'

'Who and wot's Martha when she's at home, eh?' A spiteful nudge here, and sly kick there. He was in for it, he knew. They were scuffling and larking long enough to allow Moira to go out of view.

'Bastards!' Dave Dilley screamed in fury. 'Going for one of your own kind! What about the Chink, eh? What about him? What about teaching him a lesson or two?'

The ruffians whooped with joy when they spotted the Chinaman. They started shouting obscenities and pelting him with anything and everything to hand, including balls of horse-dung dropped in the road. The Chinaman ran, the louts following him, mouths ugly, eyes cruel.

Left to himself, Dave Dilley rambled through the streets alone. Moira had long gone.

Free of his shadow, Dave Dilley began cackling to himself again. Served the little sod right. That'd teach him to be on his heels all night. Following, always following, God only knew what for. Well so be it. The bloody foreigner had no good reason, so far as he could see. He hadn't seen nothing up the

Causeway, only the Chink woman who'd vanished inside one of the buildings like a ghost. So he had waited...

His thought pattern changed and his usual mournful expression returned. The night was young and he still had a long way to go. As always searching for that gassed-up old fool Stan, or was it the girl? He had lost them both. He pressed on, arms flapping, a skinny grey figure only fitfully discernable under the lights...

'It's warmer in my room,' Harriet sternly told Moira, her dark eyes glittering. 'We've been speaking about Christmas morning and since our girl will be up before the crack of dawn, it will be cosier for her. Besides, I want to watch her face when she sees what Santa has brought.'

'She is still my charge, Harriet,' Moira replied, feeling that she was about to lose Jade for ever. 'River Pearl put her in my care.'

'Rubbish!' Harriet's hard eyes were spiteful. 'The woman's dead, done for, and I'm the one paying for her keep.'

'Jade wants to stay with me,' Moira replied doggedly. She turned to Jade, 'Don't you?'

Jade was staring from Moira to Harriet in a cool, considering way.

Oh yes. The minx is playing us one against the other again, Moira thought. Well, I'll have none of that!

She smiled brightly and heard herself breaking the silence in an all but flippant way.

'But on second thoughts, Jade, it might be a good idea if you do go in with Harriet. You always seem to take over all of *our* bed!'

'I do not!' Jade was shocked and aggrieved at this turnabout.

'Yes you do,' Moira told her brightly. 'So it will be nice for me to have a good stretch. After all, we both had our own mattresses at Flo's didn't we?' She swung back to Harriet, who was watching them closely.

'Well, that seems to be settled Harriet. If sleeping in your room is Jade's choice, then so be it.'

Moira could tell by Jade's expression that she was taken aback. And no wonder! Moira thought. I've all but toadied up to the little devil till now. It's time for her not to be so sure of

201

me. I've grovelled to her, every moment I've had the chance – and been rejected against richer rewards. Let her think I don't care!

Her heart sank because it seemed she had gambled and lost. Jade was walking over to Harriet and taking her hand. Looking up at the older woman in her enchanting, doll-like manner. 'I must stay with Moira,' she said with utter conviction. 'Honourable Lady Li River Pearl told me that I should always look to her.'

'Codswallop!' Harriet snapped and flounced off.

Moira stood there, saying nothing, even though her heart was full. Jade had actually shown that she loved her! Jade hadn't been bribed beyond recall after all.

'Come on, miss,' Moira told her charge. 'Time for bed.'

'Harriet wants to be my Number One Mother,' Jade said as they climbed the stairs side by side. 'She said that I must forget River Pearl and everyone else once she had adopted me. She said that one day you would be gone – for ever.'

'I don't think I like the sound of that!' Moira forced herself to laugh lightly, but her stomach was beginning to churn. She was thinking about the story of Mr Jones' demise. He had been sent packing – for ever. She put a teasing tone in her voice as she had added, 'And don't believe all that you hear. I would never go away and leave you. You should know that by now.'

'I know that I liked living with Honourable River Pearl Mother, at the top of the big house. I did not want us to go away from there.'

'It was not safe to stay.'

'Why?'

They had reached the bedroom they shared and Jade was looking mutinous.

'Why?' she demanded again.

'There are some people who do not like us very much because they had a serious quarrel with your dad. Then one day, Flo saw a Chinaman skulking in Ann Cherry's doorway and knew that it was time for us to go.'

'How did she know that the Chinese man was bad?'

'She didn't. Not really. But because River Pearl told us certain things, we thought it best to get away for a while. To be honest, Jade, I am not too happy about anyone from your

202

country learning of our whereabouts. I just don't like the sound of them, that's all.'

'Well I do! Harriet is getting to know a Chinaman very well, she told me so. He deals with the same person that Harriet goes to to get things to sell. He says that the Chinese call all white people foreign devils. That makes Harriet laugh. Harriet says the Chinaman wears a long robe and it's green with a yellow dragon on it. She is going to show him my emerald and ask him to read the writing on the gold on the back.'

'That's nice,' Moira replied and smiled and squeezed Jade's hand. 'Come along, you're taking too long. Let me help you.'

She settled Jade down and was smiling as she tucked her in, but inside she was terrified.

Surely Harriet wasn't that stupid? There weren't all that many Chinese gentleman around. Undoubtedly it would take only one glance to establish, through Harriet, that Jade was in the vicinity— If the brooch was recognised, or bore the family name! Dear God, Moira thought frantically, was Harriet mad? The threat of adoption was bad enough but discovery! Jade warmed to her theme.

'Harriet was told that in China children can be bought for a few pennies. Harriet wants to find out if she can buy me. Make me her very own girl!'

'That would not do, dear!' Moira said crisply. 'And I think Harriet must be careful when she speaks to that Chinaman. Going round showing off brooches can be dangerous where we are concerned.'

'I am not afraid,' Jade told her, incensed. 'Not of my people, nor of Harriet.' She smiled obliquely, 'I make Harriet do as I say! She gives me many things because I am her princess. She says that I am like a gift from heaven, that I belong to her.'

'And do you, Jade?'

'I belong to Jade,' the girl said, 'and Harriet belongs to me, like you belong to me!'

'Oh no!' Moira laughed. 'I belong only to Miss Moira O'Malley, and don't you forget it!'

Much later, once Jade was asleep, Moira made her way up to Con's attic. She opened the door and as she hesitated, he swung round. At that moment she was conscious of his unruly black hair, of his eyes the colour of the darkest irises she had seen on

the florist's stall. He was so tall and slim and lithe. So strong!
She felt confused, not quite certain why she had come to see
him.

'You're busy,' she said, 'I'll come back later.'

'Aren't you going to look at me picture' he asked. 'I'd like
your opinion.'

She hesitated, but his expression was disarming. It would
seem churlish to refuse. She walked towards him slowly and
then looked at the canvas. She saw herself. She gasped and felt
bewildered, delighted and proud all at one and the same time.
Con had made her seem beautiful! Then she felt disconcerted
by the laughter that blazed in his eyes.

'Forgive me,' he said, 'but they don't make many like you, at
all. You are extremely beautiful yet you don't believe it. The
lads at the market would be chasing you if I hadn't given them
fair warning, mavoureen.'

Moira coloured, not sure whether to feel protected, or furious that he had taken so much on himself. He saw the flash in
her eyes and changed tack.

'The painting is far from finished,' he told her, 'but even now,
with you in it, it is alive.'

It was a charming, casual compliment, meant to calm her
down. She smiled a little, recognising it for exactly what it was.

'I don't know that at all,' she told him, her voice filled with
pleasure even so. 'And you've told me that the horses you paint
are the creatures that bring your paintings to life. Kissed the
Blarney Stone you did, Con, all those years ago back in Ireland.
But you've made me feel ... feel a bit special.'

'And yet your eyes say to me,' he said, suddenly serious, 'any
minute now, Conor MacCluskey, I'm going to cut and run
right out of your life. You're worried, aren't you? What's
happened?'

Unaccountably she felt tears scalding her cheeks and dashing them away, she turned to run. In a flash his strong hands
gripped her shoulders and he was staring down at her.

'What is it? What's wrong? Has that wee madam upset you
again? Can't you see that she's a spoilt brat after getting all her
own way?'

'It's something she told me, that's all. To do with a brooch –
and with Harriet's plans.'

'Holy Mother!' He was openly impatient now. Moira's on about Jade again, he thought, and she doesn't care a fig for anything or anyone else. She's blind and deaf to everything except where that child is concerned. He heard himself exploding, 'Don't you see how it is? That wee creature needs a sharp slap where it matters most.'

'Don't go on like that,' she replied flatly. 'I came up here to see how you were getting on with your picture.' She pointedly ignored the girl in blue so prominent in the foreground and asked, 'Is that a church in the far distance? It looks rather lovely and very, very old.'

He pursed his lips, livid with her. She was deliberately changing the subject, dismissing his condemnation of Jade as though it was beneath her contempt. He couldn't get through to her at all. She'd try the patience of St Patrick, so she would.

Con looked at his picture, at the building set far away in the distance in the right hand corner, that she had pointed out. It was the little church of the Holy Virgin that he and his mother knew so well.

'The whole village round that church is old and picturesque,' he told her, trying to keep his irritation under control. 'But it's the wide sweep of the countryside that catches my fancy. It shows how life should be.'

'I don't understand what you're saying, Con.' Her tone was politeness itself. Inside she was fuming again. She could think things about Jade, but no one else had the right! And it was about time Con accepted the fact. He was speaking again, he seemed like a coiled spring beside her. She listened and tried to concentrate.

'My picture shows a countryside outwardly calm. Yet in reality it is filled to the brim with life,' he explained. 'I started out to try and get a kind of timelessness, but then changed my mind.' He warmed to his theme. 'The land will be there when we're all dead and gone. It will survive! The whole Universe throbs with the rhythm of life. And you, mavoureen, are a cabbage not to see it that way.'

'I am not a cabbage!' she flared. 'Why did you call me that?'

'Because you're content merely to dream,' he told her roughly, 'because Yani has been away all summer getting on with his own life. And now he's back, he's still dancing to his father's tune. Only a very green cabbage would not see that.'

'Stop it,' she gasped, outraged. 'It's not the truth.'

'He's to marry the Greek girl chosen for him. The two families in question have it all arranged. You've known how it's to be all along, but you won't accept it. Don't glare at me and act as though I'm the devil himself.' His large hands became clamps on her shoulders and he shook her. 'Deep down you've always known Yani was spoken for. Since he was about two years old in fact. And yet you still stay in your room once market is finished, and continue to daydream about the man. You are refusing to face the facts of life.'

'I hate you!' She brushed his hands away, cheeks fiery, eyes bright. 'I really and truly hate you!'

'And I want you!'

'Now you're trying to make a fool out of me!' she panted. 'You're a shit and—'

'Don't!' he snapped harshly, 'You're beginning to mouth on like Flo and it doesn't suit you.'

'How dare you!' Furious, taken back, on the defensive as she'd never been before, she raised her hand to strike him.

Then, somehow, Con's arms were round her, holding her tight. She was drowning in his eyes, wondering at the feel of his lips on hers. His kisses held a sweetness, a thrill, that sent waves of desire rippling through her body and soul. He was so strong, so masterful. He was pushing her head backwards, his kisses becoming more fiery by the minute. And a part of her, the base physical half, was beginning to respond. Was beginning to want and need more...

Out of the blue the flickering picture of Dave Dilley danced before Moira's eyes. The memory returned of his evil, snake-like tongue. She went rigid with shock and terror. Her eyes flew open where they had been ecstatically closed before. Filled with shame, Con let her go.

'So the dream still holds, does it?' he said harshly, completely misunderstanding. 'Well, don't worry, darlin', I'll not be bothering you again. Sneak back to your fantasy and dream on about the Greek.'

White-faced, stricken, Moira stared up at him, her hand covering her mouth. He thought that it was his kisses that had sent terror through her. Con thought it was all his fault! But it wasn't his fault! Indeed for one moment there she had wanted to give in to the rush of fire that had gone through her, had desired to melt and surrender to his masculine strength. It was her own weakness that had so shattered the mood. But she couldn't explain. Couldn't make herself speak of the abhorrance and loathing she felt for the fish fryer. Couldn't say that Dilley's awful, mournful face was always there, ghostly, at the back of her brain.

Sweat beaded her brow. Moira began to shake. She knew by his bleak expression that Con believed her revulsion to be all down to him. She could not explain, never would be able to. And the saddest thing of all was that she and Con would never be the same together again. Suddenly Moira realised how cold it was in the attic room without Con's warm arms around her. He would never want to hold her again. She felt him watching her, helpless, as she turned away blindly, and made for the door.

She ran down the attic stairs and onto the next floor. Then startled, cried out as Chumley, leaping up to his room, cannoned into her, almost knocking her flat.

'Sorry,' he said blithely. Then, on seeing her expression, 'Bli'me, cock, what's up?'

'I – I've got to leave here, that's all,' Moira stuttered. 'I've got to get away, Chumley!'

'Where to for Gawd's sake? And what the bloody hell's brought all this on? Have you been up visiting Con?'

'It's not that! It – it was something Jade said, and – and Con had a go at me. He accused me of daydreaming about Yani.' She was hiding her face against Chumley's solid chest now and weeping. 'I – I just want to go home!'

'Sorry, mate, out of the question. That Chink was spotted again, down Jordan Street the other night. Con went mad and roared like a bull and went chasing after him. But the sneaky little swine went down the alley like a blue-arsed fly and give Con the slip. Give Yani the slip too. I was behind both of them and wanting to wring the Chink's neck. While he's hanging round, Flo won't have you back.'

'She is hard and cruel and wicked to send Jade and me away.'

Her voice was muffled against his waistcoat. 'And – and I didn't know all that happened. Con never said.'

'We didn't want to scare you, mate, that why. Now, make your mind up to it. You've gotta hang on here for your own good.'

'I've got to go away from here, Chumley! Couldn't Flo or someone send for the police? Tell them about the Chinaman hanging round and—'

'No! Then the truth would come out about you and Jade, and the kid's whereabouts would be known. You can't muck about evading questions put to yer by the law. You know it and so do I and so does poor bloody Flo. That's why you had to cut and run.'

'But you don't understand!'

'No I don't mate. I thought that was why you came here in the first place? To see no one murdered the kid?'

'It was – it is! But it seems Harriet's all set to give the game away because she's trying to find out about adoption and talking to Chinese outsiders. It's not safe here, Chumley. I don't want to stay.'

Chumley held her away, so that he could look searchingly into her face. 'See here, me old sparrow, you ain't making much sense,' he told her. 'Harriet wouldn't say or do nothing what might harm the kid and—'

'I know that. I know!' Moira replied feverishly, knowing that to speak against Harriet would have Chumley immediately on the defensive. 'She loves Jade very much, but she is in danger of giving our whereabouts away. Oh, don't you see? Jade and I have got to go!'

'Ah!' Chumley said, accepting the truth of it at last. 'Well, if it's gotter be an' if you really feel it's best—' He snapped his fingers, having made up his mind. 'I could go and see Yani and see what he thinks. Though don't let on to Con that I suggested it.'

'Yani?' She was clutching at straws, then, 'But – but his father will be there and—'

'No! On the move as always is old Christos.' Chumley grinned and scratched his head, 'All about cargoes of olives, and that lousy wine that tastes like aniseed, and anything and everything to do with moving goods on his boats is Christos's business. Fair at it he always is. No time to breathe. And he won't be satisfied till old Yani's just like him.'

'Then you'll help me? Please?'

'All right, keep your hair on! Pack your things and wait. Harriet stays up all hours waiting for stuff to come in.' Chumley winked. 'Know what I mean? When the coast is clear, I'll sneak out and see Yani. I know he's there because he came in before I left. If it's all right, I'll get you there in the morning.'

'Thank you! Oh, thank you, Chumley.'

'Don't thank me, give me half a crown,' he quipped, then raised his brows, adding, 'oh – and while I'm at it, Moir, I've gotta be honest. Yani promised me a tenner if I could get you to go and see him. All right if I hold out me hand?'

'If helping me is worth ten pounds to Yani,' she whispered, 'take it by all means.'

'Go on then, buzz off. And I mean it. Not a word to Con.'

'Not even a whisper!' she replied and fled.

After that it was a question of whisking round and collecting her and Jade's things. The girl remained sleeping. She's got to do as she's told, Moira thought feverishly. Above all, she mustn't make a fuss. Harriet will go mad if she finds out.

Her stomach liquified as she remembered the blackness of Harriet's eyes. The cat-like Egyptian stare. The mental picture of Harriet cold-bloodedly pushing her own father down the stairs seemed to stand out most. If I'm not very careful, Moira thought, they'll find me at the bottom of the stairs too. I know too much!

She sat on the edge of the bed, waiting. Her heart was pounding, her mouth dry. She knew that she was terrified.

It turned out to be the longest night of her life. And all the while she was thinking of Flo, and wishing for Flo, and wondering sadly whether Flo missed her at all. Poor tarty, awful old Flo, who was common, loud-mouthed, lusty and unpredictable. Flo who was nice one minute, nasty the next, sometimes even quite evil. Not forgetting hypocritical! She unashamedly fawned on well-off people whether she liked them or not. Look how she pandered to Stavros, who she believed to be rich in spite of all he said to the contrary. Look how she toadied up to the old Greek then couldn't wait to say rude things about him behind his back!

209

Still, River Pearl was never well-off Moira chided herself, and I never had a penny to my name. Yet Flo kept me! Yes, let me stay when I could easily have been one of the homeless orphans roaming the streets ... And if Yani can't help us that's exactly where Jade and me will be.

Chapter Eighteen

'Come on!' Chumley hissed, 'Bleeding well get a move on!'

'All right!' Moira's throat was tight with terror. 'I'll just get Jade.'

'Ain't you woke her up yet?'

Moira stood in the doorway and glared.

'Would you? I've been hanging about for hours and . . .'

He grinned and looked ashamed.

'So I'm scared shitless, afraid of *her* I suppose. But it ain't what you think – for Gawd's sake get in there! Where's your things?'

It was all a panicky rush after that. Chumley, looking over his shoulder every so often, grabbed up the several brown paper carrier bags that held Moira and Jade's belongings. Moira gently woke Jade, dressed her in heart-thudding silence, aware of the child's wide-eyed stare, swung her up into her arms for all she was a big girl now, and together they fled out of the house into Market Street.

I might never see Con again, Moira thought, and felt incredibly sad. She remembered the way she had wanted to melt when his lips met hers. Thought of the rush of fire that had seared through her veins at his touch. Then she shivered, remembering how it had been when she had been woken by Dave Dilley. How she had wanted to be sick, scream and run. How she had hit him with the brass poker, needing him to be dead and done for, and out of the way like the rubbish he was. No wonder Harriet had . . .

I wish I could have made Con understand, she thought miserably, and felt tears burn against her lids. Now it's all over

211

and done with, and I'll probably never set eyes on Con again. He'll always hate me and probably cut the painting to ribbons. Oh God, he musn't do that, I'll die!

They did not stop until well into the market area of the High road.

'Wait,' Moira gasped. 'Have a heart, Chumley.' She set Jade onto her feet and smiled into the girl's wide eyes. 'It's all right, minx. Everything's going to be fine.'

She took hold of Jade's hand and they began hurrying along beside Chumley.

'Where are we going?' Jade asked.

Moira looked at Chumley who, at ease now, had his usual foxy grin lightening his face.

'Yani's arranged everything. Paying your rent and all. It's over, done with, and you're all set.' He winked knowingly, 'Play yer cards right, Moir, and who knows what might happen.'

'But where . . .'

'You've got a nice room in Cissy's mum's place. Lovely it is. Clean and well cared for.'

Moira could have wept with relief. Then a thought struck her.

'What about you, Chumley? If you're afraid of Harriet and she finds out that you've had a hand in all this, she'll go mad.'

'I ain't scared in that way, Moir. I just don't want ter hurt her feelings, that's all.' He whistled and raised his brows. 'And how d'yer think ol' Con's going to be if he thought what I had a hand in all this? String me up, he would, by the thumbs if I know him. No, it's all planned. You go to Mrs Wright's, and I'll hit the road. When I get back I'll act like nothing's happened.'

'Chumley, you can't, you mustn't, I mean . . .'

'I ain't you, ducky,' he told her bluntly. 'Always wanting to hide meself away. Scared of the open streets, scared of strange places, in fact scared of me own bleedin' shadow! You'd still go back to Flo's place given half the chance, wouldn't yer?'

'Chumley, I . . .'

'Brain-washed, that's what you've been. You're like a bird what's been born in a cage and don't know no better. Me, I'm like the common ol' sparrer. He flies free.' He chuckled. 'Free as a bird, Moir.'

'Harriet has been very kind to Jade and to me, but there's something about her that – that I can't take to. I'm so sorry to have been a pain.'

'You're a pain in the arse if you want to know,' he grinned in a wide friendly way, 'but you can't help being you, no more'n I can help being me. As for Harriet, in a class of her own, she is. A class of her own!'

'She had a bad time of it as a child, didn't she?'

'More'n you'll ever know. There's rumours what she had a hand in doing her old dad in, and she don't say as how she didn't. But I can see through her and I tell yer, it's all just an act. Harriet likes folk to be a bit scared of her. She don't want to be under anyone's thumb, not like she was under her dad's. No one's ever going to use her. No, not ever again.'

'Then you don't think . . .'

'That's what she told me and I believe her. Besides, she has to be tough since she does dealings with some bloody hard nuts. Stops up all hours, she does, and takes their swag, but always at the right price. She's immoveable. They don't argue, and no one 'ud ever try to do her down.'

'Chumley,' Moira said quietly, 'I believe you. I can understand all that. But she wants to adopt Jade.'

'So? It'd never get that far. Anne Cherry and ol' Liz would soon put paid to that idea.'

'Anne Cherry and Liz?'

'Gawd, Moir, ain't you aware of the world we live in? Anne Cherry and Liz are sisters, and them and Harriet have been right old mates for years. What's more, they could all dish the dirt about each other if they wanted. Harriet will be outnumbered wiv this one and no mistake. They couldn't have no kid break things up, could they? Lots of little secrets might come out if the bitching started.'

'You don't understand. She has spoken to a Chinaman about it!'

'Bli'me!' He scratched his head, frowning and looking thoughtful. 'I didn't know as how Harriet went as far as to open her gob to a Chink. She's been a right old crack-pot ain't she? And that ain't like her.'

'She means well, Chumley, but she must be stopped, musn't she?'

213

'Course! That's why I'm going along with yer. No one knows about Mrs Wright's place, not even Con. As for me, I'd best buzz off out of it for a while. Con knows me too well, and I just don't want ter tangle with him. Me best mate, he is. Cheer up, we ain't got too far to go...'

It was like living in another world, Moira thought a few days later. Mrs Daisy Wright was plump and homely and good-hearted. So was her out-of-work husband, Sid, who was a fun, crinkly-faced upstanding man. They hadn't thought twice about obliging young Mr Bertos, son of their daughter's boss. They asked no questions, were warm and welcoming to Moira and the little Chinese girl, and saw to it that they had all the comforts they could provide.

After that nervewracking journey, Moira relaxed. She woke up every morning in the wide brass bed that she and Jade shared, and looked round, bemused. The wallpaper was palest lavender, patterned with pansy sprays. The candlewick bed-spread was lilac mauve and the lino was of a dark fuschia shade, with a purple rug placed beside the bed. Against one wall stood a white-painted chest of drawers and matching dressing table with a tall mirror. This was covered in ornaments; lots of little white crochet doilies stood under ornaments of shepherd girls and boys, and there were china cats of all shapes and sizes with either blue or green glass eyes. There was also a dressing table set of white china decorated with violets. A gold-coloured crucifix above the bed completed the warm atmosphere. It was a lovely room, and well cared for.

'Before she left to go into service,' Daisy Wright explained as she showed Moira the room that first night, 'Cissy spent a lot of time up here. I don't suppose you can guess as how she loves cats.'

'Real ones too?'

'As my Sid knows full well,' Daisy laughed, 'since Popsy and Mopsy dig up his garden regular-like.'

'Popsy and Mopsy?'

'Fluffy they are, black and white, and too fat and lazy by half. Still, Cissy is all gooey over them, and I must say I rather like them myself.' Daisy chuckled outright, adding, 'Though I dunno about Sid. And as for Mr Braymore and his pigeons...'

214

Daisy's house was no different in size to those in Jordan Street, and the people not much better off, but there was one great shining difference. The Wrights and their neighbours in Shelley Road loved their homes, cared for them, and were proud of them. So carefully mended lace curtains hung before windows, doorsteps gleamed under the regular use of hearthstone, and aspidistras grew in china pots in front rooms. The lucky ones owned a piano, or a gramophone. Sadly, some had had to give up their every luxury. You weren't allowed a stitch when the Relief Officer came round. You couldn't get handouts for basics like a loaf of bread if you owned anything at all.

'I'm sorry, Mrs,' he would say severely, 'we cannot help you while you own this, or that, or even the old iron pot. It will have to go.'

Folk wanted to die with shame if the R.O. came round and would bite their lips and try to put on a brave face, and not mind if they'd been devious in trying to hide the only good thing they had. Above all, Relief Officers were detested for the heartless swine they were. They seemed to revel in their power. They were looked on as snotty-nosed superior sods.

The inhabitants of Shelley Road clung together, were mates, and had their pride. Woodwork was painted, shelves put up, and tiny back gardens were tended with care. Most had flowers, some held rabbit hutches and several had pigeon sheds. Racing pigeons were a man's passion in Shelley Road.

Money was hard to come by in Daisy Wright's house, since Sid only had casual work in the coal yard. But so far as Daisy was concerned, a challenge was a challenge. Her husband Sidney was the same.

Daisy was adept at making a penny do the work of two, and she was happy to share her 'little ways' with Moira, having taken her and the child to her kind heart.

Moira's first lesson was of the prime importance of the bacon bone. Large and handsome with bits of meat still clinging to it, sometimes one could get a huge bone for next to nothing. Daisy enthused over bacon bones even more than she would the crown jewels.

'No one need starve when they're to be had,' she told Moira. 'And me and Stan at the butcher's know each other very well. Went to school together we did. Stan sees to it that there's some

215

meat left on them bones. A real good'n he is. My Cissy went out with his boy Victor for a while, but I think she's seeing someone else now. Now here's what we do.'

Moira watched as every scrap of meat that could be was carefully cut away from the bone. It wasn't all that much, but the older woman's face glowed with satisfaction.

'Them bits cut up small, and mixed with lots of chopped up potato and onions will make two dinner-plate pies. Have you made dinner-plate pies?'

Moira shook her head and watched as Mrs Wright took two large enamel dinner plates out of the cupboard to show her.

'Special these are. Used to eat off them we did, when we were kids. My mum cherished them. Take a look. Not a chip on them anywhere! Anyway, I got two and my sister Maud got the other two, and we both keep them special for dinner-plate pies.'

'They're very handsome,' Moira replied, bemused.

'Here's what you do. Make a nice bit of short crust pastry – an' here's a secret worth knowing. If you make a thick, satisfying crust, be sure your filling's worth it! The way to a man's heart is through his stomach, you know. I use gravy to make the fillings nice and moist. Grease your plate well. Don't want nothing to stick, do we?' She smiled down at the avidly listening Jade. 'I'll show you how to make short crust pastry that will melt in your mouth, love. You just see if I don't.'

'Today?' Jade asked with shining eyes. 'Can we make some today?'

'Don't see why not.' Daisy turned back to Moira. 'Another trick, get a pennorth of fat from the butcher. Boil it in a saucepan of water for quite a while. Then let it get cold. The melted fat makes a thick white layer on top of the water. Scoop it out, put it in a basin, and you'll have enough there for several days cooking.'

Enthralled, Moira and Jade listened and learned.

'The bacon bone will be sawed into pieces,' Daisy went on, 'with bits of meat still on it I hope. It's put in the stewpan in cold water and left to soak all night. That's to get out the salt. Then placed in fresh water it's left to simmer for hours on the range. Then I throw in lots of shredded white cabbage, a finely diced carrot and some gravy powder for colour. Nice and filling that one.'

'Tell us some more!' Jade pleaded, eyes alight.

'All right, girl. A handful of minced meat will go twice as far if you add to it, as well as the onions and gravy powder, a handful of porridge. It'll take up the flavour and swell as it cooks, and taste really nice. Best of all, no one will know the difference.'

'It sounds delicious,' Moira told her.

Daisy smiled.

'It is, whether used for stew or pies. Sid smothers everything in pepper of course, but he reckons I'm the best cook for miles.'

Moira and Jade came to adore Sid who was a very jocular man.

'Wright by name and Wright by nature,' he laughed. 'You learn things from the Mrs and when you get married, your man'll have a treasure.'

'Moira won't get married,' Jade said quickly and her lips trembled. She warmed to her theme, her voice going high. 'Moira will never leave me. She will stay with me for ever and . . .'

'Of course she'll marry,' Daisy told her firmly, 'and make someone a truly beautiful wife and what's more, dear, so will you.'

'Don't want a lord and master,' Jade trilled passionately, aping something that Moira had often said to River Pearl. 'Men are horrible things.'

'I'm a man,' Sid pointed out. 'Am I a horrible old thing? Oh, come on, ducks! Come and see what old Sid's got for you.'

And Jade stopped being worried and went to Sid, who took from his pocket little wooden dolls he'd carved for her, no larger than pegs.

'There!' Daisy said and beamed. 'She'll be all right with us, Moira, and we'll look after her like she's made of gold. You can leave her with us any time. We'll enjoy having her. It'll be like having our Cissy with us again.'

'You're so kind,' Moira whispered and felt near to tears because Daisy's tone was so warm and motherly, 'but I won't be—'

'And when you go to meet Master Yani like he wants, you'll—'

'Meet Yani?' Moira whispered. 'Did you say . . .'

'Yes. Young Chumley left the message before he went off. He said that Master Yani will be meeting you on the forecourt of the picture house at half past six next Saturday night.'

'Oh!' Moira beamed across the room at Jade. 'Will that be all right?'

'Of course it will, love,' Sid answered for her. 'Because me and Jade are going to busy ourselves making paper chains.'

'And we'll get out our box of decorations and you can help us make the whole place look nice. There, dear,' Daisy was beaming, 'won't that be lovely?' She turned back to Moira. 'This Christmas is going to be real lovely now. We'll have you and Jade, and I think the festive season is just meant to have young people around. We always miss our Cissy most at Christmas times. That's when she works hardest of course.'

Half past six, outside the picture house, Moira was thinking. She felt as though she was riding astride a skyrocket aimed at the moon. I'm going to meet Yani. I actually have a date with Yani. Can this truly be happening? Half past six next Saturday . . .

Moira sat entranced through a re-run of *The Sheik* starring Rudolph Valentino. It seemed that the ladies requested this picture more than any other and the manager was always ready to oblige since he'd be sure of a full house.

The picture palace itself was a place to marvel at, with its golden cupids, red velvet covered seats, marvellous red gold-braided curtain and air of luxury over all. It was warm and scented, so her peacock coloured gloves and scarf were safe in her lap, alongside the magnificent beribboned box of milk chocolates that Yani had given her with such a flourish when they had first met. A very grown-up Yani now, sporting a thin moustache, which accentuated his tanned skin and marvellous white teeth even more than before. His suit was dark and expensive. He was a gentleman from the top of his brilliantined hair to his patent leather shoes.

He had purchased the most expensive tickets in the house and so they sat upstairs where Moira felt like a queen. Everything here was as different from the freezing cold outside world as sun from moon. But to Moira the most breathtaking thing of all was the fact that she was sitting in the darkness with the most handsome man in the world at her side.

She felt little squiggles of delight curling her toes because Yani's arm, a moment ago resting on the back of her seat, had surreptitiously lowered ... was now lightly looping her shoulders. She gasped at his touch and wanted to swoon as dramatically as the beautiful young woman on the screen. But the sheik was not half so handsome as Moira's own prince, and she wanted to pinch herself just to make sure that she was awake. She was most certainly alive!

The whole cinema episode wafted by and still lost in wonder, Moira stood beside Yani when the lights went up. They waited, standing upright, for the National Anthem, then Yani was leading her downstairs and into the rose perfumed foyer. He pulled her hand through his arm, as he stopped, smiled down at her, then said, 'It's early yet. Will you come with me, my darling?'

Moira was breathless with joy, but also perplexed.

'What did you call me just then?'

'My darling and you are, you know.'

'Oh!' she felt dizzy with delight, then, shyly, 'I am not sure that I understand?'

'There's nothing to understand,' he told her, his voice lowering in a thrilling way. 'Except that I cannot bear the thought of saying goodnight – yet. So, will you come with me, to the Hotel Metropole, and join me in a meal?'

'I'm not sure,' she was panicking now, her heart beating too fast. 'Is it very posh? I have never been in a hotel before.'

'You are exquisite, beloved, and I am the proudest man in this green and pleasant land. So, will you come with me?'

Moira thought rapidly. She was wearing her best dress. It was a plain dark green colour, a present from Harriet of course. Low-waisted, round-necked, she had thought it wonderful once, but now? To wear in a posh hotel? She instinctively pulled her coat more tightly round her. Yani lowered his head to look teasingly into her uncertain face.

'Please Moira?' he begged. 'Don't you know that I'm your slave?'

'If you show me what to do,' she whispered, hypnotised, 'and...'

'Don't worry,' he was gentle and coaxing now. 'I will look after you. Don't you believe me?'

'Yes,' she breathed. 'Oh yes!'

She wanted to faint with joy, then surprise, because Yani was walking her outside to where a black car driven by a uniformed chauffeur had drawn up in the kerb.

'Here we go,' Yani said, and smiled widely at her astonishment. The chauffeur left the car and walked round to open the door for them. They settled themselves and in seconds the car was gliding off.

'Does he know where to go?' Moira whispered. 'I mean, he didn't ask.'

'Don't worry, sweet, he knows exactly.'

'You were that certain, Yani?'

'No, merely hopeful,' he replied.

She forgot everything then because as she leaned back against the comfortable upholstery, Yani reached out to take hold of her hand. He squeezed her fingers in a gentle, loving way. She felt bliss flooding through her; this was love as she had imagined, and now, at long last, her dreams were coming true. Yani was in love with her and she was in love with him. One day, perhaps very soon, they would have their own, very own, happy ending...

The hotel dining room was sumptuous, very discreetly lit, and very high class. Awed, but heartened by the open admiration Moira saw in Yani's eyes, she sat at the table. It was pristine with its white linen, heavy silver cutlery and centrepiece of a single pink waterlily floating in a translucent alabaster dish. And softly soaring over all was music, violin music that was sad and romantic and almost too lovely to be true. The musicians were all but hidden behind the feathery potted palms strategically arranged on a small dais.

A waiter, napkin over one dark-suited arm, hovered. Yani picked up the menu, Moira did likewise, then froze. Stavros had not taught her foreign languages. She looked imploringly at Yani, who understood.

220

'It is written in French. Leave it to me,' he told her. 'What would you like? What is your favourite dish?'

Suddenly, inexplicably, she wanted to laugh. Her favourite dish? It had never mattered before. All that was important was the fact it was grub! She tried to think. Fish and chips? Veggy stew? What about the bacon-bone and cabbage that Daisy had dished up only yesterday. That had been a moreish as she had promised, and eaten with lots of crusty bread, had gone down a treat. Or what about dinner-plate pie?

'Well?' Yani asked.

Moira remembered the ultimate luxury.

'Yani,' she whispered nervously, 'Remember that ham they sell in the Ham and Pie shop? I'd love a slice of that. I've never had ...'

'This is not the Ham and Pie shop, sweet. This is the Metropole,' he teased. 'Leave it to me.'

He ordered chicken, which made her think it was Christmas already. It was served in a beautifully tasteful way with vegetables and savoury stuffing and a tiny star-shaped batter pudding. Surreptitiously copying Yani, who knew exactly in which order to use the knives and forks, and drinking wine when he did, Moira thoroughly enjoyed the meal. There was apple pie and cream to follow, then cheese and biscuits, and after that mint chocolates wrapped in green and silver paper.

Yani ordered a fresh bottle of sweet white wine and Moira sipped at her glass and thought she was in Paradise. Everything began to seem rosy, the world like a golden apple, and the silvery violin music soaring upwards, carried her delighted soul to the heights.

Still they lingered, aware only of each other, of the expression in each other's eyes. Yani began to speak softly, coaxingly of his island home and of the way of life there. Moira could picture the scenes he painted, of the village of Peroulades, the turquoise-blue sea and the golden cliffs that were, he said, ridged and magnificent, rising above the water like so many tawny lions.

'And the light!' he exclaimed, his voice rich and deep with emotion. 'It is like no other. Here in London there is a dullness, but on Kerkyra, some call it Corfu, the light is so clear and wonderful it can all but be tasted. It is a living thing, and it

221

dances over land and sea. It bathes the cypresses, lemons, oranges, figs and olives in white gold. It is a brilliance that I cannot possibly describe.'

'You love your homeland, don't you, Yani?' she asked wistfully.

'I am a Greek,' he told her and charmed her with his thrilling tone, 'I am wholly a Greek. And, sweet child, Greek sons do as they are told. We are a patriarchal society, you know.'

'I'm not sure I understand,' she whispered, loving him with her eyes.

'The father is very much the head of the family,' he explained. 'His word is law. His sons obey! They might argue, shout, even scream, but in the end, they obey.'

'On!' Moira's bliss was fast receding as she began to see what Yani was telling her.

'And my bride was chosen for me many years ago.'

'Oh, I see!'

'But you don't see at all.' His expression held passion as he threw down his challenge. 'I love you! I have always loved you. Right from the moment I rescued you from the gang of thugs on that very first night.'

'I – I remember,' she whispered hesitantly. 'When I ran away from Dave Dilley and that group of thugs were pushing me up against the wall, you and Freddy, Con and—'

'I rescued you,' he insisted. 'I saw that pig treating you so violently in the kitchen and gave the alarm which set everything in motion. So I am the real hero, eh?'

'Yes,' Moira whispered, wanting to cry, for she did not remember it that way.

'Then you understand?'

'I don't know what you're trying to say, Yani,' she replied carefully, thinking only of the far away promised bride.

'I am saying that you belong to me.'

'Oh!'

'That we are meant for each other.'

'But – I don't understand.' she replied painfully. 'How can that be? You're going to marry your Greek lady.'

'That will happen in Kerkyra. But I am to live and work here in England. So—'

'And so?' She was shaking and her heart plummeted like a

stone. He was not asking her to debase herself? Not asking her to . . .

'So what we do here, so many miles away, will hurt no one,' he beguiled in warm, velvety tones, his meaning only too clear.

Moira coloured, her mouth went dry. She swallowed and replied quietly enough. 'Except us!'

'We will have the big romance, eh?' he asked, smiling and quite missing the point.

'I'm sorry,' she whispered sadly. 'So sorry!'

He was taken back at the unexpected rejection. Had he misread the look in her eyes?

'Think!' His tone was urgent. He was now leaning across the table and his eyes were large and wonderful, openly imploring, 'We are in love, eh?'

'If we were, really and truly,' she whispered sadly, 'you wouldn't be marrying somebody else. Besides, if you're going to work over here, surely your wife will be at your side?'

'No! She will stay in the house that is already being built for her just outside Peroulades. My children will be born in Greece.'

'Ah!' Moira said quietly. 'The children!'

'Only because I am ordered! Because it is a family arrange-ment. Something I must live with for the rest of my life. Come, my poppet, I must make you see how it is . . .'

'What did you call me?'

'Poppet. Forgive me, it's something I heard . . .'

'Cissy has a cat named Popsy.'

'I beg your pardon?'

'I'm sorry, Yani,' Moira said, quietly wishing her dream goodbye, 'I don't know what made me think of that. Still, it leads me to this. I don't think I need to be anyone's poppet. Daisy reckons that one day I'll make someone a very good wife. I rather think I'd like that.'

'You don't understand, my darling!'

Her grief was now edged with anger, but still Moira tried to keep calm.

'You had it all worked out, didn't you?' she asked him, the smile long gone from her eyes. 'Oh yes, I understand you very well.'

'Of course you do, dearest. Of course you do! You would not

have run away from the house in Market Street otherwise, would you? You would not have sent to me for help. And earlier on, you would not have greeted me in the picture house with that oh so special look. It was then, my darling, that I saw into your heart.'

He was smiling now and looking just a little smug. And there was no mistaking the implication of his words. He was actually daring to be sure of her. Somehow, in that moment, she knew that Yani was used to women being his adoring slaves. He must have had his own way with the ladies for a very long time. And now, here he was, believing that she, Moira O'Malley, was about to fall like a ripe plum straight into his lap. She was not special to him at all, merely one of many. The scene he was playing now had been played often before, she knew it. He was certain of imminent victory, she knew that too. How humiliating and how cruel.

'Know something?' she asked quietly. 'Dear old Flo, who I'm sure you look down on, would have the nerve to call you a shit to your face. Yes, Flo! For all her mouthing and rough and ready ways, for all her drinking, she's straight forward. You know where you are with Flo. She would drop dead before acting sly!'

'Moira,' he said uneasily, looking round, 'please keep your voice down. People will hear, will get the wrong impression.'

'I don't care. You are shit!' she replied, her voice more quiet even so, but harsh with tears. 'You've tried to lead me up the garden path with all your money and smooth talking, haven't you? I don't think I'll ever forgive you for thinking I would go along with your plan. Were you so sure of me? Was it because I've been brought up by Flo? Because she ... she doesn't mind having men friends and, and ...'

'You've got it all wrong, dearest.' Yani began to bluster, shocked out of his complacency. 'I didn't mean, I would never—'

'No? Do you honestly think I'm that daft? That I'd actually be happy to be some kind of floozy?' Hurt far deeper than he would ever know, she shrugged expressively, saying, 'Oh what's the use? Take me home!'

'Moira, don't!' he said sharply. 'Don't! I didn't mean it like that. I love you! I want you. I'm trying to get you in the only

224

way I know how. Don't look at me like that. I can't bear it. I love you!'

'And the one who really knocked them all for six that night,' Moira heard herself hitting back in the only way she knew, 'was Con! He's like a giant and he weighed into them like nobody's business. He sent them flying right left and centre. Scattered them he did. I saw it all with my very own eyes, so Con was the hero, not you. You only played at the game – and talk's cheap where you're concerned. Now, take me home.'

'Which home?' he asked and his eyes were snapping with rage, 'the one in Market Street?'

'Oh no, Yani.' she replied sweetly, 'Shelley Road, Daisy's place, remember? Where the rent has been paid for the next six months. Where I have been made very welcome and accepted for being exactly what I am. Where, even though you're Cissy's boss, I don't think they'd go along with having an actual tart under their roof. Yes tart, Yani, because that's how you've made me feel.'

'No, never that. I love you!'

'But not enough. I must get my coat and be off right now!'

'Darling girl, I . . .'

She looked up at him ferociously, as she had learned from Flo, and snapped, 'Now!'

The drive back to Daisy's place was taken in silence. When the chauffeur opened the door for her and she made to step out, Yani took her hand and tried to kiss it. Moira pulled away and left him without a backward glance.

That night she hid her face in the pillow and cried herself to sleep.

The following day a florist's van stopped outside and the driver delivered a huge bouquet of red roses. They were for Moira and the message read, *Forgive me. You misunderstood. I love you. Yani.*

Moira's cheeks were as red as the roses as she handed the offering over to Daisy. The older woman looked at her and there was understanding in her eyes.

'He upset you, dear?'

'Yes.'

'And you held your own I hope?'

'Yes. Yes I did!'

225

'That's my girl!' Daisy said and chuckled. 'If you keep him at arms length you'll get him round to your way of thinking in no time at all. At heart, he's a very decent young man.'

'And you think he can be forgiven for – for trying it on, Daisy?'

'It's up to men to try, and women to say no. There's nothing more tasty than forbidden fruit. Stay out of reach, dear, and he'll respect you, and try even harder next time. And quite soon you'll have him eating out of your hands.'

'He wanted me to be belong to him, even though he's about to marry a Greek girl back home!'

'Really?' Daisy raised her eyebrows, but her eyes were twinkling even so. 'Well I've learned several things over the years, one of them being that young men try to get their way just by spinning yarns. It's up to the wise girl whether to believe those yarns or not. I wouldn't give up on him, love. At least, not yet!'

Not certain whether she was on her head or heels, unsure of whether she even liked Yani now, Moira spent her time spoiling Jade after that. And learning household hints, and fussing over the two huge cats that were soppy old things who just adored being picked up and stroked.

She read the card attached to the bouquet over and over. Finally Moira tore it up into many little pieces and watched them turn black and disintegrate in the kitchen fire...

Christmas in the Wright household was a warm and lovely affair. There was a tree heavy with tinsel and coloured lights. Chains and balloons festooned the front room and Daisy played on the old piano that held pride of place. They ate too much, the chicken dinner was a joy, and Daisy's Christmas pudding a dream. The mince pies that Jade had helped to make, melted in the mouth, and there were nuts and tangerine oranges, raisins, rosy apples and sweets.

Jade received a red velvet dress that Daisy had made from an old curtain. A beautiful dress it was too, well cut, and held together with minute stitching; it fitted Jade perfectly. There was also a just-for-run rag doll. It had long yellow wool pigtails, boot-button eyes and cherry red lips. It had a dress just like Jade's, tiny red velvet slippers, and wore a red ribbon in its hair.

Jade cradled the doll in her arms and fell instantly in love.

That doll became her most prized possession. She named it Pearl.

'River Pearl?' Moira asked softly.

Jade did not reply, just looked up into Moira's face and for just one instant, her fingers crept out and curled round Moira's. No words were necessary.

For Moira, Daisy had made a nightdress case. It was white satin and was decorated with hand-made yellow silk roses. All the materials for the presents had come from Daisy's treasured patchwork bag. This was an old potato sack filled with cast-offs and snippets of good stuff picked up from market stalls. Daisy had sat up nights making these things.

'Oh!' Moira whispered, holding the nightdress case almost reverently. 'How beautiful! I shall keep it for ever. It shall stay with my other treasure.'

'What's that, ducks?' Sid teased. 'The crown jewels?'

'No. A little picture painted on silk. Another dear and very special friend gave it to me. Also I have a little box of handkerchiefs. They have lace round the edges and violets embroidered in the corners. Now I have this truly wonderful thing and I shall treasure it along side them all the days of my life.'

'Don't go overboard. You'll have me in tears. Have a glass of port,' Sid said, 'and cheer up! It's Christmas and we'll make the most of it, eh? Come on, Dais, play us tunes we can all sing to.'

And, liking him immensely, watching him puffing away at the cigars she had brought him, having sneaked out like a thief at the crack of dawn to do her shopping days before, Moira started singing carols and popular songs – and helping Daisy to eat some of the chocolates that she, Moira, had given her. A massive box it was too, with holly and red ribbon; the money Moira had earned on the stalls had come in very handy at this time. For Jade there had been coloured pencils and a colouring book, some glass beads and a Woolworth bracelet that looked like a gold snake with a ruby eye. It was the nearest Moira could get to the holy dragon which River Pearl had always been on about...

It was a good Christmas, better in food and presents and cheer than she had ever received in her life before. But Moira's heart ached to see Flo and Freddy, Stavros and Mr Binks. She had sent cards of course – and walked for ever it seemed, to post them in the next district, just in case the postmark gave her whereabouts away. She had nearly choked herself and found it hard to breath with her hat pulled down so low, her scarf all but meeting it and covering her nose. If it hadn't been so awful it would have been absurd. She had thought so even then and vaguely wondered whether she was afraid of the dreaded murderous Chinamen, or of just being outside, alone in the streets, as Chumley had accused.

She thought often of Yani, according to Cissy now miles away in Greece, and her eyes burned with unshed tears. Then she thought of Chumley. Daisy, also via Cissy, heard that Chumley had left London, to make his fortune he said. To this end he was making his way to somewhere up north. Dear old Chumley, who reckoned Con would hang him up by the thumbs if he learned who had helped Moira and Jade escape. Con! How did she feel about him?

Moira remembered how strong his arms had been. How strange she had felt with his lips on hers. She had actually seemed to be melting and becoming impossibly weak. Then right out of the blue, she had remembered the nightmarish Dave Dilley, had froze, and Con had not understood. He had become angry, had glared at her out of his iris-blue eyes. Somehow it was terribly important that she met up with Con one day. Just to see him and try to explain...

'Let's have yer!' Sid roared out, his crinkly face beaming. 'You're letting the side down, Moir.'

'Pack up your troubles in your old kit bag and smile, smile, smile...' she sang. And before the couple's warmth, Moira forgot everything and gave herself up to the wonder of their company.

Chapter Nineteen

The January wind howled down Jordan Street and gathered up kerb-side rubbish, shook it, imbued it with life, making it seem like so many lively djinns. Freddy blinked and squinted as grit flew into his face and prickled against his eyes. Newspaper, smelling of fish and chips, swirled round his legs, and dustbin lids rattled and fell, rolling to the gutter with harsh ratty-tatty sounds.

He walked on, slowly, feeling down. He loved his mother and forgave her all her sins, but things had never been the same at home since Iddy and the Chinese child had been sent away. Oh, they had a new regular, the Irishman that everyone liked, but even he seemed to be pretty sour these days. Everyone at the lodge continued to miss Moira, especially the old Greek who was constantly seen shaking his head and muttering, 'Por, por, por.'

Binksy went about with a face like a ha'penny kite, because he didn't see his young mate Chumley since he'd gone too, and Maisy just clumped and thumped about saying barely two words. It was all very puzzling, even bothersome, because nothing made sense. If everyone missed Iddy, why was it that his mother had refused to let her come home?

There was, he had been told, danger in the air. Terrible danger for Iddy and the little girl they called Jade. But he would be on hand, always. He would see to it that Iddy would come to no harm.

In his slow thoughtful way, Freddy was trying to work out how to find his treasure and swing her up in his arms and bring her safely back to where she so rightly belonged. Where to start?

He reasoned that since he had himself carried her, rolled up in a carpet, to Anne Cherry's, the second hand shop was the first place to go. He was almost there when an almighty row coming from 313, the Yeats's place, made him pause.

Everyone in Jordan Street knew and feared the Yeats. No one, apart from Freddy, would dare to tangle with them. Crusher Bert they called the old man, a bully and a bruiser who'd made a living out of fairground boxing when young. He had a broken nose, large blue eyes under thick gingery eyebrows, and a scar that ran down the length of his face. He was known to give anyone who dared to stand up to him bear hugs that crushed and broke ribs. He was much to be feared.

The only person on God's earth to scare him was his missus, Greta. A small, skinny bantam-cock of a woman, who had fierce brown eyes and dark hair plaited and pinned round each side of her head like ear phones. She would lay in to adversaries at the drop of a hat, and had a whip-lash, sarcastic tongue.

The Yeats' had four offspring. 'All bloody B's!' Bert would yell. And as for the boys, it was the truth. Mean and spiteful, cruel and up to all nefarious tricks, they were heartily detested. They were like peas in a pod, small like Greta, skinny and dark.

Beryl, the girl, was seldom heard of. When very small she had been seen sitting on the doorstep, no shoes on her feet for all it had been winter, and hunched up, almost blue with cold. She had long fair hair and blue eyes and had seemed a pretty child. It was rumoured that she was treated like some sort of slave, but no one knew for sure. Not that it mattered. Life was a bitch anyway. It was enough to get through one's own hell-dog days and the rest could sod off.

But Freddy had always looked for Beryl, from the day he had seen her sitting on the step. He sometimes saw her when he passed. She would be peering though a filthy window, a mere pale shadow, a ghost, and he would smile his slow sweet smile and wave. Over the months and years she had plucked up the courage to wave back. She was, he thought, a dream, a whisp seen through smoke-blackened glass. She was not of his world.

Suddenly everything changed. The yelling grew louder, more

ferocious. People came out on their steps or opened windows to peer out.

The door of 313 flew open and a small figure ran out, long hair flowing and gusted by the wind. She ran neither fast nor well. One slim shoulder was higher than the other, and she limped. Even Freddy saw that she was wearing a cotton rag that could barely cover her body let alone keep out the cold. Behind her, baying like hounds came two of the Yeats's. The younger, Barry, was brandishing a strap and yelling.

'You say no to me again and I'll have the hide of your back. Cow! You come back here!'

But Beryl kept on, having given one terrified look over her shoulder. She hesitated and Bill Yeats, the older and meaner by far, bawled out.

'Do as you're told. D'yer hear me? There ain't nowhere for yer ter hide. You twisted little moo, you ain't got nowhere to go.'

They caught her and Barry began laying in with his strap as Bill felled her to the ground. They were beginning to enjoy it, safe in the knowledge that there was no one in Jordan Street daring enough to poke their noses in.

Beryl was covering her face with her hands and crying piteously. Then, like magic, her tormentors were gusted away. Went flying through the air they did, helpless and gawping as they were bounced forcefully against Anne Cherry's shop wall. Neither had breath left and Barry's nose was beginning to bleed.

Then Freddy, now an awesome figure, had scooped Beryl up into his arms and faced them both.

'She has a place to go,' he said.

Ignoring their outrage, he about-faced, carrying Beryl as easily as he might a baby, and with steady, determined tread, began walking back to the lodge. And as he walked the length of Jordan Street the women clapped and cheered. At last someone had put the Yeats bastards in their place, something everyone had prayed for. The Yeats's were the curse of the road.

'Good on yer, Freddy!' they called.

'Give the cowsons a good hiding, Fred.'

'Why don't you bash their bleeding farver in next? You'll have ter, since he'll be up your place like a blue arse fly.'

''Ere Fred, tell Flo to smash ol' Greet's face in for me while you're at it.'

'Bleeding hell, Fred, there's going ter be war!'

Fred neither heard nor saw them. He was conscious only of the small tearful figure clinging onto him. Of pain-filled blue eyes and a small shaky voice begging, 'Please don't let them take me back. Let me stay with you for ever, Fred. Please?'

'You will stay with me,' he told her, and thought he was holding the most beautiful creature in the world . . .

'Gawd!' Flo said, looking at Beryl, now planted by Fred onto one of the kitchen chairs, 'There ain't two penn'orth of you. Been treated bad ain't you?' She turned to Freddy. 'Just look at them marks on her arms! They've been giving her the strap. Bli'me, I might 'ave given you and our Moir a fourpenny one or two, but I ain't never used no cane nor strap.' She turned back to Beryl. 'What started the shemozzle today?'

'I wanted to . . . to go out. I wanted to . . .'

'Start living, girl?'

Beryl nodded while the silent tears poured down her face. She hesitantly tried to explain.

'I saw Fred going down the street and I wanted . . . I wanted to talk to him when he came back. He always smiles and waves you see.'

'And no one else ever does?'

Beryl shook her head.

'How d'yer know his name, Beryl?'

'I – I've heard people – people talking.' Beryl whispered. 'He's so big and strong and . . . When I knew he was coming I said I wanted to go and stand on the step. I wanted just to say hello.' Her breath shuddered on a deep heaving sob and continued. 'Barry said I was to get on with what I was doing. I . . . I said no! I've never dared lip him before and he went mad. When he grabbed the strap, I ran.'

'And my Freddy was on hand to save you?' Flo's wicked grin creased her face. 'Quite a hero ain't he?'

'Oh yes!'

'And you want to stay here with him?'

'Yes please. Oh please!'

'And,' Flo's tone became meaningful, 'only him? D'you get what I mean?'

'If he'll have me, I . . . Oh please!'

Freddy was beaming, but Flo had to be sure, needed to be sure, was determined to be.

'Well you don't know him like what I do. You two ain't never met before. And I ain't going to stand by and see him treated like any old port in a storm. Know what I mean?'

'Yes.'

'Well that's settled. I'll let you kip down with me, and . . .'

'Please, I want to stay with Freddy! He makes me feel safe. I only want to be with him!'

Flo gave in.

'All right, all right! We'll see how the pair of you get on. If everything is hunky-dory, we'll make it legal.' Her chins wobbled as she chuckled. 'My Gawd, what a turn up! I never thought to see the day!' She looked roguishly at Fred. 'And we'll have to get her some things over Anne Cherry's, eh? Warm togs what'll make her look nice. Got yourself a pretty little thing, ain't you?'

Neither Flo nor Freddy seemed to have noticed the poor, twisted body. A sweet face and large soulful blue eyes were enough.

'My mother,' Beryl began fearfully.

'Leave her to me, girl,' Flo's grin was wickedness itself. 'I never dreamed my Freddy would get someone, and no one on earth's going to take you away from him. Just so long as you're sure you've made up your mind?'

'Very, very sure,' Beryl breathed and clung onto Freddy's hand.

'Good!' Flo nodded and her chins wobbled again. 'It's like I said, girl. Leave it to me! Now you go down with Freddy and sort out your new home. P'raps you can make something of it. If you need anything, just ask.' She winked, ''Cause as you've probably guessed, Freddy's the only one on Gawd's earth what can get round me.'

'And Iddy.' Freddy said quietly. 'You really like her!'

'And ol' Moir of course,' Flo agreed carelessly, 'and young Beryl 'ere will like her too. The sooner we can get the Chink mess sorted, we'll get her back for you.' Flo couldn't stop herself from laughing out loud, tickled pink at the turn of events. 'And who knows, we might have her dancing at a wedding? Here, just wait till I tell ol' Maise! She'll wet herself with joy...'

A couple of hours later there was a right old barney in Jordan Street, one enjoyed by all. It was between Flo and Greet Yeats, smack outside 313, since Flo believed in carrying war into the enemy's camp. And the ensuing hollering and shouting was worth waiting for.

Greta, out-mouthed by Flo, and drowned out by the cat-calls from the watching women, threw caution to the wind. She raised her hand in fury, which was a great mistake. Flo, a heavyweight and all out to defend her Fred, weighed in.

Flo won.

'Let the rotten cruel bitch put that in her pipe and smoke it,' she called out to the hessian-aproned ladies, who were grinning round the woodbines in their mouths.

They were cheering and leering, at last satisfied that the dreaded Greet had got her come-uppance at last. There was a howl of derision as the defeated Greta crawled inside number 313.

As Flo began walking back towards the green gate, she waved regally at all the old girls. She felt a champion, she really did, and she had been accepted by them at last. Then a thought struck her. She stopped abruptly. An instant hush fell over all. Several ladies, now in awe of her, backed away. Flo raised her voice loud and piercing and above all, defiant. She threw down her challenge.

'I hope as how any Chinks what are watching get this message,' she yelled out, full blast. 'What I've done to Greet Yeats I'll do to anyone as tries it on with our Moir. Go and tell that to the slit-eyed bleeder what done for our Pearl!'

In that way she let the world know that the murdered Chinese woman had indeed once lived under her roof.

The whole street loved every minute and clapped and cheered. And if the slim Chinaman, who'd been haunting the vicinity ever since Dave Dilley had ventured to the Causeway, had been spotted, he would have been lynched. As it was, he waited until the coast was clear before slipping out from behind

234

his hiding place. It was a tall, rickety chest-of-drawers, surrounded by other ungainly odds and ends. It had been labelled by Anne Cherry as the bargain of the year, and it was grandly priced at one shilling and sixpence...

Chung Lo, number three son of Chung Weng, hurried by the wind-blown red paper lanterns and cut-outs hanging outside number 16 Limehouse Causeway. His round flat face was expressionless. Small and slight, his dark Western suit did not look well on him, seeming too large by half. He entered the dark interior, ignoring the old woman, and went straight through to find his father.

Chung Weng wore a smoking cap of black velvet. His long robe was dark blue, topped with a black padded surcoat. He was sitting at his table, a scroll of parchment on the table before him. On it were wise sayings that had sprung from the lips of Confucius, many, many years ago.

Chung Lo bowed with infinite grace and immense respect.

'Honourable father, you are at peace and harmony?'

'Lowly parent is overjoyed to see his number three son's safe return.'

'May humble and abject personage such as myself, please speak?'

'Your words will be as moths fluttering round lanterns.'

'And as impossible to gain hope from, or save from the end, honourable father.'

'Speak, my revered son. What of the English girl?'

'Nowhere to be found. Her mother is as fierce as a Manchurian tiger.' Chung Lo's eyes became twin sickle moons as he smiled. 'But today anger losened her tongue. Tsu River Pearl was indeed living with her. The young English missee told the truth. I still cannot find her whereabouts. Her mother has hidden her well.'

'Yet your honourable Number One Brother, who followed her home after she visited this place, assured lowly self that she lived with mother in house behind a wall. She is no longer there?'

'Of that I am certain.'

'And the white devil?'

'He, who is lower than the lying son of a city whore, con-

235

tinues his ramblings. I have followed him from the day we saw him here. He is clever as well as crazy, and knows his way around. He is hard to find and sometimes I lose him for hours on end. Yet when I catch up with him he is always the same. I listen to his madness and I have heard and understood some things. He was fond of his wife and he regularly visits the resting place of ancestors.'

'The young English girl is, you believe, no longer of this world?'

'She is alive, honourable father, I am sure of that. The mad dog mumbles her name constantly. He wishes to punish her, use her, then kill her. He seems to believe that one day he will catch her in the grounds of the dead. The place is named Saint Stephen's.'

'Then you must continue to watch. He will lead us to the girl, who will in turn take us to the whereabouts of the only child of the honourable, most high Lord Li Tzu. It will bring us great honour if when he returns from America, we can produce his daughter.'

'You hear from him, honourable one?'

'Of him. The lord Li Tzu is very rich, but not half so fortunate as I. He has no sons. Even so, he is a great and brilliant man. He has been away for long, long time. Has established a thriving business in his new land. I feel that perhaps, one day, he will live in America where there are now many millions of our kind. However his base is in this country and we need to learn of his child. If we do not accomplish this, we of the family of Chung will for ever lose face.'

Chung Lo's venerable father raised his hand, the slightest of gestures of dismissal, but it was enough. Chung Lo bowed with quiet reverence, then went out of the room.

He found the old woman, nodded slightly, then seated himself at a square table. He waited with an air of remote aloofness while she cooked thin slivers of pork and vegetables in a large round pan. These were served with a bowl of rice.

The young man raised his food bowl high, nearly reaching his mouth. His chopsticks moved rapidly. He completed his meal, took a sip of rice wine, then stood to his feet. The old woman watched from a respectful distance and glowed with pride. Of all her children, three married daughters, and sons

One and Two now away on family business, she loved Lo the most. And he loved her. Not a word had been spoken between them, but she knew. Just as she knew that when she woke and went to the cooking stove next morning, there inside her clean and shining wok, she would find a single fresh flower. The charming number three son never forgot...

The Duck and Drake was small, smelly and crowded, with sawdust on the floor. Its customers were mostly men, squeezed together in the confined space, else hugging the bar. For all it was stifling hot, they wore cloth caps and cotton scarves round their necks. Rough and rowdy, spitting, coughing and gasping, their jokes were crude, their attitude towards their women foul.

The Duck and Drake was situated in a bad area. One even worse than Jordan Street, Anne Cherry thought sourly as she sat at a wall table. She was drinking gin and there was a filled glass ready and waiting for when her sister came in.

Anne Cherry's hard face went scarlet as a man grasped the back of the vacant chair.

'Chair's taken,' she rasped. 'Sod off!'

The man let go, glaring and curling his lip, but one look at Anne's face had been enough.

Anne Cherry watched him contemptuously as he edged away, then she glanced at the fly-spotted clock on the wall opposite and frowned. Her sister was late. Unusual! She was usually a stickler for time; there must be something wrong. She was just about to leave when she saw the plain, ordinary-looking woman with thin lips pushing through the crowds towards her.

'What's up, Lizzie?' she asked as the woman sat down at the table. 'Been on your holidays?'

'Reet's gorn nutty, that's what. We've been going round the market, searching and questioning, and making a sodding nuisance of ourselves. I ask you! And it's been taters outside, so I'm freezing, and fair wore out.'

'Harriet? Nuts? Don't sound like her. She's usually cool as a cucumber.'

'Not any more, she ain't. Gorn flaming mad, stupid bitch, and I don't like it. I don't like it at all.'

'Come off it! You usually stick up for our darling friend

237

Reet, no matter what she says or does. You've been like her
shadow from the day Binksy fished her out of the water when
we were at school. What's got into you?'

'That bleeding kid, that's what.' Lizzie's face had gone grey
and her eyes were stony. 'Reet's like a woman possessed, she's
so determined to find that young'un. She was just mad at first,
because she'd been out-witted, then right out of the blue, she
acted scared. I tell yer, I ain't never seen her like this before.'

'Don't sound like her to get shaky. What's up with her, Liz?'

'She's got this bee in her bonnet about opening her mouth
when she shouldn't have. I can't think what's she's on about,
and she won't tell. It don't make no sense to me and I just
dunno what to do. I tell you, Reet's gorn sick in the head.'

'I don't know why you're spouting off steam, Liz Cherry.'

'O'Malley's gorn, and so's the yellow kid, that's why.
Sneaked off like thieves in the night, they did. And when Reet
found out, there was hell to pay.'

'Oh my Gawd! As bad as that?'

'Chumley's buggered off, going up north they say, so at first
she blamed him. Then nice old Con took the brunt of it.
Almighty row there was there! Harriet kept mouthing on about
how she'd bleeding well kill the little cow what had taken
darling Jade away. Con lost his paddy. Told her she'd better
keep her hands off. One thing led to another. You know how it
goes. Anyway there was a right old howd'yer do. Then he left.'

'Where?'

'I think he's taken a room in Flo Williamson's.'

'I ain't seen him in the street.'

'You will! Anyway Reet's getting worse. I think the silly
moo's reached that funny time of life or something. She's
questioning and threatening some of them what we need in our
line of business! She even told Neilson, the bloke that's got a
Chink mate, that she'll report the kid missing to the cops! She
keeps ranting on about the Chink hurting the kid. I tell you, I'm
getting sick of it.'

'She shouldn't have sparked up. Neilson will see all three of
us as a threat and have us done over as a warning. Everyone
knows him!'

'Reet's gone over the top. She took to that kid. Wants to
adopt it – and she's about as motherly as my arse! Now she's

238

scared about what's happened to the little dear. Ha! She don't give a monkey's about young O'Malley though, who I liked best of the two.'

'I still don't know why you're so worked up about it yourself.'

'Reet's getting careless. I dunno what we can do about her since she's hell bent on falling out with Neilson. Right out of the blue she's got the idea that him and his Chink mate are after that Jade for some rotten cruel plan of their own. I ask you! She'll get us in trouble, I know she will. I could ... But it's always been us three, ain't it?'

'For Gawd's sake, stop carrying on,' Anne Cherry said, exasperated. 'You've got me, ain't you? You've always got me, Liz. We'll sort it together. After all, we're family...'

Part III

Chapter Twenty

'I strongly advise you to take Rowena up on her offer,' Vivien
Bentine told Con. 'She has a wonderful studio. There's enough
room in it for a dozen artists. The room in Jordan Lodge has no
good window. At least your attic in Market Street gave good
light. Besides the area you're in now just doesn't fit. Artists are
often eccentric – but I won't have one of mine looking stupid.'

'Jaysus, you're a snob!'

'No. Realistic. You need to become a professional in look,
word and deed. Working in a back street attic is no longer
suitable for an artist who has sold three pictures for a quite
remarkable price, and who has been commissioned to do at
least three more. Indeed, the gallery will take all of your work.
You are going to make serious money!'

'With Rowena Wray, there'll be strings attached,' Con replied, his generous lips uptilted at the corners, his handsome,
expressive face showing his doubts. 'What's more, she's a spoilt
brat.'

'She was born rich, Con, and she has all the right contacts.
Yes, she's after you, and doesn't care who knows it. That's an
insult?' Vivien threw her hands out, palm upwards and looked
to the ceiling. 'My life, how stupid can you get? Rowena's
good-hearted, and generous to a fault. And most important, at
least so far as I'm concerned, is she's a brilliant water colourist.
She will go far, and, young man, so will you.'

'On her coat tails?' Con drawled, far from impressed. 'Holy
Mother! Vivien, you don't know me at all.'

'I know you're a damned good artist,' she snapped back.
'You also have an easy charm, extraordinary good looks and a

243

physique that most men would give their eye teeth for. All of which can be said about Rowena of course, though it's women rather than men who envy her. She's tall and fair and extremely beautiful. You make a natural breathtaking pair. If you listen to me and—'

'I like her studio, it's got everything, but—'

'All right! I'll warn her. No strings!'

'Sure and I don't believe what I'm hearing Vivien Bentine.' He was teasing her now.

'She listens to me.' Vivien was intent on pressing home her point. 'She really does! I'll tell her to tread carefully and she will. Like you, she puts her painting first.'

'Who's idea was it, that I share with her? Who thought of all this in the first place?'

'I did of course. You need to go on to bigger and better things.' Vivien shrugged expressively. 'I am your agent for God's sake! In this day and age, it is important that the artist promotes his own image. You need publicity, Con, and you and Rowena together could make it hands down.'

'I don't see the point.'

'Conor MacCluskey,' she snapped impatiently, 'what have you got to lose? Won't you give me the credit for knowing what's best?'

He capitulated, only because having visited Rowena's studio had made him drool, but Vivien wasn't to know that. So he smiled his roguish smile, and kissed her on her cheek.

'Sure, 'tis a fine silver tongue that you have,' he told her. 'And isn't it a fact that you can see everything that's right under your darlin' nose?'

'No need to put on the Irish, Con,' she replied, mollified now things were going her way. 'You don't need to try and prove you've kissed the Blarney Stone. Do I take it that you're prepared to move out of that dump in Market Street?'

'I said work, not live.'

'And I said live! Rowena uses the studio to work. The domestic quarters there are going begging since Rowena's used to servants and all the luxury she had in her parents' home. Don't worry, Con. No one's going all out to get you compromised.'

'Now you're hinting that I'm acting like an old woman, Viv!'

'No,' she replied, 'Just like someone who has his heart and mind set elsewhere. Who is she?'

'A girl who I've known for years. She has a great depth to her and great beauty. You can see her thoughts and dreams in her expressions. They move across her face like misty waves and I—'

'Don't stand a chance?'

'I don't think so. No. She neither likes nor trusts me now.'

'Then she's either a fool or very clever girl,' Vivien said wryly.

'Since I class all men as the same. They really believe they're born to rule. I had brothers, so I know.'

'I'm not your brother at all,' he teased, 'and wouldn't you be knowing I'm like wax in your hands?'

'And I'm not so daft as to believe that! Now, Con, let's get our heads down to the business of the day.'

By the time March came roistering in, Con was settled, and his picture was being published, alongside the willowy Rowena's in the newspapers and magazines that counted most.

Moira's rent for the room in the Wrights was nearly due, and there had been no word from Greece.

Chumley was making his way home.

When the bluebells were carpeting the woodlands of far away Wanstead, Moira was getting desperate. Not that the Wrights said a word. But Cissy did. Cissy, who Moira liked and who seemed to like her, and was as devoutly good and honest as the crucifix over her bed suggested. It was Cissy who held out hope on the day she came home on her day off. She and Moira were having a heart to heart, sitting side by side on the bed.

'Master Yani's a corker,' Cissy said. 'Oh, he's spoilt and used to having his own way, but he really and truly is the cat's whiskers. He just doesn't understand how people like us tick.'

'He wanted me to . . .'

'I know all about that! Mum told me. But you've got to accept that gents like Yani think it's their right. They try, and it's up to us to slap them down. But I know you haven't seen the last of him. I overheard him talking to his Father on the telephone once.' She looked awed. 'It must cost a fortune because Mr Christos was miles away at the time. Anyway, he was talking about how he wanted to get out of marrying someone called Dacia. I don't know what his dad said, because Mrs Lines caught me earwigging and all but done her nut. Anyway shortly after, Master Yani stormed out of the house looking like a bear with a sore head.'

'Then you really believe . . .'

'I know he always gets his own way. I know he's trying hard not to give in to what the master wants. In other words, it looks like he was telling you the truth when he said he loved you. But love to his sort don't always mean what we think, eh?' Cissy shrugged and looked sad. 'I dunno, Moira, blokes can't half mess things up!'

'I know,' Moira replied quietly, a picture of Dave Dilley's face weaving eerily as though floating in water, came into her mind. 'Some of them can be quite terrible.'

'Or stupid!' Cissy sighed deeply. 'Why can't we fall for the good fellows, eh? There's Vic now, a real nice chap, but he just don't light no fires in my hearth.'

'Don't tell me. It's never Chumley?'

'How did you guess? He can't read and he can't write. He's a devil where the girls are concerned. Worse, he's light-fingered. I'll cure him of that even if I die in the attempt. It's a pound to a penny he's had the time of his life on the road. He's the sort that turns everything into a joke, even the thought of prison. And he just doesn't care what folk think. He sends soppy messages!'

'That should make you happy!'

'I want to die the death! All kinds of tramps and hawkers go sneaking round on the look out for Wally. He's the gardener cum handyman where I work. Wally's told things, and he passes them on to me. Like what Chumley's doing and where he's going next, and that I'm not to forget him because he'll never forget me. I can just see him, smiling that smile of his, and thinking what a lark it is, sending filthy beggars and tramps trudging up to the posh Bertos house. Things like that make him roll up! I could kill him, I really could. If Mrs Lines ever found out, it'd be me for the chop.'

'And in spite of all this, of you not liking some of the things he does, you love him?'

'I'm afraid so.'

246

'That's how I still feel about Yani,' Moira admitted. 'For all he's been horrible. The trouble is, I think I've loved him ever since Stavros first told me about him. Talk about hearts ruling heads! We're both really very silly, aren't we?'

'Nutty as fruit cakes,' Cissy replied. Then sharply, 'Now, to change the subject, Mum and Dad haven't said anything, but I was wondering about what you're going to do about money?'

'I know I can earn a little by doing casual stints at the market, but I'm rather afraid to try.'

'Why? Jade will be like a bug in a rug with Mum.'

'I might be recognised, and then there's Con...'

'Chumley's bosom buddy? He won't be seen in the market these days. He's gone up in the world. Didn't you know?'

'He's sold his pictures?' Moira beamed, delighted. 'How lovely! He's a real genius. Everyone thinks so.' Her cheeks flushed and her eyes became bright. 'And he's so handsome and manly and...'

'I thought you were in love with Yani Bertos?'

'Con is different. He, he's a friend!'

'How good a friend?' Cissy was watching her closely.

Moira felt embarrassed at the directness of Cissy's gaze. Then she admitted.

'He kissed me once and it made me go weak at the knees. I didn't feel in control of myself! And...'

'You feel safer with Yani?' Cissy derided. 'Isn't that because, deep down, you're not treating dreams about Yani as real? Good Lord, Moira, and here was me thinking that I'm the only one that's confused. Well, let me tell you something. Chumley's mate's no longer anything to do with the market.'

'He isn't? How do you know? I mean...'

'He's safely up West, with a woman named Rowena Wray if all what the papers say is true. And I cannot believe that there are millions of spies all watching out for you.'

'You don't understand, Cissy.'

'I know you had to get Jade away from where you lived because Chumley's landlady wished to adopt Jade and dump you. But that's over and done with now, surely? Jade will be all right with Mum, so that leaves you free as air.'

'But there are problems. I mustn't be seen and followed. I... I don't know what to do!'

'Take the bull by the horns,' Cissy said bluntly. 'And the minute Master Yani comes back, I'm going to tell him that he owes us rent money. Yes, even if it means losing my place.'

'Don't! You mustn't! I'll sort something out, really I will.'

'Don't look like you're about to be gobbled up,' Cissy teased. 'And if the market doesn't work out, don't fret. My Mum and Dad are jolly nice people. It's because of that, that I don't want them taken for granted by master Yani.' She jumped up from the bed and surprisingly kissed Moira warmly on the cheek. 'And if you must know, wild horses wouldn't make me see you out out on a limb. And that, Moira O'Malley, is because I feel like you're the sister I always wanted.'

She bounced out of the room and ran downstairs to find Daisy who was showing Jade how to darn socks.

Moira stayed where she was. Rowena Wray, she was thinking. Who's she when she's at home? She sounds very posh, like Con is now if he's in the West End.

Suddenly, very desperately, she needed to pour her heart out to someone she could trust implicitly. Someone who would listen, but who would never talk back. Would never argue and confuse her. Who would just be there ... Robby!

She drew in a deep shuddering breath. She would go to St Stephen's the very next day.

It was unbelievable, Moira thought next morning. Just a few hours and one's whole life changed. She was sitting in the Wrights front room as Daisy had told her she should, and Sid was sitting in the old but spruce, blue upholstered armchair opposite her. A smile was crinkling up his merry face.

'Cissy told me and her Mum all about your talk,' he told her, 'and me and Dais agree that going back to the market ain't such a good idea.'

'But I need to, I really do. I can't be a hanger on and— Besides, I don't want to owe Yani anything. Not ever!'

'May a nosy old bloke ask why?'

'Because once dreaming about him was the only beautiful thing in my life.'

'And then you met him for real? Hard Chedda, Moir, but to be expected. Gawd, girl, true life happens to everyone in time.'

'But he was really marvellous once and ...'

'And then he was sent away? Is that it?'

She looked up then, sharply.

'He was sent?'

Sid nodded. 'Got too friendly, he did. With some chaps you seem to know rather well. A couple of villains, at least the bloke our Cissy likes is. And according to Cissy, Master Yani always went on and on about you. But Mr Christos Bertos rules with a rod of iron, oh yes! And he holds the purse strings. So it's curtains all round if his son wants ter step out of line. But who knows? He might finish up doing just that.'

'What are you trying to say?' Moira asked uncertainly. 'That you think I should hang on before making my mind up about anything?'

'Yes I do. And what's more, girl, I think that we will be hearing from Yani Bertos before very long. He might be a spoilt young cuss, but he's a man of his word. I'm willing to bet on that.'

Sid lapsed into silence after that. If he expected Moira to speak he was disappointed. She sat hunched in the chair, her fingers entwined together as both hands rested on her lap. She seemed rather younger than she was. She was innocent looking with her large clear eyes, he thought, but most impressive was the fact that she had made the best of herself. She spoke nice, and had taught Jade all the right things. She must have had a strong will to have survived in an area well known for its roughness and rackety ways. Another thing, you'd never guess, if you didn't know her, but there was a lot of timidity in Moira O'Malley. A kind of fear he couldn't understand, yet he knew it would take some skimming off. Her sort of fineness must have been like a bloody two-edged sword living with that harridan named Flo.

Oh yes! Cissy had heard a great deal about life in Jordan Street, and told him and Dais all about it, when she was home on her days off. Cissy had learned a sight too much from the thieving young sod she was so smitten on. His own dear Cissy really believed she could take a sow's ear and turn it into silk. Some hopes! Bloody hell, Sid thought, he'd have to do something about that young toe-rag Chumley while he was at it! Life could be a right old balls-up sometimes. Still all that'ud have to be dealt with on another day.

249

'Cat got your tongue, Moir?' he asked her in his jocular fashion. He gave her a mock bow. 'My lady of Limehouse, Mrs Wright and me will deem it a great H-onour—' he swiftly reverted to character, grinned widely and continued, 'if you put a sock in it!'

She remained still, just looking at him with wide, hurt eyes.

'Oi!' he teased, 'We've got the farmhouse dinner-plate pie and mash tonight, so we'll all have to get stuck in eat every crumb and look like we're in paradise because of it. If we don't, my Dais will have out guts for garters. All right?'

'Really? Then we'd deserve it, wouldn't we? Jade and me just lap up those pies and ... Sid? Thank you. Thank you ever so much. I think you and Daisy are the warmest, most kindest people I know.'

'And that's somethink of a laugh,' he quipped. 'You just wait and see how you feel when I start knocking Chumley's block off.'

'He deserves a chance, Sid,' she pleaded. 'He really does. He had a terrible start and he was knocked from pillar to post when very young It's just that—'

'He's a thieving sod?' He looked apologetic. 'Sorry! I shouldn't swear in front of you, Moir. Good job Jade didn't hear me. Oi! She tries to speak just like you. Adores you, she does.'

'Jade likes everyone and just about falls over herself to please anyone who's nice to her, including me,' Moira admitted honestly, 'and you and Daisy have been kinder than most. Oh Sid,' she added tremulously, 'you can't imagine the weight you've taken off my mind.'

'Good! Now buzz off and amuse young Jade. That kid'll always need you. I've seen the way she watches you. She might seem happy to be with someone else, but she's always looking over her shoulder, if you know what I mean? She don't like you out of her sight.'

'That's because she believes she owns me body and soul,' Moira laughed. 'In the country where she was born, I believe she was very rich. So rich that they had lots of underlings, and treated them as such. And all men keep themselves apart, in grand isolation; River Pearl's words, not mine; and mere lowly wives and concubines live in a separate part of the house. In

250

other words, husbands are like gods. And in turn, husbands just about go down on their knees to their sons! So, if rich Chinese ladies bear the lord and master sons, they are pampered and spoilt and given lots of lovely things.'

'Crikey! How do you know all this stuff?'

'Because River Pearl, who told me that she was Li Tzu's number three wife, said so.'

'Struth! I think you've lost me, mate. Was this River Pearl Jade's mum?'

'No, but she loved her as dearly. I think Jade is the lord Li Tzu's only child. But awful things happened in China and...'

'Well this ain't China,' Sid said flatly. 'And thank Gawd for that' He laughed out loud. ''Ere, what d'yer think would happen if I told Dais I was her lord and master? I'd get her rolling pin round me ear'ole, that's what. Now come on, Moir, don't want to keep our Dais waiting, do we? She'll think we're having a right old bull and cow if we don't go and show her our smiling clocks.'

Two days later red roses arrived for Moira from Yani and a message to meet him in the foyer of the Hotel Metropole. There was also a letter for Sid which contained a further six months rent for the room. Sid looked over to where Moira was standing by Jade and glowing as brightly as the bouquet she held in her arms.

'Look at it this way, girl,' he told her. 'You go and meet the bloke and get things clear. And if he tries to come it, you tell him no. N.O. Get it? Oh, and don't think a pound or two from him puts either you or us Wrights in his pocket. We ain't in no rich bloke's pocket like what the poor devils in China seem to be. Ready to do anything for a handful of rice? Strewth! I'd like to see the day! Anyway, Yani's only a young Greek git what's got to learn his place so far as you're concerned. All right?'

'I couldn't bear it if Cissy lost her place because of—'

'If he's that sort, my old cocker, Cissy'd be well out of it. But I reckon you're barking up the wrong tree there. This bloke, from all I hear, seems a decent sort what tried it on, made a fool of himself, and is going all out to put things right. Anyway, looks like you'll soon be finding out the truth of it. I take it you'll be going to meet him like he asks?'

There were stars in her eyes as she nodded.

Chapter Twenty-One

History seemed to be repeating itself, Moira thought. She was breathless and almost hypnotised by Yani's charm. His soulful dark eyes, his wide, white-toothed smile topped so marvellously with his pencil-thin moustache, made her go weak at the knees. They were sitting opposite each other, at the same table as before. His hand reached across the table to clasp her fingers in his.

'Moira,' he told her huskily, 'our first duty must be to our mutual love. Being away from people we both know will lighten the path. Can't you accept that?'

'I'm sorry,' she replied softly, 'I could never, ever leave Daisy. My first concern must and always be Jade. So that is why we must stay exactly where we are.'

'I know you adore the Wrights, and Cissy's a peach. But love is—'

'Very selfish, Yani, if it means blotting out duty. I left Jordan Street in order to save Jade. I left Market Street because Harriet wanted to adopt her and in so doing was in danger of giving our whereabouts away. I have never felt so happy, nor so at home since I have been living with Daisy and Sid. All of which is thanks to you.'

'But there are dangers, even in Shelley Road, my sweet,' he pointed out. 'Even in the Wright household. That's why I am begging you to come away with me. That would not be such a hardship surely. I do love you, you know and I do not wish to see either you or the Wrights in trouble.'

'Yani!' her eyes opened wide. 'Now you're trying to frighten me! That's not fair.'

'But honest even so,' he told her. 'You are living in a very decent, very upright household, Moira mine. So honest and law-abiding that Daisy has been thinking about doing the right thing. I did not want to have to tell you this, but Daisy is thinking about taking Jade to the local school and getting her into classes there.'

'No!' Moira gasped, all of Flo's dire warnings and stories about such dreaded institutions rising to the fore. 'No, I can't and won't have that. Besides, how do you know this? Daisy wouldn't go behind my back. She would have mentioned this directly to me.'

'She's worried because of something a Mrs Braymore said. A Mrs Braymore of Shelley Road?'

'Her husband is a keen gardener, like Sid,' Moira replied, nervous and puzzled, not sure of anything anymore. Yani looked so intense. 'But I don't understand what you're getting at. Mr Braymore and Sid are gardening friends.'

'And Mrs Braymore?'

'I've never met her. Daisy's not too keen on her though, since she's something of a busy-body.'

'So I've been led to understand. You see, Mrs Braymore is wondering out loud, to friends and neighbours, why Jade is not at school. Mrs Wright knows that you and Jade have run away from Harriet's place, and that there is some need for secrecy. But no matter what tales there are to tell, the law is the law. Keeping Jade away from school is against the law and Daisy is well aware of this.'

'But why didn't she she say anything to me?'

'She is going to, Moira, tonight. I confess that I'm speaking out of turn. I've known about this myself only since first thing this morning. Cissy brought me tea and toast and she asked me how her mother stood regarding having had Jade under her roof and not getting her into school. Cissy is afraid in case Mrs Wright gets into trouble, you see. Everyone has the right to an education these days, so not registering a child will go very badly for all concerned.'

'Just as Flo was always telling me,' Moira said, her throat going tight. 'Oh shit!'

'Exactly,' Yani agreed, adding, 'I rather think that poor Cissy will have serious problems with her parents when they find out that she has been talking to me. Especially about what they consider to be only your's and their business. But Cissy's problems are nothing to yours, are they? Do you think we should go along with it, and sort out this business of Jade going to school?'

'I'm afraid for her, Yani,' she gasped. 'You know something of her story, don't you? Of the risk Flo took? Oh dear, we haven't been at all fair to Daisy, have we? I mean, she and Sid, and I'm sure not even Cissy, knows about – about the hordes of murdering Chinese! Chumley wouldn't have seen fit to tell them that.'

'Not hordes,' he corrected her. 'Merely the Kung Chin clan. And surely the old man must have other things on his mind by now? After all, a rival's child is hardly fair game and— Still, I'm going along with you because I know how you feel.'

'River Pearl told me that while Kung Chin lives he will never give up needing to revenge himself on Li Tzu,' Moira replied. 'It all sounds silly and strange, doesn't it? Like it all belongs on the films or in books. But ... but nothing can wash away the fact River Pearl was done for. And, if all she said was true, Jade will be next.'

'We're in England now, not in China. Besides all that happened quite a while ago now. I can't believe you seriously think Jade's in real danger. Personally, I believe she would be as safe as houses with Daisy. But knowing how you feel about things, we have no other alternative, do we?'

'Kung Chin has made an oath and if he does not carry it out he will lose face. To lose face is for a Chinaman the most terrible sin of all. I believe what River Pearl said. That Jade will be killed as a kind of tit-for-tat gesture, because, you see, Kung Chin lost his own, very precious and dearly loved son. A son who, according to his light, brought dishonour to the Kung family name.'

'Then what do you want to do?'

She laughed, a small, shocked sound that was almost lost in the soaring melody coming from hidden violins.

'Get a message to Chumley?' she queried. 'Ask him if me and Jade can join him on the road?'

He shook his head and raised his brows unbelievingly.

'You'd go that far? Ye gods! Look! I have a better idea.' He

254

handed her an Essex newspaper. There was an advertisement pencilled round with thick blue ink. 'They are friends of mine. Their son and I were school chums and have never lost touch. He's something of an artist now, and it was through him I learned of the agent Vivien Bentine. She's the one who's making Con's name for him.'

Moira read the advertisement.

'Northmays Retreat,'
London Road,
THUNDERSLEY,
Essex,
Top of Bread and Cheese Hill.

Moira's mind was racing. Yani's air of disbelief was making her have a doubt or two. Surely the long ago story that had begun in China had worked itself out by now? People being murdered happened elsewhere, never near to hand. Surely she had left that extraordinary Chinese problem behind in Jordan Street?

She thought of Daisy's kitchen, how warm and homely and down-to-earth it was. She heard in her head Sid's jolly chuckle. He really was a very nice, very jocular man. Things like murder most foul, and doll-like young people being in danger of their lives, simply didn't belong in such a nice, ordinary place as Shelley Road. Suddenly she wanted to hide her face with her hands and cry. She felt so lost, and even in spite of Yani and the Wrights, so impossibly alone. Was she always destined to be the outsider looking in? Part and parcel of folks households, where she was accepted, but never truly belonged?

Daisy and Sid had made her so welcome, had taken her to their hearts, but she had been and still was, a lodger in their house. Oh, she had done everything possible to make herself useful. She had dusted and cleaned, had helped Sid in the garden, had avidly learned and tried out all of Daisy's wonderful recipes. Had come to adore the two lovely cats. In fact she had done anything and everything to become part of their family. And in so doing, had come almost to love them and to hope ... But she could never be loved by them like they adored their Cissy.

And what of Jade? As always, Jade had put out her winsome young self to ingratiate where she thought she was best off. And where that was, at least recently, had been firmly under Daisy Wright's motherly wing. Before that, Harriet. Previously Stavros, who handed out bread and jam, then River Pearl, and then Moira herself, being, she suspected, a very poor third in the Jordan Street household.

Did she belong nowhere, nowhere at all in the vastness of the outside world?

Deep down Moira knew that in spite of the kicks and cuffs, old Flo had actually loved her in her rough tough way. Even to doing what she thought best when she believed there was danger about. Yes, danger did not seem such an unrealistic thing down that way. Nor thieving and lying, brutality, and even murder. Anything was possible in an area like Jordan Street. Even in secretive old Jordan Lodge that had been a whorehouse once. It was a building where strangers drifted in from all over the world, where only Flo's air of ferocious command could make drunken sailors toe the line. Even so, that sombre old house so stolidly enclosed behind brick walls, had spelt safety and security for Moira herself.

Fred and Flo had been towers of strength for her to lean upon or hide behind. Dear Fred, who she could love and tease but never really talk to, because what she said would never fully sink in. She truly adored him though, and would give the earth to have him swing her up in his arms and give her that great hug of his. And dear, unpredictable Flo, look how she had defended her, even kept her away from school! A lady professing to be not very brave where officials were concerned, but even so, defying the authorities, rightly or wrongly, believing she was doing the best for young Moir.

For the umpteenth time, Moira wished herself back inside Jordan Lodge.

'Yani,' she whispered, 'could you— Could you take me back to Flo? Jade and me could hide away in the attic as before, and we'd be safe enough. I'm sure of it.'

'Was River Pearl?' he countered and shook his head. 'No, Moira mine, I think that Thundersley is the best place for us.'

'I'll have to think about it,' she told him desperately. 'Besides, how can I even try to think up a reason for leaving? I mean, one that Daisy and Sid would believe? And they must be

256

made to think we're coming back one day. It would be too hurtful else.'

'The rent's paid,' he told her casually, 'so it shouldn't matter to them too much.'

'Yani!' Moira was suddenly fiercely angry. 'You don't understand people like the Wrights at all, do you? The rent would be the furthest thing from their minds. They are mine and Jade's friends, and they'd walk through fire and water to see us all right. They have their own code of honour, you know, and sense of fair play. Sneaking off to some God-forsaken place in Essex would not be in their scheme of things.'

'I can't see your reasoning, sweet,' he pointed out. 'They will go along with any excuse you care to make. Just tell them that you have to go away for a while. Tell them that I have offered you a situation in the office.'

'That will go down very well!' she told him sharply. 'Don't you think they just might smell a rat? After all, you've been sending messages and lots of red roses to their house. Hardly the actions of someone about to offer a girl a job!' She laughed, a hard, sad little sound. 'Mightn't they believe there'd be a few strings attached?'

He frowned impatiently. She caught her breath, not liking his attitude, suspicion rising to the fore as she asked, 'Incidentally, are there? Strings, I mean. And couldn't I still stay in their home if it was only a job you were offering? How would I explain taking Jade away? Honestly! They'd never understand, nor accept such a yarn!'

'No strings I swear it,' he told her. 'Hand on heart. You have misunderstood, Moira mine, and I'm very sorry to have upset you. I'd cut out my tongue before I'd have you believe badly of me.'

She was not convinced and he knew it, since outrage was flashing like sparks in her eyes. His tone grew even more apologetic.

'I did not mean to slight them, nor offend you.'

'But you often do, don't you?' she said, fighting her tears. 'You are so set on having your own way, that you'll ride roughshod over people's feelings, no matter what. You tried to get your own way with me the last time we were here. Now I think you're trying to again. Northmays Retreat?' Her laugh

257

was a soft, pained sound. 'And to think that Cissy believes you truly love me!'

'I do really love and adore you,' he told her clearly. 'And I shall always. What is more, I intend to marry you one day.'

'Oh Yani, don't!' Moira sighed impatiently. 'I'm not so foolish as to believe that.'

'I mean it.' There was urgency in his voice as he tried to make her believe him. 'I love you, I want you, and I intend to marry you. This school business has made me jump the gun a bit, that's all.'

She merely sat there, opposite him, glaring in the way she used to when defending herself from Flo.

'Darling,' he pleaded, 'please don't look at me like that. I love you! Don't you understand? I have every intention of proving it for good and all, believe me. Not only to you, but to everyone!'

'I beg your pardon?' she faltered, uncertain now, the wind taken completely from her sails. 'You actually, I mean you intend to ignore your parents and ... marry me?'

'If you'll have me, yes! Just as soon as it can be arranged. I mean it, my sweet darling. Honestly.'

She was looking across the table at him, melting, her soul in her eyes. She saw the love in his expression and heard it in his voice. He loved her like that? Really? This was a dream. It must be! As if from far away she heard him continue.

'And sweetheart, in the meantime, please accept this.' As if in a dream, she sat there watching. He had reached into his pocket and taken from it a small black velvet-covered box. He passed it over to her. 'Open it,' he commanded softly, 'and then let me put it on your finger. Sweetheart, believe me, I love you and I'll never let you go. We will be engaged, and that will give me the strength to stand up to my family.'

'And what of your fiancé?' she quavered, still unable to take it all in.

'I love Dacia, but in a very different kind of way. We have known each other all our lives. Probably she feels the same as I do about the wedding both families are trying to foist upon us. The truth of it is, that Dacia's family owns many hundreds of olive trees. Which, my Moira, makes them very rich indeed on Kerkyra. Her family and mine, joined together can become

258

quite a force to be reckoned with. But truly, the only union I am interested in is yours and mine.'

Moira gazed speechlessly down at the diamond engagement ring flashing fire and coloured stars under the lights. Still unable to believe that all this was actually happening, she allowed Yani to take the ring from the box and slip it onto her engagement finger.

'Now, sweetheart,' he coaxed. 'Is it so unnatural for a man to wish to keep his fiancé safe? Is it so out of this world for me to wish to hold you to me for ever? To own you body and soul?'

'Don't!' she replied in panic. 'Don't rush me. I can't think!'

'What is there to think about?' he teased. 'I love you and you love me. Say it! Say that you love me!'

'I love you,' she wavered, then, 'oh blow it, Yani! I think I'm going to cry.'

'One must never cry at a celebration,' he told her firmly and signalled to the watching waiter. The man came forward to accept the order for champagne.

After that the rest of the evening passed in a dream. Moira was gusted along with Yani's enthusiasm, not even objecting when he told her of his brightest idea. That it would be kindest and best all round, to be honest about the engagement, but to pretend she was leaving the Wright's establishment, in order to meet his mother in France. His mother actually did have friends who lived in Paris, he said, and had sometimes visited them there.

'But it isn't true,' she protested.

'It is only a white lie, beloved. It will be best for people to believe that, rather than know we are with the Appletons, the people who run the retreat. Charles, their artist son and I, were students together.' He smiled into her eyes. 'Of course, we can tell my parents the truth – eventually. My mother is away, back home in Kerkyra of course. My father will not be returning to England from a business trip for at least another three weeks. When he does and learns what has happened between us, he will roar like a lion and decide to come chasing after us. So that is another reason why we must not let our whereabouts be known. We need to give him time to take it all in. He will, eventually. So that is another reason for keeping our true whereabouts quiet.'

259

'But our engagement?'

'We can tell the Wrights of course, but not even Cissy must know where we are.'

'She looks upon me as a sister and—'

'She'll tell Chumley. After that, there will be Con in on our secret, and for all we know after that, Uncle Tom Cobley and all. Will that be wise? If you are truly set on keeping Jade's whereabouts secret, I mean? No, you must say that we are going to France.'

France? Moira thought shakily. That was a pipe dream if there ever was one. She had never even been to Southend. All the talk about a place in Essex was exciting enough. Exciting, daring and yes, very frightening. But a foreign country? Still, what Yani said was making sense. She owed it to River Pearl to spirit Jade away at the first whisper of danger. And danger there was. School authorities would poke their noses in, ask questions, be open and above-board about everything. And in their determination to find out all there was about Jade, they could easily let Kung Chin into the picture too.

Even so, she thought sadly, engagements were supposed to be wonderful occasions, whereas all this seemed so muddled and sly!

'Yani,' she murmered, 'may I show Daisy my ring? As proof, I mean?'

'Por, por, por!' he exclaimed and shook his head, 'You still do not fully trust me, eh? Of course you must show everyone your engagement ring. I want the whole world to know.'

She was grateful for small mercies, but a niggling little voice kept pointing out that since both his parents were miles away, and not expected to be back for some time, no one in the Bertos family would hear the news for quite a while. Still, since getting Jade safely away was the most important thing, the little fib could be forgiven ...

Daisy and Sid looked at the engagement ring and smiled and nodded like two clockwork dolls. They were pleased for Moira, happy that they had been right, that darling Cissy's employer was a young gentleman after all. They accepted that Moira and Jade would be away for a little while. A trip to a mutual meeting place like France was far better than the long voyage to Kerkyra. And were overjoyed at the thought that Moira and Jade would be returning all in good time.

In actual fact, there was no truth in this. Yani intended to get a lovely new home for Moira, Jade and himself to share when they left Northmays. In the meantime, the fib would let the jolly nice couple down in the gentlest possible way.

Since it was now quite late, Daisy and Sid excused themselves, went to bed and left Yani and Moira to their own devices. Yani got up from his chair, stretched, and with studied care, turned off the gas light. Moira's heart began beating too quickly. Catching her look of panic, he returned to his own chair, saying nothing at all.

It was warm in the little kitchen and the range fire glowed red. Quite suddenly the room, all shadowy and orange, seemed unbearably safe and beautiful. Moira did not want to leave it. She glanced surreptitiously at Yani's profile, but could tell nothing from his expression. He seemed stern, now that the gas had been turned off and the night had hidden the usual softness of his velvet-brown eyes.

'Yani,' she heard herself whispering for no reason at all. 'They are so nice, so trusting! They'll be hurt when Cissy tells them the truth.'

'What? That my mother is not in France?' he asked easily. 'How can Cissy possibly learn that? It is not the Bertos way to tell servants about our comings and goings, unless they must make preparations for the same. Nor do we tell them about our private lives. They are told only what they need to know.'

'I'm sorry. I thought that you and Cissy...'

'Cissy and I exchange a word or two first thing sometimes, but she knows her place. She would not dare to question me about the secrecy of our engagement. There, are you satisfied?'

She felt put down by his lordly air, and rather uncomfortable, but relaxed as he added, 'Don't worry! Chumley and Con are my friends, and to a certain extent, Cissy shares my confidences too. But the time is not right for anyone to know our business, my sweet. Don't you agree?'

'Yes,' she replied, but still felt unsure.

Yani left his chair and walked towards her. His head bent slowly and without knowing how it came about Moira found herself in his arms.

261

'Come with me now,' he whispered against her ear. 'Now, tonight. Let me take you away.'

'I can't,' she whispered, stiffening. 'Jade is asleep. I must get her ready. Pack her things.'

'Without Jade,' murmered. 'Just for tonight?'

Moira froze, feeling a nameless terror. With an abruptness that was startling, Yani stood up, turned away from her and left the house.

She sat there, stunned, unable to move. She thought she heard the car engine purr into life, but was not sure. The first flutter of fear writhed in her brain. Moira ran outside, but the car, taking Yani with it, had gone. She had sent him away, just as her overreaction to Con's kiss had sent him away too. Dear God, she thought wildly, would she never learn?

Yani would believe she had rejected his offer of help, she thought and was conscious of desperation flooding through every fibre of her being. He would let her try to get out of trouble alone. What if they sent Jade to school? There would be enquiries made, official enquiries. Questions asked about the sudden appearance of a Chinese child who had, to all intent and purpose, been left in the world to survive alone. The School Board might have Jade put in a Home. A terrible soulless place like the ones Flo had always been on about. Jade would hate it all and be terribly afraid. Even worse, Li Tzu's enemies might find her, might snatch her away, hurt her as they had hurt and finally destroyed dearest River Pearl.

What on earth could she do? Where could she go without Yani to help her?

She needed Con! Dear God, how she needed the big man with iris-blue eyes and such devil-may-care ways. But he had gone out of her life for ever, she grieved. He now mixed with people in a much higher class, folk from the top drawer who lived in the posh part of London, the West End! And Con would be at ease there, she thought sadly, because Con would be at ease anywhere in the world. Con could even be happy and confident trudging the roads alongside Chumley. He was not a gentleman like Yani, not born with a silver spoon in his mouth. But his kiss had stirred a wild racing thing inside her. An emotion quite impossible to describe. One could be put in Con's pocket and feel taken care of, safe!

What of Yani? How did he really fit in her scheme of things? She loved him, of course she did. Cissy had been barking up the wrong tree. Dear old Cissy, who had as good as said it was the kind of love that one felt for the film stars up there on the screen. But what did Cissy know? Indeed, what did Moira herself know?

Moira crept up to her room and struggled to make sense of her conflicting emotions all night long...

Chapter Twenty-Two

'Wake up, wake up!' Daisy seemed to be calling from a million miles away. Moira came back to consciousness. 'Here, drink this cuppa.' Daisy told her briskly, 'Jade is all ready, and I've packed her things. She's very excited about going on a big boat, I can tell you. Oh, and we've just had a message from Master Yani. He will be sending the car for you both in an hour. Something about not missing the boat in Dover? You've lots of packing to do, Moira. My goodness! I've never known things to happen so fast.'

Moira sat up in the brass bed. The lavendar walls enclosed her and the many china cats with their twinkling glass eyes seemed to wink. Her heart began to dance. Yani had not forsaken her after all. Everything was going to be all right. But it was going to be a wrench, leaving Daisy and Sid, not forgetting Cissy who had turned out to be so nice.

'I hope you like France,' Daisy was saying as she whisked about, emptying Moira's things from the chest of drawers. 'And that Yani's mother likes you. Mind you. She'll be a stone-hearted woman if she don't. You must send Sid and me a postcard and don't forget to let me know the day you're coming back. I'll make a special dinner for us that night. How does savoury meat pudding sound?'

'Wonderful, Daisy,' Moira whispered and suddenly wanted to cry.

She did cry an hour later, as Daisy kissed her goodbye and Sid's work-worn hands enclosed hers.

'Goodbye,' she whispered. 'Thank you for everything. Oh dear! Daisy, I hate goodbyes!'

'You'll be back before you know it,' Daisy said stoutly. 'Just you wait and see. The time will fly by and you'll be with us again. 'Bye, Moira God Bless.'

'Cheerio, my two luverly ladies,' Sid roared and gave them a military salute.

The car moved off. Jade, looking solemn, watched in silence as Daisy and Sid faded from view. Then she tugged at Moira's sleeve and asked, 'How soon shall we be at the boat?'

'I don't know, Jade. But whatever happens, we must pick up Yani first. We're going on a holiday. Won't that be nice?'

'Is your young man very rich?' Jade demanded. 'Aunty Daisy said he was.'

'I think so, yes. But that doesn't matter does it, minx? What matters is that Mr Bertos is very kind and very nice.'

'Will he be kind and nice to me?'

'Why Jade?' Moira asked reprovingly. 'Isn't a lovely holiday going to be enough?'

'Oh yes,' Jade replied and smiled her enigmatic smile. 'But it will be even better if Yani—'

'Uncle Yani if you please.'

'If he's rich!'

'Sid isn't rich, yet you liked him.'

'But Uncle Sid isn't coming with us on holiday.'

'Jade,' Moira said firmly, 'you disappoint me, you really do. Instead of trying to work out all that you can squeeze out of my fiancé, wouldn't it be better for you to put your mind on the presents it would be nice to bring back? Something really nice for Daisy and very special for Sid? It isn't good to be so concerned with what you're going to get out of everything. I despair of you sometimes.'

'But you wouldn't leave me, would you?' Jade's tone became urgent. 'Would you?'

'Of course not!'

Jade's expression, which for one moment had held fear, relaxed. Then she returned to her subject.

'I can bring Uncle Sid and Aunty Daisy heaps of lovely presents,' she said in her high pretty way. 'If Uncle Yani gives me lots of money!'

'Oh!' Moira replied and shrugged despairingly. 'You never give up, do you, Jade?'

'But Harriet said...'

'I don't want to hear!' Moira snapped. 'That lady has gone from our lives.'

'Aren't you happy?' Jade asked and looked as solemn as an owl. So solemn that Moira laughed and nodded and took Jade's hand to squeeze it in her own.

The car stopped outside a bank in the main road. Yani came out of the building, waved and smiled as he joined them.

'All set?' he asked cheerfully.

'Yes,' Moira replied, feeling nervous all over again and suddenly very shy. 'It has all been a rush, but yes, we're all set.'

'When will we reach the boat that's to take us to France, uncle Yani?' Jade asked and smiled so prettily that Yani laughed and ruffled her shiny black hair.

'I don't know, poppet. We will just have to wait and see, eh?'

'I have never been to a foreign country before. I want to go on the boat and see all the different things.'

'And so you shall.' he promised. 'No problem! But first things first. I have decided to take Moira and you to a wonderful place I know of in the country. While we're there, we will visit the seaside lots of times, because it's only a stone's throw away. And while we are there we shall go on all kinds of boats, and you shall eat saucers of cockles, and we'll buy lots of toffee apples, and sticks of rock. Won't that be fun?'

'It will be wonderful,' Jade replied and her melon-seed eyes sparkled with delight. 'I have never been to the country nor to the seaside.'

'Then you are in for some lovely surprises, Jade,' he told her. He turned to Moira, 'And I hope, my darling, that so are you. You're going to love the countryside.'

'And Northmays? Is it a nice place?'

'Very. It's situated near Bread and Cheese Hill.'

'That's a funny name.'

'Appleton told me that there's an old ruin near the top of the hill, called Jarvis Hall; it was believed to have been used as a nunnery a long time ago. There was a kind of revolving table at the front of the place, which is supposed to have been for serving out meals for the hungry and poor. Probably bread and cheese. But we're not interested in the past, are we?' He was happy and teasing now. 'Surely only in the future? Our future!'

266

'Yes, oh yes!' Moira breathed and beamed at Jade before turning back to him. 'We are going to love it all, Yani. Every minute of it. And all these old grey streets will seem to be a million miles away. Even ... even Jordan Street will seem to be like a place on another world.'

'Ah! Jordan Street,' Yani replied. 'I wonder how they are all getting on? I should think they've put the fish fryer in an asylum by now. He is quite crazy they say.'

Moira's golden bubble of hope and anticipation shattered and flew away. Seeing her expression, Yani swore under his breath.

'Oh God! I'm so sorry, sweet. I quite forgot that you have a distaste for the man. It's just that I'm so pleased to have you away from that area that I had to crow. He'll never find you, darling. No one will. Besides, Dave Dilley's out of this planet. They say he wanders around, talking to himself, and cackling, and looking for that brother-in-law of his. He has not remembered that the man died in the gutter late last year, Stavros told me. So, if he's incapable of remembering that recent event, he has probably forgotten that he ever knew you.'

Moira found herself shivering and wishing that she could believe what Yani said. And in spite of the fact that the car was whizzing away from the places she knew, at that moment the evil presence of Dave Dilley seemed very near. A picture of his mournful, ghostly face was now weaving like spiders' webs in the forefront of her mind.

They sped along the London Road, away from the main thoroughfare, and now the countryside took over. For ever and ever it seemed, an endless green vista stretching far way even to the outskirts of the horizon.

Eventually they came to Thundersley village and finally turned off the main road and down a lane on the far right. Then they reached huge opened gates that were flanked by tall poplar trees. Ahead sprawled the great grey home that, according to Yani, had been the Appletons residence for at least two hundred years. The car wheels churned over a gravel pathway flanked by smooth lawns, ornamental shrubs and flower beds, towards a short flight of stone steps. Aware of the girls' awed silence as they stared through the car windows, Yani teased,

'Well, what do you think?'

267

'We ... we're to stay here?' Moira found herself all but whispering. 'Isn't it? ... I mean, it's very grand!'

'It might seem so,' he told her blithely, 'to people hailing from places like Jordan Street.' He chucked her playfully under the chin when he saw the colour staining her cheeks bright red. 'But, Moira mine, it isn't half decent enough for someone like you.'

'Uncle Yani,' Jade cut in with an air of self-importance, 'this is a very nice place. I like it.'

'I'm sure that you do, kitten,' he told her. 'You of all people seem to know a good thing when you see it. I am also sure that Mrs Appleton will be like putty in your pretty little hands.'

Moira glanced at him sharply, thinking that she had heard a hint of sarcasm in his tone. But his eyes were as velvet-soft as ever, his smile as sweet. There was of course no disguising the gleam in Jade's eye. Little minx, Moira thought, she's going to enjoy all this. Talk about delusions of grandeur, as Stavros might say. I wonder if I'm doing the right thing? Jade will hate it when we have to leave.

The car stopped and without waiting for the chauffeur to open the door, Jade turned the handle and jumped out. Moira stayed where she was.

'It certainly looks quite perfect ... for a retreat, Yani,' she said gravely. 'But, I'm not sure that...'

'Sweetheart,' he was looking at her adoringly. 'Don't keep Morris waiting. Come along.'

She looked at the chauffeur who was standing to attention by the door on her side, then back to Yani, saying, 'It is all above board, isn't it? I mean, you're not going to try to persuade me...'

'To give in to me?' he teased. 'We are engaged, aren't we? Yes, to be married one day. Do you honestly believe that I would wish to dishonour my own future wife? Por, por, por, darling. You should be ashamed!'

She allowed Morris to help her down. She waited for Yani to reach her and took his arm, then smiling up into his eyes, she apologised.

'I'm so sorry, Yani. I shouldn't have thought, have said...'

'Hush, my sweet. You have had some bally rotten knocks in your time. But that's all over now. Don't worry! Aren't you

anxious to explore Northmays? I know that I am. But first—'
He took a whole five pound note from his pocket, a fortune,
and handed it to the chauffeur. 'Thank you, Morris. You'd
better cut off now.'

The chauffeur saluted.

'Thank you sir,' he looked swiftly at Moira, adding,
'madam.' Then he turned on his heels, went to the vehicle,
started the engine and drove smoothly away. As he did so the
door of Northmays opened and an old, stoop-shouldered
craggy-looking gentleman confronted them.

'Welcome sir, madam,' he said, 'I am Carpenter. Won't you
please come in?' He snapped his fingers and servants came
forward to pick up the luggage that Morris had piled on the
bottom step, then ushered Moira, Jade and Yani inside.

With Yani's hand held possessively under her elbow, Moira
look around. It was very swish everywhere, with lots of red
carpet and dark oak panelling, gold-framed paintings and
mirrors carved beautifully with grapevines, fruits and cheru-
bim. Crystal peardrops hung from huge light shades. The
massive carved reception desk looked as though it belonged in
the study of a king. The atmosphere was warm and cosy and
overall there was a subtle, very pleasant, spicy perfume.

Before Moira could fully take in everything, a couple came to
greet them. Two people, male and female, who looked impossibly alike for all they were man and wife. Both were plump and
plain. Mr Appleton wore horn-rimmed spectacles which made
his blue eyes seem rather large; Mrs Appleton wore pinz-nez.
Moira felt shy and awkward as she took in turn the extended
hands, but her unease soon vanished at the warmth of their
greeting.

'Ah!' Mr Appleton was saying, 'Charles's friends. Welcome.'

'How nice!' Mrs Appleton enthused, her eyes fixed longest
on Jade who was now quiet, watchful, taking everything in.

'How do you do?' Yani greeted them and formally introduced everyone. 'This is Miss Moira O'Malley and her ward,
Miss Li Jade.'

'How sweet!' Mrs Appleton cooed. 'And as I understand it,
our two charming young ladies wish to share a double room?'

'If you please,' Yani replied, and Moira was hard put not to
spurt out her relief. So there were to be no tricks. She should

269

have trusted Yani. She had the grace to feel ashamed. 'And,' Yani continued, 'thank you both for taking us at such short notice. But you see, Miss O'Malley really does need to rest.'

'Of course, of course!' Mrs Appleton's tone was immediately sympathetic. 'We are a retreat in the fullest sense, and will make it our business to see that you have peace and privacy at all times. And, if it is agreeable to you, I myself would like to ensure that Miss Li thoroughly enjoys her stay.'

Good heavens, Moira thought and wanted to laugh out loud. Jade is as usual, going to fall on her feet.

'Carpenter will show you to your rooms,' Mr Appleton told them. 'And we look forward to you joining us in the dining room later on.'

'Thank you,' Yani smiled.

Carpenter had a nice look about him. His white shirt collar seemed too large for his neck, but his dark suit was of good material and well cut. His shoes squeaked as he walked. Moira rather fancied that Carpenter had been with the family for years. Jade seemed to think so too – and that as such, he was quite important. She slipped her hand into his, looked up into his face and began chatting nineteen to the dozen.

'It looks as though that young lady will be kept well amused,' Yani said quietly. 'And that, my darling, will give you and me all the time in the world.'

Moira, watching him, marvelled at how at ease he was, how wonderfully in command of the situation. Yani had been quietly courteous at all times, self-assured, and a gentleman through and through. And the most breathtaking thing of all, was that he was actually in love with her!

She caught her breath at the thought. She had never dreamed that all her childhood fantasies would one day come true, that a handsome Greek prince would come to take her away as his bride. Yet here she was, with a diamond engagement ring glittering like a beacon on her finger, walking with the love of her life holding her arm.

They followed Carpenter up a wide staircase that had oil paintings of country scenes on the walls. There was a portrait of an olden day gentleman, who looked rather like Mr Appleton, astride a horse. An ancestor, Moira thought, and believed that

270

the artist hadn't been half so talented as Con, so far as horses were concerned.

'Your room, miss,' Carpenter said and opened a door.

'And mine?' Yani asked.

'Next to this one, sir. You'll come with me?'

Alone at last Moira and Jade stood side by side, silently taking in their room. It was large and grand. The furniture was old and dark, polished till it gleamed. The overall colour scheme was beige and blue with a huge Persian carpet reflecting those colours fully covering the floor.

'I should think,' Moira said slowly, 'that this room is meant for the high and mighty, Jade, not a couple of girls from Jordan Street.'

Jade smiled and lovingly slipped her arm round Moira's waist.

'It is right for you,' she said firmly, 'and also for my own humble self.'

'Oh!' Moira's eyes went tear-bright. 'You remember River Pearl's way of saying things? Never forget her, Jade, nor that you owe her your life. If all she said is true, you belong to a place even grander than this.'

'And when my lord father finds me, and takes me to live in his palace, you shall come too. And you will stay with me for ever,' Jade said with utter conviction. 'I shall tell him of River Pearl, and I shall tell him all about you.'

'I don't know about living in your shadow for ever, my girl,' Moira laughed, 'and not so much of the old flannel, eh? Now what are you after? Stop twiddling that bell rope.'

'I'm hungry,' Jade replied. 'Carpenter said to pull the rope if I wanted something. Do you think they'll have lots of nice things to eat?'

'Slugs and snails and puppydogs' tails I wouldn't wonder,' Moira laughed. 'Now, little minx, just you stop playing with that rope and come here!'

'Shan't!' Jade's eyes were sparkling, and she wrinkled her nose in defiance.

'Right! You're for it!' Moira met her half way. Within seconds the pair of them were laughing and teasing each other and having the time of their lives. Then Yani knocked on the door and came in. He looked at them both, smiling, his expression loving and warm.

'Poppet,' he said to Moira, 'you don't look much older than your ward. Oh, my sweet, we are going to have such fun!'

Life after that, Moira thought blissfully, was like a dream come true. Yani took them on outings. Where he was concerned, money was no object, but it was the walking that Moira loved best. The shopping sprees were what Jade enjoyed most, of course. She proclaimed her intense dissatisfaction when Yani told her that, no, he did not drive motor cars himself, and indeed had no inclination to do so. Adding that he was used to taking his ease on journeys while others did the work and that, no, he would not take driving lessons and he had no intention of buying even the smallest car.

Jade sulked prettily, told Mrs Appleton how hard done by she was, the upshot being that Mrs Appleton and her husband, who both drove cars, took the girl everywhere they went.

'Thank goodness she's off our hands!' Yani said, 'come here!'

It came as a surprise to learn that Yani was in many ways quite lazy. He liked lounging about reading, or just sitting listening to music on the gramophone. He laughed and shrugged when Moira asked him to join her on her early morning walks, though afternoons and evenings were a different matter. They would walk to Tarpots, the Thundersley inn, or else ramble along overgrown pathways, climb stiles and cross the fields. They would talk heaps and Yani would make exaggerated promises about the wedding they would have, the home they would share, and the family they would raise.

'And care for Jade?' she would always ask. He would smile and shrug.

'While she needs us, of course. But she will go on to bigger and better things. Jade will always land on her feet.'

'Yani!' she had been outraged. 'You are being unkind!'

She had seethed all night over Yani's insensitivity. Men would never understand. Never see that under her calm facade, or beyond the iron self control Jade had learned at River Pearl's knee. The law was to be brave and to never, ever, lose face.

The next morning, very early, Moira crept out of bed, dressed and went downstairs to the enormous kitchen. The servants were up and at it already. Moira accepted their invitation, shyly put, and sat at the table and had a cup of tea. Within a minute or two, she and the staff had become friends. Leaving a message for Jade that she had gone for a walk, she set out. From then on, Moira loved those long, lonely walks, her explorations, her meeting with farm labourers, and women she met on the way, the people she asked for directions.

Quite soon she came to know that across the fields, and too far to view from the windows of Northmays, was the sea. It bounced and rushed backwards and forwards in such a boisterous fashion and stretched far away, white crested, sparkling until it mingled with the far distant sky. And Moira would breathe in the salt tang in the air and the smell of seaweed, sand and mud; loving it, in awe of it, respecting it, and as fascinated by it as she had been on that very first time.

It had been on the day after their arrival, when Yani had actually risen early and had been all out to impress. The morning tide was tumbling over the stones, washing them, rattling them, leaving little winding lanes of white bubbles that glittered coldly before being sucked away by the shale. And Moira had gasped and clung onto Yani's hand, wanting to cry because of the beauty of it all. Jade had just stood there, eyes wide, momentarily transfixed. Then she had quietly and with great dignity walked away from them, and began gathering shells. Yani had whispered against Moira's ear, 'This is only the beginning, Moira mine. I will show you the world.'

'Surely,' she had whispered, 'this is the world? The very heart and soul of it! I – I never knew that such majesty existed. I don't think I can ever thank you enough for bringing me here.'

'You can thank me,' he whispered hoarsely. 'You know how you can thank me! You can have no idea how much I want to make love to you.'

'And I love you,' she whispered, her heart in her eyes. 'I always have.'

'Well then? Oh my God, you do things to me! The way you're looking at me right now, I— Right now, I need you. My arms ache to hold you. I want to caress you, kiss you all over, make you mine. I want you to make love to me!'

'Yani! Sh! Jade might hear!'

'She is wise beyond her years. In her land women are

273

expected to do the right and proper thing. Please a man! Darling, I'll never rest until I know that you feel that way about me. I will never rest until I have made you mine.'

'And neither will I,' Moira had replied daringly, carried away by the moment. 'Oh Yani, isn't this a wonderful romance? You – you have made all my dreams come true.'

He held her away from him then, and had looked into her upturned face. His expression had become rueful as he replied.

'How innocent you are, my sweet. Innocent and beautiful, and I will always love and cherish you. Come along, sweetheart, we will help young Jade to gather shells.'

Life assumed a joyous unreality after that. Yani was generous to a fault, always insisting on buying Moira and Jade nice things. He and Moira spent many hours alone, since Jade's outings with Mrs Appleton had become a regular thing. Even so, moan and groan though Jade did, Moira insisted that she spent an hour each day learning things.

'I don't care that I'm a wicked old toad,' she would say firmly. 'And I couldn't care tuppence that you're wishing me dead. When your honourable lord father comes for you at last, I don't want him to find that you're a little Miss Ignorant. I promised River Pearl to look after you, so like it or lump it, my girl, you'll do as you're told.'

'I hate you!'

'That's sad because I happen to love you. Shall we get on?'

Jade obeyed.

Northmays was away from the true crest of the hill, the ruins of Jarvis Hall being higher. Moira loved walking among the old tumbled walls. The place had an atmosphere all of its own. It was crumbling and mysterious, and had been empty for ever it seemed. It was ivy-covered and a haven for birds. At the bottom of the hill the village sprawled, a picturesque mixture of old and new. Tarpots Inn, black and white, looking as though it belonged in Elizabethan times, was Yani's favourite place. It was wonderful inside, with its oak beams, pewter, horse brasses and huge open fires.

After evenings there together, Moira and Yani would walk home. When the moon rode the sky like a goddess in a silver gown, Yani would slip his arms round Moira and hold her close. It was romantic and wonderful, and the wind soughing through the trees sounded like the sea. Moira's heart would dance and she would hold up her face to be kissed. Then Yani would groan, become passionate, would beg! But always, when he became too insistent, too daring, she would hold her breath and stiffen. And hate herself though she did, she could never rid herself of the evil spectre of Dave Dilley.

At such moments her fear and confusion merged into a crying need. She would think of Con, her protector and friend, from whom she had run. Dearest Con, who was so big and masterful, yet even so, would never understand. But something rather different was squeezing up inside her now. Making her want to run away from Yani, who was proving so different from the fantasy ...

Chapter Twenty-Three

Con was bored, outraged, revolted. Society, at least Rowena's type of society made him feel bilious. He felt that almost all that her crowd said or did was completely incidental to real living. It was a round of sham, sham and, God help him, more sham!

He looked up still scowling, as the young woman who owned the building he lived and worked in, arrived. Entering like the lady she was, into the studio that they shared. It was very large and light and jam-packed with people all jabbering and drinking, and calling each other darling, dear or my sweet. Stuff and nonsense of course. Empty words, empty phrases, superficial people. Some being worse than others.

Con watched Rowena Wray, dressed in blue and wearing ridiculously expensive filagree jewellery, as she headed towards him. She had never known what it was to want for something that couldn't be paid for. It showed because she was so bloody confident. Of life, of her future, of just about everything. The poor fought and struggled every day of their lives. Fear was always present, the gnawing horror of kids going hungry, of unpaid bills, dread and awe of officials who more often than not treated them like dirt. And the inbred misgiving and distaste of the snobbery of the so-called better classes. Worse, the middle-class, the comfortably-off types who accepted the poor merely as their lackeys. Who saw them only as insignificant cogs worth less than nothing in the scheme of things.

Thank God Rowena and her family were of the genuine high class. The élite who had nothing to prove. Who just *were*! As for accepting a pseudo arty-farty crowd like this lot, he thought sourly, Rowena and her intimates had gone too far. Leaned over backwards in fact. Probably just to please Rowena. Looking round in distaste, Con realized that his friend accepted people that even the ruffians of Market Street would find hard to digest. But then, that was her way. Rowena treated everyone, rich, poor, or just plain down-to-earth sorts like himself, as equals, never losing either her charm or courtesy.

In fact, he thought moodily, the beautiful young woman sometimes got right under his skin. Then he would forget that they belonged in different worlds. He liked to see her working. Rowena had a subtle grace in her movements. She held her paint brush and moved her wrists like someone intent on bringing about gentle magic. Her completed canvases held just that. Charm and delicacy and a kind of airy beauty that made a fellow want to catch his breath.

Now he watched in silence as she advanced. Smiling at this one, exchanging a word with the next, a warm greeting to an individual she had not seen for some time. Rowena was tall, with a willowy allure that was refined rather than ostentatious. Her features were classic, her cheekbones high, and she had the kind of mouth artists dreamed of. He liked and respected her immensely, but that was all. She had been fortunate, merely coasting along, never having to meet real life head on like gutsy young Moira O'Malley. The girl he could never forget. A picture of her face, blessed with such large luminous golden-brown eyes came into his mind. He rapidly blinked it away.

Rowena was nearing, scooping up her honey-coloured Pekinese dog on the way.

'Well, darling,' she asked lightly as she reached him. 'How do you feel about the very new look? Colourful and rather fun, don't you think?'

'If you're asking for my opinion on Vivien's bright orange lips, clashing red blouse and purple skirt, not forgetting that her eyes look like the chimney sweep's punched her,' he replied sarcastically, 'the answer is, I think she's mad. I think you're mad to encourage her and—' he looked her directly in the eye, 'if you must know, I think this whole damned set-up's mad.'

'Oh dear!' Rowena said sadly, looking over his shoulder. 'It's like that is it? Now you'll be swearing like a trooper for the rest of the evening.' She glanced over her shoulder. 'Someone's uncovered your special painting. That's not good, is it?'

'No!'

'I've noticed that it's shrouded whenever strangers are about to come in. I can't think why. It's immensely beautiful, and the girl in the foreground looks out of this world! Who is she, Con? A rather special someone who actually got away?'

'She was never mine,' he replied, adding cryptically, 'sadly.'

'Poor sweet,' she was trying to be sympathetic, but there was a faint twinkle in her blue eyes. 'You really are in one of your devastatingly temperamental moods, aren't you? Would you like us all to go? Every blessed one? I can shoo them all out, take them to Greshams, who are by the way, brilliant at catering for last minute affairs?'

'And have Vivien get even madder than she usually is with me?' he asked, resigned. 'I thought this evening was meant to be for artists, about art, and for the meeting of other painters' minds. Not forgetting the scribblers who pretend to write about creativity, but always manage to dish up some dirt. And, Lord help me, they're the only reason I agreed to all this. To go along with Viv purely for the publicity she's so fond of. But who the hell invited Julian Romaro? As for his prissy friend Fenton, ugh! Vivien actually called the little prick a Beauty Specialist!'

'He is!'

'Specialist? The man's a moron, and I could do a damned sight better myself. Who gave out the invites I'd like to know?'

'I did. Everyone wants to wear Julian's creations, including me. And Fenton's make up tricks are all but art forms in themselves. Anyway, darling, they both fancy that they are artists in their different ways, so who am I to argue? If you hate them so much, shall I take them away?'

Con ignored the question, knowing full well that she would do no such thing. But he wanted to argue, had to, just to let some of his frustration and sense of inadequacy out. He didn't belong here. Try though Vivien had, and Rowena, and most of the crowd, he felt like a square peg in a round hole. These people were lightweight, inconsequential. They seemed to be skimming over life rather than grabbing it by the throat. He loved to paint, existed to create something stunning in oils, not act the fool at functions like this. It was all such a waste of time.

'Why women like you,' he said irritably, 'allow men like them, if you can call them men, to look you over like so many sheep, I'll never know. You all accept their condescensions, believe in their faulty judgements, take their insulting remarks about your appearance on the chin, and worst of all, believe them!'

'Darling, you don't know what you're talking about!'

'No? Not when it's plain as the nose on your face that you actually think they know better than you? You all go along with all the guff they spout! The women here are bright, mostly successful and comfortably off. But it still doesn't stop them from being ninnys, does it?'

'You're picking holes in us for the sake of it, Con. Really!'

'You all deserve it.' he told her bitterly. 'Fancy considering types like Fenton and Julian to be some sort of gods.'

'Now you're being absurd, my sweet, and well you know it.'

'If not gods, at the very least, magicians.'

'But darling, don't you see that—'

'Real beauty, such as you have,' he cut in, 'doesn't need paint and powder, and what you pay for one dress would keep my mother in clover for a month.'

'Ah!' She raised her finely arched brows, teasing. 'Are we all supposed to go on our knees and wail and cry out to the deities in shame? Are we supposed to wear sackcloth and ashes because of our guilt? For being incredibly selfish in fact?' She sighed. 'My dear Con, you can be so boring!'

'Thanks!'

'Anyway, I'm not taking you seriously. I know that your filthy mood always appears at functions like this. But as Viv says, we need the publicity.' She laughed softly, a rich, musical sound, and squeezed his arm in a warm, companionable way. 'Poor Viv! You always champ at the bit when she orders us around, even though you like her very much. You really hate all this, don't you?'

'That's unnatural?' he exploded. 'First it's the crowd trampling all over the studio trying to make intellectual noises – and calling our art "pretty!" Then there was your servant Smith disrupting the opening speech because he'd been ordered to take Orestes out. I had to beg their pardon and walk by everyone with the animal under my arm! Why that damned dog of yours insists on getting under my feet I don't know.'

'He likes you!'

'Well, I don't much like him.'

'Oh do stop that, Con! I've seen the sketches you have made of him. Yes dozens, tucked away in your portfolio. He's absolutely adorable and you know it.'

'Maybe he's a character, and a quite decent little devil,' Con admitted. 'But Orestes! Rowena, if you have to have a prissy, primsie Pekinese, why on earth name him after a Trojan prince who had the unsporting desire to murder his mother?'

'I didn't think you knew about such things,' she jibed, smiling directly into his eyes.

'I don't. I asked one of your intellectual friends, Charles Fillimore.' He was rewarded by her blush, and ruthlessly rubbed it home. 'That's right, dear old Charles. The chap who refuses to grovel or treat you like a goddess. Who actually dares to admit to knowing nothing at all about art. Charles, the man who is not averse to living by his own very high standards rather than bow to your wishes and accept this bunch.'

'Charles is—'

'To my mind, head and shoulders above anyone here. If you must know, I asked him about the pup's name simply because I thought the poor little blighter deserved better.'

'You are being deliberately cantankerous, aren't you?' she was rising to his bait. 'Anyway Orestes eventually ascended the throne of Argos.'

'Ye gods! A king?' Con stared unbelievingly at the small, perfect pedigree that, unsportingly, had been forced to wear a blue satin bow. 'Give me strength!'

He glared at Rowena and was happy to see his glare returned with interest. So his remarks about the good looking, very decent, noticeably absent Charles had reached home. The tall, lovely young woman, usually so forgiving and patient where his moods were concerned, had at last lost her control sufficiently to give him a withering look of patent hostility.

'Leave Orestes out of it, Con,' she said frostily. 'He is my pet. I love him and I like to think that he loves me. That's what really matters.'

'Mushy sentimentality. He's a dog, a decent little animal that should be allowed to be just that.'

He was being unfair and he knew it. None of this was Rowena's fault. It was just that he loathed outsiders staring at his picture. It was his own personal treasure, and he'd been mad to hang it where it was. He'd like to choke the living daylights out of the charmer who'd uncovered it. Probably Vivien, pushy bitch!

Of course the picture shouldn't have been hung out here in the first place. But the light was just right, also the setting; plain magnolia-coloured walls. Besides it would be ruined in the kitchen, where cooking fumes would surround it. And the bedroom was like a shoe-box and no use at all. No, Moira was there, in the studio, watching with her wide, soulful eyes while he worked. He felt she brought him luck. She certainly gave him inspiration, and he needed her.

It was his fantasy that she would walk in at any moment and smile up at him, perhaps even lip him, or confide in him as she once used to do. The crazy thing was he couldn't get her out of his mind. But he had fouled it all up, had been an oaf, and she hated him for it. So much so that she had cut and run just to get out of his way. He felt the wave of guilt and shame again. His lips went down.

'Tell me, Con,' Rowena said, and her voice was cold and crystal clear, 'why did you leave her? The girl in the picture I mean?'

Con's eyes rested on the dreamy countenance looking out from the frame.

'I told you,' he replied stiffly, feeling the old agony as he shrugged. 'I didn't! She left me. I disgusted her. All right? I don't know why it hurts so much, but it does. She trusted me and I let her down. It's as simple as that.'

'If she's so wonderful, she'll forgive and forget.'

'Perhaps,' he replied bleakly. 'She's a loyal sort of person who forgives a great deal. She still looks to Flo, a woman that would make you turn up your toes! But that's Moira for you.' He hunched his shoulders in a weary, expressive way. 'I'm sorry, love, for acting the bear. I looked round just now, and listened to all this hoo-ha and I knew just what she'd think. She'd be all eyes, and she'd weigh them up and find them wanting. For a start, she'd recognise that pansy Fenton for exactly what he is, and take Julian with a pinch of salt. One thing she'd never do; take either of them and their ridiculous posing seriously.'

'In other words, darling,' Rowena's tone was rueful, 'she is far wiser than me?'

'In many respects, yes. Though she'd be amazed to hear me say so.' He laughed harshly, 'Know something? She's worked hard on herself. Always trying to be the little lady that a bloke named Stavros said she is. Never realizing that most here are not fit to lick her shoes. She reminds me of a colt, ready to kick up its heels at the drop of a hat and race away rather than do anything underhand.'

'Con, I know you have a deep feeling for horses,' Rowena was going along with him, feeling deep down that it was Conor MacCluskey who was getting ready to kick up his heels and race away. 'But I don't think your young girlfriend would quite like you to think of her like that.'

'She'd understand. She knows how I feel about the creatures. All of them. The difference between a cart horse and a race horse is patently clear. And have you ever seen Shires all spruced up? They literally make you catch your breath with their majesty. All marvellous animals in their different ways, but they'd never be at home on the track at Epsom. No, that's the place for the racers, the whippet thin, highly strung gees, the thoroughbreds.'

'Con darling,' she said plaintively, 'I don't see how horses got into this conversation. I thought we were talking about a lovely young girl.'

'Who, for one mad moment, I forgot to treat like a lady. As for horses, I was merely pointing out that most of the social climbers here class a gentlemen in the same way they do his steed, by his breeding. Others judge him by how much money he owns, or how many hundreds of acres of land. But I've known a street sweeper who I'd call a gentleman. Yes, a damned fine one, from his finger tips to his toes. Moira's like that. A natural. A lady purely by instinct. A far finer person than some of the snots we are entertaining here.'

'I'd like to meet her one day, Con.' Rowena was still trying to go along with him. Admiring his immense talent, fearful that he was getting ready to throw his cap over the mill and let all of Viv's hard work on his behalf go hang, she didn't want him to go. She admired his work, his looks, his charismatic, mercurial character. Most of all, his inate loyalty. He would go through fire and water for his friends, and she hoped very much that he would always see her as that. In fact, in a way, she loved him. He was right of course, and usually was. Evenings like this were pretty awful, but Vivien knew what to do about the business side of things. One should never let her down.

'Moira and you would get on like a house on fire,' Con told her, not wanting to stop speaking about the girl he'd first met, and who at that time had seen as a child. 'You would give her the sort of confidence she needs. She speaks with a kind of breathlessness when she's unsure, you know. But when she's angry the sparks really fly! She was brought up by a fair old tartar. A woman who could out-cuss a navvy.' He smiled then, widely and with great charm. 'Yet when she forgets herself, Moira's greatest profanity merely sounds like a minute explosion, and holds no malice at all.'

'My God,' Rowena said softly, hearing the deepened tone in his voice, the angry need that said it all. 'What I wouldn't give to be loved like that.'

'I think you are, by Charles,' he told her, suddenly cheerful. 'Neither of you know it yet, but I think you're both dead ducks in that respect. Love can just about cut your heart out, though, can't it? Or does that sound too complex?'

'No, it sounds meaningful and sincere, and utterly Conor MacCluskey.'

He grinned. 'Meaning the same thing? Oh it's all right, Rowena me darlin', I'm out of the blues now. All the same I still think Viv's cracked, and that Orestes is a rotten handle to give a rather nice little animal. And I loathe and detest this crowd when they try to understand art. The genuine types. Like Stewart and Hanley, Maurice and his crowd, not forgetting Viv and Roseanne and Co, don't put on stupid airs. They know, and above all, feel!'

'You've just mentioned all of the most important people here,' she pointed out. 'As for the rest, I accept what you say my dear. Now we have been standing here, guarding your painting for far too long. And since I know you so well, that you'll brazen the whole thing out rather than re-cover it, shall we be Viv's good, obedient people? Try to please her and at the very least, mingle?'

'Wouldn't you be knowing I was just about to suggest that?'

he laughed. He put his arm round her slim waist and led her into the thick of the crowd.

An hour later, when things were in full swing, the studio door flew open and a newcomer bounced in. His tangled hair was almost to his shoulders, his face was weather-beaten and tanned. His clothes were tatty, none too clean and had seen far better days. He looked like a tramp; a spritely young tramp who walked with a jaunty air even though against everyone else in the room, he was the misfit of the year. Indeed, he looked exactly how Con felt in this particular gathering.

Fenton and Julian, standing too close together, were outrageously rude and did not disguise their supercillious looks. Fenton made sure that the newcomer heard his deliberately loud snort of disgust and then commented, 'A filthy gate crasher. Really this is not the done thing!'

Chumley glanced their way, grinned a foxy grin that expressed his opinion of Fenton and Julian as clearly as words, and looked round. Then he saw who he had been searching for, waved, then got his own back on those he considered to be ignorant pigs.

'Wotcher Con!' he yelled. 'Bloody hell, mate, this is a rum do! Didn't take yer for the sort as would put up with a lot of pansies.'

There was a stunned silence. News photographers clicked their cameras in the hope that something was about to happen that would spice up a run of the mill private view.

Fenton, who had been ignored by the press all evening, went even more stone-faced. So the intruder knew MacClusky! Trust the Irishman to pick up with the dregs.

'Clearly he's a painter of sorts,' Julian drawled in his know-it-all way.

'Rowena has always been a law unto herself, but this is going a teensy bit too far.'

'He knows Con.' Fenton's tone was grave-cold, 'That's why she's allowed that rag-bag in here. She's sweet on MacCluskey, but to go so far as to accept this!'

'Ah!' Julian was suddenly enlightened and snapped his fingers. 'He must be one of the clutch of eccentrics who are so busily making names for themselves.' He was watching the way Con was shaking the newcomer's hand, and noted that Con was looking alive for the first time that evening. 'I think I know who he is. He must be the cat person!'

'The chap who's made a cool fortune? Whose paintings are drooled over even by the upper crust?' Fenton's tone altered dramatically and now held awe. 'Do you know his name? Do you know him?'

'Not actually, old chap,' Julian had to admit. 'And I'll remember his name in a minute. But I have read heaps about this unconventional artist that loathes his fellow man. Lives like a hermit you know. He was born in India. His father was an army private and disgustingly low. As a youth the son visited a fakir in his cave and was told that he had the heart of a Bengal tiger and actually believed him. Imagine! Now back here, he is obsessed with their inferior cousins, cats. Paints pictures of them and nothing else. His is a very distinctive style and his subjects are odd creatures. Half cat, half tiger, big-eyed, and all in jungle settings. Although he has no class, and is as common as muck, he is accepted as an out and out genius!'

'I must shake his hand' Fenton breathed. 'Filthy rich isn't he? I could make him over. Turn him into my impression of a Wild Bill Hickock type. Really do things for him! I do hope that Rowena introduces us.'

'He seems to be more taken with our dear Con,' Julian said bitchily. 'I did hear . . .'

Unaware of Julian's dirt-dishing, not that he'd give a tuppeny cuss anyway, Chumley was saying out loud:

'Con, mate, the mongrel's done the dirty on us.' He pointed expressively to the picture that held pride of place on the far wall. 'Our girl's gorn with that bloody Greek!' A newshound edged nearer. Others followed. Chumley was unaware of them and continued. 'I got it all from Cissy. Took her and the kid off somewhere last Spring, he did. Some four months ago and no one's heard of 'em since. Supposed to be in France, Cissy said. Old man Bertos soon sussed that out as a lie, and I 'ope as 'ow he can be believed. Bleeding vast country that is.'

'France?' Con snapped, tight-lipped.

'So he said. Bloody hell, our Moir must be dying the death! I mean, she 'ates just being out of Jordan Street.' He was staring hard again, at the painting on the wall directly behind Con. 'Gawd! I don't half like that! You've made her look real!'

'Rajasthan Kotah?' Fenton was pushing through and openly fawning. 'How do you do?'

'Sod off,' Chumley replied.

'Come to the kitchen,' Con said quickly, hating them all, particularly the reporter who was sidling up to take a photograph of his painting. 'I've got to think, and there's too much row going on in here. I want you to tell me everything. Right from the beginning.' He turned to Rowena. 'Tell Viv I'm really sorry, but something's come up.'

'Which is far more important than this little gathering, eh Con?' Rowena asked, eyes bright, not caring that the reporter was scribbling.

'Exactly,' he replied, knowing that now she was now fully on his side. 'Looks like she's been spirited off by a chap that needs his teeth knocked down his throat. She'll have been taken in hook line and sinker, and I'm not going to stand by and let it go on.'

'But darling, don't you think...'

'Thinking's out,' he told her and shrugged in an apologetic way. 'I'm sorry, Rowena, Moira's missing and it's time for action.' He put his arm round Chumley's shoulder. 'And we're going to down tools and find her.'

'I was going to say don't you think you should call in the police?'

'Mr Bertos has probably done that, if he thinks it'll help,' he told her. 'Unless he suspects that his son's done something against the law, then he'd keep his mouth glued tight. Not that—' He paused, frowned, then, 'Glory be! Moira's gone missing with someone who could already be married. Yes, that's definitely on the cards. I'll kill him!'

He hurried Chumley into his private quarters, leaving them all to think what they liked. Vivien had rushed over when she had heard raised voices and was now standing beside Rowena. Rowena thought fleetingly that Con had been right in his summing up. Actually, dear Viv in her deep rose and purple, looked like an overblown fuchsia. Now the agent, never a one to miss a trick, was making the most of the fact that the reporters were avidly scribbling.

'Lost love,' Viv was saying with feeling, pointing dramatically to the painting. 'Great men always have suffered the slings and arrows, artists more than most, you know. Everything, yes everything in their lives is so deep, and so intense! Before you is Conor MacCluskey's priceless painting entitled "Unfulfilled Dreams". And now we have just learned that his beautiful model has mysteriously disappeared.'

'Dear heaven, this is sick making,' Rowena said, very quietly.

'He'll get a fortune for the painting now,' Vivien replied under her breath.

'He'll never sell, darling,' Rowena whispered back, knowing deep down that Con had at last found a very good reason to escape. A chance he would take no matter what, for above everything else, he was a free soul. She sensed that she might never see him again and hated the idea. She looked at Viv, eyes like crystals because of her unshed tears, and gasped, 'Oh do let's get out of here!'

She turned away, pulling Vivien with her. But the reporters followed, like greedy gulls screeching and flapping round a fishing fleet. Vivien turned to face them, beaming. This was publicity with a capital P, and Viv was in her element.

In the privacy of the kitchen Con shook Chumley's hand again.

'It's good to see you, boyo.'

'But bad news travels quickest, eh?'

'I can't help thinking that it might not have happened if we'd both been around.'

'I thought I was helping her by getting her away. Looks like I got it wrong.'

'Me too. I did nothing to follow through. Not even try to find out where she'd gone. God what a fool I've been! I thought she was with you.' Con was frowning again, puzzled. 'Let me get this straight. Where've you been hiding yourself all this time? More to the point, where has she? I think I know why you breezed off. You didn't want Harriet to put two and two together and realize it was you who helped Moira get away. I guessed of course. She would never have left on her own. Not with Jade.'

'Crikey, mate! You guessed, just like that? Moir swore me to secrecy and I did what I thought best. Didn't want to face you, knowing how you'd get the truth out of me all in good time. But you knew at once? Bli'me, I just dunno what to say!'

'Moira couldn't stand to be under the same roof as me, could she?' Con asked tonelessly. 'What did she tell you? That I'm lower than dirt?'

'Come off it!' Chumley suddenly guessed what was up with his pal and nudged him in the ribs. 'Old Moir could never be rotten about you. She'd forgive you anything ... well almost.' He winked in a cheeky way. 'What did yer do, make a pass at her? I would have too, given half a chance, and if it wasn't for Ciss. Moir thinks you're the cat's whiskers, you know she does! No mate, you never caused nothing. She had to get away because of Harriet.'

'For God's sake Chumley, make sense!'

'Harriet had her sights set on young Jade. Gawd's truth, she did. You know how she is! Moir was terrified that would get out of hand. You know as how she'd give her life for that kid. I was the only one around at the time. I did what I thought best because Harriet can fight real dirty, when she wants. We all know that!'

'I thought she was with you because it was curtains for me.' Con replied quietly, then, becoming agitated, 'So where the hell does Bertos come into all this?'

'He paid for a room in Cissy's Mum's house. I went off and left them to it. It didn't take the swine long to make his play by all accounts. Anyway, they got engaged. At least Moir thinks she's got a fiancé, since the bastard bought her a ring. His dad thinks different of course.'

'I must have been blind,' Con groaned. 'I never guessed things were that bad in Market Street. Moira hinted at some kind of difficulty, but I brushed it aside because I know damned well what a spoilt brat young Jade's turned out to be.' He smiled faintly, adding, 'The only bearable thing about all this, is the knowledge that Moira never cut and run because of me.'

'Strike me! Don't half fancy yourself, don't you?' Chumley grinned all over his face. 'Come on, mate, what d'yer reckon we ought to do?'

'Half kill Yani when we catch up with him,' Con's tone was savage. 'But we can't afford to leap into the deep end, we need to make sound plans. If his father hasn't turned up trumps yet it

288

means the cunning swine's worked things out very carefully. So that's what we've got to do. Hold our horses and think.'

'Oi!' Chumley looked foxier than ever. 'Since we ain't got to do anything yet, and must hang on here and make all them plans, ain't you forgot something? You might live posh mate,' he jibed, 'but you ain't got no manners. Ain't it entered that bonce of your'n that I'm bloody starving!'

'Help yourself, boyo,' Con nodded towards serving plates holding left over sandwiches, small crustless shapes of thin white bread enclosing slivers of ham and tomato.

'Come off it!' Chumley's lips turned down in disgust. 'I ain't no midget. Give us something I can get me mouth round.'

'You're on!' Con grinned, understanding his mate very well. He went to the cupboard and took out a large crusty loaf, a wedge of strong cheddar and a huge onion. 'You're like a breath of fresh air. Doorsteps?'

'As thick as you like, me old mucker. And I wouldn't mind a cuppa, a decent brew, if you know what I mean. They make gnats' pee where I've just come from.'

'On the road?'

'Hostel was the last stop. I ain't been near nor by ol' Harriet's. She couldn't keep you either, so I hear.' Chumley winked and whistled and watched Con cutting off thick, man sized slices of bread. 'I've had adventures like you'd never guess. I could write a book if I was clever, which I ain't. Anyway, the whole thing's been great, if only for people I met on the way. I've nearly froze to death, I was knifed by a nutter once, and nearly died. I've palled up with real unsavoury sorts and thought nothing of it. Not forgetting this priest what was raving mad and called 'isself God.'

'I never realized that there were so many out there on the road.'

'Thousands what are helpless, homeless and some of 'em, not so bloody harmless. An' the women! Real old witches some of 'em are an' my Gawd, can they fight! In spite of everything though, there's a kind of mateyness out there on the road. Tramps and gippos leave signs chalked on walls for them that follow, know what I mean?'

'No and it's not important to...'

'Not important?' Chumley exploded. 'Gawd 'elp us, them

signs can mean everything! Like, a sort of barred gate scrawl means Dangerous. A circle means No Good. A hammer means they'll give you work. It's a secret language, mate. One what makes life easier, and we stick together because we're all in the shit and need to feel we have mates.'

'I'm a mate. You could have come back and bunked in with me.'

'Didn't feel I could – not at first. I was scared of you, and then scared about every bloody thing. I was as green as grass at the start. I had every brass farthing pinched after only two days. The third night some son of a bitch nicked me boots, but gradually it felt good. You know, pitting me wits against all the morons that run the world. Morons what look down their noses at those less fortunate. Still, I've lived Con. And I had the time of my life sending messengers to Yani's house. Know something?'

'Tell me.' Con's grin lit his face and sparkled in his eyes. 'I know you're going to anyway.'

'It made me feel something about things as they were before I left. Like I was on easy street in Harriet's place. It made me see what I'd given up just by being a silly sod. I wanted Cissy, but not enough to try and be the bloke she wanted me to be. Moir tried to warn me, yes she did! When we were in the market one day. But I didn't rate nothing. Nothing at all. I had a roof over my head and didn't think much about it. I had grub in my belly and took it for granted. I had my best mates, you and Binksy, Harriet and Moir, and left you all without a second thought. On the road I was on me own.'

'I thought you said you made new sidekicks.'

'I did and they helped me rub the rough edges off. But when you're out on a limb, Con, you don't half appreciate what you ain't got. And though I wouldn't have missed the experience, in the end I was thinking about just what I'd given up-and bloody well hating my own guts.'

'Then why didn't you contact me there and then?'

'I still thought as how you'd kill me for taking Moir to a place what Bertos was paying for,' Chumley admitted. 'But I didn't see no harm. Our girl's got her head screwed on. She knows that there's a Greek woman somewhere on that island, with claims. I never dreamed in a million years that he'd spin our Moir a yarn. Even go as far as getting her a ring. The Wrights believe it's all for real.' He had a look of pleading on his face as he added, 'They ain't dumb, Con. Honest! It's just that they're real decent sorts. And from now on I'm going to work like the devil to try and show them I ain't so bad. I've got to, since I want Ciss.'

'Good on you. Now eat and drink and give your tongue a rest-you damned old fool.'

Chumley accepted the food Con handed over.

'Ta! 'Ere while I think of it, that old Dave Dilley's been hanging round Yani's house. I met some crazies on me travels, but he's really gone. For a reason I can't guess, that Dilley's all but a regular caller at the Bertos place.'

'And no one knows why?'

'Cissy reckons he's trying to get Wally to question the chauffeur about something. Wally's told the silly old sod to get lost of course. Strange eh?'

'Ah!' Con was grabbing at straws. 'It could mean something or nothing, but at least it will give us a start...'

Chapter Twenty-Four

The Bertos establishment, tall, detached and grandiose, enclosed Con and Chumley. It felt warm after the chilly night air outside. The carpet underfoot was rich and thick and the colour of dark tan; the wallpaper was deep cream with a gilt filigree pattern. There were Greek statues on plinths and lots of potted palms in fancy containers. An enormous grandfather clock ponderously beat the seconds away. There was an atmosphere of luxury over all.

'Cripes!' Chumley muttered. 'All right, eh?'

'Not as fancy as Rowena's parents' house,' Con replied under his breath. 'But now we know why our jack-the-lad turned his nose up at Flo's place.'

He and Con followed a servant to a large study, were shown in and left to face Yani's father. He looked small, sitting behind an enormous polished desk. His hair was white, his eyebrows were bushy and over-shadowed small black eyes. His expression was severe, and he did not rise to greet his visitors. Chumley was not bothered by this lack of courtesy. He walked forwards smiling his wily smile, hand outstretched.

'Evening, sir. Good of you to see us. This 'ere's Con, my mate.' Christos Bertos inclined his head.

'I understand that you wish to speak to me about my son,' he asked coldly. 'I cannot tell you where he is I'm afraid.'

'But you will help us?' Con asked. 'Indeed, tell us all that you have learned.'

'My son's whereabouts are not really your concern.' Christos Bertos replied and looked down his nose.

'Isn't it now?' Con asked in a companionable way, but his

body was like a coiled steel spring. 'Well I must beg to differ. It's very much our concern.' He leaned forwards and put his hands on the desk to stare at the old man in a meaningful, deliberate way. 'You see it just happens that he's taken Miss Moira O'Malley with him, and we're after bringing her safely back home.'

'I'm sorry, Mr MacCluskey.' Again that supercillious look. 'Of course, you *are* Mr MacCluskey?'

'I surely am, Mr Bertos,' Con replied and though his tone remained calm and cool, his eyes were like chips of dark blue ice. 'And you're not half so sorry as we are. You see, we're about to go to the police and tell them all that we know.' He was bluffing, but the old fellow wouldn't realize that. 'I suppose it's news to you, that your fine son liked slumming? Wore rags, he did. Ask your man Wally if you want the truth confirmed. Believe me, Yani got up to a trick or two – with us. So we are in the position to spill the beans, which we intend to do, because we are worried about our favourite girl.' He shrugged, never looking away from Christos Bertos's face for an instant, adding, 'All of which is regrettable since we once looked on your son as our friend.'

'The police? Surely, Mr MacCluskey, there is no reason to go to the police about this?' Christos Bertos replied carefully. 'Domestic issues are no concern of theirs.'

'Ah, but this may not be such a simple thing, Mr Bertos.' Con held the old Greek's gaze. 'Chumley here will be telling you about the strange happenings that have been going on behind your back. Like all the tramps that have been seen knocking on your back garden gate. Strange, homeless people all passing messages on. And there's more to it. There's been a madman hanging around. Like a mongrel sniffing the air I've been told, and getting ready to bay to the moon. What is that all about, I wonder? It's only been happening since Yani went away.'

'You are speaking of things I know nothing of,' Christos Bertos snapped. 'Now if you'll excuse me?'

'But we won't, sir.' Con replied, his voice as quietly companionable as ever. 'Because, sir, we believe the police will find it all very suspicious. And so do we, particularly now that Yani has seen fit to run off with Miss O'Malley.'

'I must point out that it takes two to bargain.' The Greek's

293

tone was now tomb cold as he tried to hide the fact that he was getting rattled. 'Are you are hinting about abduction? In my opinion the girl felt she was on to a good thing and...'

'Yes?' Con's tight expression made the older man stop in his tracks.

Chumley snorted. He had listened long enough, and old Con was coming on a bit strong.

'This ain't doing no one any good,' he said brightly. 'It's like this, me old cocker, your Yani's took off with our Moira. She thinks she's engaged. That he'll marry her. But it ain't so, is it?'

'No!' the old man said sharply.

'Over your dead body, is it?' Con put in, his voice metallic. 'Or has he already tied the knot with Dacia? Oh yes, we know all about her and the arrangements two sets of parents made. And we know how Yani feels about it too. He has told us exactly what he thinks, over and over in fact. Now, if he's done the right thing by our girl, then we'll leave well alone, but— The point is, we don't know, do we?'

'He is not married to Dacia.' Christos's voice was bitter. 'That I am certain of.'

'You swear it?'

'Absolutely.'

'So there's nothing to stop him from tying the knot with Moira, is there?'

'Yes. No. I don't know!'

'We could put a stop to all this,' Con said impatiently, 'we could go and find out personally, and we will too. Once we have the information we have come for.'

'Please make yourself clear,' Christos Bertos snapped.

Con looked at Chumley who began to explain.

'It's like this. The nut-case what's been hanging round your house has been trying to get Wally to question the chauffeur about something. Wally told him to piss off.'

'I don't see what this has to do with...'

'The moron's name is Dave Dilley. And we know that he's got this thing about Moir. Always wandering about he is, searching for her. Now from all I've heard, I reckon the bloke thinks your chauffeur knows where our girl is. Got it? We tried to question your driver, but he's kept his lip buttoned. I think as how he's scared of losing his job. He'll spill the beans if you tell him too, though.'

Christos rang a bell set on his desk. Cissy came in at once. She pretended not to see Chumley standing there, though her cheeks went red.

'Fetch Morris,' Christos snapped. 'At once...'

Jade had gone off for the day in the Appleton's posh car and would not be back till late.

Moira sat beside Yani before the fire, for the evenings were chilly. They had enjoyed a marvellous day together, shopping, yet again. Now Moira was the proud owner of a honey-brown two piece suit with accessories to match, a leather handbag and purse. When Moira had remonstrated, Yani had laughed and firmly put ten one pound notes in her purse.

'No!' she had said. 'You're making me feel like a kept woman!'

'Kept women take their men to bed,' he teased. 'You are my fiancé and must accept that I am very proud of you. You don't realize the satisfaction I feel when we're out and I have you on my arm. Indulge me, please? I can never accept your old-fashioned gimcrack ideas!'

'Yani!' she whispered, feeling warm and wanted, and that she owed him just about everything. 'You know how to to get round me, don't you?'

'I wish!' he said and gave her one of his burning, yearning looks.

They had taken a cab and passed a blazing countryside, where hedges were draped with rose-hips and ivy and trees waved their lusty bravery in the wind. She had caught her breath at the beauty of it all.

Now they were back, by the fire, lost in a world of their own. Yani had been refilling her glass with wine that was strong, sweet and very potent, and Moira was happy and relaxed. Yani leaned towards her and began whispering sweet nothings in her ear. She felt little squiggles of excitement curling her toes.

'I want you. I can't hold out much longer, darling,' he whispered urgently. 'Don't you want me?'

'Yes,' she breathed, her heart in her eyes. 'But it's out of the question right now.'

'But we're engaged to be married, my darling. We belong, so where's the harm?'

'I need time,' she pleaded. 'Deep down I want to give in, but something holds me back. Besides—' She pulled away from him and looked gravely into his eyes. 'I never want you to think that I take after Flo.'

He laughed in an exasperated way.

'Perish the thought!'

'And there's something else. When – when anyone gets too near, I – freeze up inside. I get terrified because I remember how it was when Dave Dilley came after me. The memory still makes me feel sick.'

'That happened a long time ago,' he said impatiently. 'And you said "When anyone gets too near, you freeze" Who else has tried to get to you – apart from Dilley and me?'

'I beg your pardon?'

'Who else?'

'Oh!' Moira opened her eyes wide, faintly teasing him.

'I'm not joking,' Yani said roughly. 'I never am where you're concerned. Do you hear me? I'm not joking!'

'No,' she said and suddenly felt very insecure.

'Who tried to get near you?' he asked belligerently. 'You belong to me and only to me.'

'Don't be silly. Con tried to kiss me, that's all and I ran away from him as if all the devils in hell were after me.' Her expression tightened and anger made her eyes glisten. 'And if you must know, Yani, I'll never forgive myself for that. I must have hurt his feelings, and after he had been so good and kind to me too. It's just how I am, that's all. Ever since that time with Dave Dilley behind his shop. Sometimes the mere sound of that man's name makes me feel sick!'

'Do I make you feel sick?' he was getting more angry by the minute. 'Do I? Come here!'

His arms went round her and his lips were on hers. Moira returned his kisses, desperately praying to feel as he expected her to. She owed him, and she was wearing his ring. He had rights!

She closed her eyes, willing her treacherous body to respond to his love-making. As the room swam behind her closed eyes, Moira realized, hazily, that the wine she had drunk before the

296

warmth of the fire had intoxicated her. She had never felt so strange. She could feel his rising passion, his feverish hands were beginning to roam over her breasts, the length of her body, then under her skirt, higher. Moira remained passive, fighting the panic that with every second was urging her to run though her limbs felt heavy with langour. She belonged to him, she thought dazedly. He would be her husband one day.

'Sweetheart,' he said throatily. 'Let us go where we will not be disturbed. Trust me!'

She allowed him to lead her up the stairs, moving like a sleepwalker, fighting to try to meet him half way. All the time he was telling her he loved her, of his adoration, promising her wonderful things. Only half listening, Moira felt like a parody of a person, a mere reflection viewed from a convex mirror.

In a distant kind of way Moira believed she was caught in currents too hard to fight. Was the struggle against the odds so necessary? Flo didn't fight her instincts. She gave in! She takes what she needs from men, not what they are prepared to give her, Moira thought. Not till she met Will Fenning of course. Flo really needs him!

She hesitated, then stopped in her tracks in spite of Yani urging her on. She clung onto the banister now, looking owl-ishly at the almost too handsome young man she so wanted to please – to thank!

'He's a villain,' she heard herself saying, 'do you know that? A sh— stoker on a ship and he—'

He was gently loosening her grip on the banister, urging her. 'Come along, darling. Not far to go. Do you love me as much as I adore you?'

'I love you,' she replied and felt herself smile even though there was nothing to smile about. 'Flo loves Will. Why does that bully exshite her? Are you going to ex – exshite me?'

'Yes, yes, yes! Here we are, sweetheart, at last!'

She wasn't quite sure how she came to be lying on the bed. Indeed, nothing seemed real. The whole world was flimsy, floaty, pleasantly dream-like. And dear Yani, who had defied his wicked father and utterly rejected the chosen bride, was here with her. She was a lucky, lucky girl.

Dimly, Moira realized that she was half out of her clothes. Befuddled she allowed him to continue stripping her. When naked, he spread-eagled her on the bed. Then he began stroking her and his hands were smooth, so smooth.

He began kissing her feet, and her lips curved upwards, somehow finding having her feet kissed absurd. She felt his lips touching her ankles now. Warm, wet lips, pressing, touching, gently smoothing over her skin. Her shins, knees, higher, then, to her utter shock, inside her thighs.

It came then, the sheer horror, the distaste and her own unutterable self-contempt – and the memory. Sanity returned. Moira found herself loathing and detesting Yani for expecting her to give in. He couldn't love her. If he did he wouldn't expect so much.

'Don't!' she murmured, then as he tried to persist, 'Stop it!'

'Darling,' he was panting. 'Let go! Just allow yourself to—'

'Stop it!' she was stone cold sober now. 'If you don't I'll scream for Carpenter.'

Furious, Yani sat up and began to swear. Then catching the look on her face, he stood up, shame-faced, watching her as she struggled to get dressed. Then he said quietly, 'It was the drink, Moira mine, and you are so beautiful. I don't think you realize how incredibly lovely you are. You make my blood turn to fire. You turn my head. Sweetheart, can you forgive me?'

'Yani,' she stuttered and brushed away her angry tears. 'The wine affected me too, quite strangely. I – I don't think I'll ever drink again. Please, please let me go to my room.'

He stepped aside, silently watching as Moira hurried to the door. Her hair was awry, her eyes swollen by tears. She suddenly wanted very badly to scream.

By the time Jade came to the room, late and laden down with booty bestowed upon her by the Appletons' relatives, Moira was composed. She had decided that she would have to see how Yani was in the morning. Her mouth went dry with apprehension. He would never forgive her, because he must believe that she had led him on. He might, dear God, he might hate her, might break off their engagement and tell her and Jade to go away. If that happened, what could they do? Where could they go?

It was just dawn when Moira quietly left her bed. She washed and dressed and slipped out of the house. She took the long walk to the sea. Then she sat on a rock and watched and waited while the tide rushed in.

Time passed and still she sat there, unable to face Yani, her heart pounding as forcefully as the sea, her cheeks hot with shame. Tears blurring her vision as she remembered his hands, his kisses and just for one moment, had it been his tongue? Again the vision of Dave Dilley rose up to haunt her, and the pounding of nerves in her stomach and the wave of nausea started all over again.

She heard the falling rush of small stones behind her and turned, fear in her eyes.

Yani was standing there, legs astride, arms folded. He looked stern.

'Don't you ever do this to me again,' he told her. 'I've been half out of my mind.'

'I'm sorry,' she whispered, tears starting to her eyes.

'Go on,' he said raggedly, 'tell me you never want to see me again.'

'I'd never, ever say that, Yani.'

His expression lightened.

'You mean that? You will actually forgive me?'

'If you'll forgive me,' she said quietly and was unable to meet his eyes.

He was smiling broadly now, relieved as he reached her and swung her up in his arms.

'Moira mine,' he told her, 'we have gone so far! I now love you more than ever, and my memory of last night—'

'Don't Yani! I feel ashamed.'

'Ashamed?' he held her away, looking amazed. 'Of your own perfection? Por, por, por! How extraordinary you are. I love you. I want you and I do assure you, my darling, that you have whetted my appetite.'

'Stop reminding me!' she was distressed. 'I was under the influence of drink and I feel hot and cold at my thoughts.'

He was laughing as he threw down his challenge.

'And I go all hot at mine. You make my blood race, beloved, and I do assure you, that wine or no wine, I shall try again.'

'When we're married, it will be different, Yani. Don't you understand?'

'I'll not wait,' he told her. 'I promise you. So be on your

guard from now on. I have a burning desire to kiss you all over. Every tiny particle of you, and I will not rest until I have done just that.'

'Now you're being soppy!'

'Soppy?' he teased. 'What a ridiculous word. There speaks the little girl I remember from Jordan Street. Oh my darling, I love you so much!'

'I think you really believe that,' she replied gravely. 'Yani, I...'

'Then come on, my sweet precious,' he ordered. 'Let me prove it. Oh and by the way, young Jade's impatiently waiting for us back at the house.'

They walked back to Northmays hand in hand.

It was not until the night time that Moira allowed herself to go over all that had happened. She thought of the sweet tenderness of Yani's kisses, his full sensitive lips, the velvety glow in his eyes. She felt her cheeks going hot in the darkness. It now all seemed so unreal. As unreal as the memory ... Suddenly she saw a macabre mask floating before her eyes. A mask looking like Dave Dilley bobbing up and down on an unseen string. She felt the inrush of deathly cold and thoughts of the fish fryer came to torment her again...

It was dark and Dave Dilley was smirking because it had been so easy to give the little Chinaman the slip. No one, he thought, could outwit Dave Dilley who knew the highways and byways like the back of his hand.

He continued, through a maze of streets. All uniformly dull and neutral, grey places under a pall of mildew, of abject poverty. And Dilley himself, slipping through a maze of evil alleyways, seemed to be a shadow appearing only fitfully under the pallid lamplights. Arms flapping, body even thinner, he seemed part of the night, as in keeping with his surroundings and as insubstantial as cobwebs festooning a forgotten room.

Eventually he reached the railway arches. High above, the trains thundered by, hissing and steaming and blowing out a million gold sparks. Below, beyond the brick-built arches there was a patch of waste ground sheltered by a towering warehouse. This in turn overlooked the docks. Stan had chosen well

300

... seeing that the door of his place under the arch was all but hidden by the refuse of years.

The fish fryer was not looking towards the railway arch. He was giggling as he watched the methies gathered on the waste ground. Stank the place out they did, with the smell of urine and worse. Of course the men, if you could call them that, were filthy, sore-ridden and covered with lice. They contaminated everything they touched, and the derelict buildings they crawled into, usually to die, were left fit only to be pulled down. Dave Dilley knew this particular lot, having followed Stan here in the past.

It was getting colder. Men were huddling together like hunched-up dwarfs. A small group of methies were gathered round a sparse wood fire that was giving out more smoke than heat. They were passing round a bottle holding a mixture of milk and methylated spirit. They would continue in this fashion all night, or for as long as they could stay conscious.

Some would get aggressive, but they ignored old Dave. They had hated Stan Jones, who'd haunted the place behind them for years. Worse, had made it his business to harangue them; always gave 'em a bibfull, in his gasping breathless way. Loathed and detested them he had, for drinking away their lives, for wasting themselves, for their total disregard for the good health they had once had. This when he, Stan, once a fine figure of a man, had been gassed in the war and chucked on the waste tip through no fault of his own. His hero's welcome, he always wheezed out to the world, had been a 'Thanks mate, you did well for your king and country. So sorry about your lungs, but that's how it goes, old chap.'

'In other words sod off!' Stan had been heard to gasp. 'I hate 'em all. I hate every bloody one!'

So he took it out on the methies. Openly loathing the misfits, the drop-outs, the dregs left with no courage to face the days. In turn they had wanted to kill the ex-soldier who wouldn't leave them alone. Yet they did nothing, for they were incapable, emaciated in the extreme, pale-faced, unshaven, far gone. Fit only to shamble about, broken-backed scarecrows bereft of minds.

But they had become animated for a moment or two when news of Stan's demise had leaked out. Found in the gutter he'd

301

been, with his toes turned up. And the authorities had carted him away and dumped him in a pauper's grave. Some hero! Poor, bleeding, gassed-up old fool.

But it was over, done with. Stan Jones belonged to the past. Life in all its dreary wretchedness went on.

Now, in a befuddled way, they could hear Dave Dilley's crazy mouthing; but unlike Stan, this nutter was gabbling to himself. It didn't matter. A couple more swigs of meths and nothing would...

'Stan's found somewhere else to haunt, Martha,' Dave Dilley was telling the unseen. 'But we'll find him all in good time, eh?' He cocked his head to one side in a listening attitude. 'What girl? What's that you say?'

Strange noises were floating in his ears, like wind rustling dry leaves. He realized that he was giggling to himself again, seeing the funny side. Especially over that lot in Jordan Street who carried on about him, Dave Dilly, being a crazed-up prat, for not believing that Stan Jones had gone to the grave. Rubbish! He knew that Stan was around somewhere. The gassed-up old fool had to be, since he had to do old Dilley a favour before joining his sister six feet down.

Dave Dilley smiled evilly, thinking of his brother-in-law, who had once been so fine and strong – and outspoken. Who had thought a great deal of Martha and less than nothing of Dave.

Sodding Stan, Dave sneered to himself, couldn't have all that long to live anyway. And good job too. The bleeder had had the gall to say that he, Dave, was not happy unless everyone else was miserable. That his sister was too good and too frail to go about lugging sacks of ice, and above cleaning the guts out of fish. Like she was a regular lady in fact. Definitely not the sort who had to slog herself to death morning, noon and night.

Martha, bless her cotton socks, had known better, oh yes! She had listened to her husband and obeyed. She'd carried on even when heavily pregnant like the fine woman she was. Then cruel fate had stepped in and made her die. Yes, bloody cruel fate! He'd gone down the pan when she'd upped and died on him – taking his baby with her too.

Then, as if things weren't bad enough, bleeding Stan Jones had come home from the war. Had thrown Dave's offer of home, work, and plenty of grub right back in his face. Stan who'd had the nerve to blame him for Martha's death! Had called him a miserable bastard and a right evil swine.

That had hurt. But, Dave comforted himself, it was the war that had turned Stan into a soft-head what couldn't take things in. He wouldn't listen when he explained that Martha hadn't gone after all. That she was always there, wearing her hat with a veil, and whispering in his mind. He had told Stan all about her, over and over again. And about the funny things she said. But Stan had stared and called him mad. Had not believed him when he'd replied that it was him, Dave Dilley, who was the only sane person around. That it was Stan himself that had gone bonkers because of the war.

But then everyone had a screw loose, Dave reasoned. Yes everyone! Especially that lot in Jordan Street. Dave Dilley rubbed his bony hands together and sniggered, remembering all the slights he'd received, the kicks and the buffs, the humiliation and spite which he was now so enjoying paying back.

He would have the last laugh, oh yes! Just as he had on that night. What a pea-souper that had been. You couldn't see an inch in front of your nose and air was sulphuric, cloggy and hard to breathe.

He had enjoyed the fog because it made the rest of the world seem as unreachable as the things going on in his mind. Men were grey shadows with flares held aloft, and vehicles crawled along the kerb like panting monsters with two glaring yellow eyes. Strange colour, yellow. Dried up, it looked like old paper. Yes, that's what the woman looked like now. Shrivelled and dried up. She hadn't looked like that in the beginning he remembered...

Dave Dilley pictured again how quickly she had walked through the streets. Like she'd had a message of some kind. And he'd followed close on her heels, knowing every step of the way, sure-footed in spite of the fog. Then she had stopped under a street light that made a hazy blur on top of a cotton-thin stem. That's what fog did, made wavery outlines out of what had been solid before. So the slit-eyed evil-looking sod waiting there in his foreign clothes had seemed like a phantom from hell. And the Chinese woman had screamed high and wild, but was unable to run away from the long taloned grasp.

The Chink raised his hand, unaware of Dave standing near enough to see those horrible over-long finger nails gripping round a knife.

And then triumph for old Dilley! He knew the spot, knew what to grab, a lump of fallen masonry such as abounded in the slums. A single blow on the back of the Chink's head had been enough.

Dave remembered sensing other Chinks sidling out from the curdled yellow haze and he grabbed up the China woman who'd fallen in a faint. He'd taken her away from that place and now she was safe in his care. She did as she was told, knew what would happen if she did not, and the best thing of all, it was his secret. One best kept to himself. He hadn't even told Martha, not that she'd care!

The next thing he knew was when he read in the newspaper that a defunct Chinese woman had been found in the gutter. He'd guessed that her with the knowing looks and wanton ways would believe the corpse to be her friend. Moira O'Malley would be hurting inside. She who had hit him with a poker and called him names, who had scorned him and made remarks about gherkins would suffer, and he was glad. Let her soul rot in hell.

One day the girl with cinnamon-coloured hair would be found dead too. She thought she was safe, but she never would be. Not as secure as he himself was now. No one on God's earth would know that his Chink slave was alive! But back to the girl. He would catch up with her no matter how hard she tried to hide, and then let her watch out. But first he must find Stan.

He stopped giggling and shook his head. He had forgotten just why he had to find his brother-in-law. He leaned against the railway arch and tried to think. He tried to clear his mind, suddenly uncertain of whether the fluttering figures in rags, lit up by the fire, were real. They were squatting on old sacks, drinking and slobbering, lower than the low. Stan was right. They were mad. Crazy. They ought to be shut away. Not like old Dave Dilley, who was far from daft. He began talking to himself again.

'The fish fryer knows what he knows, eh? All about the young snot that Stavros Sella's so proud of. Oh yes! The stuck-up young swine that was after Moira O'Malley. He, Dave Dilley knew all about that and what to do about it too!'

He began babbling fast and furiously, not making sense, but inside his head he knew that he had been as sharp as a needle, gifted in fact. And all his walking and talking had led him to the right place at last.

Long months of spying and wandering, listening and learning, had finally paid off. He had found the Bertos establishment and waited. Had hung about and overheard a filthy old tramp's burbling out a message from Chumley Prime. Wally the handy-man-cum-gardener had told the tramp to piss off in no uncertain way. And somehow, Dave had known that through this lot he would find Moira O'Malley. That this was the beginning of the end of his search.

So he had waited, watched and listened. Had learned of the chauffeur who had the job of driving Yani Bertos around. It had been easy to find the chauffeur's favourite pub, to sneak in at the back and listen hard.

In due course he had come to learn all about Shelley Road, the Wrights, and how they had sheltered the girl with cinnamon hair and knowing, come-to-bed eyes. But he had been too late! She had gone and it was whispered, she had been taken to a place called Thundersley.

His figure made a long shadow that stretched up, jagged and mis-shapen, against the wall. He clapped his hand against his head as realization came.

Ah! That's where Stan came in. Stan would know all about such a place, would explain how to get there. He himself must keep quiet. No one must find out about all the enquiries. Stan would do the dirty work, go and find out about Thundersley, just where it was and how to get there. He could not do it himself. Someone might overhear, get suspicious and ask questions. No! No one must know that at last Dave Dilley was all set to get his revenge...

Chapter Twenty-Five

Moira was standing by the window, looking out at the glorious scene. The autumn sun was a marigold in full bloom. Trees and hills were majestic pillars holding up the sky. She bit her lip, conscious of Yani lounging on the settee, looking sour. He usually was these days. He had changed, and now alternated from being a best friend and charmer one minute to an angry, thwarted man the next. Oh, he apologised afterwards, for being a pain, but his words no longer sounded sincere; his attitude silently proclaimed that it was really all her fault because she insisted on saying No!

He no longer put himself out, not even for Jade. Not that she worried too much; she was always off somewhere, chatting to old Carpenter, else being taken out in the car.

The door opened behind them and Carpenter came in.

'A telephone call for you, Mr Bertos,' he said. 'Will you please take it in Mr Appleton's study?'

Moira swung round and she and Yani looked at each other, shocked. A telephone call? They were discovered! This then, was the end.

With a muttered oath, Yani left the room and Moira stood there, heart pounding, her mouth dry, conscious of fear. Someone had found out where they were. It couldn't, mustn't be! The waiting seemed endless after that.

Yani came back looking shaken.

'Who – who was it?' she whispered.

'No one.' he told her. 'It was a mistake.'

'But how did they know your name? That you could be found at this number?'

'I don't know,' he replied, tight-lipped. 'And stop looking like that, caro. It does not matter.'

She found herself wanting, no, *needing* to question him. She was imagining his irate father, or even worse, a murderous Kung Chin after the honourable young Li Sweet Precious Jade. She began asking Yani again, 'Who was it, Yani? Was it a man or a woman? Was the caller English or did he speak pidgin?' He remained mute. She wrung her hands, beside herself, continuing, 'Yani! What if . . . ?'

He rounded on her.

'I told you! There is nothing to worry about. It was a mistake.'

'But you can at least tell me . . .'

'Moira mine, please forget it. Must you go on and on?'

He was staring at her accusingly now, acting as though it was all her fault. She tried again, her fear for Jade knowing no bounds.

'Well at least . . .'

'Be quiet, please,' he ordered impatiently. 'You are making my head ache! I mean it, Moira. I want you to shut up!'

From then on he steadily refused to talk.

As the day progressed his unease grew. He seemed determined to ignore her and continuously walked to the window to look out. Only the front gardens could be seen from this vantage point, so he prowled outside, nervously walking right up to the gate. Unable to stand it, Moira followed him. She found him looking along the road that wound both up and down Bread and Cheese hill.

'What is it, Yani?' she whispered fearfully. 'Tell me!'

'Ah!' he replied, not answering her. 'Here they are. I was wondering how long Mrs Appleton would be. I thought she was late bringing Jade back, that's all. Stop looking like a frightened kitten. There's no cause for alarm. Nothing to worry about at all.'

By evening his agitation had grown in spite of his efforts to hide it. The Appletons, thankfully, had retired to their own private quarters, and were quite unaware of the tension. As soon as she decently could, Moira put Jade to bed then rejoined Yani. He remained silently staring at a book, though she could tell he was not reading.

He jumped up at last and ignoring her startled cry, kissed her passionately, excused himself and went to bed. Dispirited, wondering what on earth had gone wrong, Moira herself went to her room. Jade was already fast asleep and did not wake as Moira undressed, washed and then got into bed. She tossed and turned for a long time, but finally closed her eyes.

She did not know how long she slept, but woke with a start of terror. It was night time still and she was confused, but yes, Yani's hand was pressed ruthlessly over her mouth and nose! She could barely breathe, his grip was so fierce and frightening. She tried to escape but he had pinned her down. This was a new and vile Yani, different in action and looks. Night shadows had turned his face into a ghostly mask belonging to Halloween. She couldn't bear the moonlight glinting like knives in his eyes, and blinked away. All she could see, through the window to her right, was an eerie moon staring down through a veil of clouds. Coldly malevolent, it was soulless and white and silent.

Moira writhed and fought, needing to scream but it was impossible with Yani's hand clamped over her face. She wanted to fight like a crazy thing, kick and punch and run away, but his body weight was holding her prisoner, pressing her down. There was only the sensation of mortal terror racing through her now, for he seemed to have gone crazy, almost suffocating her, his grip was so tight. Her heart was pounding, the world was falling away and she was swirling in a vortex through which she could hear Yani's words. He was hissing and panting and whispering between his teeth.

'It's all right! Stop it! Keep still!'

He was growing more confident. His free hand was squeezing her breast. He was saying in a deep guttural voice, that he had waited long enough. That he needed and wanted her. That now it must be all or nothing. That she must pay her dues...

She fiercely shook her head from side to side, gasping for air, but could not break free. And he was still going on, saying in that same strange voice that she had to give in. She must cast aside her stupid prudish ways.

'No!' she croaked against his hand. 'No!'

'For crying out loud!' he rasped, 'Can't you accept that we're engaged?'

Again she shook her head, but his mouth was now glued to

hers. She'd wanted to cry out that she would never be forced, but his lips were bruising, drowning out sound. She tried to grasp at his reasoning, but all she could think of, wildly, was that Yani had got it all wrong. That she loathed him for his and would until her dying day.

Suddenly anger replaced Moira's fear and renewed her strength. She began struggling all over again. Now consumed with the urgent desire not to wake Jade, not to have her see the ugliness that was going on. Thank God the youngster had always slept sound.

Moira's struggles seemed only to incense Yani more. He was strong and cruel, fully aroused and trying to force himself between her legs. And deep in the recesses of her mind she was sobbing for help – screaming for Con.

Suddenly she stopped struggling, going limp and so taking Yani by surprise. He was only momentarily off-guard, but it was enough. In that moment she twisted away and leapt out of bed, grabbing up a candlestick and holding it aloft. She meant business, he knew it. He had lost the advantage, he knew that too. Yani gave in.

He too stood up, panting heavily, and stepped towards the door, He was furious. He began speaking in a harsh and scornful way.

Distressed, shaken, she stood before him, listening to his tirade.

'I don't know what I saw in you.' he told her. 'You're nothing but a common tart. You've been leading me on.'

'No, Yani. No!'

'I was taken in by a tramp from Jordan Street. A cheat and liar who accepted a diamond ring and had no intention of paying for it in kind.'

'How dare you think like that. I . . .'

'You're a floozy, just like that disgusting woman who brought you up. Flo Williamson who takes, but gives nothing in return . . .'

She listened, ashen-faced, hardly able to believe that he could believe such things. Then she retaliated.

'I owe you nothing,' she whispered furiously. 'And you're a pig!'

'Every rag on your back you owe to me!' he was speaking

louder now, uncaring of the consequences of waking the household. 'Every luxury you've enjoyed, you owe to me!'

'So you're resorting to blackmail, is that it?' Moira queried, her voice thick with contempt. She stepped imperiously towards him, chin lifted, hair flying, 'Call yourself a gentleman, Yani? I've known of better men living in slums.'

'You didn't mind escaping those same slums, my girl,' his tone was thick with sarcasm. 'And don't you forget it.'

'Damn you!' she flared. 'I'm not going to stay here listening to this. I'll manage to find my own way back to Flo, believe me. And I'll enjoy telling her and Stavros what a true gentleman you are! Oh, and Flo might be rough and common in your book, but she'd never lower herself to your level. She's as open as the day about what and who she is. Yani Bertos, you're a fraud and you make me sick!'

Her fury had taken him back. In that moment she felt the winner of the game.

'Get out,' she snapped. 'Before I call the Appletons and tell then just what a worm their son's got for a friend.'

He left then, face quivering, saying that he had had enough. That he knew where he was best off.

Moira closed the door behind him and crept back into her bed. She lay there, shivering, dazed with shock. A while later she thought she heard him knocking on her door, but stayed where she was, deciding bitterly that she never wanted to see him again . . .

Dawn tip-toed into the east like a pink and silver ballerina. Moira, feeling drained, left her bed and went to the window. She watched and waited, comforted by the sound of Jade's even breathing, silently thanking God that Jade had slept through everything. Yes, even when Yani's voice had finally been raised. How he had gone on!

With a voice tight with fury he had said that had he known the true state of affairs, he would never have gone to so much trouble. That it had cost a fortune to keep their whereabouts hidden. And it wounded his soul to realize how dreadfully he had deceived his father.

Moira sighed and turned away, then saw an envelope that

had been slipped under the door. She walked over, picked it up, taking it back to read in the light coming from the window.

Yani's letter was brief and to the point.

> 'Moira, because of your unreasonable behaviour, I have no other option, but to leave. The rent is paid, so you have until the end of the month. I will be gone by the time you read this. I will always love you, but since you have so thoroughly rejected me, it is my duty to go home to the fiancé who will welcome me with open arms. Please, try to understand, and wish me well.'

She felt half hysterical laughter bubbling in her throat. He was about to do the one thing that would get his father's forgiveness, obey the rules and marry Dacia. What on earth did he expect of her, Moira, the despised? A bunch of red roses and a telegram wishing him luck?

She took in a deep shuddering breath, accepting that nevertheless she owed Yani so much! She, a city child, had been brought here, to a wonderland, to the vast, rolling countryside that flanked both river and sea. To the kind of place where she believed Robby wandered when he was not sleeping under his weeping willow tree.

Moira angrily brushed her tears away. I must remember this, she thought. No matter what happens in the future, I can always shut my eyes and picture it all.

The sun was just beginning to win the battle with the morning mists and the clouds were lifting from the summits of the hills. It was the kind of morning that made one catch one's breath. Autumnal glory had sent running fire across the countryside. Already the breezes were gusting gloriously coloured foliage to the ground. Hedges were frosted with Old Man's Beard. Hawthorn fruits were cherry-red. Blackberries were ripe for picking, and there was a polished sheen on a multitude of hipsy-haws.

The clock seemed to tick with fussy pin-points of urgency. Jade would not wake for another half hour at least, and when she did her day was already planned. Mrs Appleton and she were to go into Southend on a shopping spree. It had all been arranged. She, Moira, would not be missed. They all knew how greatly she enjoyed her solitary early morning walks. Loving the country, the feel of it, the smell of it, the sight and sound and sense of it, for once in her life she had quite forgotten her longing for the privacy of Jordan Lodge.

Before Moira realised what she was about, she had thrown on her coat and left Northmays. She walked a long way and came at last to the well of salt tears that was the sea. She stayed there for a time, but could not relax and finally retraced her steps.

She reached the gates of Northmays and hesitated. Right now she knew that she could face neither the Appletons nor their sympathy. If only she could keep what had happened to herself. But they must be told. She bit her lip, embarrassed, wondering if perhaps Yani had left them a letter too? No! That was not his way. It would be left to her, but not yet. She had to put off seeing them. At least for a little while.

She turned away from the gates and pressed onwards and upwards, heading towards the ancient ruin that looked as abandoned and dejected as she was herself. She needed to be there, on her own. Needed the peace and quiet. Needed to...

Her breath caught in her throat with dismay. Someone was there, with his back to her; an artist sitting before his easel, busily painting a picture of Jarvis Hall. He shouldn't be there, she thought, aggrieved. He shouldn't be there at all. And then she stopped in her tracks. Unsure, then shocked. Con? No it couldn't be. But yes, it *was* Con!

As Moira hesitated he swung round, saw her and jumped up, the picture of guilt, and defiance. He was devastatingly good looking, with a lock of dark hair fallen onto that noble forehead of his, above eyes of that special iris-blue; and he was tall and slim and lithe. There was something almost tigerish about him, Moira thought in confusion. He was very, very different to smooth, treacherous Yani Bertos who had such soulful, velvety eyes.

She turned away intending to beat a hasty retreat. He smiled in a rakish, but shame-faced way.

'I've been so interfering that you won't even speak to me, mavoureen?' he asked. 'Won't you stay just for a wee while?'

She nodded, remembering their last meeting, not quite certain what to say.

'Care to come and see my picture?' he was more confident now. 'I have only been here for three days – mostly snooping. Chumley was with me at the beginning, but he's left me to it. Wanted to be near young Cissy, of course. I've been trying to find out all about you. I was thinking about putting you in the painting since you look as though you belong to this place. Besides you are so beautiful and you have such an alluring face.'

She could not take in what he was talking about, and could still barely believe that it actually was Con sitting there – in answer to her prayers. But the way he was speaking, so light-hearted and everyday! He was poking fun, surely? Yet his expression was disarming enough. And oh, how wonderful it was, to come upon such a dear, familiar face!

She walked towards him slowly, speechless, not knowing whether to be astonished at his presence or to cry with utter relief. She looked at his canvas, a painting in the very early stages, of the ruin. It was good, very good. She found her voice at last and with genuine warmth Moira told him so. Then she stopped speaking, disconcerted by the laughter that blazed like twinkling lights in his eyes.

'Forgive me,' he said, 'but you do remind me of a gazelle, Moira O'Malley, and I'm delighted to see you looking so well. So it's top of the morning to you, and top of the morning to me, and St Patrick himself couldn't be happier than I am to find you all in one piece.'

'Conor MacCluskey,' she replied, and tried to act cool and dignified, 'As I live and breathe! May I ask what you are doing here?'

'The leprechauns whispered that I'd find you,' he teased, 'so I've come to rescue you from the wicked old wolf.'

'He – he's gone.' she replied gravely. 'Back to his island, I believe.'

'Ah!'

'You – you knew? You speak as if—'

'I guessed. After all, I didn't think he'd put out the welcome mat. I telephoned and told him to get his house in order by the time I called, you know. I arranged to see him today.' He looked directly into her eyes. 'He has not – hurt you?'

'He has not,' she replied, cheeks flaming anew, knowing full well what he meant. 'He has been very disappointed in me, I'm afraid. Anyway, I don't think it's your business. If you must know I – I refused him, and he said I'd led him on, and so . . . So he has gone away.'

'Then that's a blessing.' He watched her, lips uptilted at the corners. 'Not that anything you did or did not do would have worried me. So don't look at me like that.'

'How am I looking at you, Con?' she asked, suddenly defiant, realizing that Yani's behaviour the day before had all been down to Con. 'As though I'm seeing someone who scared my fiancé away?' She stepped nearer. 'What did you say to him? How did you find us? And why have you come here, Con?'

'Could it be because you and I go back a long way?' he asked her. 'And because we are friends? Not forgetting that Chumley saw fit to come chasing after me to tell me how you'd vanished, and Yani had too? Or could it be just because you're rather special and I'll always see you as the fragile innocent who was scared to death by that oaf Dilley?'

'That does not give you the right to—'

'But mostly,' he cut in, 'because I have you looking out of a frame at me every day of my recent life.' He raised one brow self-mockingly. 'It's hard to forget someone who has such a thin, bony little face, hair that seems to burn with a colour all of its own, and who can fly off the handle at the drop of a hat. Now look at you!'

'Con, I don't know what is happening to me!' she said tightly. 'And I don't know how I'm going to cope, but I will. Believe me!'

'Your eyes hold the expression in them that says, "Any minute now, I'm going to cut and run right out of your life again, Conor MacCluskey,"' he said ruthlessly. 'You're thinking of going back to being the little mouse hiding in the attic again, aren't you? And above all, you'll be thinking of all the years of your life you can spend just looking out for Jade.'

'I'll always be there when she needs me, yes.'

'She's been doing very well for herself, and with others, not you. Moira, I've been here, seeing how the land lies. When the moment is right, she will leave you without a backward glance. And you'll stick to being a recluse.'

'Oh?'

His next words made her catch her breath.

'Yes indeed, mavoureen. And it's a great pity because you're much too beautiful to be a cabbage. You have the kind of face that a man could never forget. And if I were you I'd go down on my knees and thank Yani Bertos for trying to be the seducer of the year.'

'How dare you be so – so rude!' she stammered feeling hot shame speed through her. He was actually daring to laugh at her sorry little tale. Moira felt tears of humiliation scalding her cheeks and angrily dashing them away, she turned to run. In a flash his strong brown hands gripped her shoulders and he was laughing into her upturned face.

'You can't spend your days running away and hiding in secret places and being scared stiff every time a chap makes advances, sweet thing. It simply will not do.'

'So,' she flared, 'I'm a cabbage, a cowardly cabbage! How dull and boring you make me sound.'

'Not at all. I'm merely saying that you're half asleep. You've never been awakened, Moira, and you've certainly never known love.'

'I have loved Yani all of my life. And you, Conor Mac-Cluskey, are taking too much for granted. What's more...'

His eyes reflected a sudden burst of sunlight as he stared intently into her face. His sheer animal attraction almost frightened her. Moira stood before him, willing herself to look away. But all she could hear was his rich, confident voice, and her eyes refused to focus beyond this large, magnificent man.

'You have only had daydreams,' he told her firmly, 'played fairy stories over in your mind. You believe in stuff you've read in those stupid library books Stavros used to choose. You think that when true love strikes, bells ring and bluebirds flutter in almond trees. Holy Mother, girl you are a fool. Speaking with respect, reality is nothing like that. There are no knights in shining armour. Only flesh and blood men.'

'Yani—'

'An arrogant fool.'

'You're hateful!' she gasped and turned to run from him again, but again he caught her and held her fast.

'Why not take a leaf out of Yani's book and have some fun?' he teased. 'Take another male, better still, take me! Don't waste

315

yourself on foolish dreams. And above all, don't be scared of a crazy old fish fryer while I'm around. I won't vanish like Yani, I promise you.'

All Moira's humiliation and hurt rose up in a single tempestuous wave. She thought of Yani. Smooth, gentlemanly Yani who had let her down, and now Con was laughing at her and ... It was unbearable!

Her hand flew out and fetched him a stinging blow across his cheek. Then his face blocked out the sky. She was drowning in his eyes, drowning. And then there was the stinging sweetness of his mouth against hers, followed by the sinking feeling as her heart lurched and began to thud against her sides. But it was not pounding in fear, but with a kind of excitement and a sensation that she did not understand.

Con let her go and laughed softly, wickedly, his eyes alight. In that moment he seemed very sure of himself – and of her.

'And isn't that just like a woman?' he clowned. 'To return a hit for a kiss? But don't worry, darlin' I mean you no harm. I'll wait, till Judgement Day if necessary, for when you come to me of your own free will.'

Moira stood before him, speechless, then she turned and ran as hard and fast she could. She did not stop until she reached the great wrought iron gates of Northmays.

Chapter Twenty-Six

It was evening and Jade and Moira sat at a large polished table, as invited, in the Appleton's private apartment. The older couple were there, friendly as always and making much of Jade. The girl was in her element in the setting of carved panels, polished oak, white linen and silver, not forgetting the centre-piece of deep yellow florist's roses. Jade was always so bright-eyed and confident with people she liked and they always seemed to like her. Thank goodness, Moira thought, that as yet her charge had come face to face with no bigots. There were many who would hate the youngster and spit on her for the foreigner she was.

Jade had been convinced from earliest times by River Pearl, that she belonged in a rich setting. She took to luxury like a duck to water, whereas it all made Moira herself feel out of place.

Everything about Northmays was grand, Moira thought and looked down at the place setting before her. She wanted to die the death; she could almost feel the sympathy exuding from the couple. She had kept to herself all day, but they knew, she could tell.

Nothing was said until the maid had served the soup and left. Then Mr Appleton cleared his throat.

'My dear,' he said, 'we are sorry that Yani had to leave so abruptly. An important business matter he said. A late night phone call? Ah well, that's the way it goes.'

'Yes,' she replied, relieved.

Visibly relaxing now, she sat listening to Jade's lively chatter throughout the meal, which was delicious. It was rounded off with apple pie and rich cream, which Jade lapped up. Relieved that Jade would have time to accept the fact that this life-style was drawing to a close, Moira tried to think and plan.

At least they weren't going to be turfed out neck and crop, and Yani had made the rest of the stay that much easier with his white lie. Yes, only white, since the arranged marriage with Dacia would in fact be a sort of business deal. Two great and rich families would join together and become even richer, she thought wryly. Perhaps they deserved each other.

Would Yani ever be truly happy? She doubted it, remembering what he had written to her. The letter which she had long since torn up and thrown away.

But amid all the hurt, there was the knowledge that the room was paid for until the end of the month. Better still, she would have some money to live on. And she could even thank Yani for that! All she had to do was find the nearest pawnshop and say goodbye for ever to the now offending engagement ring. She felt her cheeks flush hot.

Jade, having ignored Yani's absence, was speaking in her high, lovely way, about the wonders of Southend-on-Sea. Of course, it was not the sea, so Yani had pointed out many times. Nothing like the Ionian or the Aegean. It was in fact the estuary of the Thames, a vast place, thick with mud when the tide went out. Mud that, so it was said, had great healing properties. According to Mrs Appleton, Jade must now be the healthiest young lady in the world . . .

Moira was relieved when Jade's bed time arrived and she could make her own escape. Jade was pouting as they entered their room. Now there was no audience she let go and became her own small spoilt-brat self.

'I want Yani,' she said mutinously, and defiantly stood there in her pyjamas, arms firmly folded. 'Where is he? He is my uncle, he told me so. I want Yani. He's nice!'

'He is at that,' Moira replied easily. 'But he's had to go back to his own country, I'm afraid. A land that's a long way away. And—' she raised her brows and looked Jade straight in the eye, 'Him having to go off on business at such short notice has put the cat among the pigeons so far as we're concerned.'

'Why?' Jade was getting ready to play war and it showed.

318

'Because we'll have to leave here ourselves at the end of the month.'

'I don't want to go!'

'With Yani gone, minx,' Moira said firmly, 'we'll have to.'

Skin the colour of old ivory seemed to draw tightly over Jade's cheekbones as she allowed herself a bout of temper.

'I hate uncle Yani!' she said bitterly. 'I really do!'

'Don't be so horrible! You liked him a minute ago.'

'I didn't know he'd left us then.'

'He had to go away on business.'

'I want to stay here!'

'I don't think we can pay our way, Jade, so it's no good carrying on.'

'Mrs Appleton's rich,' Jade pointed out, and smiled ingratiatingly. 'We won't have to give her any money if I ask her.'

'You'll do no such thing,' Moira replied sharply. 'We have too much pride to be beggars. We don't have to leave straight away, so there's no need to get so het-up. Anyway Con's here, isn't that a surprise? Tomorrow we'll have to find out where he's staying. You like Con, don't you?'

Jade was too cross to reply.

Tired because of the happenings and ensuing sleeplessness of the previous night, Moira herself retired early with a book, and finally slept like a log.

The next morning she carefully dressed herself in a brown skirt and amber coloured jumper and defiantly tied a yellow ribbon in her hair. Conor MacCluskey was detestable, she loathed him, and it wasn't fair that there should be so much personal magnetism in one man. Nevertheless, he had shown her her self-pity for exactly what it was. Her chin lifted as she stared at her reflection, then took from the wardrobe her fine brown coat.

It was wonderful to have such warm, classy clothes, she thought bitterly. All presents from her fiancé of course. Only he wasn't her fiancé anymore, he belonged to someone named Dacia, who was, according to him, fading away with love. What of herself? Was she going to wilt and give in just because Yani had let her down? No, she was not! Not Moira O'Malley who had been brought up by the redoubtable Flo!

Before she could stop to think about it, Moira had left

Northmays. It began to rain. She was conscious of the sweet smell of wet grass, of the brisk, refreshing feeling of the wind against the face, of the sweeping cleanliness and invigorating air of the countryside. With quick, nervous strides she began to walk towards the village via the lane that wound gently forward until it widened into a road. Then there were the cobbles of the main thoroughfare, and Tarpots, the inn where she and Yani had spent so many happy evenings together. She hastily brushed the thought away.

People were about now, nice, friendly people whom she had met up with before and happily passed the time of day. They smiled at her as she passed. She smiled back and waved defiantly, wishing that Thundersley folk weren't quite so close. That the Northmays servants didn't all have families who lived near, and who gossiped avidly over local news, oohing and aahing and adding comments of their own. She knew this, since being at home with one and all she had treated them as equals, unlike Yani who ignored them all. They were deferential to him, just as he expected. On the other hand, they had warmed to her, had even on occasion exchanged knowing looks and shared snippets of lively conversation. So, she reasoned, it must have gone round like wildfire, how Mr Bertos had gone. Moira made her way to the post office-cum-general store that sold just about everything, and bought herself a *Daily News*. She seldom bothered with daily newspapers, but she had to buy something, anything, as an excuse to put the question she had in mind. She folded up the paper without even glancing at the front page, pretending not to notice the startled look in the proprietor's eyes. He was stout, florid and had fiery red hair; his small eyes were all but hidden by fat. He was a garrulous man.

'Everything all right miss?' he asked. 'I mean, everything?'

'Yes. Thank you, Mr Amery,' she said, intent on carrying out her plan. 'The whole of Thundersley must rely on you for just about everything. Your shelves are crammed full.'

'You can bank on us to have the lot,' he replied and winked. 'Bar the kitchen sink of course.'

'What a tip-top place you have.' She laughed lightly. 'It's a wonder you don't run a pawn-shop just to round things off.'

'Don't need to, since Ma Peacock down Marsden Lane always helps out.'

'Really?' She opened her eyes wide, hardly able to believe her luck. 'She actually hands out money for best suits and shoes and things?'

Unintentionally she had opened the floodgates. Mr Amery leaned on his counter, clearly happy to continue his theme. He seemed even more friendly than usual and she guessed he'd heard about Yani leaving. They had a very active grapevine in Thundersley.

'You'd get a fortune for some of the things you wear,' he told her in a confidential voice. 'And Ma takes watches, jewellery, all sorts of things. Must be rich as Croesus.' He gave her a strange look, adding, 'You'd think she'd be scared stiff of strangers, but not her! Mind you, I reckon the whole village would be up in arms if anyone upset her. She knows all our secrets, and we know hers, since she was born and bred here, and all her family before.'

'It's strange I've never met her.'

'Oh she's around.' He grinned, adding, 'And it's a pound to a penny she knows all about you, and will learn even more soon enough.' He leaned nearer, acting even more confidential. 'Got a lively interest in that young artist chap that's renting Blanes cottage. Stands a few yards from her place it does. Peacocks it's called. No fur, no frills, so far as the old girl's concerned. The place just bears the name she took on when she married her Will. He's gone now of course, and she plods on, a real decent old girl, yet she walks about like a tramp. I ask you! There's no understanding some folk.'

'No indeed,' she told him cheerfully, inside wanting to yell out, hurrah! What stupendous luck. She and Jade would not be destitute after all. There was someone to hand who would give her money for the ring and even for her clothes. And what a coincidence that Mrs Peacock and Con lived all but on top of each other. Talk about killing two birds with one stone! She'd walk along and take a closer look. She was almost sure she had noticed a Marsden Lane.

It was easy enough to find, she thought later. Flanked by holly and gorse bushes, Marsden Lane was secluded. Her heart leapt as she came upon Con's place. Blanes Cottage was clearly named.

The door was wide open. Without pausing to think, Moira

321

went in. The smell of frying bacon was appetising, and the place felt lovely and warm, but she was conscious only of the fact that Con was there, looking as though he expected her. He was leaning against the sitting room doorpost. His black hair was shiny with rain, his arms were folded, and there was faint mockery in his smile.

'Do you usually walk into other peoples homes, mavoureen?' he drawled.

She coloured furiously, aware of how easily Con could get under her skin. He was only teasing, but she was still confused at the recent turn of events.

He was waiting for a reply. She lifted her chin, and trying to sound calm and sophisticated, replied, 'No not often. Do you usually follow people to the ends of the earth and then telephone a person's fiancé – and frighten him off?'

He laughed and stood to one side so that she could pass him and enter the room. She had an impression of a fire and an all pervading cosiness.

'Well, you're getting back your confidence I see,' Con remarked. 'I'm glad! Oh, and I thought you might be along, sweet thing, so I've gone out of my way to prepare a welcome for you. See?'

She looked round. A cheerful fire blazed in the hearth and the table was set for a meal.

He walked towards her, hands outstretched in readiness to help her off with her coat, his size diminishing the tiny room.

'Sit yourself down,' he ordered. 'And take off your shoes. You look as though your feet are soaking. I'm about to show you that I've inherited my mother's flair with the cooking stove.' He took the paper from her and placed it on the window sill. 'Holy Mother! Mavoureen, won't you even try to relax?'

Moira sat obediently in one of the chintzy-covered chairs. She noticed that Con had made himself perfectly at home in this charming domicile. She felt the uneasy colour tinge her cheeks, for now the intensity of his eyes disturbed her. It was unnerving that he had so obviously expected her. Even worse, it really seemed as if he could read her inmost thoughts. He went into the kitchen and returned with eggs, bacon, bread, butter and a huge pot of tea.

'Go to the table, me darlin',' he ordered, 'make yourself at home and eat!'

During the meal, which she toyed with at first and then enjoyed because he all but dared her not to, Con began to speak of many things. His conversation was amusing, but underlying the pleasantries she could sense his awareness of her. He was, she felt, going to try to kiss her again. Amazingly the thought did not scare her, did not make her on the defensive as it always had with Yani. Her throat went dry and her heart was beating much too quickly. She found that she was all but holding her breath. But the moment passed.

It came as a shock, when over the washing up he said casually, 'I must apologise, Moira, for trying to kiss you yesterday. Just a prank though. By St Patrick I swear it. Just a prank! You are so easily shockable, you know.'

She looked searchingly up into his face just in time to catch the roguish twinkling of his eyes.

'Come. Let's sit by the fire and put our feet up for a minute or two. When your shoes are a little more dry I'll be taking you back to Northmays. By the way, I used the public telephone earlier on and asked to speak to Mr Appleton, but he was unavailable. I spoke to someone called Carpenter. He told me that you had gone out, he thought to the village. I went looking for you and saw you heading for the shop like a miniature Boadicea.' He laughed softly. 'I take my hat off to you. Your dignity is intact, Moira O'Malley, and you're a lady after my own heart.'

'And I must thank you for making me furious enough to do it,' she admitted and though she smiled there was a deep sadness in her eyes.

'Why did you telephone me?'

'I didn't. I was after speaking with the Appletons. We were spotted together yesterday, by an old man walking his dog. He mentioned it when I joined him in a jar at Tarpots last night.' He shrugged expressively. 'You know what hot beds for gossip villages are. So I wanted to put things right. I did not want you to feel uncomfortable on my account, so I made up my mind to say that we are friends. That I've no intention of stepping on anyone's toes, least of all their son's mate ... That I am here, having taken this cottage for a while, purely to paint pictures.

That I was hoping that you and Jade would come visiting every little while.'

'You were going to say all that for me?'

'You've suffered enough, sweet thing. I didn't want things to be made worse.'

'You were protecting me. Oh Con!' she was beaming with pleasure. 'How thoughtful and kind.'

'And you'll be as safe as houses from now on, believe me,' he said stoutly. 'Rowena would never allow it to be any other way. Indeed, once she knows that I've taken this place, she'll be driving down here just to look round. Perhaps even stay a while. I have already told her that I believe that you and she would get on.'

'Rowena?' she was taken back. 'Who is she?'

'A good friend so she is,' he replied. 'A real beauty too. Like a Helen of Troy. She comes from a fine family and she paints pictures that take your breath away. So you see, Moira, you don't have to worry or be afraid of me. I'll not do the chasing. It's you that will have to come after me.' His wide smile flashed out, 'I wouldn't want you to be compromised, no, not for a crock of gold.'

'And Rowena, Con?'

'I live in a flat that belongs to her and we share a studio. I decided to leave Harriet's place. Chumley left that establishment even before me.'

She coloured furiously.

'Oh dear! Con,' she said shakily, 'I can't keep up with all this. About Yani, and you, and the strange way that things have turned out for Jade and me.'

'Through no fault of your own,' he replied easily. 'And you have me here to help you now.'

'Oh yes!' She was all but glowing with a wave of relief at the thought. She stood up then, 'And now I must get back, Con. They'll be wondering what's happened to me.'

'As you wish, darlin'' he said easily and reached out for the newspaper, dried out now and curling at the edges. Then he swore.

A large photograph of his painting was there for all to see. The caption read, SEARCH FOR MISSING MODEL.

Underneath, the article began,

The title of this well known Con MacCluskey painting is "Unfulfilled Dreams". The girl in the picture
had been declared missing. The police are using
photographic copies of the model, taken from the
painting, to help them in their search...

'Damn!' Con said. 'Damn, damn, damn!'

He handed the paper over to Moira.

'Oh God!' she whispered, shocked. 'Now what are we going
to do?'

'Nothing except brazen it out,' he told her. 'Jaysus! That's all
we needed, eh? If the reporters get on your trail here and
publish the news...'

'Please God, no!' Moira's hands flew to her mouth to stifle
her frightened cry. 'Kung Chin will know where to find Jade!'

'I could wring Vivien's neck!' he was white with fury now.
'Ye Gods! Wouldn't you be knowing that she'd sell her soul for
publicity? She won't accept that it's all the hoo-ha I hate! But as
for that business with River Pearl, it was over and done with a
long time ago. Sweet thing, Li Tzu's enemies will have given up
by now.'

'But we can't be sure. They might...'

'Come along now! All the ifs and buts and maybe's never
amount to much. Moira, you must learn to give up fighting all
those shadows that dance in your mind! I'll not let anyone hurt
you or Jade. I promise you, everything will be all right.'

She wanted to believe him, but she was trembling as they left
Blanes cottage together...

Moira sat opposite Mr and Mrs Appleton, listening to how sad
they were at making their decision. But there was nothing else
they could do! They would pay back the money, of course, even
give a little extra for any inconvenience caused, but it was a fait
accompli so far as they were concerned.

Moira was trying hard to see things their way, but all she
could think of was, What rotten cruel hypocrites! And all in
front of Jade too!

Jade was standing close to Moira's chair, withdrawn, expressionless, looking down at the coffee table. Spread on it was
the newspaper with the photograph uppermost.

'My dear fellow,' Mr Appleton was saying crisply, 'you must accept that this is after all, a Retreat! We have people who come to us year after year. It would do us untold harm if any of this came out. That you, a runaway model used Northmays as a hide-out! The ensuing publicity ... We would become notorious and that must not be! We run a highly respected establishment, not a place mentioned in newspapers.'

The way he said "model" and "newspapers", and looked down his nose, made it sound as if he were speaking of despicable things. Moira felt sick with humiliation.

Mr Appleton coughed, a false little sound, adding,

'It would not seem quite so bad if your fiancé had been here, Miss O'Malley. The mere fact that he left us in the middle of the night...' He shrugged and lapsed into an accusing silence.

'But Jade may visit us,' Mrs Appleton said anxiously, 'Isn't that so, dear?'

She gave her suddenly tough and unforgiving husband a pleading look. He did not reply.

Then Con, who had been leaning back in his chair, arms folded, legs outstretched, took over.

'I'll have you and Jade out of there in no time at all,' he said, and smiled into Moira's wide, hurt eyes. 'And I'm hoping the wee girl will see this lady and gentleman for the shallow creatures they are, and that the Holy Mother will turn a blind eye to their mortal sins. For sinners they are! But they accepted money for your room and you don't have to go. At least not so quietly. So, if you've a mind to make a fight of it?'

'I don't want to stay!' Moira replied. 'I never want to set foot in this place again.'

'You're right, so you are. Go and help Jade pack, mavoureen. 'Twill be a simple thing to make our escape. We'll vanish like mist, and these people can swear they've not seen hide nor hair of us at all.'

Moira looked at him, her soul in her eyes. Then she replied coolly and quietly, 'I think I must begin to make decisions for myself, Con. I have let other people rule the roost all the days of my life. Times have been hard, and people cruel, but none, high class or low, have ever been so heartless where Jade's feelings are concerned.' She stood up and put her arm comfortingly round Jade's rigid shoulders. 'Come along, minx, this isn't the

326

end of the world. It's going to be fun because, like it or lump it, we will not vanish in the mist! We are going to stay quite near, in fact. We will live with Con.'

Suddenly she felt confident, strong. She had the desire to stand firmly on her own two feet. And it was, she realized, Con who had given her the courage. She smiled at him, her expression holding certainty as she added, 'But first, we'll go and confess our sins to the police.'

'Oh, but we—' Mrs Appleton began, horror on her face.

'Please don't worry,' Moira told her. 'I shall tell them that I have been with Con all of the time. That will let the Retreat off the hook, so far as the police are concerned. But there's nothing I can do about the villagers knowing the truth, I'm afraid...'

Chapter Twenty-Seven

'That's that!' Con said and grinned as they left the police station well and truly behind them. He was thoroughly enjoying the ride they had cadged.

He's having fun Moira thought. Just because he is sitting on straw at the back of a farm cart pulled by a horse! But then, he loves everything to do with horses, This one's going a fair treat, and according to Con, it's in lovely condition too.

'It's all settled,' Con went on. 'And I might say you did very, very well. But I wish you had given the Retreat as your original address. It would have served those two right. Honest and high class indeed!'

'They were very kind in the beginning and marvellous with Jade,' she reminded him. 'And at least they were truthful about how they felt! On the other hand, I have just told the police out and out lies. I was not your model in the truest sense. I never even knew that you were going to put me in your painting, and— And it's obvious that some models are not thought to be all – all that nice!'

'May the saints preserve us!' he teased. 'But you're a model now and it's official. The police accept it, the public will accept it, I certainly have, and so must you.'

'They did not like us very much, did they?' she said gravely, feeling ashamed. 'They called us publicity seekers in a very snooty way. I wanted to fall through the floor when they warned us about wasting the police force's valuable time.' She laughed apologetically, 'And remembering all of Flo's dire warnings about officials and the like, I felt that they were about to put me in prison for life.'

'That would be something,' he laughed. 'I could come and visit you in the knowledge that you couldn't run away!'

'Con,' she told him gravely, 'I was seriously afraid.'

'That sergeant was pompous.' he admitted, 'but that kind of lecture doesn't bother me. What does is the fact that there was a reporter there.'

'Oh!' Moira whispered, suddenly terrified for Jade. 'I never thought of that! Still, perhaps he was just working for the local newspaper.'

'Don't worry. We can handle things.'

'I'll never dare leave Jade again.'

'Not even with Carpenter?' he asked and raised his brows in astonishment. 'She was off with him like a shot this morning. It was good of the old chap to take her, and we are lucky as hell that this is his day off.'

'I didn't know about that reporter then. It's different now! We'll have to keep an eye on her all of the time and—'

'Whoa!' Con cut in. 'Would you be having the poor girl behind bars? Get things in perspective, mavoureen. Carpenter adores her and she's set him above the rest. Oh, and he told me that he's taking her to his daughter's place in Hadleigh. There are children there. It will be good for Jade to play with other wee things. You really must let go of the reins for a while.'

'I will,' Moira told him and determinedly lifted her chin. 'You'll just have to give me a little time, that's all.'

'All the time in the world,' he replied.

Blanes Cottage, isolated from the village, enclosed them all for the next few days. Warm and cosy, it was a haven they did not have to leave. There were plenty of food supplies in the cupboard, they wanted for nothing and were prepared to let the rest of the world go hang.

Once the shock of recent events had faded, Jade began to relax. She admired Con, for all he took no nonsense. He ignored her initial discontent in such a lordly, superior way, that she soon had a change of heart. It pleased her to watch Con, for having returned from Jarvis Hall, where he painted during the best light, he insisted on sketching Moira over and over again. She sat or else reclined in the positions he set her. Intense, roaring at her to stay still if she dared to blink an eye,

329

Moira put up with it. Jade, enjoying seeing the way Moira instantly obeyed, giggled and clapped her hands.

'He is like a lord husband,' she said mischievously, then chuckled out loud when she saw Moira flush and Con scowl.

'Like friends,' Moira told her hastily. 'Just as a lady named Rowena is Con's friend.' She looked across at him. 'Isn't that so?'

'Devil take you both,' Con replied. Then, directly to Jade, 'And while I'm at it, brat, I'm after living my own life. Right now that does not entail taking a wife. Now let me sketch in peace.'

'Why so many drawings, Con?' Moira asked, relieved that he had been so noncommital where the unknown Rowena was concerned. She risked his anger and ruefully rubbed the back of her aching neck, 'And why now? You have told me that you need to get the background of your picture just right before you even—'

'Keep still!' be ordered. 'And I'm working like this while I have the chance.'

'The chance?'

'Sure and wouldn't you be knowing that fate plays strange tricks at times? I'm capturing your moods while I can. You have a very expressive face.'

'We have a little while yet, haven't we?' she asked wistfully. 'It's so nice here.'

'Indeed it is,' he replied. 'But Fate can be cruel sometimes.'

A few days later a national newspaper picked up the story of the missing model, where she had been found, and who with. The painting was shown once more. Con's brilliance had all the publicity that Vivien's heart could desire. His model's ethereal beauty was there, on paper for all to see. There was a mystery. It must be solved. Yani's name was found out. Romantic triangle ... young Greek gentleman ... famous artist ... beautiful wayward model who had men at her feet.

Con, fiery and irascible, blamed Vivien.

'Trust her to keep her nose to the ground. I swear that she's at the bottom of this. Holy Mother, isn't a man's soul his own? And what's all this shenanigans going to do to you?'

A great deal it seemed, since the following day they had a

caller and, believing it to be Carpenter, Jade opened the door and allowed Mr Hayward Hawkins in.

Moira, thinking that it could only be someone to do with the detestable Vivien, made herself scarce by going into the kitchen to make tea. But it rankled, that the cottage was a secret hiding place no longer. A visitor. Here inside! If they had reached that stage already, she thought ruefully, the unknown Rowena couldn't be far behind.

She tried to hold Jade back, for keeping Jade out of sight had always been the priority, but the young girl stayed put, laughing and inquisitive. Moira sighed and herself remained in the kitchen. Only at Con's roar, did she hurry to put hot water in the pot.

She returned with a laden tray. The visitor stood up at her entrance, but reseated himself when she nodded. She was discomforted to see near-black eyes staring at her, and the saturnine-looking man smiling in a dour, but confident way.

'She will be perfect,' he told Con, 'an asset, Mr MacCluskey. I am sure that we can talk amicably.'

'I doubt that very much,' Con snapped, 'but seeing this is to do with Miss O'Malley and therefore her own business, she must speak for herself.'

'But you will advise her?'

'What about?' Con asked.

'Money,' came the reply.

Nonplussed, not sure of anything, Moira poured tea, set plates and handed round coconut biscuits originally bought for Jade. The two men were speaking over her head but she did not listen. Then she was taken aback by the merry twinkling of Jade's eyes every time she looked up from the book she was pretending to read.

Little minx! Moira thought indignantly. She's thoroughly enjoying watching me squirm. Then she decided enough was as good as a feast.

'Excuse me,' she said at last. 'May I ask what this has to do with me?'

'Allow me to introduce myself, Miss O'Malley.' The man said, again jumping up and extending his hand. 'I am Hayward Hawkins and my fashion house supplies shops in the West End. A great friend of mine saw your picture in the newspaper. She

331

pointed out that many of the élite who come to me, also buy paintings. So, with the curiosity that must be aroused because of your romantic story, not forgetting your very good looks, and above all, since I am a gambling man, I would like you to come and work for me. It could do us all some good.'

'No thank you,' she replied, not giving his words a second thought. 'I am much too busy here. And if you don't mind me saying so, Mr Hawkins, Mr MacCluskey does not need to find success through the back door.'

'He's making a grand offer, so he is,' Con pointed out loftily, giving Mr Hawkins a very sour look. 'On a commission basis of course – on the sale of each frock.' He looked bullish, adding, 'For all Vivien's plans, I do not paint pictures with the idea of having them sell in the same category as ladies dresses! But as for the rest, my girl, accept that it could do you some good.'

'Con!' she replied, exasperated, 'I don't know what you're talking about and I don't much care. I thought we, I mean you and me were all set to—'

'Think about it, mavoureen,' he cut in, giving a smile that could cut glass. 'You will be able to be self-sufficient. Sure and wouldn't you be knowing I'd not be the one to hold you back?'

Moira was looking from Con to Mr Hawkins then at Con again. Why was he so angry? What had gone wrong? It was a silly question. The outside world had come through the front door in the shape of Mr Hawkins. And cold reality was never part of a dream.

'My dear Miss O'Malley,' Mr Hawkins said, 'you could make a great deal of money.'

He was looking at her and clearly expecting her to all but swoon with gratitude. Well, she wasn't grateful, she thought. In fact quite the reverse. She looked from Hayward Hawkins to Con and wanted to hit him because he now seemed intent on egging her on.

'Just think what you could do with lots of money,' he told her, 'And knowing you, affording Jade private tuition would be on top of the list.'

Moira, acutely aware of Jade poking out her tongue at the idea of being tutored, felt on the defensive.

'I'm your model, Con! I am perfectly content with things as they are.'

'Are you now? No, don't look at me like that! Like a wounded deer. Remember that the time will come when we will be leaving this darlin' place and then what? I'll not say a word one way or the other. And I would never presume even to try.'

Hayward Hawkins intervened.

'As well as commission on sales, Miss O'Malley, I would be prepared to pay you a regular three pounds a week.'

Moira felt herself begin to quiver. The man was offering her a fortune. She could have Jade educated privately just as Con said.

'It is an opportunity of a lifetime,' Con said flatly. 'And you should not dismiss it lightly.' He turned to Hayward Hawkins. 'Please give Miss O'Malley the chance to think things over. If she accepts your offer, I'll bring her to you myself.' He shrugged. 'After all, the train fare to London is only two shillings and sixpence. I think we can just about manage that!'

They both turned to her enquiringly, and Moira found herself nodding agreement, for all she thought them both mad. The only interesting thing about all this, she thought, was the fact that Con had pointed out that with money to hand, Jade could be properly educated.

Shortly after that Hayward Hawkins drove off in his posh motor car and thankfully Moira heard Con close the door behind him. He came back, eyes watchful, saying, 'How does it feel to be heading for fame and fortune. eh?'

'I don't want to do it. And you shouldn't have told Mr Hawkins that I would think things over.'

''Tis a terrible thing,' he told her meaningfully, 'to be told you're a beauty! Come on, admit it. This could be a turning point in your life. There'd be no more need for the skulking in Jordan Lodge, nor grovelling to the Appletons. You'll forget your days of being all but a recluse and become instead a confident young woman of the world.'

She looked over at Jade, who was still pretending to read, but listening to every word. Then she half whispered, 'And – and Kung Chin?'

'You're still frightened of his shadow?' Con asked in his normal tone. 'After all this time?'

'I need to be sure. I want to be sure. And the memory of Dave Dilley haunts me still.'

'Well only you can do anything about all that,' he told her in his down-to-earth way. 'You'll have to stand up and face your nightmares one day. You know that, don't you?' He looked across at the silent young figure so earnestly ear-wigging. 'And this applies to you too, Jade.'

'Why?' Jade gave up all pretence and put down her book.

'Because it is a rule of life. Do you know what they teach a boy who's fallen from a horse and is therefore afraid? That he must remount at once. If he doesn't, fear will overtake him completely and he'll never ride again. Fear has to be faced and ridden out. Don't you see that? There's nothing to be achieved by running away. Nothing at all. Do you know the opposite of fear?'

'No.'

'Faith. When we have faith in ourselves there's no room for fear.'

'I have faith in Moira,' Jade replied.

'Would you like a fresh cup of tea, Con?' Moira asked hastily. 'I rather think we've been told enough for one day.'

'Tea will be fine,' he answered, 'sweet, and strong enough to bite at the tongue. And I promise you I'll lecture no more. After all, who am I to harangue a young lady whose just been told she's a raving beauty? Make no mistake, to be chosen by Hawkins is an accolade and all the opportunities he told you about happen to be true. Just think of it, darlin'. Millionaires could be in the offing!'

'You're laughing at me!'

'No,' he was all sincerity. 'I would never, ever, laugh at you, girl. I thought you had learned that by now.'

'And –' she was truly anxious, '– you still want Jade and me to stay with you?'

'You are part and parcel of my life, mavoureen.'

'And all this frock business?'

'If you choose to go and try, I'll come with you just to start you off. You can trust Carpenter to care for Jade and take her to his daughter's place in Hadleigh. What do you say?'

'I love Carpenter,' Jade cut in, only to be ignored.

'It's just that,' Moira said pensively, 'that everything is happening too fast. I've got to be quiet and ... and think about things, Con. I can't take all of this in.'

334

'There's always tomorrow, my girl,' he told her. ''Tis a grand new phase you could be entering. If you decide on it, I shall ask Rowena to put in a good word.' He frowned, looking angry again. 'Oh yes, this is Vivien's handiwork, so it will be good to have Rowena on your side.' He laughed shortly at her expression. ''Tis no wonder you're dazed. Would you like us to be visiting Tarpots for a spell? There's no point in hiding our faces now.'

Moira was laughing and relieved at the return of normality. 'And I suppose you just love lemonade, Jade! What am I going to do with you?'

'Always be my honourable mother,' Jade replied.

Chapter Twenty-Eight

Two weeks passed by and there was no further talk about Hayward Hawkins, to Moira's relief. The Thundersley people now treated her on a level footing, and she and Jade were able to walk and talk, and carry on in the usual way. By tacit consent, neither of them visited Northmays, but Carpenter called on them and completely took Jade over on his days off. Moira continued with Jade's lessons, no matter how loudly the girl argued.

Although Moira and Con never mentioned their previous conversation again, Moira could not forget what he had told her; about a man falling from his horse, getting up and re-mounting the animal, and in that way defying fear. Fear was, she thought, the most heart-stopping emotion of all. It had been fear of officials that led her into hiding at Flo's. Fear of Dave Dilley had led to her horror and distrust of men. Fear had in fact lost her Yani, for he had only wanted to be loved in a physical way. Oh, she accepted that what he had felt could not have been true love, for love, in its fullest sense, was understanding.

Yani's rejection of her still hurt, still made her burn with shame. He had told her that she was not a true woman, was stupid where the true meaning of love and giving was concerned. He had not accepted that Dave Dilley's pawing her and attempted rape, had made an indelible mark on her soul. And now here was Con, who did understand in his way, telling her bluntly that she had to stop running, had to face fear, his inference being that she should reach out and take it with both hands and shake it dead, dead, dead!

At nights she would go over and over it all in her mind, and faced the fact that, after her fear for Jade's safety, the biggest blight on her life was fear of men, of what they expected of a woman. Of what, according to Yani, was a fellow's greatest need.

At this moment in time she could not fathom what to do about the Kung Chin business, nor how to go about the finding of Li Tzu. But her fear of men? Couldn't she, shouldn't she, deliberately set out to do something about that?

Accordingly, one bright, crisp moonlight night, when both Jade and Con were fast asleep, Moira crept out of bed. She went along to Con's room and stood outside the door, tentatively knocking, intending to go in. She could hear his rhythmic breathing, could imagine his tall, bronzed figure stretched out and at ease. How would it be? If his kisses were anything to go by ... Her fingers closed round the handle, she opened the door and stepped inside.

Moonlight streamed through the window, light and shadows etching his face. She stood there, wraith-like in her long white night-dress, her hair flowing free, just watching him. He mumbled something in his sleep and turned round. She had intended to go to him, to ask him to teach her things, everything, so that she need no longer be afraid. But his movement startled her, made her heart leap into her mouth. Moira whirled round, through the door and back to her own bed before she had time to think. Then she lay awake for a long time, chastising herself for the coward she was.

The next day, having returned from shopping in the village, Moira and Jade walked into the kitchen. They saw Con sitting in the chair, arms folded and looking pleased with himself. Curious, smiling quizzically, Moira asked, 'What is it, Con? You look like a cat that's got at the cream.'

'You can read me like a book, can't you? Well, I went to the telephone kiosk and got through to Rowena and enjoyed a worthwhile conversation – about personal things. Then she put me on to Vivien who just happened to be there. 'Twas Vivien who gave me some rather fine news.'

'Oh?' The bit about Rowena registered and she felt jealousy and hardly knew why. She was almost afraid of what she was going to hear next. Her bubble of happiness seemed to be in danger of bursting.

'The gallery has sold a further two paintings of mine for rather ridiculous prices,' he told her and his whole face lit up. 'So it looks like a good Christmas for us, mavoureen.'

'How wonderful!' She was glowing with pleasure, excitement and relief. 'Oh Con, I'm so pleased for you. And so proud! Of course we'll have a marvellous time. Strangely, I was thinking of Christmas trees just now. It came to mind because the bushes outside are thick with holly berries.' Her voice faded, then she asked hesitantly, 'I suppose you'll spend part of the holidays with Rowena Wray?'

'No.'

'With Chumley and Harriet then?'

'No.'

Wild hope was surging through her.

'Con, is it to be just us the whole time, here in the cottage?'

'That's it. Absolutely,' he told her. 'And it's going to be grand. We'll make a fuss of young Jade here. We'll get a tree and balloons and make paper chains. We'll go to the local church, at least I will. I must light a candle for my mother and all those back home, and we'll have plum pudding and turkey and everything.' He was laughing like a boy. 'What shall we do about presents for you, eh Jade? What will you like?'

'A handful of diamonds?' Moira suggested before Jade could say a word and she and Con looked at each other and laughed...

By the time Christmas arrived, Moira was more self-assured and adept at making friends. She met Mrs Peacock who gave her a good price for the engagement ring, and no questions asked. Mrs Peacock was as garrulous as the man in the General Store. She took to Moira, was not over keen on Jade, and more than generous with her home-made apple and blackberry jam.

Moira marvelled over and over again about how happy and lucky she was. The only blot on the horizon was that Con had to leave Blanes by January the third. But that was not yet. She let the future take care of itself.

Now she had a little money, she caught the bus into Southend and went shopping alone, having great fun choosing "Christmas surprises".

There was one special Christmas parcel. She had searched for and finally found a charming little gold dragon brooch for Jade. It had a ruby eye. There were to be toys and games of course, but never a doll. Raggy Pearl was Jade's most dearly beloved companion and friend. Daisy's gift went with her everywhere. There was a shirt the same bright blue as his eyes, for Con. Moira had the suspicion that he would never wear it, but she could only try.

She bought and sent Christmas cards for everyone. Flo, Mrs Noice, Freddy, Stavros, Mr Binks and Chumley. Also to Daisy, Sid and one, with a black cat with a sprig of mistletoe behind its ear, for Cissy.

Then one late afternoon she asked quietly:

'Con, what are your plans after you've taken Jade and me home?'

'Home?' he roared, 'You're not talking about Jordan Street?'

'Jordan Lodge,' she corrected him, 'and yes, to Flo's. There I can work for my keep and Stavros will teach Jade.' She laughed shakily. 'Even I have to accept that all good things come to an end.' She smiled shyly. 'I – I wish we could stay here for ever, Con.'

'I'd give my soul to believe that,' he told her, and turned away.

Christmas came and went like a dream. Moira kept looking at the little gold locket Con had given her. It was silver and shaped like a star. There was a tiny diamond in the centre.

'Not in the Bertos class I'm afraid,' he said apologetically. 'But who knows? One day!'

'Oh Con!' Her eyes filled with sentimental tears, 'I'll treasure this for always.' She threw her arms round his neck and kissed him. 'Thank you!'

There was no time for anything else after that because Jade took over. A wildly ecstatic Jade who wanted them to play all the games with her, give her all their attention, and in short join her in having fun. She went to bed exhausted. Moira, dizzy with delight, took in a deep breath. Christmas in Blanes, she thought, is a memory I'll cherish all the days of my life. And what a wonderful smell Christmas has, of cooking, of oranges, and the pungeant odour of pine. The aroma of fresh evergreens festooned everywhere. What a wonderful time the three of us had gathering them. She said as much to Con who smiled his white-toothed smile.

'And now it's our time. Jaysus the energy that wee girl has. I'm glad she's abed at last. Now for our treat. I have bought some rich red wine just for us. Will you indulge?'

She looked at him, rosy-faced and bright-eyed.

'Wine gets to me, Con. And the only other time I drank too much I – I had quite a time fending off Yani.'

He stared at her very direct.

'So! You are comparing me to the Greek? Will you fend me off too?'

She took in a deep breath, dismayed because she had said the wrong thing.

'No. You misunderstood,' she replied.

'Then fetch the glasses, girl,' he said, daring her with his eyes. 'What are you waiting for?'

It was late when, in a pleasantly mellow mood, Moira found herself being led upstairs to her room. Con set her down on her bed and attempted to let go. She clung to him, feeling warm and wanton and glowing all over.

'Behave yourself,' he said quietly. 'The wine was too strong. You will feel differently in the morning, mavoureen.'

'Stay with me, Con,' she whispered. 'I want you too.'

'When you're stone cold sober you'll hate me if I take you at your word now,' he told her. 'I will not take advantage of you. It's the drink, sweet thing.'

'Stay with me – just for a little while?'

'May the saints preserve us,' Con groaned.

As he lay down beside her a thrill of excitement tinged with a little fear went through her. Moira gasped and half desperately lifted her lips to his. He began caressing her, gently and tenderly and she wanted him to go on and on. She kissed him back and crooned his name, sobbed his name, and clung on. But gradually he slowed down and finally, with deep care, he held her away.

'No, mavoureen,' he told her in a deep voice. 'This cannot be.' He swore softly. 'I have taken a mean advantage. May the Holy Mother forgive me!'

'Con,' she gasped, 'there's nothing to forgive!'

'I allowed you to drink too much wine, sweet thing,' he told her sternly. 'Now I am sane, and you'll never know how greatly I'm hating my sanity. When you are ready, really ready, you must come to me. Do you understand? You must come to *me*!'

'I'm here now!' she said urgently. 'And I'm as good as Rowena any day.'

'She is a different matter entirely. I am thinking about you and only you.' He was trying to lighten the atmosphere now, teasing, 'I'll never have you put me in Yani's category. A terrible thing that would be!' He smiled and held her close, 'It must never be said that Conor MacCluskey took a mean advantage. Come on, me darlin', help me to be a good man, and settle down before we wake up young Jade.'

Moira refused to be light-hearted. Hurt, humiliated, she felt he was holding back for Rowena's sake, in order not to be unfaithful to the rich and famous artist, she thought bitterly and had to fight back her tears.

'Moira?' he whispered. 'Settle down. There's my wee girl.'

She did as directed. Turned her face to the wall and listened as he walked out of the room...

After that, outwardly at least, things went on the same. Con avoided her eyes, but sketched her at every available moment.

Too soon, the old year died and the lease was up.

'Where to, Moira O'Malley?' Con tried to tease, though his expression was bleak. 'Will it be to the studio with me? I am quite certain that it would be all right.'

'No,' she told him gravely, knowing she would live in the gutter before going to Rowena Wray's place. 'I have decided, and did so a while ago, that Jade and I will go to Flo's.'

'But I thought you were afraid of ... Afraid for Jade?'

'No, Con,' she told him calmly. 'You taught me a lesson and taught me well. Fear must be faced and fought before it will disappear. I have made up my mind exactly what I am going to do.'

Before she left Thundersley for good, Moira visited Mrs Peacock and asked her to take the majority of her clothes. She kept her best coat, and the two-piece suit, as well as changes of ordinary everyday things. But the surplus, the luxurious items

Yani had insisted on, all were exchanged for a fair amount of money. Moira was no longer destitute.

Jade was allowed to keep everything. A strangely quiet and watchful Jade. A child who was openly shocked and hating the idea of returning to Flo's.

'She sent us away before,' she argued. 'She won't want us any more than we want horrible old her!'

'We will go inside when it's very dark and no one will see,' Moira told her. 'Don't you understand? If people have been looking for us, the Lodge would have been the first place they'd try. So they'd never think to watch the place again. No, darling, I think you'll find I'm right, and they would have given Jordan Lodge the all clear. We couldn't go to a safer place.'

'I want to stay here!'

'Oh minx,' Moira whispered, distressed. 'So do I...'

Chapter Twenty-Nine

'Stone the crows!' Flo gasped, now convinced that Moira was rich and famous because of the newspaper article. Her face was as red as a turkey cock. 'What a turn up for the books! How did you get here?' She turned to the dour Maisy Noice, 'You could knock me down with a feather! Ain't this real bloody marvelous?'

'Very,' Maisy said, and without waiting to be told, plodded over to the range to take up the already boiling kettle. 'We could do with a cuppa, eh?'

'It's good to be back, Flo,' Moira whispered tearfully, resolutely ignoring Jade's mutinous silence, her own words rushing out, tumbling over each other like a waterfall. 'We came by train. We wish to have your best front double, if it's vacant and all right with you? And if Stavros doesn't mind, I'd like him to take Jade in hand, on a professional basis of course. And while I think of it—'

'Hold your horses, Moir! Gawd's truth, you're a one. After all this time, years it's been, and here you are, bold as brass – looking like a real posh lady too. And Jade! Bli' she's grown a treat.' Flo was now openly fawning, flustered and excited. 'We've heard from ol' Con of course, about how famous you are and that, because you're his model, but we never expected to see yer here again.'

'That's unkind of you, Flo,' Moira replied and smiled, wondering how she could have ever been so afraid of this lady who could be nice or nasty at the drop of a hat. 'I've kept away, and deadly silent, for the same reason that you sent me from here.'

'I dunno as how the position's changed,' Flo said and looked uneasy. 'Come to think of it...'

'It doesn't matter very much about the situation changing, Flo,' Moira pointed out. 'Because I myself have changed. My whole outlook has, and that makes all the difference. Now, may we take off our coats and sit down please?'

'Since when did you ever ask if you could sit or take off your coat – and what a coat! You could get a quid for that off Anne Cherry.'

Moira smiled to herself, knowing very well that Flo would faint if she knew how much the coat had actually cost. And as for sitting down! She remembered obediently standing, eating a coveted slice of bread, watching and praying that Flo had stayed on gin. It didn't matter. Nothing, she thought sadly, did any more.

When she and Con had parted she had smiled up into his eyes, determined to hide her feelings. And he had been brief, to the point, and too casual to be true. Of course he was hiding the fact that he must be over the moon to be seeing Rowena Wray! Probably he was glad to be shot of her and the young Chinese kid he had insisted on calling a spoilt brat. She could almost hate him, if she didn't miss him so much.

Moira helped Jade off with her coat and took it and her own to the hanger in the hall. When she returned to the kitchen she found Jade deliberately ignoring Flo's friendly overtures.

She hates it here, Moira told herself bleakly. Well I don't – at least, not that much. And for once the little madam must buckle down.

But her own true self was arguing, whispering in her mind. All this is like going back in time. After Northmays, and beloved Blanes, Jade must think I'm pulling her down, down, down. And perhaps I am, Moira reflected.

Her treacherous thoughts filled her with guilt.

'Where's Freddy?' she asked, smiling brightly. 'I'm longing to see him.'

'He's gone to the Doc with Babs. He'll fetch your case in when he comes back.'

'Our luggage will be along later,' Moira said. 'I'm having it delivered. I just wanted to see Fred, and who's Babs?'

'Oo-er! Madam marm-stink is it?' Flo teased as she plonked

344

herself down beside Moira. 'Having luggage delivered and that! As for Fred, well he—' Her chins began to wobble merrily, ''Course! You don't know! Here, Moir, how's this for a laugh? His Babs is up the duff!' Flo nudged Moira with her elbow. 'I didn't know he had it in him!'

'His Babs?'

'Barbara Yeats! Remember her? Well, she tried to run away. The Yeats's was after her, and Freddy stepped in. Apparently her and Freddy 'ad been making sheeps eyes at each other for years. They met at last and they've been together ever since. Made that basement into a palace, she has. And I like the girl. I like her a lot.'

'Worth her weight in gold, that one,' Maisy put in.

'Mind your own!' Flo cut her down to size, 'I don't give you no three and six to but in!'

Three and six, Moira thought and wanted to hug herself. Things were looking up! And as for Freddy! How wonderful. If only . . . She came back to listen to Flo, who was as usual being down-to-earth.

'Moir's only staying till she gets a posh place of her own, Maise,' she said firmly, 'so I've gotta make hay while the sun shines.'

'Flo, I—' Moira began, feeling hot with shame; had Flo guessed? But Flo would have none of it.

'Jordan Street ain't no place for a famous lady what's been in the newspaper, girl. Even I know that.'

'Stop it, Flo,' Moira said sharply. 'And stop acting as though you've forgotten that you're the only mother I've ever known.'

'One what knows when somethink's not right. And it ain't right you stayin' here. Them nobs what help sell Con's pictures knew that! You've got to move on if you want to go up in the world.'

'That's what I thought.' Jade had come to life, and was intent on being bad-mannered and very very rude. 'Honestly!'

'You always was a proper little madam,' Flo told her and sniffed.

There was no time for more because the door opened with a bang and Freddy came in with Barbara. He gave Moira a wide, wonderful smile and in a trice she had been swung high in his arms.

345

'Now,' he said. 'I am extra happy!'

'Dear, dear Freddy,' Moira choked, remembering that sunny day in the garden and Freddy walking towards her with his gift, the ice cream she'd pigged and enjoyed so much. 'Seeing you has just made everything perfect! Put me down and introduce me to your wife.'

He set her down and looked perplexed.

'This is Babs,' he said proudly. 'But she is not my wife.'

Moira, alive and laughing now, kissed the shy-looking young woman and said, 'I've been dying to meet you for years! I used to see you sitting on the step and I wanted to talk, but— Anyway, that's beside the point. Now I have, and I've heard your news. Was the visit to the doctor's all right.'

Barbara nodded, but it was Flo who explained.

'Bab's isn't all that strong, so we've had her under special care. But we've been told that things are going along well. We've just got to look after her a bit special, that's all.'

Moira nodded, delighted, then asked Barbara direct. 'How long before . . .'

'In three months time,' Barbara whispered and went as red as fire. 'Or p'raps a little more.'

'Then we haven't much time, have we?'

'Pardon me?'

'To get you and Freddy married!'

Barbara looked nervously at Flo, and so did Freddy.

'I love weddings,' Moira said, beaming. 'We'll make arrangements and get things going. What a home-coming this is turning out to be!'

'Oi!' Flo said, 'you ain't half got to be a bossy boots in your old age. What's come over you, eh?' Her expression changed, became thoughtful. 'Getting them spliced ain't such a bad idea at that. It'll make things lawful like. Gawd, it'll be some do! It'll be bloody marvellous if Will gets back in time.'

'Not Will Fenning?' Moira's eyes opened wide. 'Oh Flo!'

'Turned up like a bad penny, he did.' Flo playfully poked Moira in the ribs, reminding her of Flo's old habit of painfully punctuating her harangues with a similar gesture. 'Right old turn up for the books that was. He goes off to sea and comes back regular-like now. I thought as how you knew.'

'How could I?' Moira choked and found herself thanking

God for small mercies. If Flo had Will, and Freddy his Babs, it wouldn't be so bad when she and Jade were able to find somewhere else to live.

After that there was lots of animated conversation and news exchanging. The luggage was delivered and Moira and Jade went upstairs to inspect their room. It was the best Flo had, clean, workmanlike but nothing special. Jade continued to look po-faced. Once they were alone she burst out. 'Why have you brought me back here? I thought it wasn't safe. I hate it, and I hate all of them, especially horrible old Flo! And—'

'Sit down, Jade.'

'I don't want to—'

'Sit down!'

Jade sat on the edge of the bed.

'Now you listen to me,' Moira told her, feeling deep-down angry, 'if it hadn't been for Flo, you and River Pearl would have died on the streets. Never forget that! Indeed, River Pearl looked near death the night Flo brought her in and in so doing, saved you both. Just as it was Flo who saved yours truly from the orphanage or worse. It was Flo who found River Pearl a job. Flo who let you both stay in her attic, yes even at risk to herself. And Flo who arranged for our escape on the night your people almost found you out.'

'But she's—'

'She is Miss Williamson to you, and deserving of your utmost respect. Do you understand?'

Jade remained silent and pulled a face.

'If you don't change your attitude at once,' Moira told her coldly, 'I shall wash my hands of you. Con's right! You are a spoiled brat. I have tried to copy River Pearl and treat you like some sort of queen, but I shouldn't have. You don't deserve it, and you make me feel ashamed.'

There came a tap on the door and at Moira's tightly controlled call, Stavros came in. Immediately the tension in the room vanished, it was so good to see him. He looked exactly the same. A wise old man, a trusted friend to whom Jade ran with outstretched arms. Then Mr Binks arrived, and surprisingly, Chumley was there too. Chumley was grinning all over his foxy-face.

'Cripes!' he told her, 'You look every inch a lady, Moir. I like your dress. Be tuppence ter talk to you now, eh?'

'Really?' she asked him and chuckled. 'Do you honestly believe that? I'm going to have to earn my keep you know. I won't be in every painting Con does.'

'Why not?' Chumley asked and noticed the swift reddening of her face.

'Chumley,' she said hesitantly, 'and you, Mr Binks, please agree with me that it's best that Harriet doesn't start coming here, upsetting Jade. At least not for a little while – until I've got my bearings I mean.'

'Even I'll drink to that one,' Mr Binks said. 'I don't know what's got into her, poor ol' thing. Prowls around she does, looking for this 'un.' He nodded towards Jade. 'She's afraid somethinks happened to her.'

'Then please explain that Jade is quite safe and well, Mr Binks, that you have seen it with your own eyes. But that she must have time to settle down. Will you do that for me?'

Mr Binks smiled and nodded his head.

Before the week was out, it was just like old times and Moira and even Jade had settled in. Moira wrote to Daisy and Sid, as well as to Cissy, to tell them that her engagement to Yani was off.

Jade spent a great deal of time with Stavros and soaked up knowledge like a sponge. She ceased to moan about being in Flo's.

Realising that she did indeed have to get a job, Moira considered what was best to do. She had heard no further word from Con. He, according to Chumley, had shut himself away and was concentrating on his painting. Moira felt a wild aching of her heart, and the heat of unshed tears, she missed him so. But Con was a singular man and wanted no further truck with her. She had known that by the distantly tight expression on his face when he had wished her goodbye.

Clearly she could not ask Con for help. And Chumley had pointed out that the market-holders would never take her seriously from now on. Worse, the Depression still held sway.

Moira still had money from the pawning of her engagement ring and her fine clothes. She was not destitute, but accepted that the funds she had would not last for ever. She had to earn some money. Had to!

She decided to go and see her old chums at the market. Just to say hello and pass the time of day. She would explain that having Con put her in a picture didn't mean anything at all!

In the end, because they were so busy getting on with their own affairs, that they didn't seem to either notice or recognise her, she funked it. Eventually deciding to wait a while before making herself known.

Moira went back to Jordan Street depressed. She looked about her, even walked quite slowly past the fried fish shop. Dave Dilley was seldom if ever there, Flo had said, and a good job too, since he was as nutty as they come. The Yeats's house looked deserted, but the hordes of ragged kids were swinging on lamp posts, playing football with newspaper balls tied round with string. The other most favourite lark was dropping cap-bangers behind girls to make them scream. The women were still there, standing on their doorsteps, bitching and brawling as was their way. Nothing had changed, Moira thought ruefully. Except that she herself was no longer so afraid.

'Who are you looking at?' a woman snapped at her as she walked by. 'What are you doing down here, lady muck? Piss off!'

They were all honing in on her now. Hard-eyed, bloody-minded, out to do an intruder down. Moira stood still, facing them, chin high.

'I won't go away because I live here,' she replied firmly. 'What's more, I always have. In Jordan Lodge, remember? And if it all boils down to it, lady, I can out-shout, out-swear, and yes, even out-fight all of you!'

'Bleeding hell, you've got a nerve!' her aggressor sneered, recognising her. 'Sod off you stuck-up little mare, before I set ol' Dilley on ter yer.'

There was a chorus of laughter and lewd remarks about Moira and the fish fryer. She felt her blood running cold at the thought, but she stood there, rock-still, showing no fear. They sniggered among themselves, stood back and let her pass.

A victory! Moira thought. Con had been right! One had to face fear, and self-disgust! Yes, she told herself, I am horrible for thinking and feeling as Jade does about all this. I'm not

349

happy in Jordan Lodge any more and it no longer feels like home. And these days I just can't stand the way the smell of boiled cabbage overrides the smell of Maisy's Mansion polish. Were they all right about me? Am I snob? I thought they were only teasing, but could they all see through the act I was putting on? Things certainly seem different now. The Lodge seems smaller and darker than I remembered, and it is scruffy, damp, depressing and cold. Dear God, was I really that impressed with all I saw at Northmays? She hated herself all the way home.

Moira went through the rest of the day only half listening, pretending an interest she didn't feel, about the men Flo had met in the pub, the rowing and bawdiness she enjoyed at the Hare and Hounds. The stalking into Dave's place like an avenging angel to get her fish and chips from the Compton's, who had been left to run the show.

'Dave's a raving looney,' Flo said, 'talks to himself and thinks silly things. He followed Pearl once, did she tell you? She made out she didn't see him. Not that he ever bothered her. And she had other things on her mind.'

'I'll never forget River Pearl,' Moira replied. 'I loved her, Flo.'

'She was all right.' Flo sniffed. 'But not my cup of tea, if you know what I mean? But we wasn't talking about her, was we?'

'You were carrying on about Dave Dilley.'

'Well, he's a nutter! You'd think he was close to that brother-in-law of his, that's a bloody joke for a start. Another thing, he won't believe old Stan's snuffed it. Goes visiting Stan's place does Dave. Mingles with them methies, and is as thick-headed as they are. He talks to Stan like he can see him, so they say. The idea fair gives me the creeps.'

'He has always been sick.' Moira told her, 'but you wouldn't see it would you? I tried to tell you once, but you wouldn't listen at all! I think the idea of that man scares me still.'

'I ain't too happy about him either,' Flo admitted. 'When I think I used to let the old sod in here. Let him— Oh shit! Thank Gawd Freddy got my door key back off him. Still, it don't matter now, does it? I've got my Will, and when he's away, there's always my Freddy to protect me. Dilley's scared stiff of

350

them both.' She smirked. 'I still insist on me gherkin, you know. What a caution Will is!'

Flo burbled on about her Will, even to the point of hoping he'd want to get spliced.

Poor Flo, Moira thought, I'll believe that when I see it! Then, because Jade was in with Stavros and all but hanging on to his coat tails, she went back to her own thoughts.

She let her memory take her back to Blanes Cottage. Remembering that marvellous night with Con, when she had wanted, no *needed* him in the fullest sense and he had spurned her. He probably remembered his darling Rowena right there and then, she thought bitterly, and wanted to break down and cry.

Still hurt, and hating Con for turning her down, she nevertheless decided to do as he advised and continue to take fear by the throat. He had been right, she had definitely won the seige in Jordan Street. And Flo talking about River Pearl had helped make up her mind.

When she woke the next day she washed and dressed and made Jade's breakfast. Jade dashed off with indecent haste to find Stavros. Flo was busy having her usual set-to with Maise.

Sitting alone, Moira was wistfully remembering the early walks she used to take. How peaceful it had been, and how wonderful to sit on the rocks and just watch the sea. Now she was back at square one and the ghost of Dave Dilley had reared its head once more – and the reminder of River Pearl hadn't helped either. Those awful Chinese men were still out there somewhere. One of them at least having committed murder. Was she man or mouse to let all this anguish and fear take over again?

On an impulse and without breathing a word to anyone, she left Jordan Lodge. Jade was by this time bending studiously over Stavros's table. His whole world that table, Moira had once thought. Sadly, it seemed quite ordinary now.

Moira's heart was hammering away as she made her way to the local police station and began speaking to the man at the desk. He was wearing a police sergeant's uniform. He had a long, lean face and crisply tight iron grey hair; his eyes were direct and silver blue. Moira took in a deep breath.

'I have come here,' she said tremulously, 'to tell you that I

351

knew the Chinese lady who was found murdered in Shaft Alley.' She hid her nervously twisting hands from his view and continued. 'Her name was River Pearl and her husband's name is Li Tzu...'

'I beg your pardon, Miss?'

He was looking into her face, his expression giving nothing away. She went over it again. He was staring at her and stroking his chin. Then at last he said evenly:

'I don't know what you're getting at, Miss. That case was cleared up over a year ago. The lady was the wife of a certain Mr Ah Weng of Peking Street. Mr Ah Weng was accused, and subsequently convicted of her murder.'

Moira stared at him, unable to take in what he said, or the implications. She finally stuttered, 'Are – are you absolutely sure?'

'Yes miss.'

'I mean, I can't believe...'

'And neither can I, miss,' he told her carefully and was still stroking his chin. 'You have just told me a very fanciful tale. One that I'm sure you'll agree, doesn't make too much sense. We have received no report of a missing Mrs Li River Pearl. Missing or murdered, no one has come forward. Not ever. Now, will you please go over all of this again?'

As she gave him the details, Moira's thoughts were flying. If it had been a Mrs Ah Weng who had been murdered, then where was River Pearl?

Shock waves undulated through her. She felt stunned, giddy, barely able to grasp what she had been told. But overriding all else was the fact that she had been wrong, wrong, wrong! And her mistake had stopped her continuing the search, and per-haps ... Dear God in Heaven! Was River Pearl alive?

'Miss?' the officer was staring as her hard.

He thinks I belong in a loony bin, Moira thought frantically. Oh he mustn't! I need his help!

'Perhaps you'll explain further, miss?' the sergeant was asking and his eyes were steel gimlets now. 'Please tell me the last time you saw Mrs Li alive. As I have said, no one was reported missing. Are you prepared to make a statement? I'll need times and dates.'

'I can't remember the actual date,' she said, panic making her mouth go dry. 'A lot has happened since then and . . .'

'Let's go over it again, shall we, miss? One step at a time?' He turned to a constable. 'Wilks, fetch D.I. Matheson. This young lady is going to make a statement.' He turned back to Moira, 'If you'll come with me, please?'

Moira followed him to an interview room. A long-nosed, hard-eyed woman constable joined them and the sergeant left. Shortly afterwards a big, podgy man with a double chin, red cheeks and warm brown eyes, came in. His attitude was such that he inspired confidence – at first. Then things began to change. His air of authority, his crisp no nonsense questions, his gradual intensity eventually making Moira feel guilty of every crime in the book.

It went on and on after that, the same old questions put in different ways, the air of disbelief, then amazingly, open suspicion! Of her? Oh God! she thought, they're actually trying to trap me! Well I'm having none of that!

Undeterred, cheeks blazing now, Moira clearly and concisely, repeated River Pearl's story, and of the avowed emnity declared by one Kung Chin. She finished by saying, 'And why you have never heard of this before is because at the time it happened, my landlady, and all in her establishment, were also under threat from Kung Chin. We believe he hates us, simply because we took in, and tried to defend River Pearl.'

'What I can't understand, Miss O'Malley,' the inspector said coldly, 'is why, after all this time, you have seen fit to come forward now? Surely even you can see that this hardly makes sense.'

'I have come off my own bat,' she told him. 'Even though I'm sure my friends won't be too happy about it when they find out. We know nothing of Chinese ways, nor do we understand their long lasting threats of vengeance. However, we have a wedding happening soon. The doors of Jordan Lodge will be more or less open for the day. We – we are asking for your help. If you please?'

There were more questions, answers and then a statement to be set down and signed. Moira left the station exhausted and a bunch of nerves. But she had accomplished much, not least that the police would now begin looking into things. They would at long last sort out Kung Chin if he was around, and find out all they could about Mr Li Tzu. It was an added bonus that they would keep a weather eye open in Jordan Street too, just in case. Then she felt sick to her stomach, suddenly realizing the implications where Jade was concerned. Had she made a terrible mistake? Had she merely jumped out of the frying pan and into the fire?

Moira dismissed that fear resolutely, more concerned with the over-riding question, where oh where was River Pearl? What happened to her? Could she really and truly be alive?

A wild hope seared through her. If River Pearl lived, Moira would find her. Just wait till she told all this to Flo!

She tried to dismiss the thought of Flo's forthcoming fury when she learned what had been done. And her creed, 'Yer keep the bobbys at arm's length,' she was wont to say. 'Bloody slimey lot!'

Now, having got the whole business off her chest, and done the right thing, Moira wished she had had the courage to defy Flo, and report everything years ago. Even so, she felt discomforted that she had not been fully open with the Inspector. She had told him everything – except about the existance of Jade. She had judged it better to keep silent on the subject of Li Tzu's only child.

Grimly, Moira thought, Jade will hate me until her dying day if the authorities put her in a Home ... I shall have to conceal her even more carefully now the police are involved.

There was a right old ding-dong when Flo heard what Moira had done.

'Gorn to the p'lice?' she shouted, going beetroot red. 'Told them about Pearl living here? Gawd forgive you, Moir, you've put me in the shit and no mistake.'

'Flo, please stop ranting and raving!' Moira pleaded. 'Think! If it wasn't River Pearl they found that day, what happened to her? Perhaps she's being held by that terrible Kung Chin. Perhaps...'

'Shut up, Moir. You're like a dripping tap. I don't think I'll ever forgive you for this.'

An hour or so later the police called at Jordan Lodge. Before she knew what was happening, Jade found herself locked up in the attic, and warned to be quiet. Statements were taken and signed by everyone in the house. Then the police left and that seemed to be that.

Nothing happened. Nothing at all.

A week later Flo, still impatient with Moira, told her to stop carrying on about River Pearl and start thinking about Babsy's "do" instead.

'Shut up, Moir, you're getting on my tits. All what you're carrying on about, Chinamen what do murders, worse, Pearl being kept alive and tortured somewhere is so much hogwash. All I know is, you've really put the cat among the pigeons. We've gotta watch out for the bobbys as well as sodding Chinks. Moira O'Malley, I could wring your bloody neck.'

'I'm sorry!' Moira whispered. 'I thought I was doing right, bringing things out into the open. Instead I've made things worse and – and none of this seems real.'

'The unborn baby's real enough, and so is Babs! Put your mind on the wedding. You're the big mouth what started all that up too! Now Freddy's set on it. Keeps on about Barbara being his wife. Yes, she's Barbara to him, not Babs. Very particular he is about that – because she's turned out to be a lady, not a mischief-making little bitch like you.'

'I'm so sorry,' Moira whispered. 'I'll look for somewhere else to live and—'

'Oh no you don't! You ain't being let off so lightly. You're going to help with the wedding you put in their minds. And you can help pay for it too. See to it that they have a good spread, because my bit of money will only go so far.'

'Anything. Anything!' Moira whispered. 'Oh, Flo!'

'And I want you to give Babs one of your dresses. She ain't got nothing fit for a bride to wear.' She glared and stood there, hands on hips meaning every word. 'And sod that missing woman! If you ask me, she's dead and done for anyway. If she was alive nothing would have kept her from that snotty little cow Jade.'

Weeping, heartbroken because in her anxiety to banish her own fears, she had made a difficult situation a million times worse, Moira was unable to reply.

'Now,' Flo snapped, 'you can turn off the water works. I've had my say and it's over and done with.' Her tone softened. 'You did what you thought right and no one can do more. And

355

we've got over a bloody sight worse in our time, eh? Now we've gotta sort out one of your frocks for Babs to wear.'

'No!' Moira faltered. 'I intend to buy her something new and very nice . . . if you don't mind?'

'Bloody hell! Mind? What a lovely idea? I'll have to see the tally man and get our Fred a decent suit if we're going all posh. It'll be perfect if Will can get back in time. He can be a witness – oh and we ain't going to invite none of them Yeats.'

'Flo, I . . .'

'For Gawd's sake, stop acting like a wet week and get on with things! Oh and when you take Babsy out, remember her favourite colour's blue. Things might be difficult – what with her shape an' all. Get her a coat if you can, it'll be brass monkeys, and what with all that standing about! Got to look after her, you know.'

'You've really taken to her, haven't you, Flo?'

'She's a wonder with Freddy, so I'm bound to take to her ain't I?' Her tone softened. 'But make no mistake, you'll always be my girl.'

The wedding was a right old turn-out. The sun shone, for all it was windy and cold. The bride and groom stood on the steps at the Registrar's, smiling. Flo was crying and clinging on to Will's arm. Jade was all dressed up, looking as dainty as a Chinese doll. Maisy was there, exclaiming how nice Babs looked in blue "and what loverly white flowers!". Stavros and Mr Binks were there, looking proud. And in spite of all Flo's plans, the Yeats turned up.

'Good on yer, girl!' Bert Yeats roared out, and Greta thumped him one for his pains.

Then everyone walked back to Jordan Lodge and the knees-up began. The beer flowed, and the gin, and everything else. The food was eaten, and at long last, Moira enjoyed some of the Pie Shop's wonderful pink ham. Old man Yeats proceeded to get drunk as a skunk, and so did Greet. A rousing good time was had by all.

Moira stood back, watching. Her heart was full, for Freddy and Babs, Will and Flo. She had loved every minute of getting the wedding arranged and paying out so that Barbara had a day to remember for the rest of her life. She laughed and kissed

356

Flo who said, 'What a right old turn-up for the books, eh Moir? I can't get over all this and the way you've changed. You've really taken charge of everything and managed so bloody well! And Will says you was dead right to spill the beans to the p'lice.'

'Thank you,' Moira replied, and wished that River Pearl could have been there if only to have seen Jade. Then, unbidden, she was remembering Con all over again. The hurt of his rejection, the strange yearning sense of loss always hovering there in the back of her mind when she thought of him.

'Why are you looking sad?' Jade asked as she came to stand at her side. 'Are you missing Con?'

'Don't be nosy, minx,' Moira replied, smiling.

'You are missing Con, I know you are,' Jade told her imperiously, 'and so am I! And I wish we were back in Blanes cottage.'

'And not grand old Northmays?' Moira teased, misty-eyed. 'What on earth's come over you?'

'We were happy in Blanes,' Jade said solemnly. 'But we are not happy here.'

'Now things are settled for all of them, and I know that they won't be hurt at our leaving,' Moira told her quietly, 'I'll start to look for somewhere else for us to live. We'll have to go anyway, because the whole world will know we're both back now. Yes, we'll have to leave.'

'Soon?' Jade asked eagerly.

'Very.' Moira replied.

That night Moira tossed and turned in her bed, thinking of Con. He had not attended the wedding, neither had Chumley and Cissy. Daisy and Sid had been invited but had made their excuses. They have probably heard what a devilish hole Jordan Street is, Moira thought. But that didn't stop Con before and it never would now. No, he never came because of me!

At that moment she would have given anything to turn back the clock. To be with Con in Blanes.

Chapter Thirty

Everyone overslept. Even Maisy was late, having enjoyed more than her usual tipple the previous day. Freddy and Barbara had gone off to Southend for a week. Flo's diamond ring and Will's contribution had paid for that treat. Having left a note for Jade, Moira sat at the kitchen table sipping tea. It still irked her that these days Flo steadily refused to allow her help with chores. With the wedding over, Moira knew that she would have less than nothing to do.

Now her mind was made up. Since she and Jade needed to move on, she would find a new place to live. After that she would haunt the market until someone gave her a job. As for Jade, she felt sure that no matter where they finished up, Stavros would come each day, to look after and educate Jade. Yes, it would work! And during any free time to be had, she would rack her brains and search high and low for clues that might help her to find out what had happened to River Pearl.

She finished her tea and decided to leave there and then and go in search of a house or a flat.

An imperative knock on the door made her jump. Moira answered it, only to find a policeman standing there.

'Miss Moira O'Malley?'

'Yes?' she replied, already on her guard. 'That's me.'

'Will you present yourself at the station at eleven o'clock sharp, miss?' His question was more of a command. 'And if possible, bring proof of your association with Mrs Li River Pearl with you.'

'Oh but – I mean, why eleven o'clock?'

'I think that's when Mr Li Tzu will be present, Miss. Make it eleven sharp, if you please.'

'Of course,' she told him and watched as he walked stolidly back down the path towards the green gate. Then she shut the door.

'It simply can't be!' Moira whispered wildly to herself. 'After all this time? River Pearl's noble lord husband has actually been found? It had taken the police no time at all! It was unbelievable. Especially when one considered how long River Pearl had tried.

If only I had known! she thought and brushed away frustrated tears. If only I had not been so stupid! That damned lord husband must be a wily devil. I bet he stayed lost because he wanted to. Just wait till I see him! I'll certainly give him the length of my tongue!

Her mind was racing now. She decided not to tell Jade in case things went wrong. Then she frowned. They needed proof. Probably the stinking, self-satisfied, arrogant noble lord was hoping that there *was* no proof! Then he could continue to wriggle out of his responsibilities, just as he had for all this time. Well that wouldn't happen, oh no! Proof? Ah, yes!

Moira was out of Jordan Lodge in a trice and almost ran all the way to Market Street and Harriet's.

If Harriet was surprised to see her, she didn't show it.

'Well, girl,' she said, her face as expressionless as an Egyptian mask, 'what brings you back here? Don't you care for your life?'

'The brooch.' Moira panted. 'Jade's brooch. Did you sell it?'

Harriet looked mean. Her mouth turned down.

'Why? What's it to you?'

'Her father's turned up. The police want proof.'

'I haven't got the brooch. Now sling your hook before I—'

'Of course,' Moira cut in smoothly, giving Harriet a direct and very confident look. 'I could have given the Inspector your address, but I thought you'd prefer me not to,' she paused significantly before adding, 'if you know what I mean?'

Harriet gave Moira a black, glittering stare, then left her to go into the back room. She returned seconds later to hand over the brooch that still remained in the little red japanned box.

'Thank you,' Moira said and ran.

She was heaving, her sides aching, when she returned to her room and took up the little Chinese picture painted on silk. She was about to leave when Jade came in wanting to talk.

'I've got to go out,' Moira told her, 'and I'm in a rush. Wait here.'

'Have you found us a new place?' Jade began, her eyes lighting up. 'Oh good! I want to come.'

'Wait here!'

'I don't want to. I said, I want to—'

'Jade – shut up!'

Moira turned tail and did not stop running until she arrived at the police station. She gave the picture and the brooch to the Inspector, who as usual had an expression that gave nothing away. Then she was led to a waiting room and invited to sit down.

So his noble lordship hasn't shown up, she fumed. Thank goodness I never told Jade. What a nasty man he must be, not at all like the great lord River Pearl told me about. Moira tried to picture her friend's husband from River Pearl's vivid descriptions. Tall and arrogant, Moira thought sourly, and impossibly good looking. Certainly very powerful and strong. A prince among men!

She was on edge, left alone by the distant-looking Inspector, who just by a mere look made her feel guilty of untold crimes. She grew more angry as the minutes ticked by. She calmed down a little when a cheery looking young constable with flaming red hair came in to give her a cup of tea.

It seemed many hours after that before the door opened again and the Inspector came in. With him was an old man, a slightly built Chinaman with a thin whispy beard, and a lined face. He was wearing a long dark blue silk robe and black padded over-jackets.

'Miss Moira O'Malley,' the Inspector introduced them in a brisk official way, 'Mr Li Tzu.'

Li Tzu put his beringed hands in his wide sleeves and bowed low, but not before Moira had seen his incredibly long finger nails.

'I am honoured to meet such good friend of greatly missed, very beautiful wife,' Li Tzu said in a high, thin voice. 'Is auspicious occasion to be introduced to young lady who was so kind to honourable Number Three. Much favoured wife gave partner of painting to own humble self. She must have greatly revered you, her true and most loyal friend.'

'River Pearl was – dear to me,' Moira told him unevenly. 'And the picture she gave me is beyond price.' She bit her lip to stop it from trembling and went on. 'She looked for you, her noble lord husband, night and day! She worked herself to skin and bone, and then in her spare time she walked the streets. Anywhere, everywhere and – and in the end—' She angrily brushed her tears away. 'And in the end, we'll never know what really happened to her. I – I believed that she had been killed.'

'Is my eternal regret that I did not know that Number Three wife survived the Chin attack. Was not until I received message from personage who runs funeral shop that I found out. Then, in all haste, I returned.'

'Then you didn't know that Kung Chin followed her here? That...'

'Message from honourable friend Chung Weng explained all things.' Li Tzu nodded like a clockwork sage. 'I have been travelling a great deal, and America is almost as vast as my own country. Mail took a long time to reach me. When letter finally reached me I made arrangements to come back here, to London, in all haste.'

'Then could you please sort out that horrible man?' Moira asked quickly. 'You know how he works. We don't and we've all been scared stiff of him. My friend, Miss Williamson, has seen Chinamen hanging about and she ... I mean we all have been on edge for a very long time!'

Li Tzu smiled a thin smile. It was only the merest hint of a grimace, but she fancied that the noble lord Li Tzu was feeling great satisfaction now. He bowed very politely, then speaking as though the policemen were not in the room, went on.

'Would perhaps interest honourable missy to know that Kung Chin began the voyage to America? This shortly after he learned that I had spent long time setting up main business interests over there. He was given to understand that I would never return to either Britain or to the Flowery Kingdom. Kung Chin's greatest enemy was own lowly self, so he made great haste to acquire passage on the S.S. *Oregon*.'

'If only River Pearl had lived to learn that!' Moira whispered and would have given her soul to have River Pearl there at her side. 'She heard that your enemy was all out to kill her to get his revenge. But that didn't stop her, oh no! She still kept on searching and trying.' Moira shrugged wearily. 'And all the time you were thousands of miles away!'

'Hai.' Li Tzu agreed.

'So it looks as though it wasn't anyone's fault.' Moira was forgiving him already and continued. 'She was so devoted to you, and heartbroken that she couldn't find you at all. I wish River Pearl had not spent all that time being so afraid. She came to look . . . look hunted in the end. And I came to hate that Kung Chin even though I never met him. He sounds a really terrible man.'

'As I have already explained to Chief Inspector,' Li Tzu said smoothly, 'unexpected accident happened to Kung Chin. By strange coincidence, Chung Han, number two son of honourable Chung Weng who you have met, was sailor on the S.S. *Oregon*. It was he who reported the accident to the ship's captain. He say that he had seen Kung Chin drinking too much saki. He was boasting that he could balance on rail when he fell overboard. His body was never found.'

'He – he's dead?' Moira gasped, and even though it was wicked to be overjoyed at someone's downfall, she felt giddy with relief.

'It may be presumed that gentleman has joined his ancestors,' Li Tzu said with quiet satisfaction, 'and is even now residing in all fourteen hells.'

'Oh!' Moira didn't know whether to laugh or cry with relief. 'You mean that we don't have to worry about him any more? Not even any of the friends who were so openly on his side?'

'All is safe,' Li Tzu replied and stared at her out of his melon seed eyes, so like Jade's. 'And when I heard, after a long time, about your visit to old friend in funeral shop, I set sail for this country at once. I presume that you heard from revered and honourable Number Three about happening in China?'

'Yes.'

'Did Number Three wife say anything about a child bearing the name Sweet Precious Jade?'

'I've got her,' Moira replied, throwing caution to the winds. Then, ignoring the listening policemen added, 'And what's more, I – I intend to keep her until I'm certain that all of this is true.' She continued apologetically, 'After all, you could be spinning a yarn and actually *be* Kung Chin for all I know.'

Li Tzu said nothing for a moment. He just stood there, expressionless, but Moira saw one tear escape. Remembering all that River Pearl had told her, Moira quickly looked away. It would be unkind to witness the old man's loss of face.

'Everything's in order, Miss O'Malley,' the Inspector said, coldly polite. 'We have ample proof of Mr Li Tzu's identity. He wishes you to go with him, to his house. He intends to show you the home he is prepared to offer to yourself, and now to his daughter.' He paused, then added meaningfully, 'Who you did not mention in your statement, Miss O'Malley. There is such a thing as withholding evidence, you know.' He watched the colour rising high on her cheekbones, and went on. 'Mr Tzu wishes to convey his gratitude for all you've done. And first of all he wishes you to inspect his home for yourself.'

'That's all very well, but—'

'Excuse me miss,' the Inspector stopped her in mid sentence, 'Mr Tzu has explained to our complete satisfaction, that he knew nothing of his wife's predicament. Nor that she had saved his daughter. By the time he learned the truth, and voyaged home here, you had disappeared. We have ample proof that all he has told us is true.'

'Really?' Moira asked, wondering wildly whether this could actually be happening. 'Then if everything is so clear cut, may I ask why you never heard anything about all this until I came in and told you? Why, I ask myself, didn't Mr Li Tzu contact you when he found River Pearl had gone missing? Not to mention me of course!'

Brown eyes gleamed sardonically.

'Tell me, Miss O'Malley, in your turn, why didn't you come to us? Clearly the gentleman made his own plans. Now please go along with him and at least visit his home. There is nothing more we can do at this stage. Besides—'

'Besides what exactly?' Moira was clutching at straws now, not at all certain of the turn of events. Feeling very unsure about going off anywhere with an unknown Chinaman.

'We do have other cases to attend to, Miss O'Malley.' The Inspector didn't even try to hide the fact that he wanted his office cleared.

363

'But you haven't sorted this one yet?' she objected. 'Haven't you forgotten the disappearance of River Pearl?'

'The matter will receive our fullest attention,' he replied. 'And we will of course be inviting you to help us with our enquiries at a later date. In the meantime, you should think hard, try to remember anything you heard or saw that might now seem suspicious? Oh, and don't hesitate to contact us if you feel you need our help.'

'Thank you,' she replied gravely. Then something made her add, 'There is something. I heard that a man named Dave Dilley followed River Pearl once. I don't believe anything happened in that direction, but ... But I feel you ought to know.'

'Thank you, Miss O'Malley' he said. She saw the sergeant behind him busily making notes and felt relieved. So they had been listening, they really had! They had indeed accepted all that she had said about River Pearl and were actually going to do something about it.

Moira felt both relieved, and utterly bewildered by the turn of events. She was not quite sure whether she liked River Pearl's lord husband, yet she felt instinctively that he had been telling the truth. But that evil little half smile had given him away. She was sure that it was on Li Tzu's orders that the unknown Kung Chin had been "helped" overboard.

Moira was not quite sure how it happened after that, but she found herself outside the police station and sitting in the back of a very large and impressive black car. Mr Li Tzu sat directly behind the uniformed driver, and at his nod the engine was started. The car, powerful and purring, sped away, another car followed with three men in it. Li Tzu's servants and a lawyer, the Inspector said, having seen Moira's look of dismay. Glancing at the servants did not reassure her. They all looked inscrutable and very Chinese, even though they did not have pigtails and wore Western clothes.

The drive was accomplished in silence through the East End. And because she was with a foreign nobleman, Moira looked at it all with new eyes, and saw the East End that, Stavros maintained, held the magic and mystery of Dickensian times in its narrow, twisting streets.

To those who knew it, it was not an alarming place, filled

with Jack the Rippers and blousey women ready to kill men for meat to make pies. It could be aggressive and tough and bloody-minded, but it held vigorous life, and above all, the bustling waterway.

The car drove through Limehouse until it reached a large establishment set on the bend of the river. It slowed before an impressive set of gates, which were opened by a manservant, and then drove through. The vehicle halted in a courtyard shaded by a large weeping willow tree. Beyond the courtyard a flight of steps flanked by stone lions led to the front door of a great stone house.

As they were helped out of the car, a woman came down the steps towards them. Clad in tunic and trousers of mid-blue, her black hair skewered on top of her head, she moved gracefully, though she was neither slim nor young. Upon reaching them she clasped her hands together and began bowing low.

'Welcome home, Lord,' she said and her voice was soft, her smile warm. She bowed again, to Moira this time. 'Missy.'

'Look after honourable guest,' Li Tzu told her. 'I will expect you to come to my study in one hour.' He then broke into Chinese, and the woman's face showed a spasm of pleasure.

He walked up the steps, his blue-veined hand holding on to the balustrade, his servants and the lawyer, like fussy hens, closely attending him. Again Moira thought he looked very frail.

The woman bowed once more. Her eyes were kind as she said to Moira, 'Come!'

After that Moira realized that River Pearl had spoken no less than the truth. There was luxury everywhere. Carpets, magnificent things of Oriental design, predominantly green and blue. Furniture, carved and black. There were ornaments of jade, screens of silk decorated with gold, tapestries on the walls that looked impossibly rich and old. A fat-bellied god who was smiling all over his face, seemed to be watching over all. Enormous vases on stands with intricately carved dragon legs were so awe-inspiringly lovely with their peacock and lotus designs that they made Moira catch her breath.

The Chinese woman led Moira to a room where the carpet was red, and there were many green and yellow dragons with fiery tongues in the decor. As elsewhere the furniture here was magnificent; black screens held gold and red lily designs, there were backless chairs, low tables, and a couch holding many coloured cushions.

'The lord Li Tzu has own private apartment,' the woman explained, as she and Moira sat down. 'This is women quarters of which I am head,' she covered her mouth with her hand, looking shy as she said, 'which took much hard work. You will meet other ladies of household at later date. We are all new here. Now, you will honour me and take tea?'

Moira smiled and nodded and knew that the last thing she wanted to do was drink tea. The woman clapped her hand and a girl of about sixteen came in laden with a tray and tea things. She set it down on a low table and left as silently as she had arrived. It was left to Moira's hostess to do the honours. Uncomfortable in the silence, Moira asked,

'May I ask your name?'

'Desert Grass.'

'That's nice.'

'Is strong, beautiful name,' came the reply. 'I was born near place where it grew.'

'How interesting. Tell me about it,' Moira replied politely, and was wondering what the dickens was expected of her. Everything in her life seemed so confusing now. The woman, clearly very anxious to please and almost desperate to entertain, continued.

'My father travelled the sands of Northern China and came to greatly value gi-gi-tsao, that is Desert Grass in my tongue. It counts as one of the most valuable harvests. When young and tender, if chopped with a fodder knife, its green shoots are suitable for horses to eat, but the plant grows quickly and before long its stalks are so hard that even camels pass it by. When it reaches its full height of seven or eight feet it is cut, garnered, and serves many useful purposes. Knotted it becomes a barrier against sand. It is woven to make mats to cover mud beds, and also to line the mud roof of the oases shack. The same mat, woven in another shape, forms the chassis of a village cart, and also makes it's awning. What is more—'

'How wonderful,' Moira was beginning to wish she hadn't asked. 'It's a very good name.'

'When young and tender, like green shoot, I was sold by my father, to a rich man. He treated me badly. I was in despair, but I learned to be like gi-gi tsao and become useful in many ways. I was eventually sold to man delivering necessary women to Chinese immigrants in America. The gods were kind and the honourable Li Tzu bought me.'

'The gods were kind?' Moira smiled unbelievingly. 'You reckon the gods were kind?'

'Was bought by good, kind man.'

'That's awful! And surely selling people is against the law?'

'Not in China. Is common practice to sell daughters when not enough food in house to feed them. But different in America. There are lots of things against the law and American policeman are very clever and have guns.' Desert Grass laughed shyly. 'But they do not know saying of wise old Chinaman who say "Softly, softly catchee monkey." Desperate men can be very cunning when it comes to buying and selling commodities. Lonely Chinamen are eager to buy wives.'

'So you caught Mr Li Tzu's eye?'

'No. Number One Master of Servants saw me. A deal was made and I was taken to the lord's house. I was afraid, for my previous master used to beat me.'

'Oh!' Moira was even more shocked. Desert Grass had been speaking in an unemotional way, and seemed to have taken everything in her stride. Now she handed Moira a thimble-sized cup with no handle. It was filled with pale green tea.

'Thank you,' Moira said, accepting the drink she didn't like the look of. 'So how did you find your new lord and master?'

'He was sad,' Desert Grass's voice held great sympathy. 'For he had learned that he had lost all his family. I had lowly position at first, but because I learned way of massaging limbs, because he was weak and frail and needed someone to care for him night and day, I became necessary to my lord. He is kind. I would give my life to see him happy. He has been very ill and sad for a long time.' She paused and looked at Moira, a question in her eyes. 'Was hoped that what he learned today would bring about miracles. We are honoured at your presence, but you are alone.'

'Oh!' Half of Moira's mind was still trying to digest the fact that this nice woman had been sold. That young women were sent, by their own nationals, to be bartered for like cattle, to a foreign land where they were bargained for by greedy men who might beat them with sticks. And she herself had thought Flo's slapping and dabbing and finger-poking was cruel!

'Lord Li Tzu,' Desert Grass went on, 'prayed before the shrine of his ancestors, for his murdered family, and for the safe keeping of his only child. Had she been found—' here Desert Grass gave Moira a quick enquiring look, but Moira remained serene, 'she would be rich and spoiled, and one day a fine handsome lord husband would be found for her.' Desert Grass sighed deeply. 'But, honourable lady, you are alone! And all the ladies of the house and I have no sweet young mistress to devote our lives to.'

'Oh crumbs,' Moira thought, 'Jade's just about going to lap this lot up! By the look of things, dear old Desert Grass can't wait to have a little mistress to fuss over and spoil. And as for Jade's poor old dad! He's certainly going to be a dead duck. Now I know why he brought me here first. I thought it odd that he didn't rush off at once to fetch Jade. He wants her to accept him joyfully. And because he actually believes she'll listen to me, he's trying to get me fully on his side! He doesn't know Jade. One look round at all this...'

She decided to play along with Desert Grass.

'Why am I really here?'

'To rest, then to see all of the house, except the lord's private quarters of course. The gardens are very beautiful. There is a pond with water lilies and many fishes that are the colour of the sun. We have many singing birds.'

'In cages?'

'Hai!'

'I like seeing London sparrows,' Moira said stoutly. 'They might be brown and only chirrup, but at least they fly free.' She changed the subject. 'Then what happens once I have seen the gardens and everything?'

'After that I do not know.'

Moira smiled to herself and soon found out...

Once again Moira sat with Li Tzu in the huge black car. Now she was wondering how on earth Jade would react. Knowing her as she did, Moira knew that whatever happened, she was certain Jade would put on a very good show. No matter. Now at last, it really did seem that all of the minx's dreams were about to come true. The driver took them smoothly to Jordan Street, swishing by the gawping onlookers, towards the Lodge.

The green gate was not wide enough for the car to pass through, so the driver left his seat to stand beside it. He adopted an evil scowl, ready and willing to scare the pants off the hordes of yelling kids. The mere look of him was enough to keep the women out of the way. The ignorant ladies of Jordan Street believed all the garbled and lurid tales they'd heard about the evil, doped-up Chinese.

Li Tzu entered Jordan Lodge leaning on Moira's arm. They went into the kitchen. Flo looked up from her cleaning and screamed.

'Will!' she yelled, terrified. 'Come quick. A Chink's got Moir and he's come to murder us!'

It took a few moments to calm her down. Then because Flo wouldn't stay in the kitchen with Li Tzu unless Moira was there, Maisy went upstairs to fetch Jade. Jade came flying down the stairs and ran straight to Moira.

'Darling,' Moira put her arm protectively round Jade's shoulders. 'This is your honourable father, the lord Li Tzu.'

Without a word, Jade clasped her hands together and bowed, just as River Pearl had taught her all that time ago.

Li Tzu also bowed, kept his distance and was very correct. But again Moira saw the weak tears in his eyes. Quick on the uptake, Jade saw too. With quiet deliberation she left Moira and walked to the man, looked up into his face and said politely,

'Honourable Father, may I have permission to kiss you in the Western way?'

It was then that Li Tzu broke down.

It was all a methodical rush after that. Their clothes were packed. Goodbyes were said, and Moira and Jade were in the car which proceeded to take them to live in 'Moongate' which was the name of Li Tzu's London house.

The residents of Jordan Street spoke of the shiny black car, and the arrival of the Chinks for many days...

Chapter Thirty-One

Of course Jade was spoiled. She was so doted on that she was allowed to go into Li Tzu's private part of the house whenever she liked. No matter what she asked for, she received, and Li Tzu didn't seem to care a jot that she wasn't a longed-for son. The ladies of the house, from Desert Grass down to the lowliest kitchen servants were so devoted to her that pleasing her became their life's work.

A high-born Chinese lady named Iris Pool, came to educate her in the niceties of Chinese society. Lots of marvellous silken Chinese clothes were acquired. A male tutor for the reading and writing of Chinese was employed, but Jade found him and the work irksome and only agreed to continue if Stavros could come and teach her things too.

Stavros came, via the black car, and was made much of. He was considered to be a very wise man. Moira learned that wisdom was revered in China more than anything else. Indeed Stavros and Li Tzu became friends, respecting each other very much, Li Tzu being no slouch in academics as well as being high up in the business world.

The only fly in the ointment, so far as Moira was concerned, was that Jade had become even more possessive with regard to herself.

'No!' she said yet again. 'You can't leave me. I won't let you!'

'Jade, what you may or may not want isn't of much conse-quence to me now,' Moira pointed out, exasperated. 'I merely looked after you for River Pearl's sake. I'm not and never will be one of your servants. All right? All this lounging about doing nothing is getting on my nerves. I shall continue to go to the market and search for work whether you like it or not.'

'You don't need to work. My honourable father sees to it that you want for nothing.'

'He is too kind and generous by half, and I feel I must be one of the luckiest girls ever. And you too are one of the most fortunate girls in the world. I can't understand why all this,' her hands indicated the magnificent room they were in, 'isn't enough for your majesty. Jade, you've got to come to terms with the fact that the day will arrive when I must leave you. I want to get on with my own life.'

'No!'

'Yes!'

'I hate the market. Hate, hate hate it! You can't go to work. I won't let you.'

Jade was so incensed that she forgot not to lose face and threw Raggy Pearl down. The doll that she loved, and which she took everywhere. The doll she treated as if it was real.

Her storm of crying was so bad after that, that Stavros was sent for. These days it was only he who could calm Jade down when she had emotional fits.

Moira began to feel trapped and told Stavros so.

'Be patient,' Stavros told her. 'This is all new to her. Her father, the life-style, this grandiose house. And we will never know how deeply the loss of River Pearl affected her. You have been the only true stability in her life.'

For the time being Moira gave in. But Jade's obsession grew rather than the reverse. Gradually Moira came to feel that the young madam was enjoying having her and everyone else on a string. Con had been right about the girl all along. But then Con was far wiser than she, Moira, had ever been. Later she sat down and wrote yet another letter telling him so. She addressed it, as always, to Rowena Wray's studio. This hurt far more than she would admit, even to herself.

Moira comforted herself that Con always replied to her letters. Warm, friendly notes, about painting, exhibitions, the nights out he enjoyed with Chumley. The evenings they all spent at Flo's. And he always agreed with Li Tzu that she should stay put for a while. That no, she should not go poking about, trying to find things out about River Pearl, that the police had everything in hand, that Moira was safe and secure where she was, and, so far as he had come to understand it, Chinese ways were not like English ways. Chinese ladies were nearly always confined to their homes, in fact treated like the treasures they were. And it would do her, Moira, a power of good to be fussed over and spoiled for a change...

Con's latest letter went along the same lines as always, so, furious, she threw it away. Jade, as watchful as ever, enquired what was wrong.

'Everything!' Moira told her tightly. 'Look here, Jade, I want you to understand something. I've had to work my passage from when I was far younger than you. I'm used to it. I know where I'm at. Lazing about reading, amusing you, and writing endless letters to Con just isn't enough!'

'Get Con to come and live with us here.'

'He'd drop dead before he'd let that happen. Con is a very self-sufficient man. Just as I intend to be a self-sufficient woman.'

'He won't even come here on a visit.'

'As far as I know, he hasn't been asked. This isn't my house. I can't invite guests. Only Li Tzu can do that.'

'He has been invited.' Jade darted Moira a speculative look. 'I wrote and asked him to come.'

'That was a sneaky thing to do!'

'I wanted to make you happy.'

In spite of being angry with Jade's cheek, Moira had to ask, 'And did he write back?'

'Hai. He wrote that it was not the thing for him to come here. That he told you once exactly what you must do.'

'Ah!'

'What does that mean?'

'It means mind your business, miss,' Moira snapped and stalked off to her room. But she was hearing Con's words on that special night. 'You must come to me,' he had said. 'Remember. You must come to me!'

I hate this, Moira thought furiously. Nothing ever changes. The world's full of people intent on telling me what I must do.

Desert Grass came to her then. A Desert Grass whose face was crumpled with woe.

372

'Sweet Precious is angry,' she said tragically. 'Sweet Precious insists that you must go to her.'

'No!' Moira exploded. 'You tell that young madam marm-stink that I'll not bow to her commands. That I am Moira O'Malley, not her slave.'

Thoroughly upset, Desert Grass went away. Moira stayed where she was, knowing very well that right about now, Jade was having one of her tantrums and that every servant, high or low, would be trying to make her happy again.

An hour later Li Tzu sent for Moira. At his invitation she sat before him in the study on his side of the house.

The old man, who was sitting at an ornately carved desk, wearing a smoking jacket and a gold-thread embroidered pill-box hat, rose at her entrance. He bowed and gave formal greetings.

Moira smiled politely and replied in the same fullsome manner. It seemed the regular Chinese thing to do, she thought, to go round the houses where a single "hello" would do. Then in answer to his usual request after Jade's tantrums, she said, 'I am sorry, very sorry indeed, Mr Li. Oh, and please do sit down. But in answer to your question, no! I will not give up my freedom of choice. Not even for Jade.'

'You do not need to go to the market,' Li Tzu told her. 'It is not necessary for you to earn your keep, as you insist on putting it. And I must confess that it worries every member of this household when you insist on going out alone. Hai! Every one, including own humble self.'

'I know,' she told him, 'and your kindness and generosity has been beyond my wildest dreams. But I love being in the market. I love going here and there and being mistress of my own destiny. I am a London sparrow at heart, not like one of your poor, very pretty caged birds.' She learned forward and went on earnestly, 'Know something Mr Li? There was once a time when I was so scared of the open streets that I always wanted to stay in and hide! I was so terrified of the outside world that by instinct I wished to be a recluse and stay in Jordan Lodge for ever. Now I feel at home when I am out there, mingling with the crowds, watching everything going on. I feel comfortable with myself!'

'Then why, when we first met, did your eyes tell me that you

373

were sad?' he asked gently. 'Even now, it makes me grieve sometimes, to see how you look when you are alone.'

'That was nothing to do with my work,' she told him, embarrassed. 'Nor with anything here – and I didn't know it showed.' She pushed the thought of Con away, adding, 'I'm not used to all this luxury, that's all.'

He was not fooled, she could tell.

'This is your home,' Li Tzu told her, 'and so are the others I own over the world. Most auspicious time soon. We are to return to America, to where new house has been built. You will be happy there. You will enjoy the sights that would have so enchanted honourable River Pearl.'

'She would have loved living in a slum had you been there,' Moira told him, and felt a wave of grief. 'I – I want to accept she's gone, but I can't! Not now. Not since the police told me that it wasn't her they found. That's one of the reasons I want to get out of here for a while every day. But Jade just plays up! Oh don't you see? I'll feel happier if I'm at least trying to find her.'

'Do not interfere with work of police,' he told her. 'Put your mind on America.'

'Me?' She was taken back at the idea. 'You are taking Jade there perhaps, but not me!'

'My daughter will need you. She is to meet respected families, for one day she will be Chief Lady of House. She must learn to become at one with her new land. You will help her to cope.'

'Really? When is all this to happen, Mr Li?'

'Within two months. You will enjoy it all very much.'

'I am sorry,' Moira told him gravely, 'very sorry, but I will be staying here in London. I need to be with my own friends. I can't bear it that Flo has never seen fit to come here, nor Daisy and Sid. And Mrs Noice who never, ever, forgot me at Christmas. And I'm aching to find out just how Babs is getting along. She's going to have a baby, you know.'

'I did not realize that you wanted visitors. I will send the car for them at once. I will—'

'That's just it! They'd feel they were ordered, and would automatically turn the invitation down. They must *want* to come, Mr Li.' She smiled ruefully. 'Clearly, right now, they are happy to stay where they are. I – I have to meet them half way, you see. It's not only posh people who have pride.'

'Then you must write to them personally. Ask them to please come and see you, if only to wish you goodbye. Explain that we are sailing for America shortly.'

'Oh, but I'm not! I mean it, I really do. I want to stay and try to find out what happened to River Pearl. I cannot leave now, Mr Li.'

'My honourable daughter will not wish this.'

'Well honourable daughter will just have to put up with it,' Moira smiled mischievously. 'And it will do her good not to have all her own way. You are spoiling her Mr Li.'

'I am trying to make up for all the years she lived in hardship.'

'Really?' Moira laughed, frankly and openly. 'How differently we look at things, you and I. I think those years must be the best things that ever happened to her. I tried to teach her not to be such a selfish little brat.' She stood up, determinedly, adding, 'And even though I adore her, and I'm now very fond of you, Mr Li, I must confess to feeling too closed in.' She paused, then added significantly. 'And it is not all that wonderful, knowing that you have me tailed every time I put my nose outside your door either.'

Two blotches of colour were burning high on Li Tzu's cheeks. Not surprising, Moira thought, since in all probability, no one had dared defy him before.

'I am not sure that I understand.' He was trying to side step. 'Tailed? Put your nose outside my door? You speak a very strange language indeed. And you have strange ways.'

'I am sure that you have too, Mr Li.' She wagged her finger at him in a reproving way. 'Chung Lo, Mr Chung's Number Three son has been allotted to guard me, hasn't he?' Greatly daring, she left her chair and walked over to him, a cool, elegant young woman these days, and she kissed him in a warm and friendly way. 'Oh my dearest Li Tzu,' she said gently. 'I never had a father, and I do so wish that I'd had one as loving and caring as you.'

Before he could reply, she whirled round and left him.

She found Jade playing a game of dominoes with Desert Grass and said bluntly, 'You're off home to America in a couple of months, Minx. I think I'd best tell you right here and now, that I am not coming with you.'

Jade jumped up, ready to do battle at once, but Moira put her arm round the young girl's waist and smiled into her eyes.

'You'll do fine, and you won't need me.'

'I will always need you. I won't go without you. I want you at my side, just as you promised River Pearl.'

'Just as I promise you now, that I will always be there, even at the ends of the earth for you, if and when necessary. For now, you have Desert Grass, and all the women, not forgetting your father who is quite wonderful. Oh, and before you start carrying on, think about this. I have the feeling that when you meet high-ups in China, you might be seen by several very eligible young beaux.'

'I don't want to meet men. I don't want—'

'Think, Jade! Your future honourable lord husband may be somewhere over there, ready and waiting to agree to a betrothal. Ready to take you to his own wonderfully rich and luxurious home the moment you come of age. I'll be dancing at your wedding yet, eh, honourable Miss Li Sweet Precious Jade?'

Moira saw the speculative look dawning in Jade's eyes, smiled to herself, and went to her own gorgeous room to sit quietly, think and plan . . .

The following day, on edge because now she knew of the forthcoming American trip she felt a sense of urgency, Moira prowled in the Moongate garden. It was Chinese in design, but she saw nothing of its beauty.

She resolutely looked away from the caged birds who were singing lustily, happy among the shady branches of trees. It was now Spring and the sun was a melting pot brimming over with gold. The birds were enjoying being outside. It always amazed Moira to see Li Tzu taking them for walks in the garden, holding each cage very carefully in his blue-veined hands. But unlike Li Tzu, Moira found no comfort in talking to birds. Indeed, she thought, I have no one I can really confide in. No one. There was only Con.

Moira returned inside and spent a while playing dominoes with Jade. They enjoyed a midday meal, then Jade went off with Desert Grass to feed the goldfish in the garden pool. Still restless, Moira was again wishing that she had someone who understood her predicament. Who knew how cut in two she felt, with Jade pulling her in one direction, and her own desire for freedom of choice in the other. If only Con . . . She determinedly banished the thought. Then she remembered Robby. The little golden-haired boy who was just a figment of her imagination, yet with whom she had held countless conversations. On the spur of the moment, she set out . . .

St Stephen's looked the same, timeless and remote, its spire like a finger pointing straight up to God. Robby's grave was only barely defined; the grass had been allowed to grow rather high under the willow tree. Moira carefully placed her offering of daffodils at the head, then she sat down, unmindful of the damp, and tried to relax.

But it was so hard not to think, to let go, to forget that night with Con – who she loved! Shocked at the thought, realizing the full truth at last, that she loved and needed Con with all her heart, Moira sat there stunned. She felt dizzy and desperate, remembering that he had sent her away.

'Oh Robby,' she whispered. 'What shall I do?'

Nothing, her treacherous inner self reminded her. He went back to Rowena Wray. Oh, she had always known that he would, deep down. How could he love a person from Jordan Street over someone who knew all the right people and the right places to be? Someone who was wise to the ways of the world, and who would never get sucked in by men in Yani's mould! Anyway, there was proof that they were together, wasn't there?

Since she had been living in Moongate, Li Tzu had arranged for all kinds of newspapers and magazines to be delivered for her amusement, the kind that had articles about famous writers sculptors, actors, photographers, models and artists. And Con had been featured, also Rowena, and where Moira read one name, it was usually closely followed by the other. The fact that Rowena Wray and Conor MacCluskey shared a studio was never, ever missed out. A "Close Association" it was called. That, Moira grieved, said it all.

Suddenly, sitting there alone under the willow tree with Robby wasn't enough. With a heavy heart she stood up, then bowing her head and speaking for the last time to the lonely

377

little boy, Moira whispered, 'I'm going now, Robby. Thank you for being my friend. I will never, ever forget you.'

Being early in the year the evenings drew in quickly and already it was nearing dusk. Moira began walking back down the path, when something made her look past the stone angel with a broken wing, beyond a lichened mausoleum, to the person talking out loud and looking down at a grave. It was Dave Dilley!

Moira froze, then very carefully edged back in order to hide behind the mausoleum. Her heart was pounding, her throat too dry even to scream. Here was her nightmare, alive and as mad as they came. He was ranting on to Martha, telling her that she'd be punished when he got home. That she was keeping Stan hidden out of his way. That she had always been a contrary cow. Why had she changed from the woman he loved? Where had she acquired her magic power? He would never forgive her for conjuring up a devil in a black car. The same devil that the whole of Jordan Street had seen. Yes, driving off with the one he'd always been looking for.

Moira's heart was pounding so hard that she feared he might hear it. She cowered away as she heard his footsteps. He was leaving, arms flapping, head bent forward, looking like a tatty bird of prey. Moira prayed then, that he would hurry and get miles out of her way. She wanted him out of her sight for ever. She wanted ...

Out of the blue she remembered what she had told the policeman. How Dave Dilley had followed River Pearl one night; there had been nothing to it, not really, but ... But even so ...

Without pausing to think, Moira began to follow him.

Now the street lamps glowed as Dave Dilley squirmed through the gates and in a second his crackly voice was lost in the night noises of the main road. He sped through alleyways and twisting streets, his thin figure driven by urgency. Now he looked neither left nor right, but when he came to the waste ground, home of the methies, he slowed his pace and looked furtively all about him. Then he slid like a dark shadow into the ramshackle residence that had once belonged to Stan.

Well back, Moira stood there, watching and waiting. She was out of breath, for she had come a long way. She sensed she

378

ought to do something, but didn't know what. She felt instinctively that something was about to happen, yet was terrified that it would. She wished with all her heart and soul that Con was there. Or Freddy. Or any loyal friend. She looked round, praying that Li Tzu had not ordered Chung Lo to keep away. Chung Lo was nowhere to be seen.

Moira saw a faint glimmer of light coming under the door. She edged forwards, keeping as quiet as she possibly could, warily watching the methies. They were intent on their drinking, and squatting as near as possible to their pathetically small fire. They took no notice of her.

As she reached the shack, Moira could hear Dave Dilley giggling and speaking, his words spilling over each other like a malicious waterfall. He was taunting his dead wife, telling her that he'd decided not to keep feeding her. That it was time for her to die all over again.

Sick at heart, Moira turned away and in doing so dislodged a rusty tin. The mouthing inside stopped. She froze. Then before she could turn and run, the door flew open and a pair of long skinny arms reached out, grabbed her, and pulled her inside. She opened her mouth to scream, but he punched her in the face and for seconds she saw stars.

Moira pulled herself together too late. A filthy, fish-smelling rag had been tied round her half opened mouth, she could neither open nor shut her jaws. She was propped up in a chair at an orange box table that was littered with remnants of stale food. And...

Dear God in Heaven!

Dave Dilley had been speaking to a corpse!

In the dim light of a candle, Moira saw sitting opposite her a skeletal figure. It was dressed in rags and its wrists were tied together. It was gagged as she was, and it wore a large black hat with a veil which covered its face. And Moira knew that she didn't want to see that face. It would be a ghoul, a horror, something totally unreal. Then she forgot the corpse and was screaming high in her mind. Dave Dilley was gibbering and laughing and holding a poker high.

'Remember this?' he was giggling? 'Remember?'

Before she could take in the monstrous thing that was about to happen to her, she thought she heard the corpse moan. Then everything was lost in a sea of agony. A world of pain engulfed her as the fish fryer, using his poker, began to exact his revenge.

He was beating her with the poker, her shoulders, her back, screaming and raining the blows down. Her vision blurred to a scarlet haze of horror, Moira begged God not to let the madman destroy her eyes, then to let her die so that she could escape the torment that was ripping her apart. A terrible crash sent strings of lights shooting away from her head. Lights blazed and blinded and flashed in her brain. A roaring sensation grew louder as a thunderball crashed onto her skull.

The world exploded into blackness and she was falling down ... down ... down.

Chapter Thirty-Two

The moon was pale and pearly, like a balloon floating in space. It was a gentle moon, a smiling moon, reminding Jade of Second Mother's face. Jade held Raggy Pearl close and her heart was so joyous it was fit to burst. She looked across at the other bed in the room, and her eyes were wet with happy tears. Most Beloved was still sleeping and when she woke she would as always see her, Jade, waiting and watching, just as she had from the moment they had brought her home.

Honourable lord father had wanted Jade to know nothing of the ugliness, but Jade was old and wise enough to know when to keep quiet. To listen, then question and find out the truth. Desert Grass had understood, had explained, and they both agreed that from now on their sacred duty was to care for River Pearl who had suffered so greatly on Jade's behalf. And the most evil fiend had not been Kung Chin after all. It had been Dave Dilley, fish fryer of Jordan Street.

Gradually the whole story had emerged. River Pearl had been followed by persons whose orders were to kill. But under the cover of fog, Dave Dilley had taken her instead, back to his home above the shop. And then the torture had begun. Not physical torture, but that of the mind. River Pearl was used as a slave. If she dared try to escape, or to let anyone know where she was, Dave Dilley had threatened that he would tell the world about Jade. The Authorities would know, Kung Chin's assassins would know, and if one didn't get her, the others would.

Dave Dilley himself didn't like to touch his captive. He did not like her eyes, nor the way those eyes watched him. Or the way her skin was pulled tight and looked like unbleached linen over her face. He had screamed at her one day and taken from its box his wife's veiled Sunday hat. River Pearl had been made to wear it from then on.

Dave Dilley had a fishing rod with which he used to poke his captive. And all the time she worked and slaved he would dig and poke at her with the end of the rod until she was black and blue. It became a habit for Dave Dilley to use that rod. He was aware of its power, almost as much as he was aware of the power of the poker that he swore he would use on Moira O'Malley one day.

'Tit for tat,' he would giggle. 'Tit for tat!'

He began to leave home and walk the streets for hours on end, always searching for the girl with wanton ways. And before he left he would tie up his captive and pull the bolt so there was no escape.

When the Comptons came, they were told never to go upstairs. The doors were locked anyway. When Dilley was heard speaking and shouting it made no difference at all. Everyone knew that the nut case was always talking to himself.

Dave Dilley, after a very long time, became convinced that River Pearl, in her hat, was indeed Martha. He needed Martha's brother and he felt that he would go to his shack under the railway arch if he knew she was there. Accordingly, in the early hours, they slipped out via the back-yard and no one saw them go.

The methies, macabre, filthy and moronic, took no notice as they passed. And there River Pearl stayed– until Moira O'Malley arrived.

River Pearl stirred, then opened her eyes. She looked over and saw that Jade was sitting up.

'Cannot sleep?' she asked.

'I am too excited. Mother,' Jade's voice was humble. 'I may come in with you?'

River Pearl pulled back the silken sheets.

'Since when has my little blossom had to ask?'

Jade padded across the room, into the bed to lay down beside Second Mother.

'When will they bring her?' she asked, nuzzling in.

'Not until noon. Why?'

382

'I need to speak to Honourable Father. I will ask him a favour.'

'For Moira?'

'No!' Jade's voice was a soft breath in the night. 'For you...'

The next day Moira was helped out of the ambulance and into the house. Her wounds had healed and she was growing stronger, but the immediate past was a muddle to her. She knew in a vague way that Con had been there, at her bedside. He had always been there, night and day. But when she had been pronounced out of danger, he had kissed her gently on the cheek, and left. He wrote from then on, and sent postcards on which he had drawn pictures, and they were always signed with love. But he never visited again.

Li Tzu was there every day and also Desert Grass and Jade. The private ward was filled with flowers, and fruit was piled high.

'Who saved me?' she whispered to Li Tzu. 'Who must I thank?'

'Chung Lo,' he told her. 'He followed you and when he saw what happened he telephoned the police. Then he burst in and fought with the madman. He was still trying to defend you when the police arrived. And you have no need to thank him. I have already done that. Chung Lo is now a very rich man.'

'And – and to think,' she choked, 'that I loathed the idea of him following me. Of being my guard. And I blamed you! Oh, Li Tzu, you are the one I should thank.'

'Then my debt to honourable, most dear friend is paid a little,' he told her. 'Sleep now and get well.'

'And – and Dave Dilley?' Moira whispered fearfully. 'I have to know!'

'Taken away in a straight-jacket, to Brentwood Asylum. Is all auspicious, since he will trouble you no more.'

'Oh!' she gasped and wept tears of relief, tears that she thought would never end, but they did at last.

And now here she was, back in Moongate, being helped to her room. And Jade was there, running to her, and throwing her arms round her in a most un-Chinese way.

'You are my thousand and one joys,' she cried. 'My Moira, welcome home!'

383

And Desert Grass was there, and the servants came in turn, all smiling and happy for Moira had come to know them well.

Jade clapped her hands for attention and everyone immediately became quiet.

'And now,' Jade told Moira, 'prepare for honourable lord father, and also someone you want so specially to see, but thought you never would again. Here is our most particular surprise.'

Con! Moira thought, beginning to tremble.

Then the door opened and Li Tzu came in. Behind him, being helped by a young girl, since she was still far from strong, was River Pearl. And she was swathed, almost swamped in what could only be *the dress!* The great heirloom of Li Tzu's house, vermilion silk embroidered with flowers and butterflies, that River Pearl had spoken of so longingly in their attic at Jordan Lodge. River Pearl was thus honoured above all others. River Pearl was the queen of them all. And the "queen" went to Moira and knelt beside the bed, and she and her dearest friend wept together . . .

Li Tzu made sure that Moira received plenty of visitors after that, but Con never came. He wrote still, and sent flowers, and always signed them "With love." And she held the cards to her heart and dreamed her dreams.

Chumley arrived, and Daisy, even Freddy's baby, Michael, gave her a smile. But Flo was a regular caller. Pop-eyed, ingratiating old Flo who, after the shock of finding herself in such a grand place, was almost syrupy. Flo was coming to quite like Mr Li, and became embarrassingly coy in his presence and even daring enough to call him dear Mr Su Su. Seeing Jade's wickedly twinkling eyes he seemed to see the joke and put his hands in his sleeves and bowed – which almost made Flo faint with delight.

After that Flo proclaimed to the world her grief and despair at seeing the state her "poor ol' Moir" was in . . .

Flo was visiting on the day the doctor had given his patient the final all clear. She was up and about again, and in full health.

Able she was told, to at last resume her normal life. But it was not that good news that was making the stars shine in Moira's eyes.

'You look like the cat what's licked the cream,' Flo observed flatly, seeing her outings to this grand place coming to an abrupt end. 'What's brought about all this undying happiness? I should 'ave thought you'd've enjoyed being treated like a queen.' She sniffed, adding impatiently, 'All set to go job hunting again, are you? Up the market, is that it? Gawd's truth, you ain't half a stupid cow! You're finally the lady of Limehouse the old Greek taught yer to be and you're going to spoil it all by yer pride.'

'No. No, Flo, it's this. Look!'

Flo looked at the magazine that had been delivered only that morning, and frowned.

'And so? I don't know these people. Should I?'

'It's a photograph of Rowena Wray and a Mr Charles Fillimore – who are now engaged to be married.'

'So?'

'She's the girl that Con shares a studio with.'

'What of it?'

'It doesn't matter, honestly!' Moira said and beamed. 'But when you go home, will you ask Binksy to go and see Chumley for me?'

'Gawd help us! Now what are you on about? Chumley?'

'Yes please.' A wide and wonderful smile lit up Moira's face. 'Of course Chumley! He'll tell me where I can find Con...'